"Are you hu[rt?]"

The worry and ca[re ...] [i]n was so clear that it made her heart ache.

"I'm sorry—" she started.

"Don't you dare apologize," he said. "Someone attacked you in your home. Anyone would have been terrified."

"I was," she said, and looked down, almost embarrassed that she'd been so scared.

He placed his finger under her chin and tilted her head back up until she met his gaze. "But you fought back and got away," he said. "You're a strong, brave woman."

Her heart pounded in her throat and more than anything, she wanted him to kiss her. No matter how hard she'd tried to resist her attraction to Zach, her body always betrayed her. It came alive when he was close to her, as never before.

She felt her body lean forward, anticipating the kiss, but instead, he released her and scanned the cabin.

THE BETRAYED

BY
JANA DeLEON

...equin (UK) policy is to use papers that are natural, renewable and
...clable products and made from wood grown in sustainable forests.
...ing and manufacturing processes conform to the legal environ...
...lations of the country of origin.

...ted and bound in Spain
...by Blackprint CPI, Barcelona

MILLS
BOON

First published in Great Britain 2013
by Mills & Boon, an imprint of Harlequin (UK) Limited,
Eton House, 18-24 Paradise Road, Richmond, Surrey TW9 1SR

© Jana DeLeon 2013

ISBN: 978 0 263 90373 7
ebook ISBN: 978 1 472 00743 8

46-0913

Harlequin... natural, renewable and
recycled products and made from wood grown in sustainable forests. The
logging... conform to the legal environmental
regulations of the country of origin.

Printed...
by B...

USA TODAY bestselling author **Jana DeLeon** grew up among the bayous and small towns of southwest Louisiana. She's never actually found a dead body or seen a ghost, but she's still hoping. Jana started writing in 2001—she focuses on murderous plots set deep in the Louisiana bayous. By day she writes very boring technical manuals for a software company in Dallas. Visit Jana on her website, www.janadeleon.com.

To my husband, Rene, who always believed in me.

Chapter One

The tortured soul wandered the mansion, calling for her children. Where had they gone? Why couldn't she hear their sweet voices? Why didn't their footsteps echo throughout the house?

Was it him? Had he done something to her babies?

The thought of it broke her heart and she screamed in anguish, vowing never to rest until her children were returned to her.

And until the man paid.

DANAE LEBEAU was running late, as usual, but today she had a good excuse. The local radio station had been abuzz since the wee hours of the morning, broadcasting information about the attack on Alaina LeBeau weeks before and the subsequent death of her attacker at the hands of the local sheriff. Until now, it had all been gossip and speculation, while everyone impatiently waited for the state police to clear those involved and declare it self-defense. Now it was the hottest bit of excitement the tiny bayou town of Calais had ever seen.

My sister could have died.

The thought ripped through her as she listened to the reporter relay the gruesome details of that horrible night at their mother's estate, the weight of the words crippling her. Her sister could have died, and Danae had never even told her they were related.

After their mother's death, the three sisters had been separated by their stepfather, Trenton Purcell, and shipped off to be raised by distant relatives. Danae was only two when it happened, not old enough to remember anything about her life in Calais. The only childhood she'd known was in California, but years ago, she'd started slowly making her way across the country to Louisiana. Even though she couldn't remember anything about her life in Calais, she'd always felt a tug—as if something was drawing her back to her birthplace.

Using an assumed name, she'd taken a job at the local café to try to find out information on her stepfather, who had lived as a recluse in her mother's family estate for over two decades. But she'd managed to find out very little about the man, given that most of the townspeople seemed to completely dislike him and were happy to see him disappear from society.

After her stepfather's death, Danae's sister Alaina showed up in Calais to meet the terms of their mother's will. According to the local gossip, each sister was required to live on the estate for a period of two weeks within one year after their stepfather's death. Once those stipulations were met, their mother's estate would pass to the sisters. It was shocking news to Danae, who'd always assumed their mother had left everything to their stepfather and that her ties to Calais had long since been severed.

Danae still remembered the day Alaina arrived in town. Through the storefront window of the café, she'd seen Alaina driving her SUV down Main Street. She'd dropped a whole stack of dishes and had her pay docked for the incident, but she hadn't been able to help it. The only thing Danae had from her past was an old photo of their mother. Alaina looked as if she'd stepped out of that photo, changed into current clothes and driven by.

When she met Alaina early one morning at the café, Danae wanted to tell her that they were sisters, but years of living on the street had taught her to always stand back and assess the situation. To always limit exposure of herself unless absolutely necessary. That level of caution had saved her life more than once, and just because she experienced a familial pull, she had no reason to sacrifice something that had always worked for her.

But now, she wondered if she should reveal herself. From the local talk, she had a good idea about the terms of the will and knew that if she wanted to take part, she'd have to come forward. The distant cousin who had taken her in when her mother died had passed away long ago, a liquor bottle clenched in her leathered hand, and Danae had never gotten close enough to anyone to make lasting friendships. If anyone tried to find her, the trail stopped cold in California.

After Danae met Alaina and got a good feeling about her as a person, she'd been tempted to talk to the estate attorney, but she'd still held back. What if their middle sister couldn't be located, either? Her understanding was that all three sisters had to meet the requirements of the will in order for any of them to inherit. If the last sister couldn't be located or didn't agree to the terms, then Danae would have exposed herself for no viable reason, and at a time when she didn't feel comfortable doing so.

But the attack on Alaina had her rethinking everything. What if her sister had died and she'd never gotten the chance to tell her who she was? She could have missed one of her only opportunities to have a real family.

As she grabbed her car keys, she glanced at her watch and cursed. She even had the advantage of working second shift that morning, but she wasn't going to make the later work time, either. Johnny, the café owner, was going to kill her for being so late. Likely, everyone in Calais would wander through the café this morning to gossip about the news report. Nothing this big had ever happened in the sleepy bayou town. It was going to be the talk for quite a while.

She flung open the front door of her rented cabin, ready to break some major speeding laws on the winding country roads, but stopped short at the sight of the plain white envelope that lay on the welcome mat.

Such a common, nonthreatening item shouldn't have set off the wave of anxiety that flooded through her, but she immediately knew something was off. She hadn't let her guard down long enough to make close friends, and even if she had, they would hardly drive ten miles into the swamp to leave an envelope at her doorstep.

Her hands shook as she reached for the envelope, and as soon as her fingers closed around it, she set off at a run for her car. Whoever had left the envelope might be watching, lurking somewhere in the swamp that enclosed the tiny cabin and blocked it off from the rest of the world.

She jumped into her ancient sedan, started it and threw it into Drive, tearing out of the dirt driveway before she'd even managed to close the car door. She pressed the accelerator just beyond the limits of safety, and her fingers ached from clenching the steering wheel as the old car skidded in the gravel. The narrow road seemed to stretch on forever, but finally, she reached the intersection for the paved road that led into Calais.

She pulled to a stop and looked over at the envelope that she'd tossed onto the passenger's seat. Habit had her checking her rearview mirror, but no one was visible behind her. She glanced back at the passenger's seat where the envelope lay, seemingly taunting her to open it. Lifting one hand, she bit her lower lip, then hesitated.

What are you—a coward?

Unable to stand it any longer, she grabbed the envelope and tore it open. A single scrap of paper containing only one sentence fell out into her hand.

I know who you are.

She sucked in a breath so hard her chest ached. All her careful planning and secrecy had been for naught. Someone had figured out her secret. But why did they leave this message? What were they hoping to accomplish by doing so? Being Ophelia LeBeau's daughter wasn't a crime, and Danae had no reason other than an overzealous sense of self-protection for hiding her true identity.

Someone must be trying to scare her. But to what end?

She shoved the paper into her purse and continued her drive to town. She'd stop at the café first and let Johnny know she had to take a bit more time that morning. He wouldn't be happy and may even fire her, but that couldn't be helped. Danae had the sudden overwhelming feeling that she had to find William Duhon, the estate attorney, and reveal her true identity.

Whatever someone hoped to accomplish with the note, she was going to cut them off at the pass.

DANAE SPOTTED ALAINA'S SUV in front of the attorney's office and felt another bout of panic. Then logic took over and she decided it was a good thing. Might as well kill two birds with one stone. She hurried into the office and told a rather grim-looking woman at the front desk that she wished to speak to Mr. Duhon.

The grim woman frowned, which surprised Danae a bit, as she'd thought the woman was already frowning before.

"Do you have an appointment?" Grim asked.

"You know that I don't," Danae replied, trying to keep her voice level. After all, this woman and everyone else knew her as Connie from the café, and probably couldn't imagine why she'd need to speak to William.

"I can make you an appointment for later this week."

"Is he talking to Alaina?"

"Mr. Duhon's clients are all afforded the privacy they deserve—"

Danae waved a hand at the woman to cut her off.

"Never mind," she said as she walked past the desk and pushed open the door to the attorney's office.

Alaina jumped around in her seat when Danae flung open the door, and the attorney jumped up from his chair, uncertain and clearly uncomfortable with the interruption.

"You can't go in there," Grim admonished behind her.

"I'm Danae LeBeau," she said before she could change her mind.

Chapter Two

Alaina and William stared at her, their expressions a mixture of disbelief and surprise. She'd expected as much. Connie Smith, café waitress, had served them both breakfast on many occasions. She'd never provided her real name to anyone in Calais before now. And as her looks were a perfect blend of both parents, she didn't favor either enough to draw suspicion.

"I have documentation," she said and pulled some faded, worn papers from her purse. "A birth certificate and a driver's license with my real name—I'd appreciate it if you don't ask where I got the one I've been using."

She stood there, holding the documents, with both William and Alaina staring at her in shock. Finally, Alaina rose from her chair and walked the couple of steps to stand in front of her.

"Danae?" Alaina said, her voice wavering. "You were just a toddler… You had on a new dress that day—"

"Yellow with white roses," Danae interrupted.

Alaina's eyes filled with tears. "Yes." She threw her arms around Danae and squeezed her tightly. "I never thought… When I came here, I didn't know what would happen."

Danae struggled to maintain her composure. "I didn't know, either."

"Why didn't you tell me when I first arrived?"

"We're fine, Ms. Morgan," William's voice sounded behind them.

Danae released Alaina and glanced back in time to see Secretary Grim pull the door closed, her frown still fixed in place. Alaina smiled at her and wiped her cheeks with the back of her hand.

"I…uh…" Danae struggled to find a way to explain. "I don't really know why I came to Calais, or even to Louisiana. I mean, I guess I thought I could talk to our stepfather and maybe find out something—anything—about my past, maybe find you and Joelle. But I never got the chance and then he died."

Danae sniffed and willed the tears that were building to stay in place. Now was not the time to go soft. "I don't really remember. I don't remember anything, and I kept thinking that it was important. That my life here mattered and I needed to know. I know it sounds silly…"

Alaina squeezed her arm. "No. It doesn't sound silly at all. Not to me."

Danae could tell by the way Alaina said it that she meant what she said. She wasn't just being nice. She understood, as only the three sisters could possibly understand. A wave of relief passed over her, and the tug at her heart, the one she'd felt for Alaina the first time she saw her, grew stronger.

"I'm sure you've heard about how our stepfather lived," Danae continued. "I never even saw him. Then he died and you turned up."

Alaina smiled. "I felt a connection to you when we first met that I didn't understand. I slipped so easily into conversation with you, which is rare. Maybe somewhere deep down, I knew."

Danae sniffed and her eyes misted up a bit. "I wanted

to say something when you arrived, but what would people think—my working here with an assumed name and all?"

She looked over at the attorney. "I swear I didn't know about the inheritance when I came to Calais."

The attorney waved a hand at the chairs in front of his desk, encouraging them to sit. "Please don't trouble yourself with those kinds of thoughts, Ms. LeBeau. You couldn't have been aware of the conditions of your mother's will. Ophelia was a very private person, and your stepfather wasn't about to tell anyone that he wasn't really the wealthy man he seemed."

As Danae slid into the chair next to Alaina, she felt some of the tension lessen in her shoulders and back. "But I still came here under false pretenses."

"No," Alaina said. "You came here looking for answers and didn't want everyone to know that evil old man was your stepfather. I hardly think anyone will fault you for your feelings."

The attorney nodded. "Your sister is correct. While some of the more dramatic of Calais's residents may find some fun in theorizing as to your hidden identity, those who partake in logical thinking will not so much as raise an eyebrow at your choices. In fact, most would assume you wise."

Danae smiled. "You're very refreshing, Mr. Duhon."

"Isn't he the best?" Alaina beamed. "Until I met him, I had no idea attorneys could be competent, nice and have a personality. I'd thought I was the only one."

"Please call me William," he said, a slight blush creeping up his neck. "Well, ladies, we have a lot to discuss, but I can cover the basics of the inheritance now and we can meet at a later date to discuss the rest."

Danae nodded. "I know I have to live on the property for two weeks and that Sheriff Trahan will verify my residency every day. At least, that's what the café gossip is."

"This time, the café gossip is correct. That was one of the things Alaina and I were discussing, among everything else."

"Why? Have the requirements changed?"

"No, but the storm last week did a lot of damage. Much of the house no longer has power, and the heating system has failed completely. Essentially, the house has gone from barely habitable to not habitable in a matter of days."

Danae pulled at a loose thread on the chair cushion. "So what do we do?" The thought of living in that big, scary house with limited power wasn't anywhere on her bucket list.

William frowned. "That is a fine question. I have already hired someone to begin the repairs, but the work could take a while to complete. I assume you'd like to get this over with."

Danae nodded.

He tapped his pen on the desk then jumped up with more speed than Danae would have thought possible for a man his age. He pulled open a drawer in the filing cabinet behind him and removed a thick folder.

He slid back into his chair and flipped through the pages, scanning and frowning as he went. Danae looked over at Alaina, but she just shrugged. Finally, he closed the document and beamed across the desk at them.

"You're renting the cabin off Bayou Glen Drive, right?" William asked.

"Yes," Danae replied, "but I don't see—"

"That cabin is part of the estate," William said. "The inheritance documents don't specify that you must occupy the main house, so I'm to assume that if you wanted to pitch a tent somewhere on estate acreage, that would also qualify. But in your case, you merely have to remain where you are for at least another two weeks, subject to monitoring and verification by our friend the sheriff."

"Oh!" Danae exclaimed. "Well, that's great."

Alaina clapped her hands. "I told you William is the best."

The ring of a cell phone interrupted their celebration. Alaina pulled her phone out of her purse and glanced at the display.

"I'm sorry," Alaina said. "I have to take this."

Alaina said very little but Danae could tell by the tone of her voice that something was wrong. Her sister frowned as she slipped the phone back into her purse.

"Is everything okay?" Danae asked.

"No. My mother—the one who raised me—fell yesterday and broke her leg. My father died a couple years back, and my stepbrother and stepsister both work full-time and can't afford to take off. They know I resigned from the firm and asked if I can stay with her for a week or so until the home health nurse is available."

Disappointment rolled over Danae and she tried to fight it down. Of course Alaina had to go help the woman who'd raised her, but she'd been hoping for long hours to catch up with her sister—to pick her memory for glimpses of their life before their mother died. Surely Alaina, the oldest of the sisters, had memories of their childhood.

Alaina put her hand on Danae's arm. "I'm so sorry to have to leave right now."

"Don't be silly," Danae said. "We have plenty of

time. I'm not going anywhere, not even after my two weeks are up."

Alaina leaned over and hugged her before rising from her chair. "I need to book a flight and pack a bag. You gave me your cell-phone number weeks ago, so I'll call you as soon as I get a chance and you'll have mine. I think there's a midmorning flight to Boston that I may be able to catch if I hurry."

Alaina hurried around the desk to plant a kiss on a blushing William's cheek, then rushed out of the office, closing the door behind her.

William watched Alaina, smiling, then looked at Danae after she'd gone. "She's quite a woman, your sister. I think you two are going to get along very well."

"I've liked her since the moment I met her. That's a real relief for me. That and the fact that she wasn't disappointed that I'm her sister."

"Why would she be?"

"I don't know—I mean, she's this big-shot attorney and I'm just a café waitress. We're hardly in the same realm."

"You had two very different upbringings after you were stripped from your home." He gave her a kindly look. "In my attempts to locate you, I learned some about your life in California. You've done well for yourself, Danae. Please don't ever doubt that."

She sniffed at the unexpected kindness. "Thanks."

A movie reel of where she'd come from up to where she was now flashed through her mind, and she realized that right now was the turning point—the time where she could choose to make everything in her life different or simply fade away into obscurity again. It was exhilarating and frightening at the same time.

"I can still have access to the house, right?" she asked.

"Yes, of course. It is—or will be—your property, after all. Is there anything in particular you wanted to do? Alaina made quite a dent in remodeling and cleaning. Her work in the kitchen transformed the room."

She smiled. "I'm sure cleaning is something I could handle, but what I really want is the ability to go through the papers and pictures—see if I can find stuff about our past with our mother. I was so young…"

"And you want to remember." William sighed. "It makes me so sad that you girls grew up without your mother. Ophelia was such a wonderful woman and her delight in you girls was apparent. Her death was a loss to the entire community but was devastating for you girls."

He removed his glasses and rubbed them with a cleaning cloth on his desk, and Danae could tell he still felt her mother's death. It made her both happy and sad that her mother was such a wonderful person she'd left such an impression, but then died without living her life to the fullest.

William slipped his glasses back on and cleared his throat. "It so happens that I need someone to go through the documents in the house. I haven't been able to find anyone willing to do the work at the house, so I was going to have everything boxed up and shipped to an analyst in New Orleans. But if you're willing to do the work, I'd be happy to pay you, instead of removing the documents."

"What are you looking for?"

"Inventory lists, receipts—anything that gives me the ability to construct a list of property. I need to have it evaluated for tax purposes and such. So much is stuffed in the attic, closets and heaven only knows where else that it would take years to uncover it all. I hoped that the most valuable of objects would be contained on an asset listing or that the receipts would be filed with important household documents. Then I could valuate those items, assuming we locate them, and assign a base value to everything else."

Danae could only imagine the mess that must be contained inside the massive old mansion. William definitely had his work cut out for him.

"I know you have your job at the café," William continued, "so please don't feel you have to accept my offer, but I wouldn't feel right if I didn't tell you the rate for the work is twenty-five dollars an hour."

"Seriously?"

"It's boring and dirty work, but requires concentration and attention to detail. The rate is standard for this sort of thing."

Danae ran a mental budget through her head. The rate was considerably more than she made at the café, but once the job was over, what would she do? If she quit now, it would be unlikely that she could get the job back. The waitress she'd replaced six months ago had moved off to New Orleans with her boyfriend, but that relationship had ended and she was back in Calais and hoping for her old job back.

"I anticipate the work will take several months," William said and Danae wondered if he could read her mind. "And during your two-week inheritance stint, you won't be required to pay rent. The estate can hardly charge you for meeting the terms of the will, but the remainder of the lease has to stay in effect."

In several months, she could easily save enough money to cover herself for more than a year. She had no debt and knew how to live on next to nothing. And maybe, if the job lasted long enough, she'd make enough to invest in the future she really wanted—to become a chef. Twenty-five an hour would go a good ways toward paying for culinary school in New Orleans.

"I think I'll take that job," she said.

William beamed. "Good. I'll have my secretary draw up the paperwork."

"Great," she said, hoping she wasn't making a mistake.

"You know, I haven't located Joelle yet, but I have a solid lead and expect to find your sister before month's end. I have no doubt I can convince her to take part in the inheritance requirements."

Danae shook her head. "What if she's got a family, a job…things she can't just up and leave?"

"Yes, all those things matter, but the reality is, with you and Alaina meeting the requirements, Joelle has no risk. Taking those two weeks out of her life will leave all three of you so wealthy that you'll never have to work again unless you choose to."

Danae sucked in a breath. "I didn't… I had no idea."

"Why would you? The estate looks like it needs a bulldozer rather than a cleaning, but the reality is your mother was an incredibly wealthy woman, and even your stepfather couldn't manage to put a dent in her accumulated fortune."

"So once Joelle finishes her two weeks, I…"

"Have the entire world at your fingertips. Whatever you desire for a future, you'll have the means to pursue it." He smiled. "Unless, of course, serving coffee and incredible pie to aging attorneys and disgruntled sheriffs is where your dreams lie."

She laughed. "You make it sound so tempting."

"Yes, well, as much as I'd love to see that beautiful smile at Johnny's Café, I prefer for you to have what you want most. It may take a while," he warned, "to locate Joelle, finish up her term and then push the entire mess through Louisiana's often frustrating legal system. But it shouldn't take more than eighteen months, even if Joelle doesn't fulfill her time right until the end of the year allotted."

"Eighteen months," Danae repeated, trying to wrap her mind around everything the attorney had told her. She'd settled in Calais hoping to find out something about her past, with the ultimate dream of locating her sisters. Her mother's will had come as a huge surprise to her and everyone else in Calais, but the knowledge that her mother's fortune remained intact astounded her.

Even in her wildest dreams—even after hearing about her mother's will—she'd never imagined much would come of it. Rather, she'd thought they would inherit a run-down monstrosity of a house that would be fraught with issues and impossible to sell. But this… this was something out of a fairy tale.

William opened his desk drawer and pulled out a huge black key. "This is the key to the front door," he said as he pushed it across the desk to her. "It's an old locking system, but it's well-oiled. You shouldn't have any problems with access."

She picked up the key, feeling the weight of the old iron in her hand, and thought about everything that single object represented. It was quite literally going to unlock the rest of her life.

"There is one other thing," William said.

A sliver of uncertainty ran through her at the apprehension she detected in the attorney's voice. "Yes?"

"I'm sure you heard that Amos broke his foot and will be staying with his niece here in town."

Danae nodded. Amos was the estate's caretaker and no less than eighty years old, hence the general run-down state of the house and grounds. Her stepfather had refused to hire additional help, and the aging caretaker had been unable to maintain it all himself.

"I'd mentioned before that I've hired a contractor to address the problems at the house," William continued. "He will arrive today and will stay in Amos's cabin. His name is Zach Sargent. He'll need daily access to the house, but I'm going to leave it up to you whether or not you provide him with a key, as you'll also be working inside. If you're uncomfortable with anyone else besides myself, Alaina and the sheriff having free access, I can arrange for someone to let him in daily."

Her gut clenched a little at the thought of a strange man who could enter the house at any time. "Actually, I can let him in and out myself," she said. "I'm an early riser and plan on spending full-time hours working on the files."

William nodded and pulled another key from his drawer. "This is a key to the caretaker's cabin," he said as he pushed it across the desk to her. "I had it stocked with basic supplies yesterday, and I've already made arrangements with the general store for any supplies or tools he needs."

"Great." At least she didn't have to manage the supplies end of things.

"The road—not much more than a path, really—to the caretaker's cabin is at the north end of the main house's driveway. The path leads straight to the cabin, so there's no chance of his getting lost. Just point him in the right direction. I'm sure he can take it from there."

Danae nodded. "You said he'll arrive today?"

"Probably later this afternoon."

"That's good," she said as she rose, the note she'd found on her doorstep weighing heavily on her. But despite her genuine fondness for the attorney, something prevented her from mentioning the incident to him.

"I better run," she said, before she changed her mind and blurted out everything about the note. "I need to square things away with Johnny at the café. How do I handle the work for you?"

William rose from his chair. "Start going through the paperwork—your stepfather's office is the logical choice to begin. Put everything you think relevant for my purposes in a box and keep a log of your time. I'll check in periodically and we'll cut you a check every Friday, if that is all right by you. Don't worry about the hours. The estate is happy to pay for whatever you're willing to work."

"That's great." She extended her hand and clasped his. "Thank you…for everything."

William gave her hand a squeeze. "It's been my pleasure."

She smiled and walked out of his office, giving Secretary Grim a nod on her way through the lobby. After she'd slid into her car, she clenched the steering wheel with both hands, trying to process everything that had happened that morning, but her whirling mind couldn't put it all into neat little boxes.

She'd almost slipped up in there—almost broken down and given William and Alaina more information than she would have normally. It was so unexpected for her to feel that comfortable with other people that she was surprised at herself. Granted, her sister and William seemed to be perfectly nice and straightforward, but her natural distrust of everyone had saved her more times than she could recall. Now was not the time to abandon a way of life that had worked well for her. At least, not until she knew more about Alaina and William.

She blew out a breath and backed her car out of the parking space. It didn't matter that she hadn't told William about the note she'd found that morning. Someone had made a lucky guess and hoped to scare her away or create drama for her. Now that she'd announced herself and stolen their thunder, likely, they'd go away.

At least, that was what she was going to keep telling herself.

Chapter Three

It was almost three o'clock when Zach Sargent pulled into the tiny bayou town of Calais. He shook his head, still not believing his luck. Landing the repair job at the LeBeau estate was an opportunity he'd never even imagined existed, much less that he'd be the one to snag it.

Granted, most men would choose higher-paying construction jobs near the New Orleans nightlife before they'd sequester themselves deep in the swamps of Mystere Parish, but Zach wasn't most men. Far more was at stake than a paycheck and a good time.

Somewhere inside the crumbling walls of the LeBeau estate, he hoped to find the answers to the questions his dad had left him with. Zach knew it was possible that his dad's words had only been the ramblings of a man drugged up and near death, but something in his dad's voice troubled him to the point that he needed to find answers.

He'd thought the words would fade after his burial, but they haunted Zach in his dreams and nagged at him while he was awake. Finally, he'd given up fighting it and started a thorough search of his dad's records from the time his dad had spoken of. It had only taken a couple of days to come across the entry in his check-book that had made Zach's breath catch in his throat. A twenty-thousand-dollar deposit with no explanation noted.

What had his dad done?

What had he regretted so much that he'd laid on his son a garbled confession of some wrongdoing?

Zach had spent many hours since discovering the unexplained deposit trying to imagine what his dad's secret could be. His father had been an honorable man, a good man, raising Zach alone after his mother passed when he was only eight. Zach simply couldn't wrap his mind around his dad doing something so horrible that he felt he had to make it right before he died.

If only he'd spoken to Zach before that last stroke, before his speech was so impaired and before he was so drugged that he couldn't maintain a semblance of coherence. But all of that was wishful thinking and a waste of time.

His dad had said only one name during his ram-blings—Ophelia LeBeau.

Somewhere in that house were the answers Zach sought. He had to believe that. It was the only thing that allowed him to sleep at night. And now he had the opportunity to find out for himself.

When he reached the second crossroads outside of Calais, he checked the map the estate attorney had pro-vided and turned to the right. His truck bumped on the sad excuse for a road, and the farther he drove, the denser the trees and foliage became. If he hadn't known it was only noon, he'd have thought it was dusk. The faintest streams of sunlight managed to peek through the top layers of the cypress trees, but by the time that light penetrated the thick moss clinging to the tree branches, it was filtered to only a dim glow.

If he'd tried, he couldn't have come farther from his Bourbon Street flat than this expanse of seemingly never-ending swamp. He'd expected remote, but he hadn't expected to feel so enclosed, so claustrophobic. After all, he lived in an eight-hundred-square-foot flat. Miles of dirt and water should make him feel less confined, not more so.

He shook his head, clearing his mind of fanciful thoughts that had no place there, and ran through his plan once he'd gained access to the house and the records. With any luck, everything would be well organized and he'd find his answer quickly. Honor and loyalty would force him to complete the work needed on the house, even if he got his answer the first day, but the work would be easier and go more quickly without the distraction of the unanswered question hanging over his head.

His truck dipped into a large pothole and he cursed as he gripped the steering wheel more firmly, trying to maintain control of the vehicle as it lurched sideways. If he had to replace anything in the house that was breakable, he'd have to creep down this road to keep from destroying things before he even got them there.

Finally, when he thought he'd driven straight across the United States to Canada, he turned a final corner, and the house loomed before him. Involuntarily, he lifted his foot from the gas, and the truck rolled almost to a stop as he stared at the imposing structure.

The architect in him formed an immediate appreciation for the bold lines and refined features of the mansion. The part of him dedicated to B horror movies was certain he'd driven straight into a midnight feature.

It was horrifying and seductive, all at the same time.

He inched the truck around the decrepit stone driveway and parked behind an ancient sedan. The attorney's car, he thought as he exited the truck and made his way to the massive double doors. He scanned the door frame for a bell, but didn't see anything resembling such a device, so he rapped on the solid wood door.

Seconds later, the door flew open and he found himself staring at someone who clearly was not the aging male attorney he'd spoken to on the phone.

The girl in front of him was small but toned, with short black hair and amber eyes that were narrowed on him. It took him a couple of seconds to realize that despite her youthful appearance, she was more woman than girl, and a bit of relief coursed through him because the male part of him had been instantly appreciative of her trim body and chiseled facial features.

The woman's shrewd eyes looked him up and down and glanced at his vehicle, quickly making an assessment, but when he expected her to speak, she just stared directly at him, her eyes locked on his, unwavering.

"I'm Zach Sargent," he said finally, extending his hand. "I'm the contractor William Duhon hired to make the repairs to the house."

The woman hesitated a second before briefly clasping his hand, then releasing it. "I'm Danae LeBeau," she said.

Zach felt his pulse quicken. Could this woman be Ophelia LeBeau's daughter? William had mentioned that one of the heiresses had been living in the house, but the name Danae didn't ring any bells.

She stepped back and opened the door for him to enter. "I have the key to the caretaker's cottage in the kitchen."

Zach stepped inside and did a double take at the

gloomy interior, layered with dust and sadly lacking in basic maintenance and care. The attorney had said the property needed a lot of work, but Zach thought it had been occupied until recently. He was somewhat shocked that a person would choose to live like this.

"You coming?" Danae asked, her eyebrows arched.

Before he could reply, she continued down a wide hallway to the left of the entry. He blew out a breath and followed her down the hall, then drew up short in the kitchen. The room was a refreshing change from the entry. Stone countertops and floors gleamed, the cabinets and dining table were polished to a high sheen and a new coat of paint covered the walls.

"Is something wrong?"

"What…? No," he replied, realizing he'd been casing the room like an eager real-estate agent or petty thief. "Sorry, I was just taking in the contrast between this room and the entry."

Danae nodded. "My sister started cleaning and re-modeling here a couple of weeks ago, but hasn't had time to get much more done."

Zach frowned. "I don't understand. William said the house had been occupied until recently."

"By our stepfather. My sisters and I haven't been allowed to set foot here since we were sent away as children…when our mother died."

Her jaw flexed when she delivered that information, and some of the bitter edge the heiress displayed began to make sense. "I'm sorry. I didn't mean to bring up a sensitive subject."

"You're not the first. Won't be the last." She pulled a key out of her purse and placed it on the end of the counter. "That's the key to the caretaker's cabin. The path to the cabin is at the north end of the main driveway. William had it stocked with basic living supplies, but he has you set up with the general store to handle anything beyond that."

He nodded. "Great. And what about a key to the main house?"

She stiffened and shook her head. "The house isn't habitable in the shape it's in, but I'm going to be working here, as well. I'll let you in every morning and lock up at night."

Zach struggled to maintain his aggravation, but knew if he made a big deal out of having free access to the house, she may start to wonder. Still, being under constant scrutiny wasn't going to get him what he'd come for. He had to find an angle that worked.

"Are you sure?" he asked, trying to sound casual. "I prefer to start early."

She'd been gazing out the back window, but when he delivered his last sentence, she looked directly at him—pinned him with those dark eyes—and he got the impression she wasn't buying what he'd said. Not completely.

"I've worked in cafés and bars for years. I'm used to getting up early and finishing up late, and as I have no other personal business in this town except the estate, your work won't interfere with my schedule."

"Okay, then. I guess I'll see you tomorrow morning at seven. If that's all right?"

"No problem at all."

"Have a good evening," he said and started down the hall to the front entry. Zach knew when he'd lost the battle. As much as he didn't need the interference, he'd have to play things Danae's way.

At least until he could find a way around her.

Chapter Four

Danae peered out a tiny crack in the front door, watching Zach drive away. He hadn't been at all what she'd expected when William had told her he'd hired a contractor. She'd thought someone older, someone not as adept at repair as they used to be, would be the only person interested in a job out in the middle of the swamp. The young, gorgeous man who'd just left was the absolute last person she'd thought would be interested in a job in a town like Calais.

With his light brown hair, piercing green eyes and stellar body, Zach belonged in the heart of New Orleans, charming all the ladies who came downtown looking for a good time. He certainly didn't fit Calais and the LeBeau estate.

Frowning, she pushed the heavy wooden door shut, unable to shake the feeling that something about the sexy contractor didn't add up. Briefly, it crossed her mind that he was running from something, but she dismissed the thought as soon as it came. He didn't have that look of flight, and she knew that look well. She'd worn it several times herself and seen it in many others.

Finally, she sighed. Likely, it was something simple and embarrassing. If bartending had taught her anything, it was that most people had some secret that they kept locked away from others. The secret wasn't often earth-shattering, but simply something the person felt would change others' opinions of them. Maybe Zach had such a secret—like a gambling or drinking problem. Something that had given him a bad reputation with construction companies in New Orleans.

She shook her head to clear her thoughts of Zach and the many different things he could be hiding and tried to focus on what she wanted to tackle next. She'd arrived at the house only twenty minutes before noon, and aside from talking to Zach, she'd spent the rest of the time doing a run-through of the downstairs rooms, checking windows and exterior doors to ensure no unwanted guests could enter.

By the time she had finished her review of the downstairs, she expected Zach to arrive at any moment and had been unwilling to start poking around upstairs. She preferred instead to get her meeting with the contractor out of the way and delve more into her past when she was alone again with the memories that she couldn't seem to access.

She had just decided to head upstairs and get a feel for the rooms there when her cell phone rang. She checked the display and frowned. It wasn't a number she recognized, but it definitely wasn't in Louisiana.

She answered and was happy to hear Alaina's voice.

"I'm so sorry," Alaina said. "I meant to call earlier, but I didn't charge my cell before leaving, so it's dead as a doornail. This is the first opportunity I've had to break away from the family and call you. I hope you didn't think I'd forgotten."

"No, of course not. How is your…er, mother?"

Even though she didn't really know Alaina at all,

it still felt strange calling another woman her sister's mother. She wondered how it felt for Alaina.

"She's doing fine, considering. My brother has a service lined up for home care until she can get around again, but they are on another job at the moment and not expected to free up for another week at least."

A twinge of something—sadness…jealousy—passed through Danae when Alaina said *my brother* but she pushed it aside. Their stepfather hadn't given any of the girls a choice when he'd sent them away. Alaina couldn't help it if she'd gotten a decent family, while Danae had gotten an addict. That was simply the luck of the draw.

"I'm glad she's okay," Danae said.

"Me, too, but the timing couldn't be worse. I'm so sorry I had to dash out this morning like I did. I have a million things to talk to you about. If I started now, I probably couldn't finish by next year."

Danae smiled. "I know."

"But first things first—I am so glad you don't have to stay in that house. When I thought about you staying there, my chest hurt so bad I felt like it was in a vise."

"I'm at the house now. It's not exactly a welcoming sort of place."

"No, but it's more than that. It's…I don't know… Oh, I'll just say it. I think there's something wrong in that house. I know you don't really know me, but I promise you, I'm not a fanciful sort of person. And given my profession, my senses are better honed than many. I know something's off. I can feel it in every inch of my body."

Danae tensed at her sister's description. It was the same way she'd felt since she'd walked into the house.

Alaina sighed. "I bet I sound like a crazy woman."

"I almost wish you did, but you're not crazy. I feel it,

too. And let's just say my survival skills are as finely tuned as your ability to recognize when things don't add up. They're firing on all eight cylinders here. But I have no idea why."

"I don't, either, and that's what concerns me the most. I'm not trying to tell you what to do, but I wish you wouldn't go there at all."

"William has hired me to go through the paperwork and attempt an inventory of the valuables, so I don't have a choice, and I really want to do the work. I want to discover things about our past. Things I'll probably never remember."

Alaina was quiet for several seconds, then finally she said, "I tried to find you—you and Joelle. I started writing letters to Purcell when I was in high school, asking him to tell me how to find you. I even tried sending him a letter on the law firm's letterhead when I got to Baton Rouge."

"But he never answered," Danae finished. "He wouldn't have. I spent months looking for that opening where I could get to him, but there wasn't one. He was a mentally disturbed old man who only cared about himself. He never would have helped any of us."

"You're probably right. I understand why you want to try to find some of the things that were torn away from you, but I still don't like the idea of you being in that house alone. Can you at least work at your cabin until I return?"

Danae felt a tickle of warmth run through her. The concern in Alaina's voice was so sincere and passionate—something she'd never experienced until now. It was everything she'd ever wanted and something she'd never counted on getting.

"When we get off the phone, I'll grab some files and

take them home with me today. The contractor starts tomorrow, so I won't be alone. He's young and looks like he'd be good in a fight."

"Well, I guess that's all right."

Alaina didn't sound the least bit convinced, but Danae couldn't exactly fault her when she wasn't convinced herself.

"Purcell's office is upstairs at the end of the right hallway," Alaina said. "The room I stayed in—our childhood room—is at the end of the left hallway, right over the kitchen. The power is out in the office area of the house, so it will be dark. There're some flashlights and a lantern in the laundry-room cabinet."

"Thanks. That helps a lot," Danae replied as she committed all the information to memory.

"Danae," Alaina said, "I know this is going to sound completely odd, but I have to ask you something."

"Okay."

"Do you believe in ghosts?"

Danae's breath caught in her throat. Of all the things she'd thought Alaina might ask, that hadn't been anywhere on the list.

Before she could formulate a reply, she heard background noise on Alaina's end.

"I'm so sorry," Alaina said, "but I'm going to have to go. I'll call you again as soon as I get a chance."

Alaina disconnected and Danae set the phone back on the counter. Ghosts? Sure, all kinds of rumors about the house and its other-than-earthly inhabitants wafted about the Calais locales, but it was the sort of thing she'd expect in a small town with a run-down, isolated house. It was not the kind of thing a reputable, hard-nosed attorney would normally come up with.

It made Danae wonder exactly how much she didn't know about the night Alaina was attacked.

She leaned back against the counter and blew out a breath. All the work she'd done to simplify her life. No strings, no baggage—at least not the physical kind. She'd even come to Calais with an assumed identity simply to avoid the looks and questions she was sure would come. And in less than a day, her life had become more complicated than it had ever been.

This is what you wanted.

And that was what she needed to keep reminding herself. In the past, she'd kept her life simple by avoiding anything beyond surface-level relationships, but she'd come to Calais to find her family. She couldn't have it both ways. If she wanted a family, she had to drop her guard, at least where her sisters were concerned.

She pushed herself off the counter and headed upstairs for the first time. She paused on the landing, trying to remember what Alaina had told her about the layout. Right was Purcell's office. Left was the girls' room—the room Alaina had been staying in when she was attacked.

Danae took one step in that direction, then froze. Was she ready to see the place where she'd spent her very limited childhood in Calais? If she had no memory of that room, then the chances of her remembering anything were so minuscule as to not exist. Not that she'd had any concrete expectation of remembering things she'd last seen at two years old, but she'd hoped for an emotional tug—something that let her know a piece of this place was part of her.

Something that let her know where she fit.

Abruptly, she turned and headed in the opposite direction, to her stepfather's office.

Coward.

Ignoring the voice in her head, she increased her pace. Plenty of time existed for her to see her childhood bedroom, she argued. She had no reason to try to force it all into one afternoon. When she was comfortable with the house, she'd go to the room.

Or when she was ready for the disappointment.

Sighing, she pushed open the last door in the hallway and reached inside for a light switch, hoping the power had been miraculously restored. No such luck. She stepped inside the room and flicked the switch up and down to no avail. It figured. First thing tomorrow, she'd ask Zach to look at the electrical problems, starting with this room.

The light from the balcony was the only source of illumination in the office. The lack of windows and cherrywood bookcases that lined every wall made it so dark it was impossible to see more than the dim outline of office furniture. She cursed under her breath at her lapse of logical judgment. Alaina had told her about the flashlights in the laundry room. She should have grabbed one before coming up here.

She backed out of the room, but as she started to turn, she caught a glimpse of something out of the corner of her eye. She froze and stared into the darkness at the far end of the room, where she'd seen the flicker of movement. Nothing moved there now, but everything in Danae screamed at her that she was not alone in the house.

She whirled around and ran all the way downstairs and back into the kitchen, where she'd left her purse. It was still on the kitchen counter, and she snatched it up. From the inside pocket, she drew out the nine millimeter she was never without.

Let that be a lesson.

With the distraction of Zach Sargent, and her first visit to her childhood home, and her conversation with her sister, she'd forgotten to keep protection within arm's reach. Her sister's attacker was dead and gone, but more than one danger could exist.

Even in the same house.

Clenching the pistol, she eased down the hallway and across the entry to the laundry room. Two flashlights and a lantern were located right where Alaina had said they'd be. She clicked on a flashlight to make sure it worked, then headed back upstairs to the office.

She crept down the hallway toward the office and paused just before the doorway, listening for any sound of movement inside. Not even a breath of air swept by, so she stepped into the doorway and turned on the flashlight, shining it in the corner where she'd seen the movement.

The corner was empty, but the last bookcase appeared to have an odd angle to it—one that didn't fit with the other wall. Clenching the flashlight in one hand and her pistol in the other, she stepped across the room to the back wall, where she was surprised to find a narrow opening at the back of the wall. When looking into the room from the doorway, the opening was almost hidden by the bookcase.

The room was pitch-black, and for a moment, she wished she'd brought the lantern as well as the flashlight. Shining the flashlight across the room, she realized this must have been her stepfather's bedroom. The office entrance was the last doorway in the hallway, so at some point, her bizarre stepfather must have closed off the main entrance to the bedroom, leaving the office as the only access to his private quarters.

Just how crazy was he?

At the first opportunity, that was a question she'd explore with William, and perhaps pay a visit to Amos, the caretaker, while he was recovering at his niece's house. She stepped into the room and slowly cast the thin flashlight beam across the room, moving left to right. On the left, at the back of the room, she saw another door and the light fell across a claw-foot tub beyond it. Then she scanned over his bed, still made up with sheets, and paused at the nightstand, with its collection of pill bottles and a half-empty glass of water still standing next to them.

Clearly, Alaina hadn't spent much time, if any, in this room. Not that she blamed her. The room was unsettling. The air was stiller, as if she'd stepped into a vacuum, and not a single sound echoed through the exterior walls and into the bedroom.

Like a tomb.

The thought ripped through her, and despite the heat of early fall, she shivered. The thought was too accurate for comfort. Her stepfather had locked himself away from society, then practically barricaded himself in this room and died. It was something a sane person simply couldn't wrap their mind around.

She lifted the flashlight beam from the nightstand and continued along the back wall to the right, where she almost missed a wooden door, carved to match the paneling. Closet, maybe?

She didn't want to take another step into the room, but she would be working just outside this room and had to know that it was secure. Her heart pounded as she inched across the bedroom, feeling as if every step took her farther and farther away from safety. When she reached the door, she placed the flashlight on the nightstand, the light shining onto the ceiling and casting a dim glow around her.

She tightened her grip on the pistol and slowly turned the doorknob and eased the door open. As the light filtered into the opening, she frowned. The clothes she'd expected to see were nowhere in sight. Instead, a steep flight of stairs led down to the first floor.

A shock wave of fear ran through her and she released the doorknob and staggered back a couple of steps. During her tour of the first floor, she'd found the servants' stairwell close to the laundry room, but she'd assumed the entry would be off the hallway upstairs. She'd never considered that the stairs would lead straight into the master bedroom.

Someone could have been here.

She grabbed the flashlight and hurried out of the room and back downstairs, rushing across the entry to the back of the house, where she'd seen the exit for the servants' stairs. The door was closed, but before she could think about all the potential dangers, she yanked it open, pointing her pistol inside.

She hadn't realized she'd been holding her breath until it rushed out in a whoosh. *Get a grip,* she told herself as she pushed the door shut, noting that it didn't make a sound as it closed. If someone had passed this way earlier, she wouldn't have heard them exit. But the big question was, if someone had been in the house, where were they now?

The laundry room was at the end of the hallway, just a few feet beyond the servants' stairs. She hurried to the laundry room to check the back door. The knob turned easily in her hand, and she pushed the door open and looked out into the backyard that had been swallowed up by the swamp. Vines and moss clung to every branch of the cypress trees that loomed above, while moss and weeds choked out any remaining sign of lawn.

She stared at the tangle of foliage and decided it made her just as uneasy as the master bedroom. It wasn't just here, either. The swamp surrounding her cabin felt equally as ominous—as if it were a living entity and resented her trespass. For a girl who'd lived in some of the toughest neighborhoods across the country, it was unnerving to get such powerful feelings from a bunch of trees and brush.

She pushed the door shut and locked the dead bolt, her mind made up. Someone had been in the house. They'd stayed hidden upstairs while she was searching the first floor, then used her trip upstairs as an opportunity to slip out of the house unseen. They probably thought she'd dismiss the unlatched back door as an oversight, but they were wrong. Street-smart women like Danae didn't have "oversights" on things as important as exterior doors, and she was certain it was locked when she'd examined the first floor earlier.

In the past, when her safety had been threatened, she'd simply packed up and moved on. She'd had no roots and nothing of value to keep her tied to any one place, especially a dangerous one. But now she had something to lose. Something huge. Running was out of the question, so she hurried back to the kitchen and pulled out her cell phone.

For the first time in her life, she was calling the police.

Chapter Five

Zach paced the tiny caretaker's cottage, aggravated with almost everything. His original enthusiasm over scoring the LeBeau estate job was seriously compromised after meeting Danae LeBeau. The heiress had enchanting features and a stellar body, but was prickly and suspicious and was already making a mess of his carefully laid plans.

How was he supposed to dig around in the house records with her looking over his shoulder? If she were going to be at the house every day alongside him, that didn't leave him any opportunity to snoop during that time. Now his only option was to find a way inside the house so that he could search for his answers at night.

Maybe he'd luck into a spare key lying around. If not, then he'd make sure to leave a window unlocked—a downstairs one with easy access, if such a thing existed. The swamp had almost swallowed the house, the brush and weeds pushing their way right up to the house walls.

He stopped pacing and ran one hand through his hair. What the hell was he supposed to do until tomorrow morning? Even if he could have distracted his overloaded mind with television, the caretaker didn't own a set. No television, no radio, not even a crossword-puzzle book. What in the world did the man do for entertainment?

He glanced at his watch for the hundredth time since leaving the mansion. Four o'clock. At this rate, he'd wear out the cabin's wooden floors before nightfall with all this pacing. Maybe Danae was still at the house. If so, he could always ask if he could take an inventory. That way, he could pick up any needed supplies in order to begin work straightaway the next morning. Surely she couldn't find fault with that logic.

Mind made up, he grabbed his keys and headed back to the mansion. As he pulled into the drive, he saw a truck with the sheriff's logo on the door. His hand tightened on the steering wheel as he pulled behind the truck and parked. What could be going on that warranted the sheriff?

He hopped out of his truck, and as he started toward the front door, it opened and a man stepped out. Zach studied the sheriff as he approached the entrance. This athletic man looked to be about the same age as him, the last thing he'd imagined for the sheriff of Calais. An aging, balding man with a potbelly was more what he would have guessed.

The sheriff caught his gaze immediately as he stepped outside and glanced back at Danae, who stood just inside the door. She said something to him and he nodded then made his way across the drive, meeting Zach halfway.

"Carter Trahan," the sheriff said and extended his hand.

"Zach Sargent," he replied and gave Carter's hand a firm shake. "I hope there wasn't any trouble here."

"Not at all. I promised Alaina I'd check up on Danae."

"Alaina?"

"Her sister." Carter grinned. "And the woman most likely to make my life miserable if I don't follow her instructions."

Zach smiled. "Is Alaina as attractive as her sister?"

"Ah, now, see, I can't answer that question without being in trouble with someone, so I'll just say they're both gorgeous in their own right and leave it at that."

"You're a wise man."

Carter nodded. "Danae tells me William hired you to make the repairs."

"Yeah," Zach said. "I just got a glance at the inside earlier, but it looks like my work's cut out for me."

"Definitely." He studied Zach for a moment. "This seems an odd choice of jobs for someone as young as you. I figured the reconstruction in New Orleans pays better and offers the nightlife."

The delivery of the statement was casual, but Zach knew a fishing expedition when he heard it. The sheriff's seemingly pleasant disposition didn't completely mask his shrewd observation skills. Zach had to be very careful, very deliberate, around this man. If he gave Carter any reason at all to suspect he wasn't exactly who he claimed to be, he'd run him out of town on a rail.

"The rates are better, that's true. But I've been in the city all my life. Sometimes a man just needs to get away from everything—slow down a bit."

Carter nodded. "I get that. Did it myself earlier this year. Resigned my detective position with the New Orleans Police Department and came back home to run herd over a town with less people than my old apartment building."

Zach struggled to keep the surprise and worry from his expression. A young, inquisitive sheriff with big-city experience and connections was the last person he needed looking into his background. This was no small-town sheriff that could be easily fooled. "Any regrets?"

"Not a single one."

"Then maybe I'm on the right track."

Carter smiled. "Did you get settled in the caretaker's cabin?"

"Didn't bring much with me except work clothes and some tools. To tell the truth, I was feeling kinda stir-crazy, so I came to see if Danae was still here. Thought I could put together a supply list and get it filled this evening. Save me some time getting started tomorrow morning."

"Efficient. I like that. Well, guess I'll leave you to it. Maybe I'll see you in town sometime—buy you a slice of pie and coffee down at the café."

"That sounds like the best offer I've had in weeks. Nice meeting you."

"You, too," Carter said as he strolled to his truck. He gave Zach a wave as he pulled away.

Zach looked over at the entry, not surprised to see Danae still standing there, observing the entire exchange. She frowned as Carter's truck pulled away, and Zach wondered if Danae wasn't thrilled with her sister's choice of men. He'd seemed nice enough but a person never really knew what went on behind closed doors.

Maybe she wants him for herself.

The thought came unbidden and he felt a twinge of jealousy, which irked him. He was in Calais to find answers and then get back to his real life in New Orleans. He'd pulled major strings to manage even a few weeks away. The absolute last thing he needed to do was waste any of his precious time with amorous thoughts of a woman who seemed annoyed at his presence.

"I wasn't expecting to see you back so soon," Danae

said as he approached the door, her tone telling him straight off she wasn't the least bit happy to see him, either.

"I was hoping to get a quick inventory—maybe get some of the supplies this evening."

"That's what I heard. I'm going to be here another hour or so. Do you think you can cover enough ground by then?"

He shrugged. "It will be more than I have now."

Danae opened the door wider and stepped back, allowing him to enter.

"So," he said as he stepped inside, "your sister and the sheriff?"

She raised one eyebrow. "I didn't take you for a romantic, Mr. Sargent."

"Please call me Zach. And maybe I was just interested in your sister."

She gave him the faintest of smiles. "Most men that have seen her are."

"Really? Then I guess it's a real shame she's settled on a guy who carries a gun for a living."

"You don't like living dangerously?"

Surprised at the slightly teasing tone of her voice, he smiled. "Not when it comes to women."

"Smart."

She turned and waved a hand toward the vast open entry. Zach couldn't help but notice how her jeans curved over her hips, how her T-shirt clung to her full chest and tiny waist.

"What did you have in mind?" she asked.

"Huh?" Her question came at the worst possible time, because at that moment, none of the things he had in mind had anything to do with the repairs.

"Well," he drawled, hurrying to recover, "I thought

I'd do a quick inventory of rooms to note the obvious items. I'm sure the list will expand as I begin work. Is there any problem in particular you'd like me to start with?"

Danae nodded. "The power is my biggest concern. I will be working through the property records for William, and the office is one of those rooms where the power is out. I can haul the files to the kitchen to work, but it would make it easier to see in there…"

Her voice trailed off and she frowned.

"Is something wrong?" he asked.

"It's stupid."

"Why don't you let me be the judge of that?"

She stared off across the entry then finally blew out a breath before turning to face him. "It's creepy, okay? I know that sounds foolish and girly and weak, but the room is creepy and the lack of lighting makes it worse." She dropped her gaze to the floor.

"It doesn't sound foolish or weak at all. For my own well-being, I'm not touching the 'girly' comment." He scanned the cavernous room, littered with columns with various sculptures and statues—all covered with layers of dust and cobwebs. "Look, I'm sure this place was beautiful once, but I have to tell you, it wouldn't be someplace I'd choose to stay."

She looked up at him, a flicker of appreciation in her expression. "Really?"

He held up one hand. "Swear. This place is gloomy and depressing. Your sister's work in the kitchen gives me an idea of what it could look like, though."

Danae gave him an appreciative smile. "You're right. I need to keep reminding myself that it will feel different after the repairs are made and we've managed a good scrubbing."

"It's none of my business, but why doesn't William hire someone to do the cleaning?"

"According to café gossip, he's tried, but none of them last more than a day."

"Why not?"

She smiled. "Because of the ghost."

Maybe it was the decrepit state of the house, or maybe it was the swamp that was slowly swallowing up the entire structure, but he actually gave her statement more than a moment's passing thought.

"Ghost, huh?" he said finally.

"That's what I hear."

"But you haven't seen it?"

"No, but then today is the first day I've been in this house since I was a toddler."

He wanted to ask her more about her stepfather and her sisters, but as soon as she'd issued that statement, her expression had gone from somewhat relaxed to completely closed off again.

"Who's the ghost supposed to be?" he asked instead.

She frowned. "I don't know. I assumed it was my stepfather. Based on the description of his lifestyle from the locals, it sounds like he was agoraphobic. I guess I figured that even in death, he didn't want to leave the house."

"Well, then, I guess I best get to work lighting up this place before I have to add a ghost to the payroll."

Danae gave him a small smile, but he could tell that something was bothering her. She appeared to be telling the truth when she said she hadn't seen a ghost, but something had happened that put her on edge—something beyond just a spooky house. She was too observant, too suspicious for the average person. Either she was paranoid or she had something to worry about. Both concerned him as either could blow his cover.

"Where would you like to start?" Danae asked.

"Well, I know the electricity is a priority, but I need to test everything before I can pin down the problem. I brought my voltage equipment with me, so I'll start that tomorrow morning. I thought I'd take a tour of the house and note the obvious needs. Then I can have supplies on hand for several jobs."

Danae nodded. "So if you have to wait on special orders, you can keep working on other things."

"Exactly."

"Then I guess we can start downstairs."

We? The last thing he needed was the cagey heiress lingering over his shoulder while he cased the house, especially now that his mind had formed a permanent imprint of her absolutely perfect rear end. But before he could formulate a logical argument, she spun around and headed to the kitchen, then came right back with a pad of paper and a pen.

"It will probably go faster if you dictate as you go," she said. "I can make the notes. That way you don't have to stop what you're doing to write."

He nodded, unable to argue with the efficiency her plan presented. "I assume you have a basic idea of the layout, so lead the way."

She pointed to rooms that lined the south side of the house. "We can start over there and work our way around."

He followed her into the first room and was pleased to find it only contained a table, dresser and a couple of boxes. The west window was intact, but a sheet of plywood covered the wall where he guessed a south-facing window was located. "What happened here?" he asked, pointing to the plywood.

"I haven't asked about it yet, but I assume the guy who attacked my sister broke it to get inside. The plywood covering it looks new."

He stared at her. "Someone attacked your sister in the house?"

"Yeah." She frowned then shook her head. "I guess I forget it's just hitting the news this morning. He attacked her here but she ran into the swamp and got away. He caught up with her trying to get away in her SUV, and that's when Carter shot and killed him."

He stared at her for a moment, trying to absorb the implications of trying to keep his cover intact at a crime scene. This entire situation was becoming more complicated by the minute. "Wow! Is she all right?"

"She's fine." Danae cocked her head to the side and studied him for a moment. "Most people would ask who was trying to kill her and why."

"You said it just hit the news. I can catch up on the local gossip later. I have a younger cousin who's more like a brother to me. I guess I was thinking about something happening to him."

"Are you always this logical?"

"I try to be. It seems to make life easier."

"Well, then, I guess we best get back to this list. I don't want to throw you off course."

He crossed to the intact window and studied it. "I'll have to remove the plywood to check the dimensions, so I'll leave off replacing the window for later. I'm going to have to special-order something to even come close to matching the others, but I know a guy in New Orleans who specializes in making windows for restoration projects. I can get some pictures tomorrow and see what he can do."

He reached up for the latches and opened the window, then pulled it upward, but it stayed firmly in place. It only took a moment to realize the sliding pane of the window had been nailed into the frame. The oxidation on the edges of the nails let him know that wasn't a recent addition.

"This window is nailed shut," he said.

"Yeah. They all are. I suppose my stepfather was agoraphobic *and* paranoid."

"He didn't want out and didn't want anyone else in." He shook his head. "That's no way to live. I'll remove the nails tomorrow—test all the windows and make sure they lift properly."

"No!"

The single word came out with such force that he spun around, surprised. She stood with her arms crossed. Her face was slightly flushed and her jaw set in a hard line.

"I can't test the windows if they're nailed shut."

"Then I guess they won't get tested—not as long as I'm working in this house. At least this way, if someone wants to get in here, I'll hear them coming or see the results of their attempt the next morning. What I don't want is for someone to have the element of surprise."

He studied her for a moment. Had he misjudged her? He'd thought her suspicious and hypercautious, but could Danae be tipping into the same realm of madness that her stepfather had lived the last of his life in?

"Are you expecting trouble?" he asked.

"No," she said a little too quickly. "It's just that the house is full of valuable antiques and if word gets out it's empty at night…"

She was lying. She was very, very good at it, but

he'd employed too many ex-cons to recognize a snow job when he was getting one. The house *was* full of antiques, and he suspected a lot of them were valuable, but that wasn't the reason she was worried about intruders.

Maybe Danae had brought trouble with her to Calais. Maybe she was afraid that trouble was about to catch up with her. Either way, in addition to tiptoeing around with his own agenda, he was going to have to constantly look over his own shoulder, watching for whatever the heiress was hiding from.

"Okay," he said finally. "It's your house."

He motioned to a door in the corner behind her. "Bathroom or closet?"

"Closet, I think. I'm sorry. There're so many rooms, I haven't gotten everything straight yet."

She turned and pulled the door open. As soon as she did, a stack of boxes tilted out and toppled onto her, sending her reeling backward. Mice scattered across the floor, scurrying in every direction, looking for an escape.

He rushed forward, catching her before she crashed to the ground. She'd twisted her body in anticipation of the fall, trying to reach for the floor before slamming into it. Now she was gathered in his arms, the front of her toned, curvy body pressed against him. That beautiful face looking up at him—so strong, yet vulnerable.

It was a bad idea, but before he could talk himself out of it, he lowered his lips to hers.

Her lips were soft and pliant as he caressed them with his own, and he felt a surge of excitement go through him that he hadn't felt before from a simple kiss. He pressed harder, deepening the kiss, and was almost surprised when she responded, her lips searching his.

Then suddenly, she jumped up and backed away from

him, one hand over her mouth. She stared at him, her face flushed, her expression a mixture of shock and anxiety.

"You should finish this yourself." She whirled around and practically ran out of the room.

He stared at the empty doorway, trying to decide if he'd been a genius or a fool. On one hand, he'd probably prevented her from asking more intrusive questions about his life. Clearly, she wanted to avoid anything personal.

On the other hand, he'd enjoyed that kiss entirely too much for his own comfort.

Get in gear, Sargent!

He grabbed the paper and pen and hustled out of the room, his mind suddenly latching onto the golden opportunity she'd presented. For the first time since he'd entered the property, Danae wasn't looking over his shoulder. She was flustered enough to rush off, so with any luck, she'd remain far away until he sought her out. That gave him a window of opportunity to create an entry into the home.

The one functional window in the first room had led straight into a huge, thorny rosebush, so it wasn't an option. He hoped his luck would be better in the second room, but it had furniture and boxes stacked to the ceiling and he could barely squeeze inside. No feasible way to reach the windows existed, so he continued to the next room. This one wasn't quite as cluttered, but it still contained stacks of paper, boxes and small furniture. He lifted several boxes away from the wall where he guessed the window was located and was pleased to find only two nails through the frame.

He hurried back to the doorway and glanced around the entry, then pulled out his pocketknife and began working the first nail from the frame. Every time the knife blade slipped from under the nail's head, he mentally cursed and wished for the pry bar in his truck, but no way was he risking the opportunity by leaving the house to get it.

Finally, the first nail worked out of the frame and he checked the entry again before starting on the second nail. This one was deeper, leaving creases in the hardwood where it had been pounded into the frame, and he struggled to get even a tiny piece of his knife blade underneath.

Suddenly, there was a loud thud overhead and he froze before closing the pocketknife and shoving it into his jeans pocket. Then he dashed back to the front of the room and grabbed the paper and pen. He peered out the door, but saw no sign of Danae. Then a second thud echoed across the entry from above, letting him know someone was moving around upstairs.

Surely it was Danae working upstairs. He started to run back to the window to finish up but hesitated. Seconds later, Danae rushed into the entry from the kitchen hallway, her eyes wide.

Chapter Six

"Did you drop something?" Danae asked, her voice shaking slightly.

Zach shook his head and put one finger over his lips then pointed at the ceiling. Her eyes widened and she sucked in a breath. Then the split second of fear was gone and her expression hardened as she pulled a nine millimeter from her waistband.

He didn't even bother to control his surprise. Minutes before, he'd had the woman wrapped in his arms and hadn't even known she was packing serious firepower. Before he could even formulate a plan, she slipped silently across the entry and up the staircase. He hesitated only a second before hurrying behind her, cursing that his pistol was locked away in his truck along with his pry bar.

He caught up with her at the top of the stairs and pointed at the far end of the hallway to the right, where he thought the noise might have originated. She nodded and hurried down the hall, using the carpeted runner in the middle of the hallway to mask her footsteps.

Zach peered into each room as they passed, but if anyone was hiding inside, it would have taken more than a peek to discover them. The rooms were just as crowded with boxes and furniture as the downstairs rooms he'd seen. As they reached the last door, Danae stopped and looked back at him. He gave her a nod, and she sprang around the doorway, gun leveled.

He was only a millisecond behind her, but his expertly executed timing was useless. This time, it was clear the room was empty, even with only the dim lighting from the entry to illuminate it. Purcell's office, he thought, as he stepped inside. A huge ornate desk stood in the center of the room, a massive chair with faded, cracked leather positioned behind it. The walls were completely covered with bookcases that were overflowing with books and paper. Plastic containers, also filled with paper, littered most of the floor, leaving only a narrow pathway behind the desk and to the far corner.

"That's the entry to the master bedroom," Danae whispered and pointed to the corner where the path ended.

He squinted into the shadows and realized that the last bookcase didn't meet quite right with the back wall. He stepped across the room and peered into an even darker room beyond the office, unable to make out anything but the faint form of bedroom furniture.

"Do you have a flashlight?" he asked.

"Downstairs, but it wouldn't matter. If anyone was here, he's gone now."

"Gone where?"

"There's a servants' staircase at the back of the bedroom. It leads downstairs into the hallway off the laundry room. I found it earlier today."

Zach clenched his pocketknife, trying to process the information. "Something caused those thumps and it wasn't footsteps."

He walked back across the office, scanning the floor

as he went, then indicated two cardboard boxes dumped sideways on the floor at the edge of the desk. The sides were split in two and the papers inside were scattered across the floor.

"Maybe it was those boxes," he said.

Danae looked over at the boxes, then up at the desk and nodded. "I saw those there earlier. I intended to take them home with me tonight."

"Did you place them too close to the edge?"

She stared at the desk and frowned. "They were already there, but maybe they were close to the edge. I was distracted when I was up here."

He nodded. "Yeah, I can see why. You were right."

"About what?"

"This room *is* creepy." He fingered a stack of papers hanging off the end of a bookcase, suspended in place by a paperweight. "It's like looking at the culmination of one man's madness. I'm guessing the bedroom is no better."

"I've only seen it by flashlight, but I'm going to go with a 'definitely not better' on that one."

Zach ran one hand through his hair and blew out a breath. "Let's go check the doors downstairs—make sure they're all still locked."

"Good idea." She grabbed a stack of the files from the floor and rushed out of the office like a shot.

Zach gave the gloomy room one more glance and hurried behind her. He hadn't been lying to pacify her. Something about those two rooms felt off. Since he'd taken his first step inside, he'd had the overwhelming feeling that he needed to leave. He was glad he didn't have to ignore it any longer.

Danae led the way, and it only took minutes to check the downstairs doors. Only minutes to ascertain that all were locked tight and showed no signs of recent passage. Danae stepped out of the laundry room and walked slowly back to the entry, frowning the entire way.

"Maybe the boxes were too close to the edge of the desk," she said finally.

"You didn't think so earlier."

She blew out a breath, clearly frustrated. "I can't be sure. I told you earlier I didn't like the room. I know it's stupid, but I accidentally moved them earlier when I was doing a cursory review. Maybe I wasn't paying attention like I thought I was."

"Maybe," he agreed, but he wasn't convinced that was the case.

"That has to be it, because there's no way he could have left the house." She nodded. "That's got to be it."

She shoved the pistol back into her waistband. "If you don't mind, I'd like to go ahead and wrap things up here. I have some things I need to take care of this evening."

"Sure."

She gave him a nod and started down the hall toward the kitchen. Zach watched her walk away and frowned. He wasn't at all convinced that she'd moved the boxes too close to the edge, but he wasn't about to tell her his theory.

That whoever was upstairs was still in the house.

DANAE PULLED UP in front of her cabin in the woods and hurried inside. As soon as she pushed the door shut behind her, she shoved the dead bolt into place and leaned back against the old wooden frame, taking a minute to catch her breath. She'd seen nothing when she pulled up in front of the cabin, nor while she dashed inside, but she couldn't seem to shake the panicked feeling she'd carried with her most of the day.

She pushed herself away from the wall and walked the few steps into the tiny kitchen to dump a stack of files from the house on her breakfast table. Only yesterday, she'd restocked her refrigerator with bottled water, and she pulled one out and took a big gulp, the cold liquid burning the back of her dry throat.

The events of the day raced through her mind on high speed. Had it really been only a day? So much had happened that it seemed as if it had taken far longer than the mere ten hours that had passed since she'd burst into William's office and announced her true identity.

You're losing it.

She didn't want to believe it—didn't want to think that the girl who had lived on her own at fifteen was falling apart over a spooky old house and an unlocked door. But as hard as she worked to dismiss everything as oversight and an overactive, overly stressed imagination, she couldn't ignore the fact that her entire mind and body screamed at her that something wasn't right.

Maybe some of the things that had happened today had been coincidence—like the boxes falling in the office. But what about the open laundry-room door she'd found earlier that day? The one that had prompted her call to Carter?

He hadn't taken her concerns lightly, nor had he even remotely appeared as if he thought she'd imagined the entire thing. In fact, he'd been adamant about not wanting her in the house alone and had appeared relieved when she mentioned the contractor who would be starting work there the next morning. Carter was logical, direct and not prone to fanciful thinking. If he wasn't willing to dismiss what she'd found, then she shouldn't be, either.

Then there was Zach Sargent. He certainly didn't look like any contractor she'd ever known. With his lazy smile, long eyelashes and chiseled features, he looked more like the privileged boys she'd served coffee and Danish pastries to at a swank eatery in Los Angeles, just a block away from one of the best private schools in the state. Certainly, he was the last thing she'd ever expected to see deep in the swamp.

And I kissed him.

She chugged back another gulp of water then poured some of the icy liquid across her clammy forehead.

What in the world was I thinking?

His kiss had been completely unexpected, but it wasn't the first time something like that had happened. Years of bartending and waitressing had left her with a history of lip-locks that she'd never have chosen for herself, and heaven knew it had gotten harder and harder to fend off advances from her drunken custodian's strung-out boyfriends, which was what prompted her to finally leave and go it alone before she was legally able to do so.

But never, in all those years of sneak attacks, had she kissed someone back.

For the first time since she was a teen, she'd lost control. And even that split second of loss had her fuming. She couldn't afford distraction, and certainly, she couldn't afford to let her guard down. Something was going on in that house. And even though she had no doubt Carter would be keeping a close watch on her, he had a job to do and couldn't stand guard over her all day.

Because he knew it as well, Carter had tried to talk her out of working at the house, volunteering to transport the paperwork to her cabin. She'd been tempted, but then that left the contractor roaming the house, unsupervised, and for some reason, she hadn't liked that idea. Now she didn't like the idea of *her* roaming the house with the contractor loose. Clearly, she'd lost all control where sexy Zach Sargent was concerned.

Alaina.

She reached for her cell phone, chiding herself for not thinking of her sister straightaway. Alaina had lived in the house for two weeks, and she was no stranger to danger or the general feeling of unease. Danae clearly remembered the morning Alaina came into the café before dawn—after the first night she'd spent in the house. Her face had been pale and drawn, and when Danae had quipped that she looked as if she'd seen a ghost, Alaina had spilled coffee on herself.

Then earlier her sister had made the cryptic ghost comment before she had to rush off the phone. Danae didn't believe in ghosts for a minute, but she did believe someone was in the house—someone that Alaina had probably misconstrued to be a ghost. It was easy to understand why. Danae didn't feel comfortable in the house during the bright light of day. She couldn't fathom spending nights there alone.

Her sister had some serious backbone.

Danae smiled, happy in the knowledge that her sister was such a strong woman. Danae admired and respected strong women and was happy that she wouldn't have to pretend to like some shrinking violet.

But as she studied her cell phone, her smile turned to a frown. No service. She should have figured. With the storm brewing overhead, reception in the swamp would be sketchy to nonexistent. She put the phone down and tapped the counter with her short fingernails until the clicking noise irritated her enough to stop.

She could drive into town and see if her cell phone could get service there. And although Johnny wasn't thrilled that she'd quit her job at the café, he'd allow her to use his landline to call Boston and pay him the charges when the bill came.

But to what end? Did she really think Alaina had the answers? Surely not, or she would have already shared them with Carter and William.

You want to feel close to her.

The thought ripped through her mind and she clenched the counter, that reality such a stark contrast to the rest of her twenty-seven years. She'd deliberately avoided creating lasting relationships. It hadn't been hard. Most people she'd come across couldn't be trusted anyway. But now, with Alaina, Carter and William, she'd found herself struggling to keep her guard up, while her heart pushed back, wanting to trust, wanting to attach.

She'd never realized how lonely she was until now. Until she'd met people she could be herself with. People who cared about her and would protect her.

A single tear fell from her eye and slid down her cheek.

Was this really the start of a normal life, with friends and family? She was scared to even dare and hope. Those desires had been pushed so far back for so long, she hadn't even realized they were still inside her.

She stared out the tiny kitchen window into the tangle of swamp that encircled the tiny cabin and sighed. What she needed was a long soak in the tub, a glass of wine and to get her head on straight. Her past was full of more difficult situations than this.

One randy contractor, a fake ghost and an unlocked door were not going to prevent her from gaining the life she'd always craved.

Chapter Seven

Zach parked his truck in front of the café and strode inside, still frustrated over the way his evening had gone. After checking the doors, Danae had insisted they clear out of the house for the day. Unable to formulate a good argument for insisting she stay when she was clearly distressed, he'd simply agreed and watched as she locked up the house and drove away.

He'd had no opportunity to finish his work on the window, so that one nail still held it fast in place. Tomorrow, he'd bring his crowbar and make quick work of it as soon as he had the opportunity, but that left him with a long night of nothing stretching in front of him.

Before his dad's death, he'd always prided himself on his patience. The intricate carpentry work he did required tons of it, as did dealing with frustrating clients that changed their minds every other day. But ever since his dad's funeral, he'd been unable to focus on his work—unable to stop the feeling of dread that flowed through him when he wondered what his dad had hidden from him.

Now he was in Calais, working at Ophelia's house. But, at that moment, he was just as far away from answers as he had been in New Orleans.

Sighing, he took a seat on a stool at the empty counter. Every table save one was occupied and the volume in the small building was fairly loud and cheerful. All around him, people relaxed and shared their day with spouses, friends and children, but relaxation and sharing were the last two things on his mind. The only person who looked unhappy was the cook, who glanced back with a half scowl when Zach slid onto the stool.

"Mind if I join you?"

A voice sounded behind him and he turned just as Carter sat on the stool next to him.

Before he could answer, a perky brunette stepped in front of them. "What can I get you two?"

Zach glanced at the menu printed on the wall behind the counter then looked over at Carter. "How's the chicken-fried steak?"

"Fantastic," Carter replied. "Make it two of the chicken-fried steak. And two beers. On me."

"That's not—"

"No arguing," Carter said. "It's the least I can do your first night in town. Might as well have a good meal and general conversation before you have to head to Amos's cabin and spend the rest of the night bored to tears. How anyone lives without a television and the internet is beyond me."

Zach smiled. "Well, I appreciate it—the food *and* the conversation."

"Did you get your supply list?" Carter asked.

"No. I got interrupted and we called it a day."

Carter frowned. "What kind of interruption?"

"A couple of boxes fell off the desk in Purcell's office. It shook Danae up a bit."

Carter's jaw flexed and he stiffened on the stool. "You sure they fell?"

"Far as I could tell. We checked the doors and they were all locked from the inside. No one was in the house besides Danae and me, and we were both downstairs at the time."

Carter studied him as he delivered the information, and Zach wondered why the sheriff looked so concerned over something that sounded so simple. Suddenly, he had the overwhelming feeling that both Danae and Carter were keeping something from him, and he didn't like it one bit.

"Any reason why you think they didn't fall?" Zach asked.

Carter stared at him for several seconds, and Zach could tell the other man was deliberating whether or not to tell him something. Finally, Carter nodded.

"I wasn't at the house today just to check in on Danae. She called me because she thought she'd seen someone in Purcell's office. She found the back door in the laundry room unlocked, but Danae was certain she'd checked it earlier and it was locked."

"I see." Finally, Danae's edgy behavior began to make more sense. "Why didn't you tell me earlier?"

"She asked me to keep it quiet, and besides, I didn't really know you then."

"You don't know me now."

Carter grinned. "That's true, but I could tell you were bothered by the noise and you took her seriously about checking for an intruder. That tells me you have a problem with people who might try to scare women, and since you'll be in the house all day, I figure it doesn't hurt to have you paying attention."

"You think someone is trying to scare her?"

"Maybe. I'm not sure how much you heard about the business with her sister Alaina."

"Only the little that Danae told me—that she was attacked in the house and you shot and killed her attacker."

"That's the short version, but there're a couple of things that still don't sit right with me."

"Like what?"

"One night someone broke one of the downstairs windows."

"I saw the window you're talking about when I was making my list. Danae assumed Alaina's attacker got in that way."

"He wanted us to think that, but the window was broken from the inside, and it was still nailed shut. He didn't do his homework on that one, and I didn't let that information leak out."

"Then how did he get in?"

"If I had to guess, I'd say he was already in there when we arrived. I changed the back door and patio locks that night, but he could have been hiding there already. Quite frankly, he could have remained hiding there even after I went looking for him."

"It wouldn't be hard to remain unseen in that mess," Zach agreed.

"Exactly, but the story gets worse. Everyone's assuming the guy I killed broke the window, but there's no way he could have. The night that happened, he was in Baton Rouge at a charity event with over a hundred witnesses."

Zach frowned. "And you have no idea who did it?"

Carter shook his head, but something in his expression made Zach wonder if the sheriff had his suspicions. "So you think someone has their own purpose for lurking."

"I have to wonder. First Alaina and now Danae are

swearing they saw someone in the house. I don't like to think either of them is imagining it."

"But after what happened to Alaina, wouldn't Danae be on edge? I mean, they're sisters. I assume they're close."

"Not at all. Until this morning, Alaina didn't even know Danae was her sister. None of us did. When Danae came to town, she did it under an assumed name and took a job waitressing at this café."

Zach stared at Carter, confused. "Why weren't they in contact before? Are you telling me Alaina didn't recognize her own sister?"

"That's exactly what I'm telling you. When their mother died, Purcell shipped the three girls off to distant relatives at all ends of the country. They had no way to contact each other. Alaina wrote letters to Purcell once she was older, trying to find her sisters, but he never answered. Danae was only two years old when their mother died. Alaina was only seven."

Zach felt a ball of anger form in his stomach and he clenched his jaw. His mother had passed when he was five, but at least he'd had his father. Those girls had been pawned off on strangers. "What a worthless son of a bitch."

"We are in complete agreement on that point."

The cook shoved two plates of food onto the sideboard and threw a dish towel onto the counter. "I'm going on break," he barked at the waitress as she came to deliver the food. He pushed past her and shoved open the back door, scowling at them before he slipped through the opening.

The waitress slid two plates covered with huge chicken-fried steaks, mashed potatoes and corn in front of them. "You two going to stop jawing long enough to eat?" she asked and grinned.

"Oh, yeah," Carter said and managed a smile.

"You got a problem with the cook?" Zach asked after the waitress walked away.

"You noticed that, huh?"

"I thought he gave me a dirty look when I sat down, but now I realize you were walking up behind me at the time. Since I've never met the man, I'm assuming the look was for you."

Carter nodded. "It was for me, all right, but don't think he's going to be any happier with you. Jack Granger spent twenty years playing errand boy for Purcell, who apparently promised him untold riches when he died."

"But the money wasn't Purcell's, right? I mean, that's what I gathered from William when we spoke about the situation in regard to the condition of the house."

"It was never Purcell's to give, but that didn't stop him from making promises. Jack recently took up with a widow with a sick girl. He was counting on that money to pay for medical care they can't afford."

"That sucks." Zach's heart went out to the surly cook and the sick girl.

"It does," Carter agreed, "and I was ready to feel all kinds of sorry for him but then he started drinking again. And when Jack is drunk, he's stupid and mean."

Suddenly, Zach understood what Carter was getting at. "You think he might be behind the break-in?"

"It's crossed my mind more than once. Especially as he threatened to 'show us all' when I tried to talk some sense into him."

"You think he's trying to scare them away from their inheritance? Would he get anything?"

Carter frowned. "I don't know what happens to the money if the sisters don't meet the terms of the will. That's something that I was going to cover with William, but everything with Alaina went down before I got to it. I hoped that it was all over with her situation, but the facts show that something else is going on in the house."

"And you're sure he's capable?"

"More than. He's tolerable when he's sober, but he's never been what you'd call a nice man."

"If it's him, what's his goal?"

Carter shook his head. "Maybe to scare them away, figuring if he can't have it, no one else should. Maybe just to steal some things he thinks are valuable and try to sell them, and they're in the way of his doing that."

"The house is crammed full of stuff. It would be impossible to know if something's missing."

"Yeah, that's the reason William has Danae going through Purcell's records. He's trying to put together an inventory of potential valuables so they can attempt to locate them in the mess."

Zach mulled over the information. All of it had been delivered in a very straightforward manner, but something was missing. Suddenly, it occurred to him.

"So if the guy you killed didn't break the window and you changed the locks, how did he get into the house later to attack Alaina? I didn't see any damage to the exterior doors and they looked like the originals."

Carter's expression darkened and he leaned over a bit toward Zach. "That's the sixty-four-thousand-dollar question," he said, his voice low. "I couldn't change the front-door lock. It's some antique that requires a specially forged key. I doubt there are a lot hanging around, but there's a slight possibility he could have acquired a front-door key, but we didn't find one on him."

"So you don't think that's the most viable option?"

"Honestly, I don't know what to think. By the looks of things, Purcell was a secretive and paranoid man. I wouldn't put it past him to have a secret entrance to the house. I think he'd feel safer knowing he had an escape hatch, so to speak. But I have yet to find such an alternate entrance and haven't had much time to look."

"Was Alaina's attacker from Calais?"

"No. Baton Rouge."

"Then how…"

"I don't know. Maybe he paid someone in Calais for the information."

"And they would have just given it to him?"

"He could have drummed up some legitimate story and thrown in a wad of cash. These are simple people who barely get by. It wouldn't take much to fool many of them."

Zach nodded. "And nobody would dare come forward and admit something like that after what went down."

"Exactly." Carter sighed and stabbed the chicken-fried steak with his fork before attacking it with his knife, taking his obvious frustration out on his dinner.

Zach took a bite of the steak. It was likely the best chicken-fried steak he'd ever had, but his mind couldn't latch onto that fact long enough for him to relax and enjoy it. It was too busy spinning with all the information Carter had given him.

He'd hoped thoughts of an intruder in the house were only Danae's stressed imagination at work, but maybe that wasn't the case. Clearly, Carter was concerned, and the man struck Zach as observant and intelligent—not at all the type to be taken in by dramatics or supposition. The disgruntled cook only supported Carter's suspicions, and if Zach had to guess, he probably wasn't the only resident Purcell had made promises to.

Then there was the fact he'd revealed about Danae when delivering the rest of the story—that she'd come to Calais pretending to be someone else. For what purpose did she come here? To see Purcell, the man who'd thrown the sisters away? If so, to what end? And why hide her true identity? Danae acted like a woman who'd seen trouble in her past—could it have followed her to town, as it did her sister?

He sighed and took another bite of his steak. Apparently, he wasn't the only one in Calais looking for answers.

DANAE STEPPED OUT of the tub and dried herself off before pulling on a thick, fuzzy robe, one of the few luxuries she'd afforded herself in the past year. She felt more relaxed, which was partially due to the hot bath, but probably mostly thanks to the two glasses of wine she'd consumed while soaking. She couldn't remember a time when she was so stressed that she'd actually gotten out of the tub for a refill, and she hoped to never experience one again.

Her mind turned to dinner as she stepped into the kitchen and opened the refrigerator to peruse her limited choices. Part of the perks of working at the café had been the free meals. Now that she was gainfully employed outside of the food industry, she was going to have to stock more than sandwich fixings and bagged salad.

She reached for the cheese and butter, figuring a grilled-cheese sandwich and chips were as good as anything else she had to choose from, and placed them on the counter next to a loaf of bread. As she reached for the skillet, which was hanging on a wall hook, her cell phone rang and she whirled around, her breath caught in her throat.

Idiot, she chastised herself as she reached for the phone on the kitchen counter, her hour-long soaking completely undone in an instant.

"It's Alaina," her sister said when she answered the phone. "The connection is really bad here. Can you hear me?"

"Barely. A thunderstorm is moving in. You know what that means."

"Unfortunately, I do. Are you at home?"

"Yes. The contractor and I left at the same time."

"Good. I don't want you there alone."

Danae bit her lip. Should she tell Alaina about the moving shadow, unlocked door and everything else she'd encountered that afternoon? Her sister already had plenty to worry about.

"Is something wrong?" Alaina asked. "I get this feeling something is wrong."

Danae shook her head. Her sister must be absolute hell in a courtroom. "It was an eventful afternoon," she said and went on to explain everything that had happened.

"I don't like it," Alaina said when she'd finished. "Not at all. Are you sure you won't delay your two weeks until I can return?"

As tempting as that was, Danae couldn't agree with her sister's suggestion. "To what end? Then both of us would potentially be in danger instead of just one. If something is going on in the house, delaying my stay won't stop it any more than delaying your stay would have stopped things for you."

The sound of static rang in Danae's ears, and for a moment, she thought they'd been disconnected.

Finally, Alaina sighed and said, "I know you're right, and I'd be saying the same thing if the situation was reversed. At least promise me that you won't be at the house alone. If the contractor leaves to buy supplies, go with him."

Danae clutched the cell phone. The last thing she wanted to do was get into close proximity to Zach again, and riding in a vehicle with him violated the "close proximity" rule. "If I have any reason for concern, I'll leave the house when he does."

"Since we're cut from the same cloth, I'm going to assume you're as hardheaded as I am and won't bother pushing for more. But please be careful. Be watchful. It took most of my life to find you. I don't want to lose you again."

Danae's eyes moistened at her sister's words. In reality, her sister was a stranger, but apparently Alaina felt the same connection she did.

"I'll sleep with my eyes open," Danae said.

"And don't be afraid to call Carter if things feel off. He'll come without question and he won't mock you if it turns out to be nothing. He's sorta great that way."

Danae smiled, happy her sister and Carter had found each other. Danae had admired Carter Trahan, both physically and mentally, since her arrival in Calais, but she'd known right away that he wasn't the man for her. He was gorgeous and smart and all white-knighty, but seeing him didn't give her that little thrill—that spark that she knew she'd feel with the right someone.

Like with Zach.

"I will call Carter anytime I'm unnerved," Danaе promised, trying to block all thoughts of Zach from her mind.

"Well, the connection is getting worse, so I guess I better let you go. Stay safe, Danaе."

"You, too." Danaе waited until the call dropped then placed her cell phone on the counter.

The cheese and butter still sat on the cabinet where she'd left them earlier, but all thoughts of food had flown from her mind during Alaina's call. She stuck the items back into the refrigerator and grabbed a bottle of water. On the upside, between general anxiety and skipping meals, it would be no time before she worked off those ten pounds she'd gained working at the café.

She set the water on the tiny breakfast table and slid into a chair. Her shoulder bag lay at the edge of the table, a stack of manila folders peeking out from underneath. It was all she'd grabbed from Purcell's office when she and Zach had investigated the noise. She could have made another trip before leaving, but the thought of going back into that room had overcome logic, and she'd left with only what she'd brought down that first trip.

Still, even a couple of files were enough to start working with. A couple of hours billed meant the day wouldn't be a complete loss. She pulled the folders over in front of her. A bunch of old paperwork should take her mind off things, maybe even bore her enough that she could sleep.

The first folder contained a list of household purchases made several months after her mother's death, and the costs—bread, milk, cereal, butter, toilet paper— all seemed like basic domestic stuff and not at all what William was looking for. The next five pages were more of the same, the date of the weekly trip noted in the upper left of each sheet of paper. It wasn't useful for the lawyer's purposes, but it did give Danae an insight into how her stepfather had lived.

Sighing, she flipped through the rest of the pages in the first folder, finding nothing of interest. It made no sense to her that her stepfather had access to all her mother's wealth, but had locked himself away in that monstrosity of a house and, based on this paperwork, lived on a diet of cereal and toast.

The second folder contained more itemized shopping lists, but these were completely different from the others. A quick check of the date let her know that the purchases were made months before her mother's death. The lists contained all the things she'd expect a household with three young children to have and stood in stark contrast to the lists in the previous folder.

The last pages contained in the folder appeared to be an investment account statement. Her eyes widened at the balance in the account, and she had to take a minute to remind herself that William had already told her the estate's holdings were significant. Still, hearing it and seeing it on paper were two completely different things. All her life, she'd gotten by on very little. It was next to impossible to imagine such riches that one no longer considered price.

She scanned the entries and found a few that might interest William. A vase that cost eight thousand dollars with the notation "Ming Dynasty." A two-thousand-dollar purchase for a grandfather clock. A three-thousand-dollar Persian rug.

Shaking her head, she tried to wrap her mind around the valuables the house contained under all those layers of dust and grime. Assuming the items weren't damaged, it might be akin to a museum when clean. She flipped the page over and scanned the next one, hoping to find more nuggets for William, but this page didn't contain any large expenses. She checked the dates and frowned. It was the week her mother died.

Determined not to let it affect her, she flipped to the next page and scanned until she found four twenty-thousand-dollar entries. Funeral expenses, maybe. But when she read the notations, her head started to pound. Four people's names—one of them, the woman she'd been sent to live with. No wonder the woman had taken her in.

Danae had always wondered, but now she knew. She should have known before now—everything with Rose was about money. Money or booze or a fix. But somehow, seeing it there in black and white made it all the more pathetic.

She pushed the stack of files away and took a sip of water. The apprehension she'd felt earlier had been replaced with anger. Anger at her stepfather for selling her out to a junkie. Anger at Rose for taking money for a child she never intended to care for. Anger at her mother for dying and leaving them helpless against their evil stepfather.

She rose and paced the tiny living room twice before stopping in front of the window. She pulled the thick curtains to the side and peered out into the darkness. He'd paid them off. He'd pawned off his wife's children for twenty thousand apiece.

Four entries.

The thought jolted through her mind and she frowned. Why four entries? There were only the three sisters. Danae had recognized one of the other names as the people who'd raised Alaina and assumed one of the other names was the person Joelle had been sent to live with. But why was there a fourth entry?

What else had her stepfather paid for?

Chapter Eight

Despite the heavy dinner and two beers he'd consumed at the café, Zach couldn't settle in the caretaker's cabin. In fact, he was more restless now than he'd been earlier that day. Of course, earlier, he'd thought his only obstacle was getting around Danae to search for the answers he sought. But when he put all the facts together, it looked as if he and Danae were not the only people interested in the house.

Whoever was lurking in the LeBeau mansion was brazen enough to attempt going about his business during the day, even when both he and Danae were right below. Zach had worked with enough cons to know that meant one of three things: he was cocky, he was desperate, or he was perfectly willing to kill them if they got in his way.

None were good options, especially as it further complicated his plans for sneaking into the house after normal working hours. What if he ran into the intruder when he himself was an intruder? If Danae or Carter caught him in a late-night excursion, they might look harder into his background.

He blew out a breath and stared at the old paneled wall from his resting place on an ancient, lumpy couch.

Finally, he jumped up from the couch and pulled on his hiking boots. No way was he going to get a moment's rest without working off some of this energy. It probably wasn't the smartest idea, but he was going to grab his flashlight and pistol and walk down the trail to the main house.

Maybe he'd get lucky and catch the intruder red-handed—wrap things up nicely so that Danae let down her guard, giving him more room to maneuver. By the way she'd responded when he'd kissed her, he knew it was possible to distract her. But certain distractions—like the intruder—would only make the cagey heiress more observant.

He grabbed his pistol from the kitchen counter and dug his flashlight from his duffel bag, then headed out into the night.

The sounds of night creatures drifted by as he inched down the overgrown path, but the swamp wasn't as active as he'd thought it would be given the density of the undergrowth. Although he lived in the city, he was no stranger to hunting and sleeping outdoors, but this swamp had a different feel to it than any other he'd ever been in.

Logically, he should be able to attribute the unsettling atmosphere to his general unease over the entire situation, but he knew it went deeper than that. This swamp felt alive in some way. Certainly, many of the things that comprised a swamp were living plants and creatures, but it was more than that. It was almost as if the swamp had taken all those living and nonliving items and somehow created its own identity.

It pressed at him as he hurried down the path as quickly as he dared. Sometimes the dense undergrowth all but covered the path, and the last thing he wanted was to wander off the trail. The swamp was inhabited by many deadly creatures as much as it consisted of plants, water and dirt.

He felt as if he'd walked forever when his shoulder slammed into something solid. He turned his flashlight beam up from the path, thinking he'd hit a tree, but was surprised to see a stone column covered in vines. He'd walked right into the overgrown patio off the kitchen of the main house.

Although he hated to do it, he shut off the flashlight and used his hands to feel his way to the stone wall of the house. The last thing he wanted to do was alert the intruder that someone was there, watching and waiting.

He used the wall to guide him around to the front of the house then stopped at the edge of the brush just before the circular driveway. His eyes were growing more accustomed to the dark, finally able to make out the shape of the decrepit fountain. A bead of sweat rolled down his forehead and he brushed it away. The humidity was getting worse—the air growing thicker and more still, like it did before a storm.

He cursed the caretaker for not having a television, but knew that reception would likely be spotty even on the clearest night. Still, he should have checked the weather when he was in the café, which surprisingly provided free Wi-Fi. He could only guess that many homes in Calais were left stranded with no way to contact the outside world during a good storm unless they had landlines.

His back began to tighten from standing in the one position, so he squatted, letting his legs do the work for a bit. Only ten minutes passed before his legs began to tighten, so he rose back up with a sigh. Apparently twelve years of general contracting wasn't as much of a workout as his days serving as catcher on his high school baseball team.

Locks of hair clung to his forehead as the humidity cranked up another notch, and he pushed the damp strands back on his head. This was stupid. He'd let a bout of nerves and boredom override good common sense. If he started back now, he might have time to get in a shower before the storm hit and likely took out the power.

Disgusted with the situation and himself, he started to turn, but as he shifted, something moved at the edge of his viewing range. His body froze even as he yanked his head in the direction of the movement. It was impossible to tell for certain, but it looked as if something or someone was directly across from him at the edge of the driveway.

Crossing the driveway put him in the open, and although it was cloudy, the sky cleared periodically, allowing thin streams of moonlight to pass through. All it would take was a second of moonlight to give him away in the open. He took a couple steps back from the edge of the driveway and began inching around it, carefully picking each step to keep the sound as quiet as possible.

When he made it about ten feet, he stepped up to the edge of the brush again and checked for movement on the other side. At that moment, the clouds moved away and moonlight filled the courtyard, casting a dim glow into the swamp on the other side of the driveway. He strained, trying to make out any form of movement in the brush, but everything was still.

Too still.

The thought occurred to him just as a scream ripped through the night sky. He pulled his pistol from his waistband and whirled around, trying to locate the source of the noise. It was a terrifying wail—like that of a doomed soul.

Then everything went completely quiet again.

In the upstairs window of the house, a light appeared—faint at first, then growing to a pulsing mass, the size of a human. Then as suddenly as it appeared, it was gone.

He heard the footsteps behind him too late. Before he could spin around, he felt the crack of something hard on the side of his head. His temple exploded as if he'd been shot and he fell to the ground, a pair of hiking boots the last thing he saw.

THE ATTACKER HURRIED down the trail deep into the swamp where he'd stashed his vehicle hours before. He'd spent a frustrating couple of hours inside the house before he caught sight of the maintenance man lurking around outside. He'd snuck out the back door and then patiently and silently crept up behind him until he was within striking distance.

Maybe the solid blow to the head would give the maintenance man a reason to hightail it back to New Orleans and get out of his way. He just hoped the blow hadn't been strong enough to kill him. It would be impossible to get things done with the police crawling all over the place. The last meddling heiress had brought enough trouble to town with her. It had been weeks since he'd felt comfortable returning to business.

If only Purcell would have held on a little longer, but the old bastard had managed to screw him, even in death.

THE LIGHT SHIMMERED above her and Danae reached up, trying to touch it. She didn't know why she wasn't afraid, why she didn't flee. All she knew was that the light made her feel safe and warm. It rose above her, almost to the ceiling of the cabin, and she gasped as it changed and shifted until the pale figure of a woman came into view.

Her face was familiar, but it took a moment for Danae to realize why. The woman looked like Alaina, but different.

"Mother." Danae's voice was barely a whisper.

The figure's mouth moved, as if speaking, but Danae couldn't hear even a whisper of sound.

"I can't hear you. What are you saying?"

A single tear ran down her mother's face and she began to fade.

"No!" Danae sat upright, her hands reaching for the shimmering light as it faded away.

"So close...so close...close." The whisper came as the light faded.

Danae leaped from the couch, landing on her feet with her heart beating so loudly she swore she could hear it. She blinked a couple of times, trying to get her bearings, then realized she was standing in the living room of her rented cabin, file folders scattered across the coffee table in front of her.

I must have fallen asleep on the couch. It was a dream.

But even as she thought it, she frowned. It had seemed so real—as if her mother were really there in the room with her. As if she'd tried to speak to her.

So close.

That was what her mother had said in the dream, but close to what? Close to finding her past? Close to finding herself? She'd been searching for both for so long that some days she wasn't certain exactly what she was looking for any longer. Some days, she just felt tired. Tired of being on constant alert. Tired of regarding everyone she met as suspicious. Tired of erecting walls that no one could scale.

Tired of being alone.

As that last thought occurred to her, a mental image of Zach flashed through her mind. He was one of the most attractive men she'd ever met, and in her line of work, she'd met a lot. There was something about his easy smile that made her relax around him even when her mind was telling her to keep her guard up. Something about his obvious concern that made her feel he cared.

Two stellar reasons to keep her distance from the sexy contractor.

She glanced at her watch and sighed. Not even 5:00 a.m. The café would be opening soon, but she didn't feel like having a run-in with Jack this early in the morning. Ever since Carter had filled her in on the situation with the cook and her stepfather, she'd felt bad for the man, but that didn't mean she was going to give him the chance to snipe at her. Jack hadn't been the most pleasant of people to work with when he'd thought she was just Connie the café waitress. Her emergence as Danae LeBeau, heiress, had probably tipped him right past rude and into angry.

Her pantry was sorely in need of restocking, but she could manage eggs and toast. There was no point in attempting to sleep any longer. She was too edgy— whether it was from everything that had happened since yesterday morning or the dream, she wasn't sure, but either way, sleep was a thing of the past.

She took a step toward the kitchen then froze. Was that a noise outside her cabin? It sounded like scratching. She held her breath, trying to lock in on where the noise had originated, but only the buzz of the ancient refrigerator echoed back at her. She took two cautious steps toward the living-room window and peered outside.

The morning sun hadn't yet peeked over the thick cypress trees, so it was too dark to see anything outside except for the faint silhouette of the tree line, but she felt someone there. Watching. Waiting.

She dropped the curtain back in place and crossed her arms over her chest as a chill ran through her. What did he want with her? What was he waiting for?

So close.

Unbidden, her mother's words echoed through her mind once more.

But she still had no idea what they meant.

AS THE SUN BROKE over the cypress trees, Danae turned her car into the circular drive of her family home. It was barely 6:00 a.m. and she knew Zach wouldn't show up for another hour, but she couldn't sit in her cabin any longer. She was no stranger to dangerous situations, and the reality was, she was just as much a sitting duck at her cabin as she was in the house. But at least in the house, she could look for answers—try to put together the pieces of her past.

As she stepped out of her car, something out of the corner of her eye caught her attention. She looked over at the brush near the north side of the house and saw a boot sticking out of the edge of the overgrown weeds. In a single fluid movement, she pulled her pistol from her purse and took one hesitant step toward the boot.

Call Carter.

Her mind screamed at her to let the sheriff do his job,

but with the cloudy sky, she knew cell-phone service would be nil. If she had to drive into town, whoever was in the brush might be gone before she got back.

She began inching toward the boot. Maybe she'd get lucky and it was her intruder. Maybe he'd been struck by lightning or had a heart attack while trying to sneak into the house.

Sure, and maybe he'll have a full confession typed up in his pocket.

She clenched the pistol, silently willing her optimistic and sarcastic selves to give her a break as she stepped next to the boot and peered into the dense foliage.

Zach!

She shoved the pistol into her purse as she dropped down beside him, placing her fingers on his neck. A wave of relief washed through her when she felt his pulse, steady and strong. Some dried blood pooled on leaves under his head, and she warred with herself over whether to move him to check his head or run for help.

Then he stirred and groaned.

She placed her hand on his chest as his eyes fluttered open. "Don't move," she said.

His eyes widened and he looked wildly around but Danae noticed he didn't turn his head.

"What happened?" he asked.

"I don't know. Can you move your head?"

He turned it slowly from left to right. "It's throbbing a bit, but everything is moving okay."

"Good. Do you think you can sit up? I need to get you inside so I can take a look at the injury and see how bad it is."

He sat up okay, but when he tried to stand, he staggered a bit. Afraid he would fall, Danae wrapped her arm around his waist to steady him and guided him toward the house. At first, he was wobbly, but as they entered and walked to the kitchen, he started to steady.

He slumped in a chair at the breakfast table and she hurried to gather a wet cloth, aspirin and a glass of water. She handed him the aspirin and he swallowed them down. His hands seemed steady as he held the glass, which was a good sign.

"This may sting a bit," she said as she patted his head just above the ear, trying to remove the dried blood. "The blood is caked in your hair, so I can't see the injury. But it's all dried, so that's a good sign."

"It doesn't feel like a good sign."

"Give the aspirin time to work."

She blotted at the blood again and finally removed enough to lift his hair and get a good look at the cut. "It's a pretty good gash. About an inch long, but it's not bleeding anymore. It needs to be cleaned, though, and you might need stitches."

His eyes widened. "No. I'm sure I'll be fine if it's cleaned up."

Instantly, Danae's senses went on high alert. The man was a contractor, and based on the scars she'd seen on his arms and hands, he was no stranger to injury on the job. Was she really supposed to believe that he was scared of doctors? Something about Zach didn't add up—hadn't added up from the beginning—but she'd been unable to put her finger on what.

"How did this happen?" she asked.

His eyes flickered a little, and she knew he was trying to decide what to say. She'd altered, edited and otherwise rewrote the truth so many times before that she recognized a cover story in progress, but Zach wasn't as adept as she was. Wasn't used to lying, so he gave himself away.

"I was restless last night and couldn't sleep, so I came to the house hoping to catch the intruder in the act."

She studied his face, but all she could see was the look of failure and a bit of embarrassment. It appeared he'd decided to tell the truth, which sent her right from concerned to angry.

"You have no business poking into things you weren't hired for," she said.

"I disagree. If someone was in the house yesterday, then that means they were inside when I was working. That puts me at as big a disadvantage as you, and I don't think I should have to work that way any more than you should."

She clenched her jaw, but couldn't formulate a good argument. Zach did have the right to feel safe in his work environment, but she still couldn't approve of what he'd done, especially as he hadn't even bothered to talk to her before doing it.

"So you thought you'd do what—take a picture? It's not like you know enough people in Calais that you could identify the intruder, even if you managed to see him."

He shrugged. "I guess I figured I'd catch him and put the whole thing to bed."

She stared. "Have you lost your mind?"

He gave her a half smile and pointed to the gash. "Maybe a bit of it leaked out."

"That's not even remotely funny. You could have been killed, and don't bother trying to tell me that you fell and hit a rock. I looked and there wasn't a rock anywhere near you, much less under your head. Besides, I've seen plenty of people clocked with a beer bottle and know what a blow to the side of the head looks like."

The smile slipped from his face. "I was hiding there,

at the brush in the edge of the driveway, and I saw something move on the far side in the swamp. I waited for the clouds to clear to get a better look, but he must have left by the time the moonlight came."

"And then someone hit you?"

He frowned and stared down at the floor, his brow scrunched. Finally he shook his head. "Not then. First, the scream came."

Danae's heart leaped in her chest. "What scream?"

"I don't know. It sounded like it came from inside the house, but it echoed everywhere. It was awful—like someone in agony. Then a light appeared in the top window of the house and the scream stopped. A second later, I heard footsteps behind me, but before I could turn around, he clocked me."

She struggled to process the information, trying to put it all in a rational perspective. "What kind of light—flashlight, a room light?"

"Neither. It was more of a small glow that grew in size, pulsing as it got bigger. I could see it upstairs, through the window on the landing."

"Then what was it?"

He hesitated, and she could tell he didn't want to say.

"Zach, what did you see?"

"It looked human."

Danae barely managed to keep her shock from showing. Under other circumstances, she would pass off Zach's claim as a symptom of his head injury. He'd simply seen the light after someone cracked him on the head and was confused now.

But what were the odds that they had both seen a corporeal entity on the same night? She needed to know just how bad that crack on Zach's head was.

"Are you still dizzy?" she asked.

"Yeah, a little."

"I'm going to take you to Doc Broussard."

His eyes widened. "No, I don't need to see a doctor. I'll be fine."

"I'm not asking you. You were injured on my property while under the employment of the estate I'll inherit. It's a liability issue, so you'll see the doctor. We can wait for a decent hour to call William, but I bet he says the same thing."

Zach frowned but he'd been in construction long enough to know the drill. "Surely the doc won't be up yet, either, much less open for business."

"He's an early riser, and he's always open for emergencies. I'll call him from my car as soon as I can get a signal. Can you walk?"

He rose slowly from the chair. "Yeah, the dizziness is starting to go away."

"Good," she said.

Maybe when it cleared completely they could make more sense of it all.

Chapter Nine

Doc Broussard was a kind-looking silver-haired gentleman who smiled at Danae and nodded at Zach as they walked into his clinic. Zach's head still pounded from the hit, but he wasn't about to admit that to the doctor or Danae. If Danae even suspected he wasn't up to par, she could easily have him removed from the job, and that would ruin everything.

Doc Broussard introduced himself and directed Zach to sit on an examining table. "Looks like you took a crack to the head. William said he was hiring someone to work on the house. It wasn't supposed to work on you."

Zach glanced at Danae, but her jaw was set. Clearly, she wasn't interested in volunteering details. He didn't understand her reasons, but figured it was smart to follow her lead. Danae had lived here for six months and knew everyone. If she wanted to keep the whole thing quiet, then that was what he'd do.

Doc Broussard parted Zach's hair and studied the gash. "You've got a pretty good cut here. I could put a couple of stitches in to help it close faster. Wouldn't take more than a few minutes."

Zach looked over at Danae.

"That would be great," she said, "and please be sure to send William the bill. The estate will pick up the cost."

"Of course," Doc Broussard said as he began threading a needle. "Injured on the job and all that. Of course, this happened sometime last night and that gash was made by something smooth, like a crowbar. But I'm going to assume you have your reasons for wanting people to think he was injured while making repairs."

Danae sighed. "We've had some...unexplained things happening at the house. Zach thought he'd play hero last night and see if he could catch someone in the act."

Doc Broussard looked at Zach. "And you caught the raw end of it."

"I'm afraid so," Zach said.

"Humph." Doc Broussard shook his head and started stitching. "You're not the first to sit on my table and tell me a story about strange things in that house, and I'm guessing you won't be the last."

Danae's eyes widened. "What do you mean? Who else?"

"A couple of the women hired to clean. One had a pretty good scrape and the other bruised her knees pretty good."

"What happened to them?" Danae asked.

"They claim they saw a ghost."

Danae sucked in a breath. "I heard the rumors, but I always dismissed them as the fancies of simple minds. Was the ghost a woman?"

Doc Broussard shook his head. "They didn't specify. They said it appeared right in front of them and they took off out of the house. One fell in the entry and bruised her knees on the marble floors, and the other caught her arm on the end of one of those ornamental columns in the entry and that gave her the scratch."

Danae frowned. "William said he couldn't find anyone in Calais to clean. They were all scared."

Doc Broussard nodded. "They weren't the first to hightail it out of that house crying 'Ghost.' I guess the others managed to do so without injuring themselves. And then there was your sister."

"Alaina?" Danae stared at the doctor, her shock clear. "I never heard of anything happening to her. I mean... except for the attack."

"I think she and Carter were trying to keep it all quiet until they figured out what was going on, but she took a tumble down the stairs early on in her stay. Gave her a pretty good crack on the head, like our contractor friend here." He cut the stitching thread and patted Zach on the back.

"Were you...?" Danae's voice trailed off. "Were you my doctor...before?"

"No. Ophelia's parents had doctors in New Orleans that they'd used for years and always took her there for checkups. She did the same with you girls." He smiled. "At first, I was a bit offended, but then I noticed that a trip to the doctor always ended with a shopping spree for you girls. Ophelia always bought you the prettiest dresses."

Danae smiled. "That's a nice memory. Thank you for sharing that."

"You're welcome."

"Can I ask you another question?" Danae asked.

"Of course."

"Did you know my stepfather? I know he was private, possibly even agoraphobic, but I figure someone had to look after him when he was sick...."

Doc Broussard nodded. "I made a trip to see Trenton once a month—more if he was ill."

"Was he ill a lot?"

"Not really. If I had to guess, he was a good twenty years older than your mother and had the usual things that come with age and lack of proper diet and exercise—high blood pressure, high cholesterol and the like. Any of those combined with age and a weak heart could take someone out."

Danae frowned.

"I know you want to figure out something about your past," Doc Broussard said. "I'd want to do the same thing in your position, but I honestly don't know what I can give you."

"Surely you can tell me something about him. Anything?"

The doctor sighed. "You'd think after all that time I'd have an idea what made the man tick, maybe have an inkling of how he spent his time, but I don't. He lay there in his bed wearing striped pajamas, completely silent while I did my exam. The only time he spoke was to tell me of a symptom or ask about a dosage."

"That's just strange," Zach said.

"Definitely," Doc Broussard agreed. "He was an odd man, but I never got a handle on why."

"What do you mean?" Danae asked. "I thought he was mental."

"Perhaps. Certainly, the indicators were there, but I always wondered what would show if he'd agreed to the tests I suggested."

"You think he was faking?"

"Not necessarily. I think he was definitely suffering under some neurosis, but there was a cunning in him— something so imperceptible in the way he looked at things that later on, you'd convince yourself you hadn't seen it."

"You think he was hiding something?" Zach asked.

Doc Broussard shrugged. "Aren't we all? But I couldn't begin to guess what secrets lay in Purcell's past that caused him to lock himself away in that house for over two decades. I'm afraid to even try."

"It sometimes seems," Danae said, her tone conveying her frustration, "that Purcell went to the grave still taking from everyone and not giving a single thing."

"I'm really sorry," Doc Broussard said and placed his hand on Danae's arm. "I wish I could give you some answers."

Danae gave his hand a squeeze. "I do, too, but I'm not giving up. I'll find them. It just might take a while."

Doc Broussard smiled. "I believe you." He walked back over to Zach and took a look at his earlier work. "Well, this guy is patched up nicely, if I do say so myself. Just keep it clean and dry for a couple of days and let me know if your headache gets worse."

"Thanks, Doc," Zach said, gently probing his head. "Hey, I'm curious. You said you didn't think I'd be the last person to sit here after being injured at the house. Any particular reason why?"

The doctor frowned. "Just a feeling, I suppose."

"What kind of feeling?" Danae asked. "Surely you don't believe those women or Alaina saw a ghost?"

Doc Broussard stared at the wall for a couple of seconds, rubbing his jaw, then finally looked back at Danae. "I guess I figure the house has been sitting there like a tomb all these years. Purcell was there, but he wasn't living so much as he was existing."

He took off his glasses and rubbed them with the

hem of his shirt. "Maybe the house is coming alive after all these years…and bringing something with it."

Zach narrowed his eyes at the doctor. "You don't really believe that, do you? I mean, you're a scientist."

"That's true enough, but the swamps of Mystere Parish are different than most. Things happen in them that can't be explained in earthly ways. I figure that house has been so swallowed up by the swamp that maybe it's become like it."

Zach was momentarily taken aback. Last night, when he was walking the trail to the main house, he'd been thinking how different this swamp felt. How it felt alive. Now this seemingly sane and obviously well-educated man was saying the same thing. The problem was, it still made no sense, regardless of what feelings he might have.

"What kind of unexplained things?" he asked.

"Oh, ghostly lights and noises that can't be attributed to man or beast…the usual sort of thing you'd expect to find in an area of the country where things are steeped in lore and some still practice the old ways."

"But that's not why you think they're different," Zach said. "Is it?"

Doc Broussard smiled. "You don't miss much, do you? No, I have my own reasons for thinking the way I do. My own unexplained story."

"I'd love to hear it," Danae said. "I mean, if you don't mind telling it."

"Not at all. It was about this time twenty-five years ago and I was deer hunting. A fellow doctor friend of mine had canceled at the last minute, and my wife tried to convince me not to hunt alone, but I was determined. I was on call the following two weeks and I intended to get my one clear day in."

He stared out the window and into the row of cypress trees across the street from his office. "I was tracking a buck—a good size based on the tracks—when all of a sudden, I got the feeling I was being watched. Well, there's plenty of creatures in the swamp that you don't want keeping that close an eye on you, so I stopped short and tried to get tuned to what it was."

Zach nodded. "That's smart."

"Usually, but this time, it made me a sitting duck. There wasn't a whisper of sound, not a single insect or even a breath of breeze. It was the most silence I've ever experienced and it was unnerving because it was so unnatural. I had just made up my mind to get the heck out of there when something hit me on the back of the head and sent me tumbling down an embankment."

Danae gasped and covered her mouth with her hand.

"My deer-hunting cap probably kept my head from splitting open, but I broke my leg in three places on the way down. Put me in the hospital in New Orleans for a month and rehab another two after that so I could learn to walk again."

"You don't know who hit you?"

Doc Broussard shook his head. "That's where the unexplained part comes in. The sheriff—not Carter, as he was just a boy back then, but the sheriff then—was an expert tracker. He covered every square inch of that swamp in a mile radius from where I was hit. He didn't find a single track besides my own, and there was nothing—not a rock or a branch or even a dead bird—to explain what hit me."

"But," Zach said, "there had to be something. You didn't send yourself tumbling down an embankment."

"No, sir, I did not. But whatever did didn't leave a trace. Now, what exists in the swamps of Louisiana that can knock a two-hundred-pound man down without leaving a single track?"

"I don't know," Zach replied.

"The answer is, nothing on this earth."

DANAE INSISTED THEY GO to the café for breakfast. Zach was a little rumpled, but his clothes weren't stained, so he'd pass muster for the early-morning crowd, anyway. He needed to eat in order to take the pain medicine Doc Broussard had given him. Plus, she had an ulterior motive or two. First, she wanted to gauge Jack's reaction to her now that the gossip had spread, and second, she was hoping to catch Carter before he left for his usual rounds.

Jack glanced at them as they entered the café, then turned immediately back to the grill, but not before Danae caught his scowl. Apparently, the cook was aware of her ascension from café waitress to small-town heiress, and he looked none too happy about it.

Fortunately, Carter was sitting at the counter, the empty plate in front of him letting her know they'd caught him just in time. She slid onto the stool on one side of him and motioned Zach to the other. Carter glanced at both of them, looking surprised.

"You two are out early," he said. His voice was casual, but Danae knew the question was in his statement.

"I was hoping to catch you," Danae said, keeping her voice low.

Sonia, the waitress who had replaced Danae, stepped up to the counter, a big smile on her face.

"Can I get you guys some breakfast?"

"Just some coffee for now," Danae said, "and breakfast in a few."

Zach nodded, cluing in to her desire to send the waitress out of earshot.

"I'm glad to see you here early, Jack," Danae said as the waitress poured them coffee.

The cook turned to glare at her then mumbled something to the waitress and stormed out the back door. The waitress slid the coffee in front of them and gave them an apologetic smile.

"Apparently, Jack went on break, so I'm glad you two don't want breakfast right away." She grabbed the pot of coffee and headed to the other side of the diner.

Danae waited until she was out of hearing range then gave Carter a quick rundown of what happened to Zach. Within seconds, Carter's face went from early-morning blank to completely alert and concerned.

"Damn it," Carter cursed, keeping his voice low. "I have got to figure out how he's getting into the house. I didn't think many copies of that front-door key could be floating around, but maybe I was mistaken."

"There's probably not a lot," Zach said. "I know a guy in New Orleans who can make duplicates, but he has to have an original to work from. My guess is that the house only had two originals when the lock was installed."

Carter nodded. "And I figured because of the trouble and cost, servants would have received keys to the back door but not the front."

"Probably true," Danae said. "But you changed all the other door locks. Even if he has a front-door key, I seriously doubt he strolled up to the door, through the foyer and up the stairs yesterday with Zach and I right there."

Zach glanced at Carter, who frowned.

"What are you not telling me?" she asked, looking

from one man to the other. "Oh, wait. How could I be so stupid? He was already in the house, wasn't he?"

"It makes the most sense," Carter said. "He might have entered the house that morning, and when you arrived, he had to wait for an opportunity to leave."

"But all the doors were locked after the boxes fell. Zach and I checked." She sucked in a breath. "He was still there. Hiding somewhere in the house while we were checking the doors. Do you think he's still in there now?"

"I don't know," Carter said. "I hope not."

He rose from his stool and tossed some money onto the counter. "I have a couple of things I need to get out of the way this morning. Eat your breakfast and I'll meet you at the house as soon as I can get away."

"Thanks," Danae said.

Carter gave them a nod and headed out of the café. Sonia stepped back behind the counter and refilled their coffee, so Danae and Zach slipped back into silence. As she was restocking the napkin holder, Jack came back in from his break.

"Do you want breakfast now?" Sonia asked.

"I'll have a vegetarian egg-white omelet," Danae said.

"Sounds good," Zach said. "I'll take the same with a side of wheat toast."

Jack shook his head.

"Is there a problem, Jack?" Danae asked, determined to get the unpleasantness out of the way.

Jack turned around and gave her a dirty look. "Yeah, there's a problem, Miss Fancy Omelet. I should have known the first time you ordered it that you thought you were too good for this town. Plain ol' eggs and bacon can't touch those heiress lips of yours or you might explode, right?"

"Look," Danae said, "I know what my stepfather did to you and it was wrong, but I had nothing to do with that. If you have a problem with the way things turned out, then I suggest you take that up with the estate attorney, but I will not take crap from you because you got a raw deal."

Jack's face flushed red. "You got a smart mouth now that you got a little money."

Anger from her entire life flooded through her, and she clenched her hands to keep from throwing something at the man she used to work next to six days a week.

"You think you got screwed? Purcell sold us for twenty thousand each. Paid strangers less than what a bass boat costs to rip us from the only home we'd ever known. If there was a way to bring that bastard back and kill him myself, I would. Damn Purcell to hell all you want, but the line starts behind me and my sisters."

Jack's jaw dropped and he blinked before tossing his spatula on the grill and storming out of the café for the second time that morning.

It took Danae a second to realize that the entire café had gone silent. Without turning around, she knew every eye in the place was on her. Embarrassment washed over her like a tidal wave, and she grabbed her purse and ran out of the café.

Chapter Ten

Zach hesitated only long enough to toss some money onto the counter before he hurried out of the café after Danae. Her car was still parked at the end of the block in front of Doc Broussard's office, and she made it almost all the way there before Zach managed to catch up with her.

"Hey," he said, putting his hand on her shoulder. "Wait up."

"I'm sorry," she said, staring at the ground. "I didn't mean to embarrass you. I shouldn't have poked at him. He's always been mean-spirited, but I'm usually in a better place to tolerate it."

Zach felt his heart tug at her obvious distress. He put his hand under her chin and pulled her head up until she was looking at him.

"You have nothing to apologize for," he said. "Jack was out of line, and everyone in there knows it."

"I made a fool out of myself, airing my family's dirty laundry."

"You're not a fool. You're hurt and you have every reason to be. I take it you didn't know about the pay-off until now?"

She sniffed, and he could tell she was trying to hold back the tears that were pooling in her eyes.

"I found a check register in the files I took home with me last night," she said. "There were four entries for twenty thousand dollars. I recognized two of the names. One was the woman who took me and the other was the people who took Alaina."

Zach stiffened. It was the same amount he'd seen in his father's records. "And the other names?"

She shook her head. "I didn't recognize them and the last is barely legible, but I figure one of them is the family that took Joelle."

Zach struggled to control his own anxiety. The last thing he wanted to do was tip off Danae to exactly how interested he was. Then another thought occurred to him. "There are only three of you, right?"

Danae's eyes widened. "Yes. Well, I guess as far as I know there are only three of us. I was too young to remember anything."

She clutched Zach's arm. "What if there was a baby? Oh, no, I need to call Alaina. Surely she would remember if our mother was pregnant after I was born."

Instantly, Zach felt guilty for causing her more distress. He put his hands on her shoulders and gave them a squeeze. "Don't outdrive your headlights. If your mother had another child, wouldn't William know?"

"I don't know. Everyone said Purcell locked us up in that house and no one saw my mother or us kids for a long time. Maybe long enough for her to have his child."

"Okay. So as soon as you think it's appropriate, you'll call Alaina and ask her."

Danae nodded. "You're right."

She took a deep breath and blew it out, then gave him a small smile. "Thank you."

"I didn't do anything."

"You calmed me down and reminded me that I'm

not in this alone. I have Alaina and I need to remember that."

"And you have me."

Her eyes widened a bit, but he saw the flicker of hope in them before the wall went back up.

"None of this is your problem. I can't ask you to get involved. You've already done too much and you're injured because of it."

"You didn't ask. I'm volunteering."

She cocked her head to one side and studied him for a couple of seconds. "Why would you volunteer for this?"

"Maybe because I find it all kinda fascinating, like an old movie-of-the-week story. Maybe because I always wanted to be Sherlock Holmes. Maybe because I like you and want to help."

She stared a second more then gave him a small smile. "You need to get out more. If you like me, then your friend card must be seriously low."

"There's always room on my card for beautiful maidens."

She raised one eyebrow. "Are you going to rescue me from the dragon?"

He smiled. "I didn't bring my chain mail with me, but I can have it delivered."

She laughed. "I bet you can. Well, I suppose we better get back to the house. I need to cook you some breakfast, since I'm responsible for your missing the special. Alaina stocked basics at the house. I can rummage up something."

She stepped back and out of his grasp and pulled her keys from her purse as she turned toward the car. He watched her for a moment, thinking how lovely she looked when she actually let her guard down. When she trusted someone else with a small piece of herself.

Part of him felt incredibly guilty about being one more in a likely long list of people who'd deceived and used her, but he couldn't afford to tell her his true agenda. What if his father had somehow been part of selling off the sisters? How could he expect her to remain impartial to him?

He stepped over to the car and slid into the passenger's seat. The only way this would work was if Danae never knew who he really was. After he got what he wanted, he needed to disappear back to New Orleans and forget he'd ever met her.

If that were even possible.

CARTER FILLED WILLIAM IN on everything that Danae and Zach had told him at the café. The attorney's expression shifted from concerned to angry to fearful in a matter of minutes.

"Is Mr. Sargent all right?" William asked when Carter finished.

"Yeah. He took a good crack on the head, but Doc Broussard doesn't seem to think there's any permanent damage."

William shook his head. "It's like everything's repeating."

Carter nodded. "I thought the same thing. Even though I know someone else broke that window, I guess I was hoping the entire mess would go away when Alaina's situation was resolved. Shortsighted of me, I know."

"Not shortsighted. More like wishful thinking, and you can put me on the list right next to you. I really hoped all the attention Alaina's situation drew would prompt whoever else was lurking around the estate to rethink their plan. Apparently, he's as brazen as ever."

"Maybe even more so, and that's what concerns me

the most. Before we latched onto the situation with Alaina, I was going to talk to you about potential suspects from an inheritance angle. We already know Jack is none too happy about the situation, but I thought there could be others. And I'd like to know what happens to the estate if the sisters don't meet the conditions of the will."

William nodded. "All very good questions, and a line of thinking I'd already taken to just before Alaina's situation was resolved."

The attorney pulled a pad of paper from his desk drawer. "I made some notes as I went through the terms of the will. First off, the cash and securities are to be distributed among several New Orleans charities and two churches."

"Are the directors of any of the charities or the ministers aware of the terms?"

"I don't see how they could be. Even if there was gossip to that effect here in Calais, it would be a long shot that any of it made it back to key people in those organizations."

"And the house?"

"The house and land, including mineral rights, would go to the town of Calais."

Carter frowned. "What was the point of that?"

"It was Ophelia's way of preserving the town as she knew it and wanted it to remain. If developers or oil companies came in, they might tear down the house and strip the land, and that would change what Calais was."

"She was assuming that the Calais city council felt the same way. They could just as easily choose to do that themselves, make a ton of money, vote themselves huge raises and bonuses, and retire in Fiji."

"Yes, that's absolutely true. I'm afraid Ophelia was

overprotected by her own parents. She had the naïveté of a far younger person, and such a thing wouldn't have occurred to her."

"Does anyone on the council know about this?"

"It's quite possible. Of course, I've not told anyone the terms of the will except you, Alaina and Danae, but Purcell could have told someone."

"That wouldn't have been in his best interests, though," Carter pointed out. "If Purcell let others know he didn't have control of disbursing the estate, then people like Jack wouldn't have worked for him all those years for nothing. Surely Jack wasn't the only one to be taken in by the man."

"No. Bert Thibodeaux was in my office a few days ago, yelling."

"Really?" Carter's interest perked up. Bert was a fifty-year-old long-haul trucker with a list of offenses a mile long. He'd even taken a swing at Carter the year before when he'd told him he couldn't park his semi on Main Street, where it blocked the alley.

"Yes, seems he did some delivery-service work for Purcell between here and New Orleans. Claims to have done quite a lot of it over the last ten years."

"And Purcell was supposed to leave him money?"

"That's his claim. Says Purcell promised him the money for a brand-new semi in lieu of charging him for all the deliveries."

Carter whistled. "There's no small price tag on those trucks."

"Definitely not."

"This is what I don't get. Why did Purcell promise them all money when he could have just paid them? Was it some perverse game on his part?"

"To an extent, certainly, but it went beyond that, I believe."

"What do you mean?"

"Purcell had access to the estate, but not in the form of large cash withdrawals. It was a very irregular arrangement, and the more I learn about it, the more I understand some of Purcell's more odd behaviors."

"Like what?"

"Like remaining in Calais, for starters. The way the estate was set up, Purcell could purchase whatever objects he desired as long as the value was sufficient to substantiate the cost, and the estate accountant in New Orleans would write a check for it. But other than a reasonable living allowance, he couldn't withdraw cash from the estate at all."

Carter leaned back in his chair and stared at William. "So he closed himself up in that house and bought a bunch of stuff with the estate money because that was the only way he could get his hands on it, then sent Bert running to New Orleans to get it?"

William nodded. "After gaining a full understanding of how the estate has been managed, that's what I believe."

"How is it that you didn't know all this before?"

"Remember, I wasn't Ophelia's attorney. Her parents established a relationship with the firm in New Orleans long before her birth, and Ophelia maintained that relationship with them. She was young when she passed. I tried to convince her to make an appointment with me and let me review all the documents, but she never did."

Carter sighed. "She didn't think she was going to die. She thought she had plenty of time to deal with that sort of thing."

"Yes," William said, and Carter could hear the sadness in the older man's voice.

"So the firm that manages the estate hired you to oversee it—is that how this works?"

"Exactly. I have formed a relationship with the firm over the years, and they felt it was a good answer to the problems created with the stipulations for the inheritance. My living here makes it easier on everyone."

"Ha, and easier for you to cajole the local sheriff into being hall monitor for the sisters."

"Yes, well…that was supposed to have been a bit easier than it's turned out to be—the hall-monitoring part, that is."

Carter held in a smile at the attorney's obvious chagrin. "You think? There's still an intruder on the loose, I've had to kill a man and now I have a fiancé. I hold you responsible for all of this."

William looked so stricken that Carter's smile finally broke through.

"I'm joking," Carter said. "About holding you responsible, anyway. The rest of it's kinda true."

William laughed, then sobered. "I know this isn't what you signed up for, and it's not what I had in mind, but I'm glad you're here in the middle of this, Carter. You're a good man and a good cop. I wouldn't trust those women with anyone else."

Carter rose and shook William's hand. "I'm going to get to the bottom of this."

"I'm counting on it."

DANAE PLACED A PLATE of eggs and toast in front of Zach along with a glass of milk and one of the pain pills Doc Broussard had given him. "Eat some of that before you take the pain pill," she said.

"Thanks," he said and gave her a smile. "What about your breakfast?"

"I'm too wound up to eat. I need to work off some of this nervous energy, then I'll have something."

"You sure? There's plenty here. I don't know if I can finish it all."

"I'm going to try to give Alaina a call."

"Okay. I'll be here if you need me."

She gave him a nod and left the kitchen, pulling her cell phone from her jeans pocket as she walked down the hall. She glanced at the display and blew out a breath of relief—it had a signal.

Seven-thirty a.m. She bit her lip. Alaina was an hour ahead in Boston. Hopefully, she'd be up. Danae pressed her sister's number on the display and put the phone to her ear, clenching it harder with every ring that went unanswered.

Just when she figured it was going to go to voice mail, Alaina answered, sounding a bit breathless.

"Did I wake you?" Danae asked.

"No, I've been up for hours. My brother came this morning to take our mother to her doctor's appointment and to have her hair done, and I just finished up a quick morning run. I was going to call you later. Is everything okay?"

"Yes… No. I don't know." Danae filled Alaina in on the intruder the day before and the attack on Zach, leaving out the part about ghostly lights and terror-filled screams.

"Oh! Is he all right?"

"Doc Broussard says he'll have a headache for a couple of days, but he'll be fine."

"What did Carter say to do?"

"He hasn't said much yet, but he's supposed to meet us here later this morning."

"Good."

Danae bit her lip, trying to come up with a good way to ask her next question, but she couldn't think of one. Finally, she just blurted it out. "Did Mom have another baby after me?"

Alaina sucked in a breath. "Heavens, Danae, where did that come from?"

"Just answer me. Did she?"

"No. Not that I remember. I mean, my memories are sketchy, but I don't think I could have blocked out her having another baby."

Relief swept through Danae and she sank onto the steps in the foyer.

"You're kinda freaking me out. Why did you ask that?"

"I was going over some of the house records last night at my cabin," Danae said and went on to explain the four entries she'd discovered.

When she finished, the phone was silent for so long that Danae checked to make sure the connection hadn't dropped.

"They took money?" Alaina's voice was barely a whisper. "All of them?"

"Yeah. I saw the woman who took me listed and your parents' names and two others. You can't really read one of them anymore but I'm assuming one of the others is the people who took Joelle."

"But there were four? You're sure?"

"Positive. It's hard to miss four entries in a row for twenty thousand dollars, especially when everything else on the list was minor."

"Did you tell Carter?"

"No. I...I couldn't. It's so demeaning. I just couldn't say it out loud."

But you were able to say it to Zach.

Danae pushed that thought from her mind. Her attraction to the contractor was enough to make her uncomfortable all on its own and something she definitely didn't have the head space to address. Not right now.

"I understand," Alaina said. "But it might be important for him and William to know. They might be able to help."

"I know. I'll tell Carter when he comes this morning."

"He won't judge you. Not Carter."

Danae smiled at the absolute certainty in Alaina's voice. Her sister was already deeply in love with the gorgeous sheriff. It made Danae happy to see the two of them together—talking about building a life together. Alaina was right. Carter was a good man.

Before she could change her mind, Danae launched into her next topic. "I...I saw something last night. When you called that first time yesterday, you asked if I believed in ghosts, but then you had to hurry off the phone. I'd forgotten about it when we talked last night, but I have to know why you asked."

"Why is it so important now?"

Danae took a breath. "Because I saw something in my cabin. No one else knows, so I'd prefer if we keep this between us for the time being. I'm trying to get my footing in Calais. I don't want everyone to think I'm crazy, like our stepfather."

"Of course. Trust me, I don't want anyone to know, either. It's not exactly the thing that improves a reputation. What did you see?"

Danae told her about falling asleep on the couch

and waking up to the vision above her. "I think it was Mom. She looked like the picture I have, which looks a lot like you."

"What was she wearing?"

"A long white nightgown. Her black hair hung loose around her shoulders and she was speaking, but I couldn't hear her."

Alaina sucked in a breath. "She spoke?"

"She was trying, but no sound came out until she started to fade away. Then it's almost like in my mind I heard her saying 'So close' over and over. Is that what you saw?"

"I'm sure one of the things I saw was Mom, but she never spoke. So close to what?"

"It could be anything—home, each other... I just don't know."

"I wonder..."

Danae frowned, finally focusing on her sister's very deliberate wording. "You said Mom was one of the things you saw. Does that mean you saw something else? Some other ghost?"

"Yes. That first night I stayed in the house. Remember I came in the café before dawn the next morning?"

"I remember. You'd slept in your SUV that night because something had spooked you, but you never said what it was."

"I don't know. A ghost, I guess, but it didn't look anything like Mom. This one was gray with red eyes, and there was so much anger in it. I could almost feel it spilling out on me. It looked... I know it sounds crazy, but it looked like it wanted to kill me."

Danae gasped. "Oh, no! No wonder you were terrified, and I made a joke about seeing ghosts when you walked into the café. I'm so sorry."

"You have nothing to apologize for. How could you have known? This isn't exactly the kind of conversation you have with just anyone."

"That's true. There's something else—something I left out of Zach's story." She told Alaina about the scream Zach heard right before the attack and the pulsing light that appeared on the landing.

"That scream would have sent me off on a dead run," Alaina said. "He's got some serious backbone if he stood there trying to figure that out."

Danae smiled, unable to stop from admiring the contractor's fearless if dangerous approach to problem solving. "He seems to be made of stern stuff."

"Good. Because I don't want you there alone. Not ever. Not even for a minute. And get out of that house before dark. Promise me."

"I promise. Alaina, what's happening here? What's happening to us?"

"I don't know, little sister, but we're going to figure it out."

Chapter Eleven

Carter pulled up in front of Bert Thibodeaux's run-down shack, pleased that the trucker's old rig and pickup truck were both parked next to it. It was early, but Carter wanted to make sure he caught Bert before he went out on a run. The trucker was often gone for days at a time, so it was a stroke of good luck that Carter found him at home.

He knocked on the door and waited. Nothing stirred inside, so he knocked again, this time louder. Something crashed to the floor and he heard cursing. A couple of seconds later, the door flew open and Bert glared out at him.

He was a beefy man and had a good three inches on Carter. He wore soiled jeans and a white T-shirt, but his bare feet, uncombed hair and red, watery eyes let Carter know he'd woken up Bert. The angry expression on the trucker's face told Carter exactly how Bert felt about it.

"Good morning, Bert. Can I come in? I need to talk to you."

"Hell, no, you can't come in. It's hardly a time of the morning to be entertaining. What do you want with me? Ain't no warrants out for me. All my tickets are paid."

Carter glanced behind the man into his cabin. It was

a mess of dirty clothes and torn furniture. Empty beer cans, chip bags and frozen-pizza boxes littered every surface and most of the floor. A lacy red bra hung from one of the lamps, and Carter wondered briefly what kind of woman would get undressed in there. Perhaps one who'd had a tetanus shot.

Bert noticed Carter's gaze and pulled the door close to his side so that his massive body was blocking any view inside. "What do you want?"

"William Duhon tells me you used to do some work for Purcell—that you made a little scene in his office over the way the estate is being handled."

"That worthless SOB promised me the money for a brand-new rig. I ran up and down the highway to New Orleans for him for over ten years. I got a right to make a scene."

"No, you don't. William isn't responsible for what Purcell did, and he's just doing his job administering the estate. He's bound to the terms of the will, same as everyone else."

"That still don't make it right."

"I agree. None of it is right or fair, but what Purcell did to those girls after their mother died wasn't fair, either."

"I guess not, but they'll get theirs in the end. What do I get? What does Jack Granger get? All that work—all those years—and what do we have to show for it but a whole lot of nothing?"

"Would you mind telling me exactly what you did for Purcell all those years?"

Bert narrowed his eyes at Carter. "Why you asking?"

"Because some questions have arisen about Purcell's use of estate funds. I'm trying to get answers for William."

"I ain't saying nothing, then. If Purcell was up to illegal stuff, I'm not going to take the rap for that in addition to getting screwed out of a decade of pay."

"If Purcell did anything illegal, that's not on you. I'm just trying to get a better feel for the man—figure out what it was that made him tick."

Bert studied Carter for a minute, then finally shrugged. "Beats the hell out of me. He was a strange one. He bought stuff all the time—at auctions and those fancy stores in New Orleans with ugly art that costs a fortune. God only knows how much he spent on that stuff."

"So you transported the things he bought from New Orleans to here."

Bert nodded. "And back again when he sold them."

All of a sudden, Carter got it—the remarkably simple answer to the question he'd had about Purcell and the money.

"He sold the stuff he bought?" Carter asked. "You're sure?"

"I didn't see the actual things I was carrying, if that's what you mean. They were always wrapped or in crates, but nothing went inside that house that me, Jack or Amos didn't carry in, and I was the only one who made regular trips to New Orleans. He was either selling the stuff he bought or stuff that was already there."

Carter nodded. "I appreciate your time."

"Don't thank me, and tell that attorney not to thank me, either. I'm going to see a lawyer about this. I'll tie that estate up in court until those girls are dead before I let Purcell get away with screwing me from the grave."

He slammed the door and Carter got back into his truck and drove away. One question had been answered—he now knew how Purcell made money off an estate that he couldn't withdraw large blocks of cash from. But that only led to another question. Where was that cash now?

DANAE FLIPPED THROUGH stack after stack of paper, trying to find more documents from around the time of her mother's death. The lantern was the only source of light in the dark office, and it wasn't nearly strong enough to illuminate the mess that Purcell had created. She'd thought the room was cluttered, but the reality was it was practically littered with paper.

Stacks of paper covered almost every inch of the floor and oozed out of every drawer in the desk. The top of the desk was piled two feet high with folders and paper, except for the small section she'd cleared the day before to stack the boxes on. The bookcases contained few books. Mostly, they held stacks of paper and folders. Even the areas that held books had paper stacked on top of books.

It would take her forever to make sense of it all. She'd originally thought the rate for the work overly generous, but now she understood why William had to pay such an amount to get quality work. It would take everything she had not to run screaming from the mess inside of an hour.

She slumped into the office chair and assessed the small stack of papers that she'd located from the time period surrounding her mother's death. All around her were discarded piles that hadn't fallen into that time line. No one would ever guess that she'd already spent the better part of an hour digging through the mess.

"You doing all right in here?" Zach's voice sounded from the doorway.

"I guess. It's such a mess I feel like I'm spinning my wheels."

"Maybe you should try to separate it by date first, then concentrate on one piece at a time."

She sighed. "There's decades of paperwork in here. Apparently, my stepfather, my mother, my grandparents and heaven only knows who else thought they should keep every scrap of paper their hands ever touched."

Zach scanned the room. "It does look a bit over-whelming. Tell you what—I found a stack of cardboard boxes and packing tape in one of the downstairs rooms. I could line them down the hallway, and you can label them by decade or whatever works."

"That's not a bad idea. At least I'd be getting the paperwork out of the room. As it is, it's so cluttered that I can't move it far enough away to get to it all."

Zach nodded. "I'll go get the boxes."

As Zach assembled boxes, Danae lined them down the hallway, against the wall, and labeled each with a different decade spanning seventy years.

"It's a good thing we don't have to meet a fire code," Zach said as he finished with the last box.

Danae glanced at the line of boxes that stretched almost the length of the hallway, only skipping over entrances to rooms. "I'll probably need multiple boxes for some periods, too. In fact, I'm sure of it. I don't think everything in the office will fit in the amount of boxes we have here."

Zach nodded. "I hope you wanted long-term employment when you agreed to this."

"I'm going to hazard a guess that William will say to look at the more recent time frames and forgo things that happened when my grandparents were in charge. Too many things could have happened to assets purchased that long ago."

"That's true enough. Do you want me to take a look at the electricity while you're working up here?"

"I don't want you overexerting yourself. Take it easy, at least for a day."

"The voltage meter fits in the palm of my hand and I only need to remove a couple of screws."

"Then I guess that's okay."

He smiled. "I'll go get my equipment."

Danae walked back into the dim office and sighed at the long day that stretched in front of her. She was twitchy, jumping at every little noise, and had checked her watch every two minutes since hanging up on the call with Alaina. It was almost eleven o'clock and she wondered why Carter hadn't made it to the house yet. She vacillated between hoping he'd found out something important and hoping he hadn't run into trouble.

She picked up a stack of paper on the desk and started flipping through it, checking the dates to ensure they all fell in the same decade. When she finished that stack, she placed it facedown in one of the few bare spots on the desk and picked up another stack.

The second stack of paper was also from the 1950s and she flipped it over on top of the first stack and decided to try another location. The bookcase behind the desk was crammed with nothing but paper. Maybe she would find more updated documentation there. She stepped behind the desk and slid a tall stack of papers off a shelf and carried it back to the desk.

When she saw the dates on the first paper, her pulse quickened. It was from the year her mother died, just a couple of months before. She was definitely getting closer. She flipped through the pages, noting date after date that led up until the time of her mother's death and right after. When she got to the last page, she went back to the first and started studying the transactions, but the dim light in the room made it hard to read the faded cursive.

Carrying a couple of the sheets, she walked into the hall, where the light was better. The cursive was much easier to make out, but the faded spots were many and it was still difficult for her to make out all the words. As soon as she got a chance, she'd pick up a magnifier at the general store. The store probably didn't have anything that would please Sherlock Holmes, but she knew they kept small magnifiers in stock for sewing.

From what she could make out, large deposits were made into the account randomly, and never for the same amount. Royalties, maybe? But then, she wasn't aware that Purcell had any money or investments of his own, and wouldn't royalty payments have recurring dates? She sighed and dropped the papers in the appropriate boxes, mentally adding one more thing to the list of things she needed to discuss with William. Sitting in his office yesterday, everything had seemed so simple.

Too simple.

The thought echoed through her mind, forcing her to acknowledge one of the driving mottoes she'd always lived by—if something appeared too simple, it was always going to be a bear. Still, it seemed horribly unfair that she'd come to Calais for answers and all she'd found were more questions.

"Hey." Zach's voice broke into her thoughts. "Sorry, I didn't mean to startle you."

"You didn't. Just interrupted a bunch of negative thinking that needed to stop."

He held up the voltage meter. "Well, positive or negative, I can pick up the energy signal. I'm not going to get in your way, am I?"

"Not at all, but we need to clear you a path to the light switch, unless you want to try to hook up that thing leaned over ten thousand sheets of paper."

"It's usually better to have a clear view and both feet planted on the floor when playing with electricity."

She smiled. "If we move those three piles nearest the wall, that will probably be enough. Let me grab one of the extra boxes."

She snagged one of the empty boxes from the hall and grabbed a stack of the paper and dropped it inside.

"Do you want to try to keep this in order?" he asked.

"I don't see the point. Most of the stuff I've looked at isn't sequential. It's like God came into the office and shuffled all the paper like a deck of playing cards."

He laughed. "Now, there's an interesting visual."

When they removed the last of the large stacks away from the light switch, she dragged the box back into the hall to get it out of the way, then returned to the papers on the desk as Zach removed the plate from the light switch.

It was comforting having him right there next to her, even though she'd never admit it out loud and was a little perturbed that she felt that way. In every crisis she'd come across before now, she'd always been the strong one—the person everyone else looked to. Her own personal crisis had been borne silently and without aid, not even so much as a cry on an understanding shoulder.

It almost seemed as if revealing her true self had weakened the wall surrounding her, and now everyone and everything was systematically chipping away at it, exposing more of herself than she felt comfortable showing. For the first time since she was a child living in Rose's house, she didn't feel in control, and that bothered her.

"What the—" Zach's voice broke into her thoughts.

He was staring down at his voltage meter, a stunned look on his face.

"What's wrong?"

"It's spiking like crazy, registering way more voltage than is normally found in home wiring."

He held up the box and she saw the needle jerking back and forth in the center of the display.

"Maybe that's what is causing the problem—the wiring's shot," she said.

He raised his head and looked directly at her, his eyes wide. "You don't understand. I haven't hooked it up to the light switch yet." He lifted the loose wires up in his free hand.

She gasped as one hand involuntarily covered her mouth. It wasn't possible that the device could register electrical charge when it wasn't even connected to an outlet, but it was happening right in front of her.

"How…how can that be?" she asked, her voice barely a whisper.

He shook his head. "I have no idea. Nothing like this has ever happened before."

He moved the box around, but the needle still swung back and forth over the center of the screen. When he waved it in the direction of the bedroom doorway, it spiked even higher. He frowned and stepped toward the bedroom. When he stopped in the doorway, he lifted the two loose wires in the air and pointed them inside. The needle sprang to the right side of the meter and stayed pinned against the side, not moving at all.

"It's in there," she said. "Whatever is causing it is in the bedroom."

She looked down at the box, and suddenly, the needle fell from the right to the left. Zach shook the box and lifted the wires farther into the room, but the needle remained at zero. He stepped back into the office and walked over to the light switch, but the needle didn't move even a millimeter.

"It's gone. How can that be?" she asked.

"Given that it should never have happened to begin with, I couldn't even begin to guess why it stopped. Electricity is a moving current, but it doesn't move in those extremes—not inside of houses. And it certainly doesn't move through air."

"Except lightning."

"I didn't see any lightning in the bedroom, did you?"

"You know I didn't." She blew out a breath. "I don't know how much more of this I can take. I live a simple life, and ever since I claimed my birthright, everything has become so complicated and confusing. I'm beginning to think I should never have told William who I was and continued living a perfectly decent life as a waitress."

He placed the voltmeter on the desk and laid his hand on her arm. "We're going to figure this out."

A spark ignited in her at his touch and her arm tingled where his hand lay. It had been a long time since she'd allowed a man to touch her in an intimate way, even one as simple as a sign of reassurance, and he was the first man she actually believed when he said he'd be there for her. He was a good and honorable man who would probably do the same for anyone else, but she knew his touch held the promise of so much more.

Realizing she hadn't responded, she said, "Figuring out my problems is hardly in your job description."

He looked down at her, his green eyes staring directly into hers. "It's more interesting than repairs."

She tapped the side of her head, reminding him of his injury. "But not nearly as safe."

He stepped closer to her, and her breath caught in her throat. "Sometimes a guy just doesn't want to play it safe," he said.

She knew he was going to kiss her, and she could have moved away, but instead, her body betrayed her and leaned into him as he lowered his lips to hers. The gentle brush of his lips sent so many emotions racing through her—care, passion and desire—and she closed her eyes, drowning in this one perfect moment.

He stroked her hair and deepened the kiss, and she leaned farther into him, pressing her body against his as he gathered her in his arms. She wrapped her arms around him, her hands caressing his strong, muscular back. Her skin tingled as the blood rushed to her head, leaving her almost dizzy with desire.

"Hellooooo!" Carter's voice sounded from downstairs like a boom of thunder.

She released Zach immediately, the shock of her more-than-compliant reaction just now setting in. He held her a second longer, clearly reluctant to let the moment go, but not about to press the issue with Carter downstairs.

"Up here," she yelled as she walked out of the office and looked over the balcony. "We'll be right down."

Carter nodded. "I'll meet you in the kitchen."

She glanced back at Zach, who was staring at her with a pensive look. Was he already regretting his action?

"Should we tell him about what happened here?" he asked.

Unbidden, a flush rose up her neck at the thought of explaining to Carter what he'd interrupted, then she realized Zach meant what happened with the voltage meter, and a second wave of embarrassment washed over her as she realized her mind and body were still more engaged with the kiss and not the business at hand.

"I guess so," she said. "He won't think we're crazy. He'll just go looking for an answer. That's the way he is."

Zach nodded. "Then I guess we better get downstairs."

She hurried down the balcony hallway to the stairwell, wondering all the way just how far she would have taken things with Zach if Carter hadn't interrupted. Something told her that if the sheriff had been ten minutes later, he might have caught them in various stages of undress.

The worst part was, she was almost disappointed that he hadn't.

Chapter Twelve

Alaina LeBeau stood at the front door and lifted a hand as her stepbrother drove away. As his taillights faded into the distance, she pushed the door shut and locked it behind her, her earlier conversation with Danae weighing heavily on her mind.

She turned around and cast her gaze over the cozy living room of her adoptive parents' tiny Boston home. Real estate was at a premium where they lived and always had been. Five people shoved into twelve hundred square feet had been a challenge at times, but they'd managed to make it work, and Alaina and her brother and sister had attended great schools with stellar reputations—allowing them all to enter top-tier universities with scholarships to pay for their degrees.

Alaina had been fed, clothed, required to make good grades, praised when she'd done well and disciplined when she'd gotten out of line. On paper, she had nothing to complain about, even though she'd always known her adoptive parents never loved her as they did their own children. They cared, but that wasn't the same thing.

With Danae, Alaina got the impression that her sister's childhood had been rough, possibly even abusive. Danae had that tough outer shell and guarded her speech like so many street kids Alaina had interviewed in the past for testimony. But Alaina also knew that behind that wall her sister had erected was a vulnerable, damaged human being, and her heart ached for the sister she'd always loved and wanted to protect. Now more than anything, she wished she was back in Calais, but she couldn't see any way out of her obligations here— at least, not for a week or so.

She heard her mother shifting in her bed, trying to get comfortable, even though it was practically impossible with her broken leg. Alaina stepped into the kitchen and poured her a glass of milk and gathered her medicine. She'd made vegetable soup while they were gone and her brother had stayed long enough to enjoy the meal with them and help her get their mother settled in her bedroom.

You should wait.

The words came to her every time she thought about the conversation she needed to have with her mother— the one where she asked if the only reason they took her in was for money. The one where she asked if Purcell continued to pay them to keep her.

She and Danae needed answers. She knew next to nothing about Danae's past, but her little sister had offered up that the woman who'd taken her was now dead. No answers were forthcoming from that source. William had yet to locate Joelle, although he thought he was getting closer. But even when their middle sister was found, no guarantees existed that her adoptive family was still alive or would be willing to answer the questions they had.

She sighed. Truth be told, no guarantees existed that her own adoptive mother would be forthcoming, but at least Alaina had the advantage of being able to read people well. She'd know if she was getting the truth or a lie. She'd know if her mother was telling her everything or holding something back, and if she had to, Alaina would twist and manipulate her into letting it all out just as she did those on the jury stand. Now was not the time to worry about past hurts. Lives were at stake.

Her mother was propped up on her back wedge, a rerun of one of those singing reality shows running on the television. Alaina handed her the milk and pills, and her mother took them both and dutifully swallowed the medicine as Alaina pulled a chair over next to the bed to sit.

"Your soup was excellent," her mother said. "I have to admit, I was a bit surprised. I don't remember you being all that interested in cooking."

Alaina smiled. "Carter's mother gave me some of her recipes and some tips. She's a genius in the kitchen and makes it look so easy."

Her mother raised one eyebrow. "So all it took was a good-looking man to get an apron on you?"

"How do you know he's good-looking?"

Her mother laughed and patted her hand. "You're a beautiful, intelligent woman, Alaina. If a man caught your attention to the point that you've got his mother giving you cooking tips, then I have no doubt he is every bit a Hollywood hero."

"You watch too much television," Alaina said, but her mother's words pleased her.

"Well, I would go bungee jumping instead, but my doctor might object."

Alaina laughed, then before she could change her mind she said, "Mom, I need to ask you something, and it might make you uncomfortable, but it's very important that you answer me honestly."

Her mother frowned. "I've never lied to you before. If I have answers you need, you'll get them."

"Did my stepfather…did he…pay you to take me?"

Her mother's eyes widened and she sucked in a breath. "Why would you ask something like that?"

"Because my sister is going through the household records for the estate attorneys and she found entries in a checkbook—large payments to you and to the woman who took her in, made just after our mother died."

Her mother sighed then gave her a single nod. "This is one conversation I hoped I'd never have to have, but I promised you I wouldn't lie and I won't. Right after your mother died, Purcell started contacting her relatives. None of us really knew your mother—her family had moved to Louisiana so long ago and never visited—but your stepfather figured family could get legal custody more easily."

Alaina swallowed. "And family who got paid for it might be willing to take on a stranger's children."

"When Purcell called us, the first thing we thought was what a horrible man, and I'll go to the grave without changing my mind on that one, but our motives weren't pure, either. We were living in a two-bedroom house on the south side of town at the time, and despite working extra jobs, we couldn't afford to get out. The school system was horrible and we worried constantly what would happen to your brother and sister if they grew up in that neighborhood."

"So you took the money."

Her mother nodded. "This house had just gone on the market, and we could stretch to make the monthly note, but we needed the down payment and money to move. Purcell's offer seemed prophetic. We needed the cash to make a better life for our own children, and you girls needed a home, but we knew we couldn't take in all three of you."

"So you got me. How was that decided?"

"We requested you because you were closest to our own children's ages. We thought it would be an easier transition for you, and we didn't want to go through toddler stages again."

Alaina took a deep breath and blew it out, trying to process the fact that she'd drawn the good family completely by default. If she'd been the youngest, she would have gotten Danae's life instead of this one. The unfairness of it all left a bitter taste in her mouth.

"Did he keep paying you? I mean, after that first payment?"

"No. It was a onetime offer and we were instructed never to contact him again. We asked for information on your sisters, but he said it was not our concern and wouldn't tell us where they'd gone."

Her mother squeezed her hand. "I'm so sorry, Alaina. It's true we made the decision to take you in because we needed the money, but I promise you we love you and are proud of you. We've never once regretted our decision."

Alaina nodded, afraid her voice would break if she spoke. She knew what her mother said was true—they did love her—but it wasn't the same for her as it was for her stepbrother and stepsister. It never could be. She knew part of that was because she wasn't their biological child, but the other part was all on her.

She still remembered her mother, and snatches of her childhood were returning to her since she'd moved to Calais. Some of the distance was her fault, because she knew where she really belonged, and it wasn't in

Boston. Ever since she'd set foot in Calais, Alaina had known she was where she was meant to be.

"Are you all right?" The worry in her mom's voice was clear.

Alaina nodded and squeezed her hand. "I don't blame you for your choices. You did what was right for your family, and I benefited from your dedication to raising your children in a safe place with a good school system."

"But you're worried about something. I've known since you walked in my door that something was wrong. I hoped with that man dead, all the trouble was behind you now."

"Apparently not." Alaina gave her mother a brief rundown of the odd things happening at the estate, leaving out anything to do with the supernatural. Her mother was a staunch believer in only what she could see and quantify.

"I don't like it," her mother said when she was finished. "Can't you girls go somewhere else until the police have figured all this out?"

"I'm not positive it would do any good. If someone simply wants to prevent us from inheriting, then I don't see any reason why the harassment would stop if we left Calais."

"But you're not safe there."

"Actually, in many ways we're safer in Calais. It's a small place, so things that are out of the ordinary are easier to spot, and Carter knows everyone and everything that goes on. He's watching everything like a hawk. He'll figure this out."

Alaina made sure her voice sounded convincing, but the look on her mother's face told her she wasn't certain.

The worst part was, Alaina wasn't certain, either.

IT TOOK THE BETTER PART of an hour for Zach, Danae and Carter to exchange information, and with every passing tidbit that Carter added, Zach found himself more confused by what might be going on in the house. When Danae told Carter what happened with the voltage meter, he listened intently, occasionally asking questions, but not once did the sheriff appear even remotely concerned about their sanity.

When Danae finished, Carter looked over at Zach. "You got any idea what could have caused something like that?"

"None whatsoever," Zach said. "Unless there's a problem with my equipment, which would surprise me, I don't have a clue."

Carter nodded. "I have a voltage meter at home. I'll bring it by tomorrow for a test. I don't suppose someone could have created enough electricity in the room to set it off, could they?"

"Maybe, but our hair would have been standing on end if that much electricity was wafting through open space. And besides, the people you've got your eye on don't sound like the kind that could rig such an event, and even if they were, how would they know I'd use the voltage meter in that particular room and at what time?"

Danae's eyes widened. "You don't think he's still in the house, do you? I mean, if it was a prank of some sort, he'd have to time it correctly, but surely…"

Carter glanced at Zach and he knew the sheriff didn't want to tell Danae what he thought, but he wouldn't lie to her, either.

"Anything's possible," Carter said finally. "I wish I could tell you we're alone in the house, but the reality is, there're a million places to hide in here and no way for us to check them all. And that's just the areas we're aware of. There could be more servants' passages or secret rooms."

"Wouldn't Amos know?" Danae asked.

"No," Carter said. "I talked to him after leaving Bert's place. He knew about the servants' stairs but he has no knowledge of any exterior entries to the house other than the obvious ones."

"I hate this!" Danae jumped up from the dining chair and paced the kitchen. "It almost feels like we're being... I don't know, herded?"

Zach nodded. "Like a puppeteer—someone behind the scenes, pulling the strings."

"Exactly," Danae agreed. "Like's it all been staged just for me."

"I think it probably has been," Carter said. "Not you, personally, but the sisters."

"Do you really think a long-haul trucker or an alcoholic short-order cook could pull off something this elaborate?" Danae asked.

Carter shook his head. "But either of them could have hired someone. Or one of the organizations that will inherit could have found out about the terms of the will. It could be anyone from an employee to the board of directors to a local politician."

"Too many people," Zach said. "Too many possibilities."

"Yes," Carter agreed. "My next objective is to work on whittling down that list."

"Can we help?" Danae asked.

"Maybe. I know there are lots of options but I can't help feeling that the key to everything is Trenton Purcell. I've been looking into the man, and it's all very sketchy. It's like one day he materialized in Calais but there's not even a hint of his existence prior to then."

"So what are you thinking?" Zach asked.

"I don't have a supposition yet, but I'm hoping this house contains the answers to Purcell's secrets. Those journal entries that Danae found are a good start. Based on what I learned from William and Bert, I'd guess that what you found was Purcell's logs for his own funds."

"His accounting for the cash he made selling off estate assets?" Danae asked.

"Exactly, an entirely different issue than the estate accounts, which are managed by the law firm in New Orleans."

"Makes you wonder what happened to the cash after he died."

"Maybe that's what the intruder is looking for," Carter said. "From the looks of the office, Purcell didn't throw much away. Surely there's enough information in here to piece together what he was up to and everyone in Calais who was involved."

"Should I…" Danae began. "I guess I should start going through things in his bedroom."

A mere glance let Zach know that the last thing Danae wanted to do was spend time in Purcell's bedroom. From the weird, creepy perspective, he didn't blame her, but he couldn't afford for the voltage-meter incident to deter him from the job at hand.

"I'll do it," Zach said. "I'll search for records in the bedroom and haul them out as I find them. That way Danae doesn't have to go in there."

Danae's face flushed. "I am perfectly capable of doing the job I've been hired to do—"

"I know," Zach interrupted. "I'm not suggesting anything different, but the office is going to take forever, and I need to figure out the problem with the electricity in the bedroom anyway. Without moving some of that stuff out of there, I'll never be able to get to the sockets to test."

"He's right," Carter said. "And I'd feel better about you being in the house if Zach was nearby. The sooner we figure out what's going on here, the sooner I can make it stop. I'll talk to William and explain that Zach will be working on some nonconstruction-related things. You know he'll support that decision."

Danae sighed. "I know. We'll start this afternoon."

"Good," Carter said. "If you two are okay here, I'm going to head to New Orleans this afternoon to talk to a couple of people—see if I can turn up anything on Purcell there."

"We'll be fine," Zach assured him.

Carter rose from his chair and placed his hand on Danae's shoulder, giving it a squeeze. "We're going to get through this. I promise you."

He looked over at Zach. "Would you mind getting me a couple of items from Purcell's bedroom? Things he would have touched on a regular basis."

Zach stood, understanding immediately what Carter wanted. "You think the print will turn up something?"

"It's worth a shot."

Danae jumped up from her chair and opened the pantry. "I have some sandwich bags in here. Be careful not to touch anything yourself." She handed the box of sandwich bags to Zach.

Zach grabbed the box and headed upstairs, Carter and Danae trailing behind. Maybe this was the answer to some of the questions. If Carter could figure out where Purcell came from and why, then they might be able to get a better handle on the horrible things he did.

What worried him more was how Danae would take it if it resulted in just another dead end.

"THIS IS THE LAST of the records from the dresser," Zach said as he stacked the spiral notebooks on the desk in front of Danae. It had been a long, dusty afternoon and he wanted nothing more at the moment than a hot shower. Unfortunately, the shower was going to have to wait.

As soon as Danae called it quits and headed home, he was going to make good use of the window he'd freed that morning and grab the box of paperwork from the time surrounding Ophelia's death. He'd get it back in place long before work time, and Danae would never be the wiser. He might not have an internet connection in the caretaker's cabin, but he'd had the forethought to bring his laptop and a scanner. If he found anything interesting, he would make a copy.

Danae looked at the stack of dusty notebooks and sighed. "So that's everything from the dresser and nightstands, right?"

"Yeah, but I think there's more under the bed, and I didn't have the heart to even peek into the closet."

She glanced at her watch. "No wonder. It's six o'clock already. You should have let me know it was so late."

"We were both absorbed, and besides, it's not like my Calais social calendar is bursting at the seams."

"Well, then, let me do something about the social calendar to make up for working you like a slave. Dinner at the café—my treat?"

"You don't have to do that."

"I want to. You've done so much for me today. Besides, I don't like eating alone, and my cupboard is bare."

Zach laughed. "So essentially, you're still working me." He said it in a joking tone, but he could tell that what Danae was really avoiding was going home alone. With her independent nature, she'd never admit it, though.

She smiled. "Then I'll throw in a couple of beers and, if you're really good company, a bowl of banana pudding."

"You had me at *dinner,* but I'm not going to turn down the rest. I had a bowl of banana pudding there last night with Carter and have already decided it should be illegal. Seriously, if I lived here, I'd be fat as a tick."

"Not if I keep working you like a mule. Let's get out of here. It's probably dark already."

She rose from the desk and headed out of the office. Zach watched her as she walked away, momentarily mesmerized by the gentle sway of her hips in snug jeans. After talking with Carter, Danae had gone straight to work, and Zach could tell her protective wall was back in place. He'd pushed all thoughts of their shared kiss to the back of his mind while he worked, concentrating instead on the real reason he was in Calais.

All afternoon, he'd been thinking about getting ahold of that paperwork and wondering what he would find, but the moment Danae asked him to dinner, his fickle thoughts had switched right back to that kiss. He could still feel the heat from her body pressed into his, her lips soft and smooth.

He shook his head and hurried out of the office before she wondered what was holding him up. Stealing paperwork and taking that kiss to the next level were the only two answers he could honestly give, and he was pretty sure she wouldn't like either one.

As he stepped out of the office, he almost collided

with Danae. "Sorry," he said as he grabbed her shoulders to avoid slamming into her.

"No, it's my fault," she said as she stepped around him and grabbed the notebooks off the desk in the bedroom. "I want to bring some of the records home with me tonight."

Zach clenched his hands as she tossed the notebooks into the box with records from the period surrounding Ophelia's death and then bent over to lift it.

"Let me get that," he said and hefted the box up in front of his face, afraid his frustration was showing.

He carried the box outside and placed it in her car while she locked up the house. With every step, he tried to come up with another idea. So far, Danae had refused his offers to help go through the paperwork, and he understood that. She was a very guarded person and that paperwork might contain information that was private—things she might not feel comfortable letting others know.

He'd seen how uncomfortable she was telling Carter about the payments to the families who had adopted the girls. Carter, of course, had taken it in without even blinking and had moved straight toward analysis rather than lingering over the emotional impact of her findings. But Zach had seen the flex of his jaw and knew the good sheriff was beyond angry. He was just smart enough to know that his anger would only make Danae feel worse.

Zach had liked Carter from the moment he'd met him, but at that moment, his respect for the man had doubled. If anyone was going to get to the bottom of everything happening in Calais, he had no doubt Carter Trahan would be that person. Which left Zach with two objectives—find the information he came for in the first place and prevent anyone from harming Danae.

"I'll follow you to the café," he said and jumped into his truck.

THE INTRUDER WATCHED from between the blinds of an upstairs window as the heiress and her maintenance boy drove away. From his hiding place in the attic, he'd heard every conversation that had occurred in Purcell's office. When the sheriff arrived, he was tempted to leave the attic and sneak down the servants' stairs off the kitchen to see if he could hear the discussion, but it was too much of a risk.

The house was old and many places creaked, which made it nearly impossible to change location without alerting others that he was there. Lately, it had gotten much harder to get in and out without detection. He was fortunate he still had the front-door key that he'd stolen years ago, and he'd thought when the first heiress finished out her days in the house he could get back to work.

Now he not only had another meddling woman in his way, but also a nosy contractor who seemed more interested in the woman than repairing the house. But that wasn't even the worst part. The worst part was that the woman had just driven off with a box that probably contained the paperwork he'd been looking for.

He banged his hand on the window, damning the day the woman had come to Calais. First, he'd finish the work he needed to do here today, then he'd pay the heiress a visit at her cabin.

And collect what was his.

Chapter Thirteen

All twenty minutes of the slow, bumpy drive, Zach thought about how he was going to access the records. Sneaking into the empty main house and stealing them was one thing, but he could hardly break into Danae's tiny cabin with her in there. The memory of her nine millimeter was stamped on his mind.

When he parked in front of the café, he was no closer to an answer than he'd been when they left the house.

Several tables were occupied, but the far corner held an empty booth with no one seated nearby. Zach pointed to it and Danae nodded. Unless they were yelling, they wouldn't be overheard. As soon as they took their seats, the waitress walked over, a big smile on her face.

"It's great to see you again," Sonia said to Danae. "I didn't get a chance to thank you this morning for quitting. I really needed my job back and there's only so many available in Calais."

Danae smiled. "I'm glad it worked out for everyone."

"I do have a favor to ask, though. I have some personal business to take care of tomorrow. Is there any way you can cover for me? I know it's Saturday, and I don't want to ruin your weekend, but it's just the midmorning shift, so you wouldn't start until nine. Irene said she can come in early and cover starting at eleven."

"Is Johnny okay with it?"

Zach's pulse sped up a tick and he knew he was holding his breath, waiting for the answer. If Danae was out of her cabin for the morning, that would give him time to get in there and look at some of the documents.

Sonia rolled her eyes. "You know Johnny. He said he doesn't care as long as the food gets out before it gets cold."

Danae nodded. "That sounds about right. Sure, I can do it. I hope it's nothing too serious."

Sonia looked down at the floor for a moment and Zach could see a blush creeping up her neck. "Just some old business that needs to be handled. You know how it is."

"I do. Well, good luck with it."

"Thanks. Can I get you guys something to eat? Pot roast is the special, and I have to say, Jack's outdone himself. It's fantastic."

Zach nodded and Danae held up two fingers. "Make it two, please?" she said.

"Got it," Sonia said and hurried back to the grill to put in the order.

She'd barely left when one of the men at the table nearest them rose from his chair and sauntered over.

Danae looked up and smiled. "Hi, Mr. Martin."

"Roger, please," he said to Danae and then stuck his hand out to Zach. "Roger Martin."

Zach shook the man's hand, wondering what he wanted. His companions, two older men, watched from their table, and Zach could see them speaking to each other, their shoulders almost touching.

"Zach Sargent. It's nice to meet you."

"I don't think I've seen you around before. You a relative?"

Zach shook his head. "I'm a contractor. Mr. Duhon hired me to make some repairs at the LeBeau estate."

"I heard the place was in a real state of disrepair. No way Amos could have kept all that up at his age." Roger turned to Danae, studying her for a moment. "So, I hear you're one of Ophelia's missing daughters."

Danae sat up a bit straighter, clearly uncomfortable under Roger's scrutiny. "I guess it seems strange to everyone that I never said anything."

"Not to me. Purcell wasn't well liked and you couldn't have known what you might walk into here. I don't blame you for taking in the lay of the land before offering up that bit of information."

Zach saw Danae relax a bit.

"Well," Danae said, "I hope others share your feelings."

"I'm sure most do. Anyway, I wanted to apologize for not recognizing you. You were just a baby when I saw you last and you don't look much like your mother...."

"No, I don't. Did you know my mother well?"

Roger nodded. "I was the sheriff for thirty years. I knew everyone. Of course, no one saw her much after she married Purcell. He was a bit of an odd duck. Kept you all locked in that house like the apocalypse was coming."

"That's what I hear. I don't really remember anything."

"No, I guess you wouldn't. She was a nice woman, your mother. What my mother would have called a real lady. Anyway, I just wanted to say that if you need anything, I'm happy to help."

"Thank you."

Roger gave Zach a nod then walked back to his table.

"That was weird," Danae said, glancing back at Roger before turning back to face Zach.

"I take it you weren't friendly before?" Zach asked.

"I was as friendly as I am to all the customers, but I never got to know him like some of the other residents. Until now, he's never spoken to me other than to give his order. I didn't even know he was once the sheriff."

Zach glanced across the café and saw Roger frowning at Danae, his brow scrunched as if in thought. "I wonder what he wanted."

"You got that feeling, too?"

"That he had an ulterior motive for the conversation—sure."

She sighed. "Me, too, but I have no idea what."

"Maybe he just wants some gossip to spread around," Zach said. "I'm guessing there's not a whole lot to talk about in Calais."

"You may be right. The two men with him are both widowers and worse gossips than most women I've known. Roger isn't married now, but I suppose he could have been married before. Maybe they're just bored."

"Or maybe he was looking to hook up with an heiress," Zach teased.

Danae stared at him, her dismay so obvious, he laughed.

"That's just wrong," she said. "He's old enough to be my father."

"A lot of women see that as a plus."

"Weak, lazy women who have daddy issues. I hardly need a man to take care of me." She stopped speaking abruptly and stared at him for a moment. "You're picking on me, and I totally took the bait."

"Sorry, but I couldn't resist, especially as I can't imagine you hooking up with a man for any reason other than you wanted to." Before he could stop himself, his thoughts tumbled out of his mouth. "You're an admirable woman, Danae. I wouldn't blame a man, regardless of age, for taking a shot at you."

She shifted in her seat, looking both flattered and uncomfortable. "Thank you, but I've been surrounded by bulletproof glass for a long time. Anyone shooting at me wouldn't stand a chance."

"Maybe," he said and smiled. What she said was probably true of her past, but he'd already put a crack in that shield. Danae wasn't as insulated as she wanted to believe. Her statement also made him wonder what had happened in her past that made her so cagey, so protective.

"Can I ask you a personal question?" he asked.

"Sure, but I reserve the right not to answer it and to rescind my offer to pay for dinner."

"I'll take my chances." He studied her for a moment, trying to decide the best way to approach the subject, then finally just blurted it out. "What happened to make you so closed off? You don't strike me as a woman who would take abuse, but I figure it had to be something horrible. What did he do—cheat on you? Steal your money?"

Danae's eyes widened. Clearly, the question had been an unexpected one. "I've never been married or even in a serious relationship."

"That surprises me."

"Why?"

"You're a beautiful woman. I can't imagine you don't know that or that other men haven't noticed. You mentioned working in bars and cafés—how many times do you get hit on in a week?"

"That doesn't count. That's just men behaving like boys."

"Yes, but men don't behave like boys unless they think a woman is attractive, something I'm sure you've seen played out a thousand times in your lines of work."

She shrugged and looked down at the table.

"So what caused you to close off this way?" he asked. "You're an intelligent, beautiful, engaging woman, but you've made yourself an island surrounded by suspicion and distrust."

She looked back up at him, but her gaze seemed to go right through him. Whatever haunted Danae LeBeau went much deeper than a failed romance or the betrayal of a friend. Finally, her vision sharpened and she narrowed her eyes at him.

"My choices are not up for discussion," she said.

Before he could reply, Sonia slid two plates of food in front of them. "Y'all need anything else?"

Zach waited a second for Danae to reply, but when she remained silent, he looked up at the smiling waitress and shook his head. "No, thank you."

"Okay. Holler if you do." She jaunted off across the café, leaving them wrapped in silence so thick he could cut it.

DANAE JUMPED INTO her car in front of the café, barely lifting her hand to Zach as he pulled away in his truck. They'd finished the meal in silence except for the barest of sentences, like "Please pass the salt." She knew Zach was disappointed that she wouldn't engage in any of the topics he'd put forward, but she simply wasn't ready.

Yes, she was attracted to him—how could she not be? He was strong, sexy and hell-bent on protecting her. And even though the last thing she needed was a white knight, her heart beat a little bit stronger just knowing that such a man wanted to be her savior.

Then there was the kiss.

She'd been kissed before—probably not as much as people thought, but certainly, she was no innocent maiden. But something about Zach's kisses was different. Her whole body responded to him, every single square inch as if it were awakening for the first time. It was exhilarating and frightening all at the same time.

Then he'd asked her why she didn't let people in, and all romantic thoughts had flown out the window. Her gut had involuntarily clenched as every horrible moment from her past ran through her mind on speed play. Then, for a millisecond, she thought about telling Zach everything.

A second later, the thought fled as if on fire and she returned to her good senses, wondering what in the world had gotten into her. Sure, Zach was gorgeous and she'd be lying if she said she wasn't interested in a physical relationship, but she'd always guarded her past like Fort Knox, intending for it to go to the grave along with her. What in the world had caused her to think, even for a split second, that she should share her past with a man who was essentially a stranger?

Sighing, she rolled down the window to let the cool autumn breeze waft over her. Maybe the air would clear her head. As she put the car in Drive, a hand clutched her shoulder and she jumped.

"Sorry." Amos, the ancient LeBeau estate caretaker, stood outside her car door, leaning on a crutch with his free hand, the other crutch tucked under his arm.

"Amos! You shouldn't be walking around like this. It can't possibly be good for your foot."

He waved a hand in dismissal. "If I have to rest another minute, I'm going to just go ahead and die. My niece is one of those hoverers. Darn woman spends all day standing over me or peeking at me around corners. A man needs some room for his thoughts. Ain't had a single one of my own since I moved in with her."

Danae held in a smile at the crotchety man's delivery. She knew the niece and didn't doubt for a minute that she was hovering—she was decidedly that kind of woman—but she also knew Amos probably made the worst patient ever.

"Anyway," he continued, "I saw your car here from her living-room window, and I've been waiting for her to take her nightly bath so I could sneak out and talk to you. You got a minute for a foolish old man?"

"Of course."

Amos scooted away from the door so that Danae could exit the car, then he pointed to a park bench on the sidewalk in front of the café. She took his arm and guided him over to it, then sat beside him.

"I guess you heard the gossip," she said.

Amos nodded. "I should have figured it out before. I felt something—a connection, I guess—with you the first time I saw you at the café. But I didn't understand why. I mean, you're a nice girl and a pretty one, but it was something more than that."

"I was only a baby when Purcell sent me away, and I don't look like either of my parents, not enough to call attention. It's not surprising that you didn't recognize me. Alaina didn't, either."

"You got her smile—your mom's, that is. Did even when you was a baby. You used to follow me all around the house when I was trying to do my work. If I ignored you, you'd clutch my leg and I'd go dragging you down the hall, you riding my leg and giggling so hard it gave you the hiccups."

Danae smiled. "I wish I could remember that."

"Maybe you will someday. I know you was just a little thing, but being here, in the house, you might get a flash of memory now and then."

Amos sat up a little straighter and rubbed his old blue jeans with one hand. "You're staying at the house, right?"

"No. I'm still living in my rental. It's on estate property and William said that was good enough to satisfy the requirements of the will."

The relief on the old caretaker's face was apparent. "That's good. I don't like the idea of you being in that house."

"I am there during the day, though. William hired me to go through paperwork for the estate, but I'm not alone. The contractor William hired is there with me."

"I guess that's all right, then." But he didn't look convinced.

"Is there any reason you don't want me to be there?"

Amos stared at the sidewalk and nodded. "I haven't told no one. They'll all think it's just the ramblings of an old man, but I know what happened."

"What happened when?"

"When I broke my foot."

"I thought you fell down the stairs. That's what William said."

"Because that's what I told everyone, but the truth is, I ain't walked up them stairs in ten years or better. Sometimes went a month or more without seeing your stepfather. Hadn't seen him in months when I found him dead on the floor right there in the entry."

Her mind immediately created a visual image of Purcell's cold, lifeless body splayed across the marble floor of the entry, and she crossed her arms over her chest, suddenly feeling a chill.

"So how *did* you break your foot?"

"I was leaving the house by the back door, like I always do. It was still daylight, so I could see clearly. I stepped outside and fumbled a bit for my keys. When I started to turn around to lock the door, someone shoved me."

Danae sucked in a breath.

"Hit both my shoulders like a freight train," Amos continued. "I took a step back, trying to get my balance, but he'd hit me too hard. I twisted my ankle on the way down, then banged it pretty good on the stone patio."

"Who shoved you? Why didn't you call the police?"

"Because no one would have believed me."

"Why not? You were turning around. You had a clear view of your attacker."

Amos shook his head, his eyes wide. "Wasn't no one there."

"I don't understand. You said someone pushed you…"

"Yep, and that's the God's honest truth. Felt his fingers pushing into the tops of my shoulders, but couldn't see a thing."

She sucked in a breath. "You're saying a ghost pushed you?"

"I know what it sounds like, which is why I lied. But I don't want to lie to Ophelia's girls, and I don't want any of you in danger in that house."

"And you think we're in danger?"

Amos nodded. "Your stepfather was a nasty man. I ain't got no proof of it, but I'd dare and say he was evil. I stuck around all those years because I knew one day you and your sisters would return. I knew it in my heart. But after your mother passed, things felt different. Heavy, like something was constantly pressing down on me, trying to smother me."

Danae nodded. "It's an oppressive atmosphere."

"Exactly. Your stepfather never liked you girls. Never liked anyone being in the house unless it couldn't be helped and took darn near an act of God to get him out of it."

She stared at him. "You think my stepfather is haunting the house?"

"I know it sounds crazy, but I don't think he's ever left. That feeling I always got when I was alone in the house with him is still there. And I could swear I smelled Wild Turkey when I fell. He was always drinking Wild Turkey. I haven't been able to stand the smell for over twenty years."

Danae took a deep breath and blew it slowly out, trying to make sense of what the caretaker said. His expression—half earnest, half afraid—told her that he believed every word he'd said. But was his aging mind playing tricks on him?

"Why would my stepfather haunt the house?"

Amos shook his head. "My granny used to say that your spirit only stuck around on this earth if your body died and your soul was vexed."

"Like if someone was in a highly emotional state or a crisis?"

"Yep."

"But that doesn't make sense for Purcell. He had a mansion to live in and didn't have to work. What could be keeping him here?"

"Anger."

She stared at Amos, the conversation with Carter playing back in her mind. "Carter found out Purcell didn't have free access to the estate money—just an allowance and the ability to buy assets of approved value. Carter thinks he was buying stuff and then selling it for the cash."

Amos nodded. "That very well could be. Whenever he'd show himself, he was usually grumbling about being stuck in the house. I always thought it was odd that he stayed as he didn't seem to like anything about it, but if what you say is true, then I guess he couldn't leave."

"Not unless he wanted to support himself, and apparently, he was willing to give up his life to avoid work." She shook her head. "I've known some lazy people in my day, but never anything like that. It doesn't make sense."

Amos narrowed his eyes at her. "It does if he was hiding from someone even worse than him."

The conversation with Amos ran through Danae's mind a hundred times on the drive to her cabin. Carter's cursory check into Purcell's background had yielded almost nothing but maybe he'd find more in New Orleans. Maybe the fingerprints would give them some information about the mysterious man who'd removed her mother from society and given away her children as if they were unwanted pets.

Maybe Amos was right. Maybe Purcell used Ophelia's remote estate to escape a worse fate. When she'd died, he probably thought he would collect an amount of money that allowed him to go to the far reaches of the earth to hide from his past. And when he heard the terms of the will, he got angry.

His escape to Calais became his prison.

Chapter Fourteen

Carter paced the interview room at the New Orleans Police Station, his coffee sitting forgotten and cold on the table. His former captain hadn't even hesitated when Carter had asked him to lift and run the prints, and he'd been astounded when Carter told him about all the trouble going on in the tiny town of Calais.

The captain had warned him the lab was backed up and it might take a while, but Carter didn't have any business in New Orleans other than Purcell and no other leads if the fingerprints didn't provide them. He reached for the coffee and sighed when he felt the cold cup. Maybe he should take a walk around the block—something just to get out of the building.

Just as he made up his mind to leave, the door opened and the captain walked in, carrying a stack of paper. His expression left no doubt that not only had he found something, but that he also didn't like it.

"You've really stepped in the middle of a hornet's nest," the captain said. "Those prints hadn't been loaded five minutes before the computer screen started whirling so fast I was afraid it would fry. I printed it all out and hurried in here before the phone calls start."

Carter stared. "Who was he—D. B. Cooper?"

"Close enough. His real name was Raymond Lambert, and he was a hit man for the Primeaux family. They run a lot of the adult-trade business in New Orleans and dabble a bit in threats and extortion. Got a couple of politicians in their pocket, if you ask me, but I haven't been able to put a case together yet."

Carter slumped onto the table. "You're kidding me. What the hell was a hit man doing in Calais?"

"My guess is he was hiding. Says here that word on the street was old man Primeaux put a price on his head, but no one has ever heard why. Lambert simply disappeared twenty-five years ago and everyone figured someone from the Primeaux family had caught up with him."

"That definitely fits with what little I know about the man. Everyone assumed he was agoraphobic, but maybe he was just lying low to avoid the risk of being identified."

"Seems an odd choice to make for a man in his mid-forties, but some people will do almost anything to avoid an honest day's work. He probably figured he could eventually talk the widow into leaving Louisiana."

"Probably," Carter agreed. "The police didn't look into his disappearance?"

"Of course—we're cops. But you know how those families operate. They close ranks and you can't get anyone talking, not even about each other."

"So he left New Orleans and became Trenton Purcell and romanced a young widow for her fortune."

"Looks like. What I don't understand is, why didn't he leave Calais after the widow died?"

"I can answer that one," Carter said and gave the captain a rundown of the terms of the estate.

When he finished, the captain whistled. "I bet he was madder than a hornet. Probably thought he'd won the lottery when she passed so young, and then finds out he's tied to those four walls in the middle of the swamp unless he wants to leave with the shirt on his back. That probably didn't do anything to improve his disposition."

"He was a nasty man. The more I find out about him, the more I wish he was still alive so that I could throttle him myself."

The captain nodded. "There's a name in the file—an FBI agent who was working up a case against the family about the time Lambert disappeared. He's retired now, but still lives in New Orleans. I wrote his name and phone number on the top of the printout. Thought if you had time, you might want to talk to him."

Carter took the printout from the captain and glanced at the name and telephone number penciled on the top sheet. "Yeah, that would be great."

The captain extended his hand to Carter. "It was good seeing you, Trahan. If you ever change your mind about coming back to the force, I'd be happy to have you."

Carter shook his hand and nodded. "Thanks, sir, but I think Calais is where I belong."

The captain shook his head. "Seems your attempt to move to a simpler place has failed you all the way around."

"Seems like," Carter agreed. "But I'm going to fix that."

DANAE STUCK HER HAND out of the shower and reached for the towel hanging on the hook next to it. The hot water had done wonders for her neck and back, both of which had grown increasingly tighter as the day had worn on, culminating with all-out knots after her conversation with Amos.

She dried off her body then wrapped the towel around her head before stepping out of the tub to grab the shorts and T-shirt she'd draped across the vanity. A draft of chilly night air wafted through the bathroom and she quickly pulled the clothes on. The days were still warm and humid, but the temperatures dropped at night, especially in the swamp.

As she reached for her hairbrush, she heard the floor creak at the front of the cabin. Immediately, she froze, trying to lock in on the noise. Then it came again, the faintest creak of the floorboards.

Someone was in the cabin with her.

Mentally cursing herself for leaving her pistol in her purse, she scanned the bathroom for anything that made a viable weapon and grabbed the scissors from the vanity. She inched over to the bathroom door and eased it open, praying that the hinges didn't squeak. When the door was open enough for her to edge through it, she peered down the hall toward the living room, but couldn't see anything moving.

The sounds of the swamp were the only things that broke the still night air, and she wondered if the intruder had gone. Or maybe she'd been wrong and no one had ever been inside with her. Maybe the stress of her situation and her overworked imagination were getting the best of her.

She eased down the hall toward the living room, clutching the scissors and praying she'd blown the entire thing out of proportion. When she reached the opening to the living room, she scanned the room as much as possible without stepping into it, but nothing appeared out of place.

You're an idiot.

Shaking her head, she stepped from the hallway into the living room, and that was when he sprang. In an instant, he grabbed her shoulder with one hand and wrapped his arm around her neck, pulling it so tightly she couldn't breathe.

Before her mind could even process what was happening, instinct kicked in and she stabbed his arm with the scissors. He let out a roar and released her, shoving her into the hallway as he ran for the door.

She stumbled backward, barely managing not to fall, then rushed back into the living room as the intruder yanked open the front door. She lunged for the kitchen table and grabbed her purse, pulling her pistol from inside. Before she could get off a round, the intruder dashed out the front door.

She ran across the room and scanned the front of the cabin, but couldn't see anything in the inky blackness. Still clutching her pistol, she slammed the door and locked it, then grabbed her cell phone and started to dial Carter when she remembered he was in New Orleans. Cursing, she punched in Zach's number, praying that the connection was strong enough on both ends for the call to go through.

It was all she could do to keep from crying out in relief when he answered on the second ring.

"There was someone in my cabin," she blurted out before he even finished his greeting. "I heard something when I got out of the shower and I thought I'd imagined it, but then he grabbed me and I stabbed him with my scissors. Then he ran and I grabbed my gun, but it was too late. He disappeared into the swamp before I could fire."

Her breath came out in a giant whoosh and she realized she'd been holding it through the entire delivery.

"Are you all right?" Zach's voice sounded as panicked as she felt. "I'm on my way. Lock the doors and don't you dare put down that gun. I'll be there in a couple of minutes."

"Don't hang up, okay?"

"I won't."

Danae hurried to the corner of the living room opposite the door and sank down into a squatting position next to the couch. This way, she had the advantage over anyone entering the room. A quick scan of the living room and kitchen revealed no broken glass, and she was certain she'd drawn the dead bolt on the front door as soon as she'd entered the cabin. Clearly he hadn't entered that way, but it didn't look as if he'd come through a window, either, so where had he gained access?

Part of her wanted to get up and look for the point of entry, but the other part wanted everything to do with self-preservation and nothing to do with things that could wait until Zach arrived.

"Are you still there?" she asked.

"Yeah, I'm in my truck, but I'm going to have to put the phone down. I need both hands to negotiate the roads at high speed."

"Okay," she said and clutched the phone even tighter. She could hear Zach's truck engine and silently willed it to move faster, but she knew speed was next to impossible on the winding, bumpy roads.

A second later, her phone beeped once then went silent.

"No!" She looked at the display, but service had dropped to nothing.

Surely he was almost there. It had been several minutes since she'd called, right? It felt like longer than that, so he had to be close.

Breathe.

Realizing that she was beginning to panic, she took a deep breath and slowly blew it out. Never had she felt so vulnerable, so completely exposed, as she did right now, and it was a feeling she didn't know how to handle.

The crunch of gravel had her springing up from her hiding place, and she ran to the window to peek outside. Relief flooded her when she saw Zach jump out of his truck and run for the door. She managed to get it open just as he arrived and he rushed inside, then clutched her shoulders, looking her up and down.

"Are you hurt?" he asked.

The worry and care in his voice and expression were so clear that it made her heart ache. She shook her head, afraid to speak, and a single sob escaped. Instantly, he drew her into his arms and held her close to him, running his hand down her hair and whispering in her ear that she was safe.

She clutched him, her arms clenched around his strong back, and buried her head in his shoulder, crying openly and afraid she'd never be able to let him go.

Finally, the last tear ran down her cheek and her breathing began to return to normal. She pushed herself back enough to look at him.

"I'm sorry—" she began.

"Don't you dare apologize," he said. "Someone attacked you in your home. Anyone would have been terrified."

"I was," she said and looked down, almost embarrassed that she'd been so scared.

He placed his finger under her chin and tilted her head back up until she met his gaze. "But you fought back and got away," he said. "You're a strong, brave woman."

Her heart pounded in her throat, and more than anything, she wanted him to kiss her. No matter how hard she'd tried to resist her attraction to Zach, her body always betrayed her. It came alive when he was close to her, in a way she'd never felt before. Her heart beat stronger, her skin was more sensitive and her head felt as if she were walking on the moon.

She felt her body lean forward, anticipating the kiss, but instead, he released her and scanned the cabin.

"How did he get in?" he asked.

Her mind leaped back to reality and she realized they could be at risk standing here.

"I don't know," she said, her fear returning. "I started to look around after I called you but then I thought it was smarter to remain stationary with a clear view of all entry points."

He smiled. "Definitely smarter. Most people wouldn't have thought of it. Let's check the cabin."

She nodded. "There's not much to it, so that's an advantage. I drew the dead bolt on the front door as soon as I walked inside, so he didn't get in that way."

He scanned the floors in the kitchen and living room. "I don't see any glass, but let's check the windows. I'm sure you keep them locked, right?"

"You know it," she said as she moved to check the window on the far wall as Zach checked the front living-room window.

"All locked tight," he said and moved into the kitchen to check the small window over the sink. "This one, too."

They walked down the hall and checked the two bedroom windows but they were locked tight.

"I don't understand," Danae said. "The bathroom window is no more than a vent slot. Only a very small child could fit through there and they'd have to have a ladder to reach it. So how did he get in?"

Zach frowned. "My guess is through the front door."

She sucked in a breath. "He was already inside when I got home. I literally locked him inside with me. How many keys to LeBeau property are walking around this town?"

She dropped down onto the edge of the bed, her mind racing with all the possibilities of what could have happened. "But that makes no sense. When I got home, I headed straight for the shower. He could have attacked me then and there's no way I could have defended myself."

"I know, which leaves us with two possibilities—either he was trying to scare you or you aren't what he was here for."

"But what else is there? This cabin doesn't hold the collectibles that the main house does. Every stitch of furniture and decor in this place probably wouldn't bring a hundred dollars at a garage sale."

"Maybe he thinks you have something valuable."

"A café waitress? Not likely."

"An heiress," he corrected. "Far more likely."

She shook her head. "Not yet. Everyone in town knows we haven't inherited yet. There's no reason for them to expect I have anything of more value than I came to town with, and I haven't had any trouble until now."

"Maybe he thinks you took something of value from the house."

She frowned. "I suppose that's possible, but all I took was paperwork. The paperwork!"

She jumped up from the bed and ran into the kitchen, but the box of paperwork still sat next to the dining table.

"Is it all there?" Zach asked.

She reached into the box and pulled out a stack of paper. "It looks like it, but I thought I put those notebooks you took from Purcell's bedroom on top. Now they're wedged below some other papers."

"Maybe he was going through the paperwork while you were in the shower and wasn't able to find what he was looking for before you finished. When you came down the hall, he couldn't get out in time, so he attacked you instead."

Her heart began to pound in her temples. "He was inside the main house today. That's the only way he could know I took the paperwork home with me."

Zach nodded. "That's what Carter and I believe."

"We're going to have to watch everything we say—whisper or go into our cars to talk—but I refuse to stop my investigation. I must be onto something if he's willing to risk coming inside my cabin. If I'd been able to get my pistol in time, I would have shot him without hesitation."

"I know you would have. It's one of the things I like best about you."

Despite the seriousness of the situation, the unexpected comment made her smile. "So what now? Carter won't be back until tomorrow, and I don't see the point in calling this in. He was wearing gloves, and I haven't found the scissors, so I have to assume he took them with him. He didn't even stick around long enough to leave a speck of blood."

"We'll tell Carter tomorrow when he gets back. In

the meantime, pack up some clothes. You can stay with me in the caretaker's cabin."

"No." Her reaction was instant. "Surely he's not stupid enough to come back here tonight."

"I'm not going to bet on it. The caretaker's cabin is basically one big room and a bathroom. It's even easier to secure than this place, plus I have some spare locks that I can use to change the ones on your place and the house tomorrow."

"You carry around spare locks?"

"Contractor, remember? I do a lot of rehab work. The last thing I want is equipment walking away in the middle of the night because I was foolish enough to leave the old locks in place."

Tired, frustrated and knowing she didn't have a good argument to the contrary, she rose from the bed and pulled a backpack out of the tiny closet.

"Give me a minute to pack," she said. "And I want to bring the paperwork with us. If that's what he's after, then the last thing I want to do is make it easy on him."

Chapter Fifteen

Zach pushed open the door to the caretaker's cabin with one hand and clutched his shotgun with the other. It only took him a minute to ensure the cabin was empty, then he hurried back to his truck to open the door for Danae.

"Go ahead inside," he said. "I'll grab the box."

She jumped out of the truck, hesitating long enough to scan the swamp on each side of the cabin, then hustled inside. He grabbed the box from the backseat and followed close behind her.

She stood in the middle of the small room, clutching her backpack and looking extremely uneasy.

"There's only the pullout sofa," he said as he placed the box on the kitchen counter. "Amos gives *minimalist living* a whole new definition, but I can take the recliner. It appears to be the one thing the man splurged on."

"I can't ask you to give up your bed."

"Who said you are? Make yourself comfortable...if that's possible. Are you hungry?"

"No," she said as she dropped her backpack on the floor and sank onto the couch "My stomach's kind of in a knot."

"A drink, then." He grabbed a couple of glasses from the cabinet and poured them both half-full with scotch.

"A happy client gave this to me," he said as he handed her the glass and took a seat beside her. "I'm normally a beer guy, but I have to admit, this is really smooth."

She took a sip and nodded. "I've bartended long enough to know this is expensive. He must have been really happy."

Zach took a sip and nodded. "Happy and loaded. I figured it wasn't cheap as he took it out of his own collection, but I've been afraid to look it up. I figure I'll never be able to afford another bottle."

She took another drink and stared straight ahead, and for a moment, he wondered if she'd even heard a word he'd just said.

"She was an addict," Danae said quietly. "Rose—the woman who took me in. It started with alcohol, but eventually, it wasn't enough."

He froze, wavering between being thrilled that Danae was finally talking to him and wanting to express outrage at what she'd just said.

"I'm sorry," he said, deciding keeping it simple was best. "I can't imagine how difficult it must have been for you."

"Awful, horrible, terrible… All those words put together aren't enough to describe it. *Living hell* may be as close as I could come."

She took a deep breath and blew it out. Wisely, he kept silent, afraid that if he asked a question, she would stop talking.

"We had a house at first," she continued. "A shack, really, about this size, but it had four walls and a good roof, and we were happy there. Until we weren't. With her issues, Rose didn't hold jobs for very long, but she managed okay when it was just alcohol. When I hit junior high, she tried cocaine, and later, heroin."

Her eyes grew misty and he slid closer to her, taking her hand in his and giving it a squeeze.

"I wasn't really surprised when we lost the house. The landlord had been more than understanding, but he had bills to pay, as well. We lived at a shelter for a while, but when they caught Rose using, they kicked us out. For a while we lived in her car. Then she met some guy at the truck stop she was waitressing at, and we moved in with him. I think she'd known him less than a week."

"That's so dangerous," he said.

Danae nodded. "It was—is—but that didn't stop Rose. The worst part is, I can't even tell you his name. He was the first of many men that Rose used for shelter and money. The fix was really all she cared about."

"Was she physically abusive?"

"Not often, but it happened. Usually, she wasn't mean when she was high or drunk. She was just…I don't know—checked out, I guess. I don't think Rose's childhood was all that great. I always figured she was hiding from her past with a bottle or a needle."

"She should never have taken you in, knowing she had problems."

"I'm sure she did it for the money. Twenty thousand dollars probably covered Rose's meager expenses and alcohol for years. She never cared anything about having me around, except to wait on her and clean house, but she was only physically abusive a couple of times. The men were another story."

Zach felt his back tighten. "Did they…?" He clenched his free hand into a fist, unable to even finish the question.

"No, nothing like that."

Relief coursed through him so strong it made him dizzy. "Thank God."

"But that's the direction it was going. Once I turned thirteen and started to develop, I saw the way they looked at me. Even then, I understood what it meant and how wrong it was. I also knew that not only would Rose not be strong enough to defend me, but that for the right offer at the right time, she may even sell me. So I left when I was fifteen."

"And went where?"

"A rent-by-the week motel far enough away from Rose that she wouldn't find me. I'd been hustling on the street for a while. Nothing illegal—at least, not that I'm aware of. Mostly delivery for local businesses. I was cheaper than delivery services or gas and parking fees."

Zach stared, trying to wrap his mind around a fifteen-year-old girl managing on her own. "What kind of motel rents a room to a minor?"

"Probably any in that area of town, but I had ID that said I was eighteen. That's the only illegal thing I've ever done. There was a guy who lived down the block from one of Rose's many shack-ups. He dealt in fake IDs, social security cards, that sort of thing."

Suddenly, something that Zach had wondered about fell into place. "That's how you were able to come here under an assumed name and not raise any questions. You had identification."

She gave him a questioning look.

"Carter told me," he explained. "Jack scowled at him a couple of times and I asked about it. He brought me up to speed on the local gossip."

"Before I came to Calais, I wandered around from town to town, but nothing ever felt right. I met some nice people, but I didn't get close to anyone. I couldn't afford to when I was a minor. I was afraid I'd be put into the system. I'd met street kids who'd been in the system and it didn't sound any better than living with Rose."

She sighed. "It was self-preservation at first, but I guess it became habit. Not that it didn't prevent me from making some mistakes. I trusted the wrong people a time or two and quickly learned my lesson. A lot of people are not anything like what they appear. My distance allowed me the time to see them for who they truly were."

"And in all that time, no man ever passed your assessment?"

"No." She looked over at him. "I mean, I've been with other men… I'm not… It just didn't go anywhere. No matter how sincere they appeared, I couldn't trust them. Then I came to Calais and everything felt different. Maybe I was simply tired of living a shadow of a life."

"Maybe it's because Calais is where you belong."

"Do you really think so?"

The hope in her expression as she looked at him made his heart break for the lost little girl who had spent a lifetime looking for her place in the world.

"Yes, I do. Everyone here seems to like you. I haven't met your sister, but I like Carter, and he doesn't seem like the kind of man who would settle down with a questionable woman. So I'll go out on a limb and say that Alaina is probably a good person and happy you're here."

Her eyes misted up and she nodded. "Alaina is a great person—one of the best I've ever met. I felt a connection with her immediately. She's worried about me, and I can tell it's real because it feels so strange. Nice strange, if that makes sense."

"It does. Danae, you're a wonderful woman who's overcome a past that most people would have crumbled under. I know it's not in your nature to let people in, but your life would become so much more if you took that risk. Sometimes it comes with great heartache, but without risking heartache, you can't experience great joy."

She sniffed and gave him a small smile. "How did a contractor get so philosophical?"

"My dad was a funeral director, and my mom died when I was five. I learned about the fragility of life at a young age. All of us have only so much time on this earth, and none of us know how much time that is."

"So I should live life as if it were my last day?"

"Well, maybe not your last day, but perhaps second-to-last?"

She laughed softly as she stared at him, her amber eyes looking so deeply into his that he wondered if she could read his mind. He hoped not, because at the moment, his thoughts were anything but pure.

She was so beautiful—the fine bone structure of her face, her full lips and glossy black hair. Sitting on a broken-down couch, wearing shorts and a T-shirt, she was the most gorgeous woman he'd ever seen.

"Maybe I'll start living that second-to-last day now," she whispered and leaned over, brushing her lips against his.

He told himself it was a bad idea—to take when she was so vulnerable—but nothing could have stopped him from responding. Danae had awakened parts of him that he'd never known were there. She'd already taken his heart and soul. The only thing left to give was his physical self, and he'd been fighting that urge for too long.

He wrapped his arms around her and deepened the kiss. She ran her hands up his back, and immediately, he wanted her hands everywhere—his hands everywhere. He lowered his mouth to kiss the nape of her neck and she groaned, leaning her head back so that he could trail kisses across her chest.

He slipped one hand under her T-shirt and found her bare breast, giving silent thanks that she'd dressed in haste and left off the bra. Her smooth skin sent his body into overdrive, and he decided there was entirely too much cloth between them.

With a single flourish, he pulled her shirt over her head and dropped it on the floor. When he took her full breast into his mouth, she trembled and tugged at his shirt.

"I want you now," she whispered.

No more prompting needed, he rose and pulled off his clothes, then snagged a condom from his wallet. Danae pulled off her shorts and he pushed her gently back on the couch before rising above her.

In one fluid motion, he entered her and gasped.

She clutched his back and he kissed her again, then set the pace that quickly sent both of them over the edge.

CARTER PULLED INTO CALAIS around 2:00 a.m. He'd originally planned to stay the night in New Orleans, but his day had revealed so much information, he knew he'd be too restless to sleep for a long while. Finally deciding there was no use paying for a hotel room when he wasn't going to use the bed for hours, he jumped into his truck and headed back home. His bed there was more comfortable and free, and this way, he'd be able to talk to Danae first thing in the morning.

He debated between a shower or food—it had been a long time since he'd had either—but food finally won out and he fixed a sandwich and ate it standing over the sink. If Alaina were there, she'd fuss at him for the bachelor behavior and he smiled thinking about it. He missed his fiancée, more than he'd ever thought possible. She'd slipped so easily into his life, making it complete when he hadn't even realized something was missing.

A few minutes later the hot spray and shower steam relaxed his muscles, which had tightened during the seemingly never-ending drive on the lonely highways from New Orleans to Calais. It had been a really long but productive day, and he was glad he'd finally gotten to the bottom of the odd habits of Trenton Purcell, aka Raymond Lambert. He couldn't wait to tell his mother, who'd always loathed the man, that her instincts were right, as always.

He was almost waterlogged when he heard his cell phone ringing. Frowning, he jumped out of the shower, grabbing a towel as he hurried into the kitchen to grab his phone. He'd notified dispatch when he was on his way back to Calais, but tomorrow was his day off, and the deputy he'd hired a couple weeks before was on call.

The display showed the sheriff's department number, and he felt his heart rate tick up a beat as he answered. Something was seriously wrong for them to call at this hour.

"I'm sorry to call you in the middle of the night," said Margaret, the night dispatcher, "but we've got a bad situation at Jack Granger's place."

Carter clenched the phone, praying that the cook hadn't gotten drunk and done something incredibly stupid. He'd never been brought up for domestic violence before, but he was a mean drunk and had been a pressure cooker of emotion lately.

"What did he do?" Carter asked.

"He was murdered."

Involuntarily, his jaw dropped, and for a moment, his mind went completely blank. "Come again?"

"He was murdered. The deputy's on the scene, but he's panicking."

"You think?" Ten days on the job in a town that usually boasted drunk-driving citations, poaching and the occasional bar brawl, and the completely green twenty-two-year-old had been called to a murder scene in the middle of the night.

"Give me a second to throw on clothes. I'll call you from the road and you can fill me in on what you know."

He tossed the phone onto the kitchen table and ran into the bedroom to throw on jeans, tennis shoes and a T-shirt. Not even taking time to run a brush through his wet hair, he strapped on his pistol, grabbed his phone and ran out the door and into his truck. He dialed dispatch as soon as he pulled out of the driveway.

"What do you know?" he asked, wanting to get as much information as possible before he walked onto the scene.

"His girlfriend, Cherise, was out of town with the kids, helping her sister, who'd just had surgery. She called that evening for Jack, but he never answered and no one at the café had seen him since he left work. She waited awhile, but by ten o'clock, decided something might be wrong and headed back here to check."

"Please tell me she didn't have the kids with her."

"She was smart enough to leave them sleeping at her sister's, and it's a good thing. Deputy Finley said he'd been stabbed repeatedly—*hacked* was the word he used. He sounded like he was going to pass out when he called in. I figured Cherise was in even worse condition than the deputy, so I called Doc Broussard while I was waiting on you to call back. He's on his way."

"Good." Carter would need the doctor not only to calm Cherise, but also to give him an idea on time of death and weapon. Doc Broussard wasn't well versed in forensics, but he'd seen enough knife wounds that he might be able to give them an idea what weapon was used.

"Is there anything else I can do?" Margaret asked.

"Yeah, call my mom. Give her a rundown of the situation and tell her to prepare a room for Cherise. She'll need a place to rest and someone to keep watch over her for a bit."

"I'll do it as soon as I hang up with you."

Several seconds of silence followed, and for a moment, he thought they'd been disconnected.

Then Margaret's voice came through again, and this time, he could hear the fear in her voice.

"Carter, what's going on in this town?"

"I don't know, but I'm going to find out."

Chapter Sixteen

Danae handed Zach a refill of coffee as he sat on a stool in front of her cabin door, changing out the locks. As usual, she'd awakened early, but for the first time in her life, she hadn't awakened alone. Wrapped in Zach's arms, even the lumpy old pullout couch felt like the bed in a five-star hotel.

She'd snuggled against him and felt him stir, lower parts first, then working upward. They'd made love again, this time slow and easy, with him taking the time to enjoy every curve of her body. She'd languished in the attention and the way her body responded to his touch.

Before the sun even peeked over the cypress trees, they'd eaten breakfast, and Zach had changed the locks on the caretaker's cabin before they'd headed back to her cabin to do the same.

In the bright daylight, the cabin looked so innocent, so free of trouble, but the previous night was so clear in her mind, the attack might as well have happened five minutes ago. Still clutching her coffee mug, she crossed her arms as the cool morning air wafted inside the cabin and ran across her bare skin.

"When should we call Carter?"

Zach placed a screw in the door frame and tightened the lock onto the door. "He said he would head back early this morning. It's almost seven a.m. We can try him now, if you want."

She nodded and stepped into the kitchen to retrieve her cell phone. "If we don't catch him before he leaves New Orleans, we may not be able to for a while. I don't think there's much signal to speak of on the highways in between."

"Probably not."

She pushed in Carter's number and was relieved when he answered on the first ring, although he sounded beat. A flash of guilt passed over her that she'd woken him up when he probably could have used the sleep.

"I'm sorry to wake you," she said.

"You didn't. I haven't been to bed yet."

A million things flashed through her mind, none of them good. "Is Alaina all right?" she asked, getting her most important worry out of the way.

"She's fine. Nothing to do with her, but I need to talk to you."

"Good. I need to talk to you, too."

"I'm about to finish up here. I can be there in about thirty minutes. Are you at the house or your cabin?"

She was momentarily shocked to hear he was back in Calais, which opened up an entirely new avenue of possibilities for his lack of sleep. "I'm at my cabin. So is Zach. We'll wait for you here."

"I'll see you in thirty."

She slipped the phone into her pocket and looked over at Zach, who'd stopped working.

"What's wrong?" he asked.

"I don't know," she said and relayed Carter's whereabouts and lack of sleep to Zach.

His face darkened. "That doesn't sound good."

"I know. I could hear it in his voice. He sounded exhausted, but also frustrated, angry and sad, all rolled into one. What could have happened?"

"Your sister's all right, though?"

She nodded. "If he needs to talk to me, then it's something to do with me, right?"

"Or just the estate in general."

"William handles the estate and I can't think of a legal matter that would keep him up all night."

Zach rose from the stool and wrapped his arms around her. "There's no use worrying about it now. We'll know everything in thirty minutes."

"You're right. I'm going to take a shower before he gets here. Maybe the steam will help clear my mind."

He kissed her before releasing her.

"I'm almost done with the locks. I'll do another check of the windows while you're showering."

"Thanks," she said and headed for the shower.

She was pulling her hair back into a ponytail when she heard Zach call out that Carter was there. She took a deep breath and headed into the living room, where Carter stood next to Zach.

He looked as if he'd been through hell. His face was drawn and dark circles pooled below his eyes. His posture was stiff and she could see his jaw flexing.

"Do you want something to drink?" she asked. "I put on coffee."

He looked so grateful, she felt sorry for him.

"That would be great," he said.

"Take a seat," she said and waved her hand at the kitchen table. "You look like you're about to keel over."

He slid into one of the chairs and Zach took a seat

across from him as she poured three cups of coffee and carried them to the table.

"I feel like I'm about to keel over. I'm going straight to bed for a couple hours when I leave here, but I had to talk to you first." He took a big sip of the coffee. "You said you had something to tell me?"

Danae slid into the chair next to him. "Yes," she said and filled him in on what had happened the night before, only leaving out the part about her and Zach getting naked.

Carter stiffened as she described the attack and then slammed one hand on the table and cursed. "He could have killed you!"

"Zach and I talked about that," Danae said. "But if he wanted to kill me, he could have when I was in the shower."

Carter shook his head. "Doesn't matter. You came out of the bathroom before he'd finished whatever he was doing. You changed the game, and he had to change accordingly. If you hadn't taken the scissors with you…"

Danae clutched her coffee mug with both hands, just realizing they were shaking.

Carter placed his hand on her arm. "You were smart and it might have saved your life. I don't suppose you can tell me exactly where you stabbed him, can you?"

"I think so." She motioned to Zach. "Can you stand behind me and put your arm around my neck?"

They stood and Zach did as she'd described.

"I had the scissors in my right hand," she said. "I brought my arm up and stabbed like this." She mimicked the movement.

Carter nodded. "Probably the middle of the forearm."

"Are you going to try to find someone with that injury in Calais?" Zach asked as they took their seats again.

"I might not have to." He blew out a breath and ran one hand through his hair. "Look, I was going to come talk to you even before you called. Something happened last night and I don't want you hearing it around town."

Danae felt her stomach clutch.

"Jack Granger was murdered."

A waved of nausea rolled over her and she put her hands on the table to steady herself as the blood rushed from her head.

"How...? You're sure it was...?"

Carter nodded. "He was stabbed, which is why I asked about the location of the wound on your attacker."

"If you find one on his arm," Zach said, "then you'll know he was the one stalking Danae, right?"

"Not necessarily," Carter said and frowned. "I don't want to distress you any more than I already have. I know Jack was a friend, of sorts, anyway. Let's just say that he didn't go down without a fight."

Danae gasped, the image of the disgruntled cook fighting to his death rolling through her mind like a horror movie. "Oh, my God. Who found him?"

"His girlfriend, Cherise. She's a bit of a wreck. Doc Broussard gave her something to knock her out and my mom's taking care of her for now."

Danae nodded, trying to force her overwhelmed mind to focus. "That's good. Your mother will know what to do. She always does."

You're rattling.

She clenched her hands and released then clenched again, trying to work out some of her frustration, fear and anger without losing control.

"There's more," Carter said. "We searched his

house—standard procedure—and we found a key to the front door of the LeBeau mansion."

"He did errands for Purcell, right?" Danae asked. "So I guess it's not completely shocking that he had a key, although I think William asked him about it a while back and he said he didn't have one."

"That's right," Carter confirmed. "In addition to the key, we found the phone number for the guy who attacked Alaina on a pad of paper in his desk drawer."

She gasped. "You think he helped that man get to Alaina?"

Carter sighed, his expression sad. "I don't want to, but I think Jack was at a place where he would have done anything for money. It wouldn't have taken much for someone to find out his situation and capitalize on it."

"How could he?" Danae asked. "How could he help someone with murder?"

Carter shook his head. "I'd like to think he was told it was just a prank or that Alaina had something her attacker needed to steal. I don't think Jack was so far gone that he'd willingly agree to murder. At least, I don't want to think that."

"But if he attacked me last night…"

"You said yourself that if he wanted to kill you, he could have," Carter pointed out. "The bigger question is, who killed Jack?"

Zach nodded. "Someone who thought he was getting sloppy."

Carter looked Danae straight in the eyes. "I need you to be very careful. Whoever was pulling Jack's strings doesn't have a problem with eliminating anything that stands in his way."

"I WISH YOU WOULDN'T do this," Zach said as he held open Danae's car door so that she could slip inside.

"I promised I'd work Sonia's shift. Johnny will have to pull double duty after what happened to Jack and he's going to need all the help he can get. Carter will keep it quiet as long as he can, but it's going to make the rounds. By lunchtime, everyone in Calais will start cycling through there to find out what happened."

"Okay. I'll finish nailing the windows shut, and then I'll be right behind you. I'm not letting you out of my sight, even if it means sitting in the café half the day."

He leaned in to kiss her gently on the lips. "Be careful. Keep your cell phone right next to you and call me if anything seems even remotely out of place."

"I will."

He closed the door and stood there watching until her car disappeared into the swamp, then he hustled back inside the cabin and straight to the box of paperwork on the table. He didn't have much time to go through it before he needed to leave for the café, but he had to take advantage of every opportunity, no matter how slight.

The first hundred pages were receipts, and he flipped through them quickly, then tossed them aside. Somewhere in this mess had to be check registers or logs— some detailed list of expenditures.

He'd already seen the ledger with the payments to the families that had taken the sisters. Danae had placed those on the top of the other paperwork and he'd been able to quickly review it while she was showering. But the dates were all wrong. Those payments were made more than a month after Zach's father deposited the lump of cash into his checking account.

Purcell's notebooks.

He reached back into the box and pulled out the notebooks he'd retrieved from Purcell's bedroom.

Pay dirt!

The notebooks contained page after page of descriptions and costs. He flipped through the first notebook, checking the dates, but they were too recent, as were the entries in the second. The third notebook he pulled out of the stack was wavy, as if it had gotten damp then dried, and the edges of the paper had yellowed.

He flipped it open and his pulse ticked up a notch. This one was from the right time period—just before Ophelia's death. Running his finger down the right column, he scanned each amount paid, then turned the page and did it again and again.

On the fifth page, he froze, his finger hovering over a twenty-thousand-dollar entry.

He knew he wasn't breathing when he finally forced himself to look to the left and read the notation. All it contained was a set of initials. D.S.

David Sargent.

The date was five days before his dad made the deposit.

A wave of anger and disgust ran through him and he closed the notebook, then slammed his fist on the table. It was everything he'd been afraid of.

You knew the risk when you came here.

That much was true. He'd known the risks of finding out something about his father that changed the way he viewed the man he'd always held in such high esteem. But even that paled in comparison to the bigger problem.

Telling Danae that he'd lied to her and, even worse, exactly why.

He hadn't expected to fall for her. Initially, he'd pursued her as a form of distraction, but the more he'd been around her, the more he genuinely wanted her. She was beautiful and intelligent, but beneath that strong exterior was a fragile woman who'd never been able to rely on another person. She'd lowered her guard and trusted him. He'd repaid her by lying. More than anything, he wished he could take that part back.

He dropped the notebooks back into the box and hefted the entire thing up to take with him to the café. As soon as Danae got a break, he'd pull out the notebook and explain everything to her, but he didn't hold out much hope for a future that included her. It wasn't just the lying.

It was what his father might have done.

Chapter Seventeen

Danae poured coffee for a group of fishermen and tried to smile at their dated jokes. News of the murder hadn't gotten around just yet, and she was trying to appear normal. Most likely, one of the people she'd served coffee or pie had killed Jack. She couldn't help but think that if she observed everyone closely, maybe she'd be able to pick out the killer.

Sighing, she walked back behind the counter to start a new pot of coffee. Who was she kidding? If someone in Calais was a killer, that ability had been in them long before now, and she'd never noticed.

In the movies, it was always the person you least suspected, but in this case, she doubted that would apply. Amos wasn't capable of overpowering Jack even if his foot wasn't broken and even if Jack was passed out drunk. Carter, his mother and William were all on the list of least suspicious, but if it turned out to be one of them, she was packing her bags and moving to a remote cabin in Alaska where she never had to see people again. If her discernment was that poor, she needed to remain alone the rest of her life.

Johnny, the café owner, looked over at her as she refilled the coffeepot. His face was drawn and several shades lighter than normal. Carter had talked to him early that morning, so he was aware of the situation and didn't appear to be taking it very well.

"I still can't believe it," he said, his voice low. "It really happened, right?"

She nodded.

He blew out a breath. "Part of me keeps hoping Carter will come in here with that silly grin—you know the one—and tell me he was pulling my leg. But the other part of me knows Carter would never joke about something like this. It's just so hard to take in."

"I know. I'm having trouble processing it myself."

He looked across the half-empty café. "It's quiet now, but by lunchtime, it will get around. More people will show up, wanting the news. Heaven help me, I don't know that I can give it to them."

Danae placed her hand on Johnny's arm. "No one would fault you if you closed today, especially once they all find out what happened. Maybe you should do it before it gets busy."

"Thirty years I've owned this place and the only time I closed was for Hurricane Katrina," he mused. "Maybe you're right. I'll think on it while I scrub these pots. Got to keep moving so I can keep my mind off it."

He moved over to the double sink and started washing pots. Danae went back into the sitting area to clear dishes from the vacated tables. An elderly couple sat at a table near the door, and they were the only other occupants at the moment.

As she stacked the dishes in a plastic container, her mind raced. So many things had happened since last night, and she couldn't get them all sorted out. Her attacker, her night with Zach and Jack's murder all pushed and shoved, vying for her attention. If the murder didn't weigh so heavily on her, she might take time to marvel at the fact that her night with Zach didn't bother her like it would have a week ago.

That in itself should be enough to send her into a panic, but instead, the thought of the two of them, wrapped around each other on that lumpy bed, made her feel warm and safe. She'd never met someone who made her feel as if everything could be all right simply because they were there. Usually, her experience with people had been exactly the opposite, but with Zach, she'd gone places with her heart that she never expected to go.

As she was finishing up the second table, the bells on the front door jangled and Zach stepped inside. She smiled, already feeling better because he was there.

"Not busy, I see," he said.

"No. The breakfast rush happened early, and the news hasn't gotten around, yet. But it's only a matter of time. I'm trying to convince Johnny to close for the day. He's not taking Jack's death very well."

"That's probably not a bad idea." He pointed to a table in the corner. "Is it all right if I rent that booth for a while?"

"Make yourself comfortable. Do you want something to eat?"

"No, but a coffee would be great." He glanced around. "And if you can take a break, there's something I need to talk to you about."

"Okay." She headed back behind the counter and poured two coffees.

"I'm taking a break, Johnny."

He nodded. "Nothing going on anyway."

She carried the coffees over to the booth and slipped in across from him. "Are those the journals from Purcell's bedroom?" she asked, pointing to the notebooks he'd placed on the table.

"Yeah, I put the box in the backseat of your car and locked it. The back window on my truck's broken, and I didn't want to risk anyone stealing it."

"Good." If someone wanted the paperwork, then that meant they thought it contained something important. Maybe the answers they were looking for.

The bells over the café door jangled again and Danae looked up to see Carter enter. He didn't look happy. She jumped up from her seat.

"Is something wrong?" she asked.

"Yeah." He glanced at Zach then back at her.

She sat back down and Carter pulled a chair over to sit at the end of the booth.

"Yesterday," Carter began, "when I talked to that FBI agent who investigated Purcell-Lambert, we met at a coffee shop on Maxwell Street. A new bank building is going up across the street."

Carter's jaw flexed and he stared at Zach, whose eyes widened.

"You want to tell me," Carter said, "why you're here, posing as a handyman, when you own one of the biggest commercial construction companies in New Orleans?"

Danae sucked in a breath, feeling like a metal wrecking ball had just slammed into her chest. Surely Carter was mistaken.

But one look at the guilty expression Zach wore and she knew it was true.

"How could you?" she managed to ask, even more angry that her voice shook as she spoke.

Zach sighed. "I was about to tell you, I swear. That's what I wanted to talk to you about."

Danae glared at him, wondering why her instincts

had let her down this way. She'd let him into her heart, and all this time, it had been a lie.

"You're going to tell me why you lied and pretended to care about me? This ought to be good."

"I do care about you. That's what made my lie even worse. I didn't want to hurt you, but I was afraid telling you the truth would hurt you even more."

"I don't see how."

"You owe her the truth," Carter said. "It's too late to worry about hurting her. That's already done. She deserves to know why."

Zach nodded. "My dad died a year ago. He was ill for a long time, and toward the end, he wasn't always lucid. But right before he passed, he awakened and told me he regretted something—told me like he was confessing before he died. The only thing I understood in his mumblings was your mother's name, Ophelia LeBeau."

"How did he know my mother?"

Zach shook his head. "I'd never heard the name before, but if you could have seen him—he was insane with worry. My father was a kind and gentle man. He raised me alone after my mom died. I've never even seen him raise his voice, but…"

"What did you father do for a living?"

"He was a funeral-home director."

"So maybe he handled Ophelia's funeral arrangements," Carter suggested.

"That's what I thought at first," Zach said, "but it bothered me so much, I did some digging. Around the time Ophelia passed, my dad made a large deposit into his personal checking account—twenty thousand dollars."

Danae gasped. "Just like the people paid to take us."

Zach nodded. "It gave me a start when you said there

were four entries in that journal, but I looked at it this morning when you were in the shower and the dates for those payments are dated after the one my father deposited."

Zach opened one of the journals he'd brought into the café and pointed to a twenty-thousand-dollar entry. "That payment is dated five days before my father deposited the money. Look at the initials—D.S. My father's name was David."

"I still don't understand the problem," Danae said. "Purcell had to pay for the funeral."

Zach shook his head. "My father didn't own the funeral home. He was just the director. He would never deposit funeral money into his personal account, and if it was that aboveboard, it wouldn't have weighed so heavily on him at his death."

Carter's expression was grave. "I've wondered for a while if it's possible that Purcell killed Ophelia and made it look like an accident. But maybe that wasn't it at all. Maybe he killed her and simply paid off the people who would talk. Maybe that's why he was buying expensive art with estate money then turning around and selling it but with nothing to show for it personally."

"He was paying them to keep silent," Danae said, her stomach churning at Carter's suggestion that made so much sense.

She slid out of the booth. "I can't deal with this right now. You two can hash out the horrible details. I just need some time away from this—it's all too sordid."

She gave Zach a painful parting glance before crossing the café and entering the storeroom. Then the tears she'd been holding in burst through, and she sank down on the storeroom floor and cried so hard she thought she'd collapse from the effort.

All those years spent protecting herself, and the one time she lowered her guard, it had brought her nothing but pain. She'd come to Calais looking for herself, but all she'd found were horrible actions and unbearable grief.

She pulled her legs up and circled her arms around them, wishing she'd never come home.

ZACH WATCHED as Danae walked away and he started to follow her, but Carter grabbed his arm and stopped him.

"Let her go," Carter said. "She's not ready to talk to you, or me, for that matter."

"I wasn't using her."

"I know," Carter said. "I could see it in your face. You care about her, but you hurt her. Probably more than anyone else except Purcell."

Zach stared at the table, feeling sick to his stomach. "Because she trusted me and that's something she never does." He looked up at Carter. "When my feelings for her started to change, I wanted to tell her, but then I was afraid she'd hate me—not for lying, but for what my father might have done. If he was involved…"

"I get it," Carter said. "That doesn't mean I condone the way you went about things, but I understand why you felt you had to."

"Do you think she'll ever forgive me?"

Carter shook his head. "It's hard to say as I don't really know her that well. If I had to guess, I'd say that eventually she will, but that doesn't mean she'll want to have anything to do with you."

Carter's words cut through Zach like a razor blade, but he knew the other man was only telling him the truth. And it wasn't anything Zach hadn't already thought, although he wasn't quite ready to face the potential finality.

"Sorry to interrupt." Johnny's voice sounded behind them. "Carter, I put together a container of soup and a casserole for your mom. I wanted to do something to help Cherise, but the only thing I'm good at is feeding people. I know your mother doesn't need any help cooking, but it's one less thing she'll have to see to—for a couple of meals, at least."

Zach looked up at the café owner and could tell the man wasn't taking Jack's murder well. He was pale and his voice and hands shook as he spoke.

"That's very considerate of you," Carter said, "and I'm sure my mom will appreciate it. Do you need me to deliver the stuff?"

"No, Danae's going to do it. I'm closing for the rest of the day, and she burned her arm getting the casserole out of the oven. Doc Broussard is at your mom's house right now, checking on Cherise, so Danae is going to deliver the food and have him take a look at the burn."

"Is it bad?" Zach asked, his stomach clutching at the thought of Danae in any more pain.

"No," Johnny assured him, "but I want Doc to take a look and give her something to put on it—injured on the job and all that." He tried to smile, but wasn't successful, then gave them a nod before shuffling back to the kitchen.

A shadow passed across the café's plate-glass window and Zach looked over in time to see Danae walk by on the sidewalk, carrying the food containers to her car. He clenched his hands, mentally forcing himself from jumping up from the table and running after her. She'd gone to the trouble of walking out the back door and around the building. Zach could only assume she'd done so to avoid looking at him.

He couldn't really blame her.

"Let's get out of here so Johnny can close," Carter said.

Zach rose from the booth and glanced around the café, just realizing it was completely empty aside from the two of them. He shook his head. He'd been so absorbed in the conversation and his own thoughts that he'd never even seen the older couple leave.

"I think we should talk to William," Carter said as they exited the café. "We can bring him up-to-date on your situation. He will know what arrangements were made for Ophelia's funeral and can probably gain access to Ophelia's autopsy reports."

Carter pulled out his cell phone and spoke briefly to the attorney.

"He's at his office," Carter said, "and can talk to us now."

"Great," Zach said, but he was already ashamed to tell the attorney how he'd lied. "Does he know about Jack?"

"Yeah. Given the circumstances, I thought it best that he be in the loop."

Zach nodded. "Do you think... Danae's all right going to your mother's house alone, right?"

"She'll be fine. Besides, Doc Broussard is there, too."

"Yeah, I guess so." But it didn't stop him from worrying, which was foolish. Three other adults were plenty of protection for Danae. More protection than him. The way things had turned out, he'd hurt her far more than the attacker.

Carter's cell phone rang and he pulled it from his

pocket and answered it. The conversation was brief, but Zach could tell he was frustrated.

"That was the state police. They want me to meet them at the crime scene and answer some questions. I tried to keep them out of this, but with the potential connection to Alaina's attack, I couldn't. I've got to run but you go ahead and meet with William. Tell him everything."

"Good luck," Zach said.

Carter lifted one hand as he hurried away.

Zach watched him for a couple of seconds, delaying the inevitable. The last thing he wanted was to tell another person how he'd lied—tell another person that he suspected his father had been involved in something sordid. But it had to be done.

He'd opened Pandora's box by coming here. Now more people than just him were awaiting answers.

And if it was the last thing he did, he was going to see that they got them.

WILLAMINA TRAHAN LIVED at the end of a dead-end road, in a beautifully maintained farmhouse on five acres of cleared land, surrounded by the swamp. Her nearest neighbor was Carter, who lived a mile up the road from his mother. Danae drove slowly down the road to Willamina's house, trying to get a grip before she had to face the older woman. Willamina was one of the most observant and compassionate people Danae had ever met. One look at her right now, and Willamina would immediately know something was wrong. The last thing Danae wanted to do was dump her problems on Willamina when she already had her hands full caring for Cherise.

As she pulled into the driveway and parked next to

Doc Broussard's car, she took a deep breath and practiced a smile. It looked more like a grimace, but maybe Willamina would be too distracted by everything else to notice. She gathered the food containers and made her way to the front door.

Not wanting to awaken Cherise if she was sleeping, she balanced the containers on her leg and rapped lightly with one hand. Footsteps sounded on the hardwood floors inside, and a couple of seconds later, Willamina opened the door and gave her a smile.

"Connie, come in." Willamina held the door open for her to enter.

"I'm sorry," Willamina said as she pointed to the kitchen. "I should be calling you Danae. With everything going on, it slipped my mind."

"That's all right," Danae said as she slid the containers onto the kitchen counter. "It will probably take everyone some time to get used to it all. How is Cherise?"

Willamina frowned. "Doc Broussard is in with her now. She seems physically okay, but I think she's in shock. Doc is going to try to talk to her. The state police are pushing for an interview. I know the sooner they get information, the more likely they are to catch whoever did this, but she's so fragile."

"I can't imagine finding Jack that way...."

"I can't, either. Would you like something to drink? I just brewed some sweet tea. I'm coffee'd out."

"That would be nice. Thank you."

Willamina prepared two glasses of sweet tea and pointed to the patio doors. "Let's take it outside. I could use some fresh air, and Doc Broussard may be in there awhile. Johnny said you burned yourself. How bad is it?"

Danae followed Willamina onto the patio and sank

into one of the cushioned lawn chairs. "It's not bad at all. Johnny is just stressed over everything. He wants to do something, which is why he prepared the food, but I don't think he could face bringing it over himself."

"So he made an excuse to send you. Sounds like a typical male."

"I don't mind. I would have offered anyway. I talked Johnny into closing the café, and I don't really feel like sinking back into my own work at the moment."

Willamina handed her a glass of tea and sat in the chair next to her. "So are you going to tell me what's wrong or do I have to guess?"

Danae sighed. "I should have known I couldn't hide anything from you."

"I don't know why you tried. You know I'm always here for anyone who needs to talk things out. Talking is my second-best skill."

"What's first?"

"Well, that depends on who you ask. I say listening is first, but Carter says it's giving unsolicited advice."

"Typical male." They both said it at the same time and Danae smiled.

"Carter's a good man," Danae said. "Whatever you did worked."

"A mother's work is never done, but at least I have Alaina to pull some of the weight. Now, why don't you tell me what man's got you riled?"

Danae shook her head, amazed again at Willamina's perception. "With everything going on in my life, how do you know it's man problems?"

Willamina patted her hand. "Oh, honey, I saw that look on your face when I opened the door. Only a man can cause that particular look of anger, frustration and heartbreak all at the same time."

"When you're right, you're right." She took a deep breath and started telling Willamina about Zach. It was easier than she'd thought it would be, and once she got started, she didn't stop until she'd laid the whole sordid mess at Willamina's feet.

Willamina listened intently the entire time, never interrupting, but Danae could tell by her expression what she was thinking. When she finally ran out of words, Willamina leaned over and hugged her.

"The two of you are breaking my heart," she said.

"The two of us?"

Willamina released her and nodded. "Here you are with a stolen childhood and that wall of steel you put up around yourself, then the one man who managed to scale it is at the precipice of having everything he thought he knew about his childhood destroyed."

Danae frowned. She hadn't really thought about Zach that way, but what Willamina said made sense. He must be horribly worried that the father he loved and thought he knew wasn't the man Zach thought he was.

"I'm struggling to find my identity," Danae said, "and he's struggling not to lose his."

Willamina looked pleased. "That's it exactly. Now, you and I both know that even if Zach's father was involved in something nefarious all those years ago, that's no reflection on the man Zach is today. Nor is it, in my opinion, a reflection on what kind of father he was to Zach, but he's not likely to see it that way. Not yet."

"He's just thinking it's all a lie."

"Yes, but it's more than that."

"What do you mean?"

"Now he's also afraid that his father was involved in the worst thing that ever happened to the woman he loves."

Danae stared at Willamina. "Loves? No, he doesn't... He can't... I barely know him."

"I knew an hour after I met Carter's father that he was the one."

Her mind raced, trying to process Willamina's words. "Even if that's true and his father did something wrong, that doesn't have anything to do with Zach. I would never hold that against him."

Willamina gave her a sad smile. "I know that, dear, but he doesn't. So he got scared and made a foolish mistake—he hid the truth from you. I don't agree with his method, but I do understand the thought process behind it."

Danae reached over to squeeze Willamina's hand, as the older woman had done to her earlier. "How did you get so smart?"

"My mama was a pistol. I got it all from her. She would have loved you."

Tears welled up in Danae's eyes, and before she could get control of them, they spilled over onto her face.

Willamina rose from her chair and leaned over to kiss the top of Danae's head. "You sit here for a while with your thoughts. I've got to run into Calais real quick and drop off the church keys to Celia. Someone else is going to have to run the bake sale this afternoon. I'm needed here."

Danae sniffed and wiped the tears from her face with her hand. "Thank you. For everything."

"I'll tell Doc Broussard you need to see him before he leaves. I'll be back in fifteen minutes or so." She gave Danae's shoulder a squeeze before walking away.

Willamina's car started up a minute later, and Danae heard it pull away. She stared into the swamp, wondering how her previously simple life had gotten so complicated. A minute later, she rose and strolled across the backyard, taking in the layers of texture and color that Willamina had worked into her landscape. The woman had a real gift for design.

As she neared the side of the house, she heard a tinkling sound from the front yard, like the sound of glass breaking. Without thinking, she rushed around the side of the house and almost collided with the man standing next to her car and holding a crowbar.

Chapter Eighteen

William must have been watching for him, because he opened the front door of the law office as Zach approached.

"Carter had to go meet the state police," Zach explained, "but I'm supposed to bring you up to speed."

"Of course, come in." William waved a hand toward his office. "I'm going to lock this so that no one interrupts us. I'm not really open on Saturdays, but it doesn't stop people from dropping by if they think I'm here."

"No, I guess it wouldn't." The attorney was one of those likable father-figure types. Zach could imagine that most of Calais's residents had probably stopped in at some time or another for advice.

Zach slid into a chair in front of William's antique desk as the attorney took a seat behind it. Deciding it was best to simply lay everything out on the table, Zach told William everything—his father's deathbed confession and Zach's real reason for coming to Calais. Then he showed the attorney Purcell's journals and explained the entry matching the time line and amount of the deposit his father made.

"I can't think of any legitimate reason," Zach said, "that my father would have been paid by Purcell."

The grave look on the attorney's face let Zach know the older man thought the situation looked as dire as Zach did.

"Yes, well," William said, "I can see why you'd find that troubling. You said your father was a funeral director. Did he deal with the preparation of the bodies?"

"No, but he knew a lot about it. I guess you pick up things after so many years."

William nodded. "Quite so, I'm sure, but would it be enough for him to notice if something weren't appropriate?"

"You mean something the embalmer didn't notice?"

"Not necessarily. We've already found evidence of Purcell paying different people for less-than-desirable services. It could be that he paid off the embalmer as well as your father."

"That hadn't occurred to me," Zach said, the one sliver of hope that his father hadn't involved himself in something horrible completely slipping away.

"The only thing," Zach continued, "worth paying an embalmer and funeral director to lie about is murder. You, me, Carter…we've all danced around the word, but we're all thinking it."

The sympathy on the attorney's face was clear. "Yes, I'm afraid you're right."

"Carter wanted you to get a copy of the autopsy. I guess he's hoping we could find something the medical examiner missed."

"An autopsy wasn't performed."

Zach stared. "What? Why not?"

"There was no suspicion of foul play. Ophelia had been to see a doctor in New Orleans just two days before, complaining of chest pains and being short of breath. The doctor did a cursory exam and concluded she had pneumonia and requested she come back for further testing after the pneumonia had run its course."

"So everyone assumed she died from the pneumonia."

"That or she had an underlying heart condition that was exacerbated by the pneumonia."

Zach shook his head, something about it all still not adding up. "But Ophelia was a young woman. I still can't imagine a coroner making such a leap."

"It wasn't the coroner who made it," William said. "The only coroner back then was in New Orleans."

"Then who would have called the death?"

"The local doctor."

A wave of panic ran through Zach. "Doc Broussard?"

William's eyes widened and he nodded. "He's been the only doctor here for a good forty years. Oh, my...I never thought..."

Zach jumped up from his chair. "Call Carter and tell him to get to his mother's house. Danae is there...with Doc Broussard."

William's face paled as he reached for the phone. Zach tore out of the office and jumped into his truck, cursing himself for putting the box of papers in Danae's car. Killing Jack had already given away his level of desperation. He wouldn't stop at killing again to keep his secret hidden.

GLASS FROM THE BROKEN car window glinted in the gravel driveway, leaving her no doubt as to what had happened, but she was floored by the man himself, former sheriff Roger Martin.

"You?" She took a step back from him, but he grabbed her arm, preventing her from escaping. "But why?"

"You meddling little bitch." He pulled a pistol from his waistband and opened the car door. "Give me the keys and get in."

Danae scrambled to come up with an alternative escape. If she cried out, Doc Broussard might hear her, but Martin had a clear shot at him when he came out of the house. Her cell phone was sitting on the back patio, of no use to her, and her pistol was in her purse, sitting on Willamina's kitchen counter.

A glance around the lawn didn't reveal Martin's car, but the bayou ran behind Willamina's house, just past the cleared land. He could have easily taken his boat here in order to gain entry to the property unobserved.

"I don't have the keys," she lied, trying to stall. "They're inside."

"I see them in your pocket. Give them to me, or I shoot you here."

One look at the pure hatred and rage in his expression, and Danae knew he wasn't joking. If she fought back, Doc Broussard and Cherise might hear, or Willamina might return. The only way she could ensure their safety was to leave with the man she was certain had killed Jack.

She pulled the keys from her pocket and handed them to him before sliding into the car, her tennis shoes crunching on the broken glass on the floorboard. Martin hurried around the front of the car, keeping his pistol trained on her, and climbed into the driver's side. As he backed up, Willamina's front door opened and Doc Broussard looked out.

"Get down!" Martin yelled before Danae could signal for help.

He grabbed her hair and yanked her down in the seat. At the same time, he punched the accelerator, and the car launched forward, the spray of gravel pinging against the car's undercarriage and sides.

Danae crouched on the floorboard, her head pounding where Martin had yanked her hair. "Where are you taking me?"

"Home to the LeBeau estate. Where it all began and where it's all going to end."

"What are you going to do?"

"Something I should have done as soon as Purcell died. Burn it to the ground."

"What you're looking for is in that box in the backseat."

He looked down at her and sneered. "That's not all I was looking for, and I'm not about to risk that you found everything implicating me. Purcell was crazy. Who knows what kind of scribbled ramblings he has shoved into that mountain of crap in that house."

"You're not going to get away with this."

He laughed. "Of course I am. I've gotten away with it all this time. If that idiot Jack had done his job properly, you wouldn't be in this position. Blame him for your early demise. But when everyone hears the sad and damaged heiress burned herself down in the house, they're not going to blink."

Danae's stomach turned. Martin wasn't even on the list of their suspects. No one would have any reason to connect him with the fire. Except for the remote chance that Doc Broussard got a glimpse of him as he drove away, Martin was right—he was going to get away with everything.

"Purcell killed my mother, didn't he? And you covered it up. You and the coroner and the funeral director and God only knows who else."

"You'll never know, and neither will anyone else

when I'm done. I should have known better than to trust Purcell. He's managed to screw us all from the grave."

The car dropped down into a rut and her head slammed into the center console, blurring her vision. She closed her eyes, hoping the blurring cleared before they got to the house. The last thing she intended to do was go quietly inside to be lit on fire.

If she was going down, she was going down with a fight.

Sitting on the patio with Willamina, Danae had felt cheated by life once more, sad and angry over what she'd viewed as betrayal by Zach. But Willamina had put things in perspective…reminded her that most people tried to hide the parts of their past they weren't proud of.

Despite all his suspicions, Zach had helped her continue her search of the records. He'd put himself at risk to protect her, knowing all the while that what she was doing might lead to the worst possible information about his own father. Last night had been real. Someone who'd been faking her entire life recognized the difference. It was thrilling and frightening, but more than anything, she didn't want it to be over.

At any other time, the drive from Calais to the estate would have seemed to take forever, but this time, it felt like only a few minutes. When the car screeched to a halt, Danae started to rise, but Martin pointed the gun back at her.

"Not so quick, sweetheart." He reached into his pocket with his free hand and tossed a set of handcuffs onto the floorboard. "Put those on."

Her heart sank as she clicked the metal around her wrists, eliminating any possibility of gaining the upper hand in a fight. Even her ability to run was seriously compromised. There was nothing left to do but go along with him for the time being and watch closely for an opportunity to escape.

And pray.

ZACH'S TRUCK SLID to a stop in front of Willamina's house and he jumped out, his pistol clenched in his right hand. Before he reached the front door, Doc Broussard opened it and hurried outside.

"Hold it right there," Zach said and pointed his gun at the doctor.

Doc Broussard's face paled and his eyes widened, as he froze in place. "What in the world is wrong with you?"

"What did you do with Danae?"

"I didn't do anything with her. I was with Cherise when I heard a commotion outside. When I looked out, Danae's car was racing away."

"She figured out it was you, didn't she?"

"What was me? You're beginning to worry me."

"You knew Purcell murdered Ophelia. You called her death natural causes so that there wouldn't be an autopsy."

Doc Broussard's jaw dropped and he stared at Zach for several seconds. "Murdered?"

Zach studied the other man closely, but if he was acting, he was really good at it. "Yes, murdered. Purcell's been paying for the cover-up for years, including your part."

Doc Broussard shook his head, the disbelief clear in his expression. "But I didn't pronounce Ophelia. I'd broken my leg hunting—"

"Damn!" Suddenly, everything snapped together and the picture was clear.

"Was she alone in the car?"

"I… It looked like two people, but I couldn't be sure."

"Call Carter," he yelled at the stunned doctor. "Tell him everything."

"Wait! Where are you going?"

"I've got to find Danae before Roger Martin kills her."

Chapter Nineteen

Zach slammed his truck in Reverse, then floored it down the gravel road, his mind processing all the pieces that had just fallen neatly into place. Doc Broussard had told them the story about breaking his leg hunting, and how he knew something hit him, but no tracks or weapon had been found. It was the sheriff who'd searched the woods.

Sheriff Roger Martin.

He'd claimed he found nothing, but Zach would bet anything it was because Martin was the one who'd clocked Doc Broussard. With the doctor out of the way, the sheriff would have called Ophelia's death.

All those years ago, those men had staged the perfect crime. If Trenton Purcell hadn't insisted on keeping records, Roger Martin might have gone to the grave without anyone the wiser.

Like his dad.

Zach clenched his jaw, pushing that thought to the back of his mind. It was something he'd have to find a way to deal with, but that could wait. First, he had to save Danae.

If Doc Broussard saw two people in her car, he had no doubt the other was Martin, but where would he take her? In fact, the documents Martin wanted were in the backseat of Danae's car, so why take her at all? The only thing Zach could figure was that she caught him trying to take the documents.

So if he had the documents, where was he taking her now?

The house!

The answer came to him in a flash and he cursed himself for being so stupid. There could be other documents in the house that implicated Martin. He would have to return to the house and make sure those documents were never found.

He punched the accelerator down and gripped the steering wheel with both hands, struggling to keep the car from jolting off the cavity-filled road. Never had the drive to the house seemed longer or the road in worse shape than right now, and he prayed he wasn't too late.

Martin had no idea anyone was onto him. He wouldn't hesitate to eliminate Danae if he thought she was his only living threat. Zach would bet money that was exactly what happened to Jack.

He stopped just short of the house, figuring if Martin didn't know he was there, he would have the advantage. Hoping like hell the window he'd released was still unlocked, he ran through the patch of swamp between the road and the house. He approached from the side, praying they were in Purcell's office, where no windows existed.

Danae's car was parked in the center of the drive in front of the main entry. Shards from the broken window glinted in the sunlight, giving Zach a good idea of what Danae had walked up on.

He didn't even hesitate before running across the small open area to the side of the house. Gripping the window with both hands, he eased it up, trying not to make any noise. The window stuck a couple of times, but he pushed a bit harder and managed to get it up enough to crawl inside.

He raced to the doorway and stopped to listen. Faint scuffling sounded on the second floor, but not directly above him. His instincts had been right. They were in Purcell's office. He slipped out of the bedroom and flattened himself against the wall, careful to stay well below the second-floor balcony. He paused directly below Purcell's office only long enough to ascertain that Martin was up there, then continued along the wall until he reached the hallway to the laundry room.

He couldn't approach the office from the balcony without being seen, but if he took the servants' stairs into Purcell's bedroom, he might be able to get the jump on Martin. He had no doubt the other man had a gun—otherwise Danae would have fought him at Willamina's—so he had to be careful. The last thing he wanted was for Danae to be injured in the cross fire.

The door to the servants' stairs opened without a sound, further convincing Zach that Martin or Jack had been in residence when he and Danae were in the house. The hinges were well-oiled, and none of the wooden steps were loose—a far cry from the condition of the rest of the house.

He stopped at the top of the stairs and put his ear to the door, trying to determine whether anyone was in the bedroom. The noises he heard didn't sound as if they were right on the other side of the door, but with the high ceilings and impossible drafts, it was hard to be certain.

Taking a deep breath, he cracked open the door and peered out into the dim bedroom. What he could see of the room was empty, so he widened the crack enough to see the entry to the office. The light from the balcony streamed into the office, giving it more illumination than the dank bedroom. It was just enough light to create shadows.

Zach waited until the shadows moved, then eased the door open wide enough to slip into the bedroom. He crept across the bedroom floor to the office entry and listened, trying to gauge Martin's position in the room.

"Where is the money?" Martin asked. "I know Purcell hid the cash somewhere in here."

"I didn't find any cash," Danae said.

"Lying whore. I know what you are, with your thrift-shop clothes and your cheap haircut. You hid the money for yourself. Now tell me where it is!"

"Even if I had it, why would I tell you? You're going to kill me anyway. Just get on with it. Set the place on fire and burn me down with your blood money."

Zach's stomach clenched and he gripped his pistol tighter. Martin's plan was perfect, but he'd been mistaken on one key element—that Danae had people who loved her and were hot on his trail.

He couldn't tell by the voices where either Martin or Danae were positioned in the office, but he couldn't wait any longer. It was a risk he'd have to take. Clutching his pistol in the ready position, he sprang around the corner and came face-to-face with the worst possible scenario.

Martin stood in the doorway between the office and the balcony, his gun pointed directly at Danae, who stood handcuffed in the middle of the office, facing Zach. He didn't have a clear shot at Martin, and Martin could shoot a lot quicker than Danae could duck.

"Well, what do we have here?" Martin said. "Looks

like the heiress has a rescuer. What a shame that he's not better suited for the job. Now, I want you to put your pistol on the desk and step back or your girlfriend takes one to the head. You don't want to see that, do you?"

The blood rushed from Danae's face and Zach's trigger finger twitched, aching for the clear shot that simply wasn't going to come. He didn't doubt for a moment that Martin would do exactly what he threatened, but even if Zach complied, he had no doubt the end result would be the same.

If he dived and attempted a shot, at least he had a chance. If he put his pistol on the desk, it was all over.

He looked at Danae, hoping she understood what he was about to do and why. Hoping she had some idea of what she meant to him. A single tear ran down her cheek and she gave him an almost imperceptible nod. He clenched the pistol and prepared to dive.

But before he could act, a shimmering light appeared above them, bright as a spotlight and growing in size.

"What the hell?" Martin shouted. "What kind of trick is this? Do what I say now or I kill you both right here."

A crackle of electricity broke through the room, flashing so bright it was as if lightning had struck right there inside the office. Zach put his free hand up to shield himself from the brightness and saw hands reach out from the light and shove Danae to the ground.

He couldn't see through the light at all, but instantly, Zach fired at the doorway. Martin yelled and Zach fired again and again, praying that he'd at least managed to disarm him.

He heard the crack of wood, like a branch splintering, a scream and then a loud thud. The crackle of electricity vanished as quickly as it came, and the light began to fade. Zach rushed out of the office to the broken railing and looked over. A growing pool of blood seeped from under Martin's head, matching the three holes in his chest.

Zach ran back into the office and sank down onto the floor to gather Danae in his arms.

"Look," she whispered and pointed to the fading light.

Zach looked over and gasped. Inside the light was the figure of a woman. She wore a long white gown and smiled at Danae before fading completely away.

"It was my mother," Danae said. "The two of you saved me."

"I was so afraid I'd lost you."

"I was afraid, too, but somewhere deep down, I knew you'd come for me. I've never felt that with someone before. I was scared of the feelings."

"You don't have to explain."

"No, but I have to say this—I don't blame you for hiding the truth when you came to Calais. I wanted to be upset, but the reality is, I did the same thing. I understand your reasons, and I want you to know that I don't hold you responsible for anything your father might have done. His choices were his own."

The great weight on Zach's shoulders disappeared in an instant. The past troubled him, and probably always would, but it didn't compare to the worry he'd had that the only person who mattered to his future might not be able to reconcile the past with the future.

"I tried to avoid my feelings, too," Zach said, "but somewhere along the line, I fell in love with you. When I saw you standing there, with that gun pointed at you, it was as if my entire life were over. I don't want to be without you, Danae."

"I don't want to be without you, either."

He cupped his hands around her face and leaned over to gently kiss her.

So much work remained—working for the estate, uncovering the past—but with Danae in his arms and his heart, Zach knew it would be okay.

Epilogue

One month later

Danae clutched Zach's hand as they waited outside of William Duhon's law office for Alaina and Carter, who were crossing the street. Alaina lifted her hand to wave at them and Danae smiled and waved back with her free hand, marveling at how much her life had changed in thirty days.

Carter, along with the state police, investigated everything and found the weapon used to murder Jack in Roger Martin's boat. He'd tried to clean it off, but his fingerprints were right there, along with microscopic traces of Jack's blood. Based on the way things turned out and Danae's account of Martin saying Jack paid for his incompetence, the state police were happy to mark the file solved and get back to New Orleans.

Danae finished out her two weeks in her cabin with Zach at her side and in her bed. Alaina returned days after Zach killed Roger Martin, and the two sisters had spent long hours talking about their past, present and future. Danae was amazed at how quickly her attachment to Alaina had formed and now couldn't imagine a life without her sister. Both of them prayed daily that

William would locate Joelle soon, as she was the missing piece that would make everything whole.

If anyone had told Danae when she came to Calais that she'd acquire a family and a fortune, she would have laughed. Of the two, she was happiest with the family.

She'd talked at length with Zach and Alaina about what happened that day in the office—about what she and Zach saw in the light. Danae was certain it was her mother and could still feel her mother's hands on her, pushing her out of harm's way. Alaina, normally focused only on facts and proof, didn't hesitate to believe everything they said. They'd spent many hours in the house since then, hoping that their mother would appear to them again, but it seemed as if she'd vanished as quickly as she'd appeared.

She continued her work for William but so far hadn't found anything that shed more light on her mother's death or how Zach's father was involved. But she'd already promised she wouldn't stop looking until she'd reviewed every last sheet of paper in the house.

Beginning next week, that review would take place in Zach's flat in New Orleans so that Zach could return to his real-life responsibilities of managing huge construction projects. They'd spend weekends in Calais, working on the house, continuing the inventory work and spending time with Alaina and Carter.

Then next spring, Danae would start culinary school, fulfilling a lifelong dream.

Despite what they were about to do, Danae couldn't keep herself from grinning as Alaina stepped onto the sidewalk and gave Danae and Zach a hug. Carter shook Zach's hand and kissed Danae's cheek. All of them looked a little nervous.

"Are you sure you want to do this?" Carter asked.

Alaina slipped her hand into Danae's and squeezed as she studied her sister's face and nodded.

"We're sure," Danae said.

Carter opened the door to the law office so they could enter. "Then let's go make it happen."

The secretary was expecting them and directed them straight to William's office. The attorney jumped up from his chair and hurried over to greet them, a big smile on his face.

"It's so good to see all of you…and especially together," William said. "Ophelia would have been pleased with her daughters' choices in men." He sniffed and took his seat, waving at them to sit in the chairs in front of the desk.

"When I heard you all wanted to speak to me," William said after they were seated, "I couldn't imagine what it was about. Something good, I hope? Marriage-license information? Joint retirement accounts?"

Zach and Carter glanced at each other, looking a bit uncomfortable, and Alaina laughed. "You're going to scare them out of here, William. Besides, Willamina has already claimed control of all till-death-do-us-part stuff."

William smiled. "Then I'll leave her to it. I learned a long time ago not to step into women's territory, especially Willamina's. So if it's not couples' business, what can I help you with?"

Danae looked over at Alaina. "Go ahead," she said. This was legal business, and she wanted her sister the attorney to take the lead.

"It depends on your definition of *good*," Alaina said, "but we do think it's necessary."

William nodded. "I'll do my best to provide anything you need."

Alaina reached over for Danae's hand once more, and Danae could feel her sister's hand trembling as she clutched her own.

"We want to exhume our mother."

* * * * *

"Do you feel it?"

"Feel what?"

"Someone watching." She tipped her head back to see his sharp gaze swinging back and forth. He was looking, too. "Do you think I'm paranoid?"

That clear blue gaze settled on her. "No. I've felt it, too." His hands tightened at her waist and he pulled her into his chest, winding his arms behind her back and resting his chin at the crown of her hair.

Her arms caught between them and she whispered against the KCPD logo embroidered on his chest. "Did you see someone? What do you need me to do?"

"Easy, partner. I need you to let me hold you for a minute. Okay?"

Hope nodded. She willed herself to relax against him. "I'm okay with that."

"You're not alone, Hope. It's you and me, remember? This guy's going to try to come after you, but he won't get to you, understand? I won't let him."

Whatever the reason behind this show of support, Hope curled her fingers into the back of his shirt and held on. She needed to feel safe for a few moments. She needed to know she'd made the right decision to agree to helping the police.

She needed to hear him say it again, in that deep, husky voice that danced across her eardrums and soothed the fear from her heart. "You're not alone."

TASK FORCE BRIDE

BY
JULIE MILLER

MILLS & BOON

First published in Great Britain 2013
by Mills & Boon, an imprint of Harlequin (UK) Limited,
Eton House, 18-24 Paradise Road, Richmond, Surrey TW9 1SR

© Julie Miller 2013

ISBN: 978 0 263 90373 7
ebook ISBN: 978 1 472 00744 5

46-0913

Harlequin (UK) policy is to use papers that are natural, renewable and recyclable products and made from wood grown in sustainable forests. The logging and manufacturing processes conform to the legal environmental regulations of the country of origin.

Printed and bound in Spain
by Blackprint CPI, Barcelona

USA TODAY bestselling author **Julie Miller** attributes her passion for writing romance to all those books she read growing up. When shyness and asthma kept her from becoming the action-adventure heroine she longed to be, Julie created stories in her head to keep herself entertained. Encouragement from her family to write down the feelings and ideas she couldn't express became a love for the written word. She gets continued support from her fellow members of the Prairieland Romance Writers, where this teacher serves as the resident "grammar goddess." Inspired by the likes of Agatha Christie and Encyclopedia Brown, Julie believes the only thing better than a good mystery is a good romance.

Born and raised in Missouri, this award-winning author now lives in Nebraska with her husband, son and an assortment of spoiled pets. To contact Julie or to learn more about her books, write to PO Box 5162, Grand Island, NE 68802-5162, USA or check out her website and monthly newsletter at www.juliemiller.org..

For the wonderful pets who have blessed my life:
Purr, Bobbi, Boots, Frosty, Cocky, Peanut Butter,
George, Anxious, Butterscotch, Reitzie, Duke, Patches,
Sherlock, Shasta, Padre, Maxie and Maggie.

Please consider supporting your local animal shelter,
and open your heart to a new furry friend.

Prologue

Today was a bad day to be a bride.

"Hello?" Hope Lockhart pressed her phone to her ear and inched her way toward the door, quietly seeking an escape as her perfectly executed plan for her client's wedding blew up in an explosion of harsh words and wailing tears. "Hello?"

Click.

Hope cringed as the mysterious caller hung up without saying a word. She didn't need this today. She tucked her phone into the hip pocket of the gray suit she wore and hurried her steps.

"Cold feet is not an option, young lady," Dale Barrister lectured his daughter over the chamber music drifting down from the sanctuary upstairs while the mother of the bride wept right alongside her daughter. He pointed his white-gloved finger to the ceiling. "Everyone who's anyone in Kansas City is in that church right now, waiting for us."

"Daddy!" Deanna Barrister wailed, pushing her veil away from the mascara running down her cheeks. "I don't think I can do this. Not today."

"Well, we're not doing it tomorrow or any other day." The skin above his starched white collar turned red with anger. "I spent more money on this shindig than you're worth, and this is how you repay me?"

Hope curled her fingers around the doorknob behind her and paused at the cruel words. Raised voices always twisted her stomach into knots. Tension like this usually suffocated the breath from her chest and scattered coherent thoughts right out of her head. The anger, pain and frustration filling the room reminded her of things she'd worked long and hard to forget.

"You stupid cow! When I tell you to do a thing, I expect—"

Uh-uh. Hope slammed the door on that particular memory and forced herself to take a deep breath and intervene. "Mr. Barrister, perhaps if we give Deanna a few minutes—"

"Miss Lockhart!"

It wasn't a great day to be a wedding planner, either.

Hope flattened her back against the door as the father of the bride whirled around and stalked across the dressing room toward her. "I'm paying you a boatload of money."

She turned her head from the finger jabbing near her face.

"You make today happen."

As much as every frayed nerve inside her longed to bolt to a place of silence and solitude, she'd also worked long and hard to learn how to cope with volatile emotions and uncomfortable situations like this. She was stronger than her past. She could do this. Her client needed her. And if someone needed her, she had to help. That had always been her Achilles' heel. Hope released the door, keeping her voice calm and her smile serene.

"Of course." She gestured to the woman wiping at the tears that dripped on her taupe lace gown. "Perhaps you could take your wife to the restroom to freshen her face," she suggested, needing to clear some of the emotions from the room if she was to have any chance of saving the big day. Ignoring both the father's impatient curse and the doubt in the reluctant bride's red-rimmed eyes, Hope pulled out her phone and texted her assistant upstairs. Tell organist to play another 15 min. Send groom down. Keep smiling. Pray.

Hope hit Send and looked up to see the fractured family all staring expectantly at her. A mixture of compassion and trepidation filled her. She'd worked miracles in the past to make a bride's wedding dreams come true. She hoped she had another miracle up her sleeve today. "Mr. Barrister? Please."

With a grunt and a nod, he swung open the door and pulled his wife into the hallway with him. Hope closed the door softly, studying the grain in the fine old walnut, racking her brain for the next step in this impromptu wedding rescue.

A soft sniffle from the young woman behind her provided an inspiration. Adjusting her narrow-framed glasses on the bridge of her nose, Hope spotted a box of tissues on a shelf and retrieved them before sitting in the Sunday school chair beside her client. "Here."

Deanna pulled a handful of tissues from the box to wipe her face and blow her nose. "It's too much. I can't take this kind of pressure. What if I'm wrong?"

"About Jeff?"

"About getting married. I'm only twenty-two."

A decade younger than Hope. Her client had so much life ahead of her. She had two parents who loved her, even if they were having a hard time expressing it on this particularly stressful day. She was slender, beautiful—stunning in the mermaid-style gown Hope had helped her select. Deanna had a handsome young doctor who wanted her to be his wife.

Not for the first time in her life, a pang of envy nipped at Hope's thoughts. And not for the first time, she pushed aside that longing and focused on what needed to be done at that moment.

She found a discarded florist's box for Deanna to toss her soiled tissues into, and offered her another handful as the tears quieted into silent sobs. "You know, Deanna," Hope began, "today isn't about those people upstairs. Or the gifts or the doves or the champagne we'll serve at the reception. It isn't about how worried your father is that this won't turn out to be the happiest day of your life."

"He just wants it to be over."

"He wants it to be perfect. He's about to lose his little girl to another man, and today is his way of showing the world how much he loves you and how much he's going to miss you. He's worried that you won't be happy."

"Dad's angry with me, not worried. Today is a business opportunity for him, publicity for his company. He doesn't care what I'm feeling."

Hope's phone vibrated with an incoming call, setting off a chain reaction of startled gasps. She apologized before reading the incoming number, and then felt the warmth drain from her blood. How? Why? She had a pretty good idea who the unknown caller harassing her today might be. The Fates must be mocking her for sitting here and defending fathers.

"Do you need to take that?"

"No." Hope purposefully ended the call as temper brought heat back to her body. She'd have to change her cell number. Again. She buried the phone in her jacket pocket, politely masking the urge to hurl it across the room. Hope inhaled a deep breath and remained calm for the woman beside her. "Some men—some people—don't know how to express what they're feeling in a way we all understand. For fathers, I think the wedding day is that one last hurrah that he can do for you. He's trying to show his love by giving you everything he thinks you want. But I'm guessing—behind the frustration and anger—that he's afraid."

Deanna sniffed. "Of what?"

"That he's failed you. That if he'd done something more or less or different, then you wouldn't be having second thoughts about getting married."

Deanna blinked a few last tears from her dark brown eyes and looked at Hope. "Dad never failed me." Lucky woman. "It's just that today has gotten so out of hand. There's so much that has to happen."

"There's only one thing that has to happen." Hope reached over and patted Deanna's hand. "Don't think about the pressures of the day—that's what I'm here for. Think about yourself, and the future you'll have with your husband."

A soft knock at the door ended the conversation. "Dee?" The groom covered his eyes as Hope let him in. "Your dad said you were freaking out. Is everything okay?" he asked, peeking between the fingers of his crisp white gloves.

Hope pointed to the woman rising to her feet. "I thought maybe you two could use a quiet minute alone."

He dropped his hand and turned to his bride-to-be. "Wow."

Deanna blushed at his unabashed appreciation for the image she created in the subtly blinged gown she wore. "Jeff. You shouldn't see me before the wedding."

"There *is* going to be a wedding, right?"

Hope politely faded into the woodwork when the bride's and groom's eyes locked onto each other's. There was so much love, acceptance and desire in Jeff Stelling's eyes that she didn't see how any woman could hesitate to commit to a man who looked at her that way.

"That's all that has to happen today." Deanna repeated Hope's words and met her fiancé in the middle of the room. "You and me. I want to spend my life with you."

"I love you, Dee. Come upstairs and start that life together with me. Please?"

"I love you." He leaned in for a kiss before Deanna shooed him out. "Okay. Go up to the church. Tell Dad I'll meet him upstairs. Hope? Can you make me gorgeous again in five minutes?"

Crisis averted. Tally up one more happily-ever-after. For someone else. The phone was vibrating against her hip again. Her past was calling. Ignoring it, Hope smiled. "You bet."

Chapter One

"Really?" Hope squinted and averted her eyes from the bright headlights that filled up her rearview mirror. "You're following a little close, buddy."

She gripped the steering wheel more tightly and pressed on the gas to put some distance between them. She wasn't a nervous driver at all. But normally she wasn't out this late, and she didn't take the shortcut off the interstate through the heart of the city. But cleanup after the Barrister-Stelling wedding had run long past the end of the dinner and dancing. And though she wasn't the one actually bussing the tables, there were family pictures and table decorations she'd promised to hold on to until after the honeymoon. Then the gifts had to be delivered to their parents' hotel rooms. Other than the hotel staff, she'd been the last person to leave the reception.

So what if her panty hose had long since cut off the circulation to her toes? Or if she'd have to unload every last box in the trunk and backseat of her car herself because she'd sent her assistant home. Hope had earned a tidy fortune with this event. Earned every last penny playing fashion consultant, wedding planner and family counselor. The sooner she got home, the sooner she could celebrate with a glass of wine and a long, hot bubble bath. Or maybe she'd skip them both and just fall straight into bed and sleep until Monday.

"What the heck?"

The same lights rushed up behind her a second time, nearly blinding her. "Jackass."

Hope blamed the unlady-like condemnation on the length of the day and the unwanted calls piling up on her cell phone that bothered her more than she cared to admit. She must have a stamp on her forehead that said "Pick on me" today. Just because she tended to be shy and soft-spoken didn't mean she lacked backbone or a brain or a temper. When the driver flashed his lights through her rear window, she muttered another word in the Ozark accent that crept into her voice whenever she got a little too angry or afraid. She double-checked her speed. She wasn't poking along, by any means. Still, if the guy was in that much of a hurry…

Pulling closer to the parking lane so he could pass, Hope adjusted her charcoal-framed glasses to try to catch a look at the driver and license plate on the beat-up white van. But it veered so close as it sped past that it nearly clipped the side mirror on her car. "Hey!"

The van shot back into the lane in front of her, forcing Hope to stomp on the brake and skid to a stop. Glass rattled and boxes shifted behind her as several brief images printed like snapshots in her brain. A shadowy figure dressed in dark clothes sat behind the steering wheel. He wore a black knit cap pulled low over his forehead and a white scarf across his nose and mouth, hiding all but his eyes. In those brief milliseconds when he'd looked down into her car, she was certain their gazes had met, although he flew on by before the details completely registered. A shiny silver bumper that seemed at odds with the rusting wheel wells and dinged-up back doors was the last image she saw before it disappeared into the night.

"Where's a cop when you need one?" She sighed, fighting a niggling sense of unease that her sleep-deprived brain was keeping her from recognizing something important.

"Need some help, sugar?" A trio of young men, dressed in hoods and jeans and more jewelry than she owned, knocked on her passenger-side window.

Startled by their approach and frightened by their leering smiles, Hope stepped on the accelerator and did a little speeding herself—leaving a trail of rubber, laughter and catcalls in her wake.

She drove three more blocks before she eased up on the gas. Hope inhaled a deep breath and ordered herself to get a grip. It was probably just the neighborhood she was driving through that had made her suspicious of the van and driver. Besides the three young men, she'd passed a homeless man pushing his cart along the sidewalk, and at least one scantily clad woman who'd been leaning into a parked car—either picking up a client, making a drug buy or both.

If Hope wasn't so darned nearsighted, maybe she could have read the van's license plate, even on the dimly lit street. If she wasn't so distracted by those unwanted phone calls, she could have gotten a useful description of the driver. If she wasn't so worn-out, maybe she would have taken the long way home and bypassed this run-down neighborhood where she had no business driving alone, anyway.

Hope breathed a sigh of relief as she finally left the less savory section of the city behind her and drove past the familiar landmarks of renovated art deco buildings, solid midcentury brownstones and converted warehouses that now housed trendy new businesses and condo apartments like her own. Her company improved, too. Instead of the prostitute and gangbangers, and rude drivers crowding her on the street, she drove past a busy bar with a neon green shamrock sign and a group of friends standing outside the front door, sharing a laugh and a smoke.

She stopped at the next light and waited for a young twentysomething couple to cross in front of her. They were holding hands, out on a Saturday night date to a restaurant or coffeehouse in the next block. Or perhaps they were meeting a group of friends to go dancing at one of the newly opened clubs in the trendy Kansas City neighborhood where Hope lived over her own shop.

A little pang of longing squeezed at Hope's restless heart. Even if she had a date, or a whirlwind social life that included dancing and barhopping, she was too tired to do more than drive herself home tonight. She couldn't wait to kick off her heels, slide into that bath and curl up with a good book.

Still, it would be nice if just once she had something more to look forward to than a hard day of work and a quiet night at home. She wanted something more— something a little more exciting, something a little less lonely.

Almost as soon as she thought the wish, she regretted it.

She knew she was lucky to have built a successful business. Lucky to have a solid roof over her head and plenty to eat every day. She was lucky to have a few friends and a younger brother she was so proud of serving in the Marines. Hope's gaze dropped to her right hand where it rested on the steering wheel. A familiar web of pale scar tissue peeked above the cuff of her tan trench coat. She touched her fingers to the collar of her silk blouse, knowing there was more scarring underneath. All along her arm, her foot, her thigh—there were scars there, too.

She was lucky to be alive.

Hope was grateful to be where she was now, considering where she'd started. She was pushing her luck to dream of something more—like holding hands or being the recipient of a look like the one Jeff Stelling had given his bride, Deanna, today.

"Damn lucky," she whispered out loud as the light changed. And she meant it. As long as other people kept falling in love, she'd have a job—and the security she'd been denied growing up. What would she do with a man, anyway? Embarrass herself? Shy, plump and partially disfigured—what man wouldn't want to get all over that?

With a healthy dose of mental sarcasm to sharpen her dreamy focus, Hope turned onto her street. The familiar brick facade and storefront windows she'd decorated herself welcomed her as she slowed to pull into the parking lot beside Fairy Tale Bridal.

Hope parked her car in the reserved space next to the side entrance and climbed out, keys and pepper spray in hand. As stylish and reborn as this neighborhood might be, it, unfortunately, had become the hunting ground of a serial rapist that the press had dubbed the Rose Red Rapist. She had the unwanted distinction of being responsible for the horrid nickname because one of his first victims had been abducted right outside her shop. So much for fairy tales. Several more women, including a friend who'd worked just across the street at the Robin's Nest Floral shop, had been blitz attacked, driven to another location, sexually assaulted and then dumped back here on this very block as if they were so much trash.

A client of hers, Bailey Austin, had been that first victim. Hope still felt guilty about the night more than a year ago when Bailey—then an engaged woman having a tiff with her fiancé at the shop—had stormed out of Fairy Tale Bridal and been assaulted. Although the younger woman had assured Hope that she in no way held her responsible for the attack, Hope was still looking for a way to make restitution.

Hope unlocked the vestibule and picked up the mail off the floor that had come through the slot. Then she unlocked the inner door to her shop and set the bills and letters along with her purse inside before returning to her car to unload the boxes from the wedding reception. She tilted her gaze to make sure the security lights and camera monitoring the entrance were working before opening her trunk and grabbing the first box of family mementos from her car.

With each trip to and from the shop, she made a point of scanning her surroundings and locking her car. KCPD had formed a task force to track down and arrest the elusive rapist, and they had stepped up patrols in this particular neighborhood. The Rose Red Rapist had received plenty of press on television and in the local papers, although facts about the attacks often got less coverage than the reporters' negative opinions on the police department's handling of the case. But every woman in town knew the dangers lurking in the darkness. Every woman who lived here knew the details of the crimes—what to look for and what to avoid.

She was one woman, alone in the city. And even though she was no slim, head-turning beauty, she wasn't so naive to think she couldn't become a victim, too. She fit the profile of the professional women the rapist targeted. She was successful and confident—when it came to her business, at any rate. Hope was smart enough to be on guard, especially at this time of night. But she couldn't very well surrender to the terror she faced as a single woman in this neighborhood. Her entire life's savings was tied up in this shop. Anything she could call her own was in that apartment upstairs.

Besides, she was experienced enough in life to know that danger could find a person anywhere—in the heart of the city, or on a dusty back road in the middle of nowhere. This building was her home and her livelihood, and no man—no threat—was going to frighten her into giving up everything she'd worked so hard for. She just had to be aware. She had to pay attention to the alerts and details the police had shared with the public.

Details.

Driven to another location...

Hope shifted the box of photos to one arm and closed the trunk as a shiver of awareness raised goose bumps across her skin. *That* was what she should have remembered about the white van that had cruised past her. She'd read a witness account in the paper with vague details about coming to inside a white van before being dumped in the alley across the street after her assault.

White van? A driver hiding his face on a cool autumn night?

There had to be hundreds of white vans in the city. Just because one had crept up on her bumper...twice...

And the man in black and white behind the wheel? Surely he wasn't... Hope's stomach knotted with fear. Surely she hadn't gotten a glimpse of the Rose Red Rapist himself.

En route to another abduction.

Returning from the scene of an assault.

"No. Surely not." No one had seen the serial rapist. One reason he'd never been arrested was that no victim had been able to identify him—no surviving victim. She hugged the box to her chest and tried to talk herself off the ledge of fearful possibility she was climbing on to. "He was just some jackass who was in a hurry."

A blur of white in Hope's peripheral vision drew her attention out to the street.

A white van moved with the late-night traffic past the entrance to the parking lot. *The* white van? Was the Rose Red Rapist on the prowl for his next victim?

Hope's breathing locked up the way it had at the church. She was squarely and completely trapped on that ledge. "That can't be him."

Cruising through *her* neighborhood? Had the driver followed her home? Was he hunting *her?*

Hope barely managed to save the box and its fragile contents from crashing to the asphalt. "You don't even know if it's him," she warned herself on a whisper. "It's just a white van. It's just some guy in a van. It's probably not even the same one."

Refusing to let her imagination turn her observation into a panic, she carefully set the box down on the trunk and took a couple of steps toward the street. Rusting wheel wells. Shiny silver bumper.

She glanced up into the cab. Dark stocking cap and…not a scarf.

A surgical mask.

Shadowed eyes met hers.

"Oh, my God."

Hope slipped her hand into her coat pocket to pull out her phone as the van suddenly picked up speed and headed toward the next intersection. She hurried out to the sidewalk to see which direction the vehicle would turn and punched in 911. The driver might not be the Rose Red Rapist, but it was definitely the same van that had nearly crowded her off the road tonight.

"Nine-eleven Dispatch," a succinct female voice answered. "What is the nature of your emergency?"

"I don't know if this is exactly an emergency, but I'm not sure who to report this to." Hope turned up the collar of her trench coat and huddled against the suddenly brisk chill in the autumn air. "I just saw a white van that matches the description the police gave in the paper about the vehicle the Rose Red Rapist drives. The man inside had his face covered."

"Are you in danger, ma'am?"

"I…" There were a few people hanging out down at the corner where the van was waiting for the light to change. A group of young women wandered out of the dance club. Was the driver watching them? Choosing one for his next victim? "I'm not. But someone else may be." Hope glanced around at the cars parked on the street, at the closed shops, at the deserted sidewalks here in the middle of the block. She was safe, wasn't she? The van turned right, slowly circling past the group of women waiting at the crosswalk. "I think you should send the police."

"Yes, ma'am. Where are you now?"

Hope relayed her location, refusing to take her eyes off the van until it disappeared from sight. A man wearing a surgical mask wasn't necessarily a threat. Maybe it was part of his work—such as an exterminator, or someone who worked with food might wear. Or maybe he was one of those people who was phobic about catching germs. Still…it just didn't feel right.

"We already have an officer in the area, ma'am," the dispatcher assured her. "I'll send him to your shop right now."

Good idea. Go back inside her shop. Lock the doors. "Thank you."

Hope disconnected the call, waiting a few seconds longer until the young women changed their minds and went back into the club for more dancing. The breeze whipped loose a long tendril of hair that had been pinned up in a French roll all day. The long curl hooked inside the temple of her glasses and caught in her lashes, forcing her to squint until she pulled it free and tucked it back behind her ear. Good. The women were all safely inside. She'd be smart to do the same until the police arrived to take her statement.

"Staring into space like you always did."

Hope jumped inside her pumps and whirled around to see the gray-haired man standing behind her.

"I've been waitin' for you, girl."

"DAMN IT, HANK."

"Don't you get fresh with me, girl. I'm your father." Not anymore, he wasn't. And though he wasn't much taller than Hope, he could still point his finger and somehow manage to look down at her. "You watch your tongue. Here."

He held out a small box wrapped in brown paper and packing tape. Hope pulled her hands back to her stomach, instinctively retreating from his touch. "Go away."

"Hey, if you don't answer my phone calls, then I've got to come find you in person." His twangy, low-pitched drawl grated against her eardrums. His face was clean-shaven; his clothes were clean. But Hope could smell the booze on him. Or maybe those were the bad memories. What some people might describe as folksy charm, she knew to be a lie, a facade that hid the monster underneath.

"So it *was* you," she accused, referring to the countless unanswered calls and hang-ups she'd gotten on her phone today. "We have nothing to say."

She turned to the parking lot, but stopped after a few steps when she realized he was following. Apparently, changing phone numbers and ignoring his calls hadn't sent the message she wanted any more than moving away from the Ozarks when she was eighteen had. Getting rid of her father tonight would require one of those confrontations she hated.

Hope tugged the sleeves of her blouse and suit jacket over her wrists, and turned up the collar of her trench coat. "What are you doing in Kansas City?" As if she couldn't guess.

"Truck broke down. I need some cash to get parts to fix it."

"How did you get to K.C. if your truck's broken?" She followed his glance over his shoulder to see the a middle-aged woman with brassy hair tapping her dark red nails against the steering wheel of the compact car she sat in. "Friend of yours?"

The woman waved when he winked a smoky gray eye, one of the few traits Hope had inherited from him. "Don't you be rude, girl. I've been seeing Nelda for a couple of weeks now. She was nice enough to drive me up to the city from Wentworth. We're staying with a cousin of hers here in town. Oh, I'll be owin' her for gas, too."

"Then get a job."

He folded his stout arms over his belly, reminding her of the wrapped package he'd brought her. He nodded toward the front of her shop. "Why don't you give me one? You seem to be doin' well enough."

"I'm not hiring you."

"I could do odd jobs around the place for you. Sweep up at night. Fix the plumbing and electrical. Help haul all that stuff inside." He'd been watching her unload her car? Hope started to shake, although she wasn't sure if it was anger at his lazy rudeness, just sitting there and watching her work, or fear that he'd been spying on her, lying in wait, and she hadn't noticed—hadn't even suspected—that heated her blood. "You need a man around the place."

She didn't need *him*. Hope swallowed her emotions and kept her voice calm. "I have someone who takes care of those jobs. I have nothing for you." And that's when she saw the canceled stamps above her name on the package. It wasn't a gift he'd brought to try and buy his way back into her life. "You picked up my mail?"

"Just this." This time, she took the parcel when he held it out to her. "It wouldn't fit through the mail slot and was sitting outside your door. Didn't want someone to take it." Unfortunately, someone *had* taken it.

She studied the box for a moment, idly noting the lack of a return address, wondering at the plain brown wrapping when everything she ordered for her store came through a professional delivery service. Whatever was inside didn't weigh much, but the contents seemed to shift each time she turned the box. She hoped it hadn't come from her brother, who was currently stationed in the Middle East, because she suspected that whatever was inside had broken. "You do know it's a federal offense to take someone's mail? I have every right to call the police."

That made his silver brows bristle. "I'm your father. I was doing you a favor."

Hope shook her head. "It's not worth what you're asking me for. There's a reason I don't answer the phone when you call. And it's not because I want to see you in person, instead. You're not a part of my life anymore. Not legally, and certainly not emotionally."

"That's a lie, girl. I know how that heart of yours works. I know you want to be a part of something." He stepped closer and Hope flinched. His eyes sparkled with satisfaction. He probably knew he'd finally pushed the right button to get around her resolve. His gaze darted to the bare fingers on her left hand. "I know you ain't got a man in your life."

"And you think being a family with you and—" she gestured to the car at the curb "—Nelda is some kind of consolation prize? No, thanks."

Ending the late-night conversation, Hope turned away. But five strong fingers clamped down like a vise on her arm. She instantly tugged at his grip, but he jerked her shoulder back into his chest and whispered beside her ear, "We're family. I paid my debt for what I did. How many ways can I say I'm sorry?"

Her pulse throbbed beneath the scars at her wrist and neck and suddenly she was ten again. Suddenly she felt weak. Trapped. Afraid. "Hank, I—"

"Hank!" A car horn honked at the same time a siren whooped through one warning cycle. Flashing lights reflected in Hope's glasses and bounced off the windows of her shop as a black-and-white pickup truck screeched to a stop in the parking lot entrance behind them.

Hank Lockhart released his daughter's arm and shushed the brassy-haired woman who'd sounded the alarm. Hope clutched the package in her hand and rubbed at the bruised skin above her elbow.

She, too, backed off a step when she heard the fierce barking coming from the cage in the backseat of the truck. She held her breath as a wheaten-haired cop in a black uniform and KCPD ball cap jumped out of the hastily parked truck and circled around the front. She recognized the blue eyes and rugged features and felt an embarrassed awareness choke her throat. *This* was the cop KCPD had sent? Could her night get any worse?

Pike Taylor rested his hand on the gun at his waist as his broad shoulders came up behind her father and dwarfed him. "Is everything all right, Miss Lockhart?"

Chapter Two

Why did that woman jump every time he spoke to her?

Edison "Pike" Taylor bit down on the urge to curse and concentrated on the wiry older man who'd put his hands on Hope Lockhart. With his canine partner, Hans, loudly making it known that Pike had backup—in case six feet four inches of armed cop wasn't intimidating enough—he subtly maneuvered around the gray-haired coot who smelled as if he'd just walked out of a bar. Despite a nonchalant adjustment to the bill of his KCPD ball cap, Pike turned his shoulder into the space between Hope and her assailant, blocking any chance of the man reaching for her again.

Damn it. She drifted back another step, as if she was just as afraid of him as she was this guy. He and Hans had been patrolling this neighborhood for months now. And, as members of KCPD's Rose Red Rapist task force, they had answered every call to the scene of a female assault victim in the area, including one this past summer to the flower shop across the street that Hope's friend Robin Carter—well, Robin Lonergan now that she'd recently married—owned.

Up until that night, Hope Lockhart had been this prim, uptight shop owner—a stereotyped old maid who wore glasses, buttoned-up suits and her hair in a bun. She'd said barely more than "Hello, Officer" to him whenever they ran into each other on the street. She was either too busy, too snooty or too disinterested to make friendly conversation with him, despite his best efforts. It had become a challenge of sorts every day or night he worked for Pike to walk Hans by her storefront and wave or tip his hat to her through the display windows to see her sputter or blush or quickly turn away.

But on the night of the flower shop attack, when Hope had come over to check on the well-being of her friend Robin, and Robin's infant daughter, he'd suddenly seen her in a whole new light.

Hope Lockhart wasn't a snob at all. She was shy—a woman on the quiet side—maybe about as awkward making conversation with him as he'd been trying to tease and get a rise out of her. Hope Lockhart was guarded, a little mysterious, even. She was pretty, too. Not in a knock-your-socks-off kind of way. But if a man looked—and he'd been doing more looking than he should have that night—he'd notice there was more to Hope than a tight bun and those boring suits she wore like some kind of uniform.

That night she'd worn the same trench coat she had on now, hastily tied over a nightgown, showing a V of creamy skin that dropped down between some seriously generous breasts. Without the pins and barrettes, long, curly hair tumbled over her shoulders in sexy, toffee-colored waves. He'd noticed her eyes behind those skinny glasses that night, too. They were big and gray and deep like a placid fishing lake early in the morning before any boats or lines had disturbed the surface. But she'd about bolted from the room and gone all shades of pale when he'd tried to talk to her. Kind of hard on a man's ego.

Shyness didn't explain why she didn't like him much. But with her unwillingness to get better acquainted, he had no idea why. An aversion to cops? Was she intimidated by big men? Had he said something to offend her? Hope's reaction to him that night—and every other time he and Hans had crossed her path since—read fear to him. And that kind of fear—when he was damn sure he was one of the good guys—rubbed him the wrong way.

Pike glanced down over the jut of his shoulder to see Hope massaging the arm this man had grabbed. "Are you hurt, ma'am?"

That gray gaze darted up to meet his for a split second before dropping down to the pavement. "I'm okay."

Anything creamy or sexy or pretty was locked up tight beneath the buttoned-up coat and tightly pinned hair she wore tonight. Pike discovered that that bothered him, too. Why would a woman go to so much effort to hide what were potentially the prettiest things about her?

Hiding? Afraid?

Ah, hell. Why hadn't he fit the puzzle pieces together sooner? If Hope's covered-up appearance and skittish behavior didn't speak to some history of abuse, Pike didn't know what did.

Pike focused squarely on the man in front of him, even though he spoke to Hope. "Do you want him to stay?"

"We were just having a conversation, Officer, um..." The older man squinted the name on Pike's shirt into focus. "Taylor. I'm Hank Lockhart—Henry Lockhart the first." He extended a hand that Pike ignored. "I'm

Hope's daddy. I happened to be in town and thought I'd drop by and have a visit."

Her *daddy?* Paying a surprise visit after midnight?

"Hank?" A blonde woman, wearing a top that was too tight and skimpy for her age and the autumn weather, climbed out from behind the wheel of a parked Toyota. "Is everything all right? You said this would only take a minute. You've kept me waiting for more than an hour."

"Not now, Nelda." Hank waved off the woman, who'd tried to signal Pike's arrival when he pulled up.

"You didn't say she was friends with the cops. You said this was going to be easy—"

Hank swung around, pointing a bony finger at the woman. "Get back in the car."

With an annoyed huff, the woman tossed back her overbleached hair and slid behind the wheel.

Friends with the cops.

Pike slipped another peek at the woman cradling a small package in her hand and warily keeping an eye on everyone involved in this late-night tête-à-tête, including him. Hope didn't seem any more open to the idea of becoming friends now than she'd been during the other brief encounters they'd shared. And though he wished he knew what he'd done to earn such a cool reception from the bridal shop owner, Pike knew he didn't have to be liked by all the residents he'd sworn to protect and serve—he just had to protect and serve them.

"Did you want to press charges against him, ma'am?" Pike asked.

"Charges?" both Lockharts answered in unison.

But while Hope didn't seem to know how to answer the question, Hank had no trouble arguing his innocence in the matter. "Charge me with what? We were having a family discussion. A private one, I might add. I don't know where you came from or why you're here. But I haven't done anything wrong."

"Hope?" Pike prodded, willing her to snap out of her meek silence. He'd come here, looking for a suspicious white van, and he'd shown up right in the middle of some kind of domestic dispute. He could arrest this guy and make him go away for the night, but not for any longer if she refused to speak up. Pike hooked his thumbs into the top of his utility belt and waited for an answer. "What do you want me to do?"

Nelda honked the horn again and Hank swore beneath his breath.

To Pike's surprise, he heard a soft voice behind him. "My father was just leaving."

So the old man hadn't completely knocked the spirit out of her.

"We're not finished, girl," Hank dared to argue. When he turned that bony finger on Hope and took a step toward her, Pike quickly shifted to block his path. "About that job we were discussing—"

"I said he was leaving."

The rising confidence in Hope's tone made it that much easier to back her up—and made it clear that in this situation, at least, she'd appreciate a little help from him. Pike nodded toward the irritated blonde. "I wouldn't want to keep you, Mr. Lockhart."

The grizzled older man sized up Pike with one contemptuous glance, then angled his head to make a final plea to his daughter. "Don't you do this to me. You can't punish me forever. You know I need—"

"I suppose it's about time to walk my dog." Pike pulled out his black, reinforced leather gloves and nodded to the muscular German shepherd fogging up the rear window of his departmental vehicle, intently watching Pike's every move. Right on cue, the dog started barking again. "Hans has been cooped up inside my truck for a long time tonight."

He watched the color bleed from Hank Lockhart's cheeks, making the broken capillaries in his alcoholic's nose stand out in redder, sharper detail. That's what he figured. Pike's canine partner had a knack for convincing people to do exactly what Pike asked.

"I get your message loud and clear." Offering a placating hand that sported half a dozen homemade tattoos that indicated the man had done some jail time, Hank Lockhart finally retreated. "I'll talk to you later."

A soft trace of vanilla joined the damp scent of dying leaves on the late-night breeze as Hope stepped onto the sidewalk beside Pike to watch Hank and his lady friend drive off down the street. The sounds of a heated argument leaked through the open car windows and faded as the car turned the corner and vanished into the night.

Pike stuffed his gloves back into his pocket. "He's hurt you before, hasn't he?"

Hope's breathy sigh was confirmation enough. So maybe he'd been a little blunt with his speculation. Knowing she'd grown up with an abusive man went a long way toward explaining her ready distrust of him. And made him more determined than ever to prove that he wasn't the bad guy here.

A long twist of honey-brown hair had freed itself from the severe confinement of the clip at the back of her head and lifted like a feathery banner in the breeze. As she captured the wayward curl and tucked it behind her ear, Pike realized that that was where the sweet scent from a moment ago had come from. Once again, he wondered why Hope Lockhart would hide something so feminine and pretty as that glorious hair from the world.

Either unaware of or uninterested in the stirrings of awareness she sparked inside him, Hope turned away to the parking lot, dismissing him. "Good night, Officer Taylor."

Pike got the brush-off message but followed her, anyway. "Do you have a restraining order against him?"

She set aside a small package on the rear fender of her car and reached for a bigger, heavier box. "I haven't seen him for a couple of years. He doesn't even live in Kansas City."

"He's here now. I'd consider filing for one." Pike nudged her aside and picked up the box for her. "Where to?"

Her mouth opened to voice a protest, but once she understood he wasn't leaving her here alone at this time of night, she pointed to the side entrance of her shop. "Thank you."

"Miss Lockhart—Hope—is it okay if I call you that?" After a momentary hesitation, she nodded and opened the door for him. "You want to tell me about that 911 call?"

She held open the interior door, as well. "It had nothing to do with my father, Officer Taylor."

"Pike."

"Pike," she repeated, then paused, knotting the smooth skin above the nosepiece of her glasses. "What kind of name is Pike?"

He grinned, seeing the first opportunity for a normal, friendly conversation between them. "There's a story behind it. Taylor is my adoptive parents' name. But I was born Edison Pike."

No comment. But the curiosity was still there.

So he forged ahead. "Like Thomas Edison. I think my grandmother who raised me was hoping for an inventor—someone brainier than I turned out to be. And for a while, I did think about going into veterinary medicine. But what can I say? I come from a family of cops and firefighters. I always liked the action more than the books. But I kept the nickname as a way of honoring the woman who took care of me for the first few years of my life."

She tilted her eyes up to his, flashing him a look that said his words didn't make sense, before she led him through her shop to the back room. "Your grandmother raised you—but you're adopted?"

Well, at least he knew she'd been listening. Pike ignored the gowns, mannequins and fancy accessories surrounding him and focused in on the curly lock bouncing against Hope's neck as she walked. "Gran died when I was ten. I went into foster care, where I met my mom and dad and my three brothers. They're adopted, too. Alex is the oldest. Then there's me, Matthew and Mark."

Hope turned on the light and hugged the door frame to stay out of his way as he carried the box into the storage room. He set the box of picture frames and photo albums down on the shelf she indicated. "There was no other family to take me when Gran got sick. I lucked out, though. My mom, Meghan, had been a foster child in the same house when she was younger, and she liked to come back and help out whenever she could. She brought me my first dog—a smaller, mutt version of Hans—that she'd rescued from a fire. I named her Crispy. I think Mom kind of adopted us even before she married Gideon Taylor."

Pike paused when he realized he was rambling to

fill up the silence. He reached over Hope's shoulder to turn off the light switch and watched her scuttle out of the room, leaving a trail of vanilla deliciousness in her wake. Hmm. Maybe the KCPD brass had made a mistake in selecting him and Hans to do frontline PR and security work between the task force and the community. Apparently, his presence was more unsettling than reassuring—at least with this particular community member.

Protect and serve. Forget the sweet fragrance and tempting lock of hair. He just had to earn Hope's trust and keep her safe. She didn't have to like him.

Inhaling a deep, resigning breath, Pike followed Hope out to the counter at the center of the shop. "I'm doing all the talking. If you don't say something soon, I'll never shut up."

Was that…? No. A smile?

"I don't mind. I like to listen."

Some unknown weight lifted off his chest and Pike grinned right back. He'd almost made her laugh.

But just as soon as it had softened her mouth, Hope's smile disappeared. She pulled her purse from beneath the counter and looped the strap over her shoulder. "I was a foster kid, too. My mother passed when my brother was born. And Hank wasn't… He couldn't handle her death and we… Harry—my brother—is just a year younger. When I aged out of the system, I filed for guardianship and we moved to Kansas City. I went to school and Harry enlisted in the Marines."

"Sounds a lot like my mom's story."

Ah, hell. Wrong thing to say. Telling a young woman she reminded him of his mother—no matter how much he loved that mother—wasn't the smoothest line a man could use.

Just as he thought he was getting somewhere with Hope, her body language became all stern business again, and she spun toward the parking lot exit. "I called because there was a van following me home from the wedding I worked today. At least, I thought it might be. When I saw it drive past my shop several minutes later, I realized it matches the description of the van your task force may be looking for."

Pike shook his head at the abrupt change in topic. But then the import of what she was saying hit and he hurried after her to catch her before she reached the door. He turned in front of her, blocking her path. "This van was following you?"

She tipped her head back, adjusting her glasses at her temple to look him in the eye even though she was sliding back a step. "I don't know that he was intentionally following *me.* But he was driving behind me, maybe a little closer than I'd like, on the street. When I saw him drive by again and circle the block, that's when I called KCPD."

This was exactly the type of lead the task force had been looking for. And he'd been worried about making nice with her? "Did you get a license plate? A description of the driver?"

She shook her head. "I can't tell you much. He was dressed in black. Wore a stocking cap pulled down over his forehead and..."

"And what?"

Her shoulders lifted as though she doubted what she'd seen. "At first I thought he was wearing a white scarf around his neck. But I got a closer look the second time he drove by. He had on a surgeon's mask." She raised her hand to her face to indicate how little she'd been able to see. "It covered his nose, mouth and chin."

Wait a minute. Pike propped his hands on his belt, tuning in to the details beyond her description of the driver. "The second time?"

She nodded. "He circled the block and came back by the shop."

"Did he see you? Do you think he was looking for you?"

"I don't know. I know we made eye contact, but then he sped off and my father showed up and..." She shrugged again. "Sorry I can't tell you more. But I can give a pretty accurate description of the van if that helps."

"We'll take whatever help we can get if it leads us to our rapist." Pike hesitated a moment before stepping aside and following her into the vestibule and waiting for her to lock the shop door. He guessed the other interior door, built of antique walnut and bolted tight, led upstairs to the apartment above the shop. Had she carried in all those other boxes, packed with the similar white netting and tissue paper tonight? By herself? After midnight?

With a serial rapist at large in the city?

How many other nights had she worked this late and come home alone? Even if the guy in the van wasn't the Rose Red Rapist, and her father hadn't been on-site to bully her, she'd been at risk.

Swallowing the acrid taste that suspicion left in his throat, Pike gave one last glance at the racks of fancy dresses and froufrouy displays that marked her bridal shop as foreign territory. He was too big, too male, too comfortable in his black uniform to ever fit in with all the lace and glitz and monkey suits there. Maybe that's why she'd barely spoken a dozen words to him over the past few months. They had next to nothing in common.

But ignoring the extra security he provided this neighborhood wasn't an option. Not anymore. Hope Lockhart needed to accept somebody's help in making her habits smarter and safer.

"How often do you come home late like this?" he asked, holding the outside door open for her.

"Once or twice a month," she answered, walking to the trunk of her car. "Depending on how elaborate the wedding is and how late the ceremony or reception runs."

Pike reached behind the badge on his belt to pull out a KCPD business card with his contact information on it. "Next time you've got a car full of stuff to unload by yourself late at night, you call me."

"I'm perfectly capable of—"

"I'm not talking muscle." The breeze lifted the distracting swirl of caramel hair again and Pike was reaching for it before he'd even thought the impulse through. He caught the silky twist and wound it around his fingertip, watching twin dots of color warm her cheeks as he tucked it behind her ear. Yeah, maybe his hand lingered a little longer than it should have, but those curls were just as soft as they looked. "I'm talking company. You shouldn't be alone on the streets or in this parking lot after dark. It'd make my job a lot easier if I knew I didn't have to worry about one of the locals getting herself into trouble with a serial rapist—or a long-lost father."

"I'll try not to be a bother." She pressed her hand against her ear and the nape of her neck, as though checking to see if the wayward strand he'd touched was still there. Her eyes darkened and she turned away, acting as if his curious touch had somehow upset her.

"That's not what I meant."

She hurried to retrieve the small parcel still sitting there, never giving him a chance to apologize.

"I know what you…" The box toppled off the trunk of her car before her fingers ever touched it. It landed flat on the ground, came to a complete rest, then wobbled on the asphalt. The thing rocked back and forth, moving several inches, as though it had sprouted feet and was slinking away. "That's weird."

When she went to pick it up, Pike latched onto her arm and pulled her back. "Hold on. Is that box from the wedding?"

"No." She quickly moved away, hugging an arm around her waist and clutching her collar together at the neck. "My father had it when I came home."

Pike let her go and squatted down to get a closer look at the package. Loosely taped. Plain brown wrapping. Moving away like a drunken snail. Something was wrong here. "Gift from your dad?"

"He handed it to me. Said he picked it up outside my door. I'm not sure where it came from."

Pike read Hope's name and this address scribbled directly onto the brown paper. "You got any friends who are into practical jokes? Maybe it's full of Mexican jumping beans."

But Hope wasn't laughing. "I thought it might be from my brother overseas. He's in the Marines. But there's no APO address, country of origin or customs label, either."

"There's no cancelation stamp, period. This didn't come through the mail. If your dad didn't bring it, then someone left it here." Pulling his gloves from his hip pocket, Pike rose to his feet. "Let me get Hans out to check it before you open it."

"That's not necessary. I…"

But Pike was already heading to his truck. He pulled Hans's leash from the front seat before opening the back door. "Hey, big guy. Want to go to work?"

The familiar whines of anticipation were as clear as a verbal yes. Pike rubbed his hands around the German shepherd's jowls and neck, reinforcing their bond and cueing his intention before he clipped the work leash to the harness between Hans's shoulders. Pike rotated the dog's collar so his brass badge hung in front of his deep chest. Then he patted the tan fur twice and issued the command to exit the truck.

Jogging at a pace that gave Hans a chance to stretch his muscles, Pike took him in a circle around the perimeter of the parking lot before he tugged on the lead and slowed the dog to put his sensitive black nose to work. "Find it, boy. *Such!*"

Working in methodical steps along the building's south brick wall and around Hope's car, Pike let Hans sniff the ground and vehicle. This was a game for the dog. In addition to his security work, he'd been trained to search for certain particular scents, and once he found one and sat to indicate his discovery, he'd be rewarded with a game of tug-of-war with his favorite toy. If Pike led him straight to the box, Hans might not identify it as anything suspicious because he hadn't had the chance to track the scent first.

"There he goes." Hans's rudderlike tail wagged with excitement as he zeroed in on the trunk of the car. His breathing quickened and his nose stayed down as he picked up the trail of the mysterious package. "Find, it, Hansie," Pike encouraged, repeating the command in German. *"Such!"*

His black nose hovered over the package, touched the ground beside it. He whined at a high pitch, then jumped back as the package moved again. Hans was panting heavily now, more worked up with excitement than with the duration of the search.

"What is it, boy?" The dog lifted his dark brown eyes to Pike and sat. "He's not hitting on it like he does when there are drugs or explosives inside." The dog's high-pitched squeal indicated a degree of discomfort or uncertainty. "This is something different. I don't think it's anything dangerous or he'd let us know, but I'm damn curious to open it."

After tossing Hans his toy, and giving him a few seconds of play time to reward him for completing his job, Pike pulled his utility knife from his belt and flipped it open. "I'm going to go ahead and open it. Unless you want to?"

With a cautious hand, Pike slit open the packing tape and peeled off the outer wrapping. As he set the paper aside, he turned his ear to a clicking noise coming from the tottering box. He leaned closer. Not clicking. Chattering. Shuffling, maybe. Oh, man. Was there something alive in there? Forgetting caution and feeling pity for whatever poor creature had been trapped inside, he sliced through the cardboard and pulled open the flap.

"Whoa." Pike landed on his backside as he jerked away from the bugs tumbling out through the opening in the box. Hans barked at Pike's surprise as the insects poured out, scurrying across the asphalt, seeking their freedom. Dozens of them. Hundreds, maybe. Cockroaches. Crickets. Centipedes. Creepies and crawlies he couldn't identify. "What sick son of a...?"

He scrambled to his feet and backed toward Hope, positioning himself between her and the swarm of shock and terror. "Don't come over here. You don't need to see this... Hope?" Pike spun around, desper-

ate for a glimpse of prim-looking glasses and tied-up
hair. "Hope!"

She was gone.

Chapter Three

"Hope? Hope!"

"Get back here, girl! You runnin' from me?"

Hope bolted the door behind her and scrambled up the stairs, desperate to put some distance between her and that huge, horrible monster.

The bugs were gross, a sick joke—maybe even from her dad. Probably meant to scare her into thinking she needed a man here. Maybe he'd even hoped she'd open the box inside her shop or apartment and then she'd hire him to exterminate every last one of them. Never. A bug she could step on.

But the dog...

"Hope?" The pounding on the door pushed her across the landing, past the double door leading to a loft storage area and straight to the restored antique door to her apartment. She dropped her keys when a thundering bark joined the pounding. "Are you in there? Are you okay?"

Knowing she was acting on blind panic, but feeling just as helpless to stop it, she scooped up the fallen keys and unlocked the door.

"Hope? Answer me!" Wood splintered around the

lock below as she pushed open the door and ran straight to her kitchen. "Go, boy! *Voran!* Hope?"

She yelped when she heard the galloping up the stairs, the long legs running her down. The rapid drumbeat filled up her ears and she could barely catch her breath. She swiped away the foolish tears that stung her eyes and reached for the biggest weapon she could find.

Pulling a carving knife from the butcher block on the counter, Hope swung around into the open dining and living area to meet the beast at her front door. A man in black filled up the opening, but he was just the imposing backdrop to the real threat.

Gripping the knife in both hands, Hope prepared to defend herself. Far better than she had done twenty years ago. This time, she was no little girl. This time, she wasn't weak from starvation. This time, she was armed.

She heard the growl. Saw the rush of movement. Screamed.

"Hans! *Platz!*"

The charging dog halted as if he'd jerked to the end of an invisible chain and plopped back onto his haunches. He slowly walked his feet forward until he was lying down beside the black military-grade boots of the man in the doorway. Hope didn't believe that relaxed posture for a moment. The dog was breathing just as hard as she was, and those big, midnight-brown eyes still had her in his sights.

"Miss Lockhart?" The man raised one hand in a placating motion, then stooped down to clip a leash to the harness the dog wore. He dropped his voice to a deep, husky pitch. "Hope?"

Something short-circuited in her brain, cutting off the instinctive fight-or-flight response long enough for her to see what was really happening here. Pushing the falling hair off her face, still breathing deeply and erratically, still holding the knife, Hope blinked Edison Pike Taylor into focus. Clear blue eyes in a rugged, masculine face. Broad shoulders. Black ball cap. KCPD embroidered on the shirt that stretched over a black turtleneck and protective vest. A badge and gun on his belt.

Not her father. Not the damned babysitters. *"Get her!"*

Hope cringed and looked away from the ugly nightmare that tried to surface.

Pike Taylor slowly straightened, filling up the doorway again. "Why did you run? I turned around and you were gone. I thought you'd been abducted or something— that maybe your dad had come back or…" He took a step toward her and she lifted the knife, gripping it between both hands. He stopped, put up his leather-gloved hand again and drilled her with those startling blue eyes. "Don't be afraid of me."

The sharp words, more command than request, pierced the fog of fear that lingered in her brain. "I…I'm not. I don't think I am."

"Could have fooled me." His gaze dropped briefly to the knife she still wielded, and she suddenly realized that with a gun and a guard dog and the sheer size and strength he had over her, she hadn't stood much chance of defending herself, anyway. But he still didn't make another move toward her. "Did you see something out there? That van? Was it the bugs? Trust me, they've scattered."

"They're not especially pleasant, but—"

"Is it me?"

She was the target of Pike Taylor's piercing blue eyes again. "Not exactly."

She couldn't handle the intensity there—the suspicion? The anger? Hope blinked. She blinked again, trying to understand exactly what was happening here. Damn, he was big—more man than had ever been in her apartment before. He'd come by her shop nearly every day for months now—had always tipped his hat and said hello or winked as if they were some kind of friends. And now he was in her apartment, shrinking the wide-open space down to the few feet that separated them.

Why had he touched her hair tonight? And why had she…? Her heart had never raced like that before—not with anything except fear. Why had his fingers tangling into her wayward hair felt like a caress? As if she had the experience to recognize a man's gentle caress.

Hope shook her head, dispelling the unfamiliar imprint of a man's warm hand brushing across her cheek and ear. Blue eyes and distracting touches didn't matter. She couldn't afford to take her gaze off the black and tan dog. She could smell him now—the heat of his panting breath, the outdoor scents that clung to his thick fur. Hope finally lowered the knife, but only to slide her fingers beneath the sleeves on her right arm and rub at her wrist. The ridges and dots had softened and faded over the years, but she could feel the pain and itch of every scar as if they were new.

"Is it Hans?" At this hushed volume, Pike's deep voice danced along her fried nerves like a soothing balm.

As embarrassing as her phobia might be to admit, her behavior put her past the point of lying or making a joke about it. Hope nodded. "I'm sorry. I guess I had a panic attack."

"You think?"

"I haven't had one for a long time. I usually can control it. But with the running and...and he was tracking so hard, so relentlessly. He's so strong—all muscle, isn't he?" She pushed her glasses into place at her temple, then found her fingers sliding beneath the collar of her blouse and loose hair to touch the scar there. She'd lost her big hair clip somewhere, and had probably left a trail of bobby pins on the stairs. Her hair was most likely sticking out in all directions, looking as wild as the pulse beat at the side of her neck felt. "I'm sure it seems irrational to you. I know he's specially trained, he's a member of the police force, and that he helps—"

"He's not going to hurt you."

"You don't know that." She blinked away flashback images of tearing flesh and searing pain. Of a gunshot that jerked through her even now. The final tragedy of two desperate children's struggle for survival.

"Stay with me, Hope." Pike stepped forward and Hope retreated.

"I am." She managed to keep the knife pointed to the floor, although she couldn't seem to ignore the phantom throb beneath the scars on her wrist. She pulled up a coat sleeve, a jacket sleeve and unbuttoned the cuff of her blouse to massage the skin there. "I will."

Tall, Blond and Rugged was moving closer again. Hope focused on the black button at the center of Pike's shirt. She could still hear the dog panting, but she could no longer see him past the width of those shoulders and chest.

"I trust Hans with my life. I trust he'll do whatever I say. He's trained to be an extension of me on the job, not a rogue wild animal." Pike pulled off his cap and rubbed at his short dark gold hair, leaving rumpled spikes in its wake. He dropped his gaze to the leash in his hand and followed it back to the dog lying in the doorway behind him. The dog's black muzzle lifted up and he tilted his head in some sort of anticipation.

Hope's fingers tightened around the knife handle.

But Pike raised his hand and the dog settled down again, resting his head on his front legs. When Pike faced Hope again, his narrowed, probing eyes looked straight into hers. "I never had a chance at getting you to trust me, did I. All these months I've been patrolling this neighborhood, I've been trying to get to know you. Trying to find out if you were stuck-up or just unaware of my efforts."

Regret followed closely on the heels of her simmering panic, sapping the remainder of Hope's strength. It was a shy person's worst nightmare to have her quiet moods and awkward social skills mistaken for arrogance or indifference. It compounded her frustration to discover that the time she needed to process her thoughts, emotions and reactions could be interpreted as a lack of caring. It hurt to know that the fight it took to assert herself sometimes came off as disdain.

"I've even been a little ornery about it," Pike went on. "Making up excuses to come by your shop, demanding that you give me your trust and respect. But you were never going to give me a real chance."

"I'm not stuck-up," she whispered, mindlessly massaging the scars again.

"No. You're terrified. Doesn't make me feel like much of a cop—or much of a man—to see you look at me like that. I'd like to fix your perception of Hans and me." He reached out, and for a moment, she thought he intended to disarm her. Instead, he reached past the knife and slowly closed his fingers around her wrist, brushing the warm pad of his thumb across the pale web of scars there. "What happened to you?"

"I…" Gentle though his inquisitive touch might be, Hope jerked her arm away and quickly pulled down her sleeves. What did she tell him? Long version? Short version? Was there any version that didn't make her sound sad or eccentric or worth anything more than his pity?

Hans raised his head and woofed a split second before Pike turned his head and Hope heard a whisper of sound from the foot of the stairs. The outside door opened.

No version.

She clutched the knife in both hands again. There were knocks at both the shop and stairwell doors.

"Taylor!" a man shouted from the vestibule downstairs. "Pike! You here?"

"We're not done with this conversation." Pike adjusted his ball cap on his head and turned to the door. "I'm here!" he shouted. "Hans. *Fuss!*" The dog jumped to his feet and fell into step beside him. "Detective Montgomery? Nick? What are you doing here?"

Hope followed them out the door to see man and dog jog around the landing and down to the entryway below.

She heard a second man's voice now. "We saw your rig out front. Thought maybe you knew something we didn't."

"Knew something about what?" Pike asked.

Hope crept to the top of the stairs behind him. "He took someone else, didn't he? That's why he was here."

"The Rose Red Rapist?" At the foot of the stairs, Pike stood taller than either of the two men, one in a gray wool suit and tie, the other wearing jeans and a black leather jacket. The badges they wore identified them as cops, too.

Hope sank onto the top step, still holding the knife. "That was his van I saw, wasn't it? That was *him*."

The shorter of the two detectives pulled back the front of his leather jacket and reached for his gun, his gaze zeroing in on Hope—or, more specifically, on the carving knife she still held in her fist. "Ma'am? I need you to put that down."

Hope's breath locked up in her chest and she instinctively recoiled.

Pike put up a hand and warned the dark-haired detective not to unholster his weapon. "It's okay, Nick. She's a witness, not a threat. I..." His head tipped down toward Hans. "We...scared her."

The air gradually eased from her lungs at Pike's politely vague explanation. She'd pulled a knife and freaked out on him, yet he was still kind enough to defend her. And although she appreciated having that blockade of Pike Taylor's shoulders between her and the two plainclothes detectives, Hope wisely set the knife down on the floor beside her. She spotted two bobby pins on the next step down and remembered that she probably looked as if she'd been fighting something more than her own fears tonight.

The red-haired detective who seemed to be in charge slid his gaze up to her, too, assessing her unkempt appearance and dismissing her before giving a concise, emotionless report to Pike. "We've got a body dump around the corner in the alley. Red rose inside her coat."

Body dump? That meant the victim was dead, didn't it? Raped *and* murdered. Hope's audible gasp echoed through the walnut banister and across the crisply painted white landing. The dog's ear pricked to attention, but none of the men seemed to notice. Hope pressed her fingers to her lips and whispered, "Oh, God. She was inside there, wasn't she? She was in that van."

The red-haired detective heard her hushed voice and looked up the stairs. "A LaDonna Chambers. Do you know her?"

"LaDonna?" For a moment, the detective's hard eyes swam out of focus. But she blinked away the emotions that made her light-headed and nodded, picturing the friendly acquaintance she'd seen just yesterday morning. "Not well. She's interning at a law office on the next street over. I've waited in line with her at the coffee shop several times."

The detective in the suit jotted something into his notebook before tucking it inside his jacket pocket and turning his attention back to Pike. "Some college kids who'd been at Harpo's Dance Club found her. That's not the call you're answering?"

Pike shook his head. "Miss Lockhart called in that she'd seen a suspicious white van on her way home tonight. I came to take her statement."

"She saw the van?" The redhead pulled back the front of his jacket and splayed his hands at either side of his waist. "*His* van?"

Pike answered. "Could be, sir. She gave me a detailed description, but no plate number."

The dark-haired detective looked agitated. "When? Did she see our guy? Can she ID the driver? Is that what spooked her?"

Clearly, the two detectives suspected there was more to her story than a helpful citizen's phone call. But Pike didn't mention her father, the sick present she'd gotten or her off-the-charts paranoid reaction to his efforts to help her. Thankfully, neither detective had questioned her erratic behavior, either. Until now.

They had bigger problems than hers tonight.

"I'm Detective Spencer Montgomery, KCPD task force, ma'am. This is my partner, Detective Nick Fensom. We work with Officer Taylor here." Detective Montgomery flashed his badge and looked over Pike's shoulder, right at her. Somehow the intensity of that slate-colored gaze was even more unsettling than the threat of Detective Fensom's pulling his gun had been. "We need to talk to you."

"WELL, THAT WAS a lousy plan. Do you think she recognized you?"

"I don't know." He breezed past the woman in the negligee and robe and headed straight for the bathroom.

"You don't know?" She followed him in. "You already made one mistake tonight. I don't think we can afford another."

He unhooked his belt and slung it at her feet. "We?"

She crossed her arms beneath her breasts, refusing to let the subject drop. "I did my part. LaDonna Chambers can never hurt you again. But you don't even know if this woman—"

"Shut up. I need to think." He opened the shower door and turned on the shower until the water ran blisteringly hot. He stepped underneath the spray, clothes and all. He braced his hands on the tile wall and bent his head. The water beat against his scalp, drowning out the sounds of her calling him all kinds of stupid for going to the bridal shop tonight. Finally, she got the hint and returned to his bedroom. He stood there for countless minutes, letting the hot water sluice through his hair and soak through his clothes while the trapped, steamy air opened the pores of his skin. He stood like that until most of the rage was purged from him.

Once the haze of emotion had cleared his brain and reason returned, he peeled off his sodden clothes and dumped them into the hamper beside the shower. Then he unwrapped a fresh bar of soap and started to wash, cleaning beneath every nail, massaging every hair follicle, rinsing his skin twice and then again.

When he was done, exhausted by the furious emotions and the long night, he pulled a clean towel from the linen closet and wrapped it around his waist. He pulled out a matching towel to wipe down the shower walls and glass door. Then, with a third towel, he dropped down to his hands and knees, sopping up the puddle of water beneath the hamper.

He hated that he'd have to do something about Hope. He knew most of the women he hunted by their face, their habits, their location. But he rarely knew their names until their pictures were splashed across the television screen or centered in a newspaper article. He knew Hope, liked her well enough, he supposed. She stirred nothing inside him—no desire, no rage—but now he could see he'd been wrong to think she was of no consequence.

Hope Lockhart ran a successful business. She was loved by clients and respected by leaders in Kansas City business and society. Who'd have thought she'd have the guts to look him in the eye and call the police?

He'd have to find out exactly what she knew about him, exactly what she'd seen. If he was lucky, she'd still be of no consequence. But if she was a threat to him...

The damp towels fisted in his hands and he felt the stirrings of that damned hunger stirring inside him again.

"I suppose you need me to take care of this problem, too?"

She was in the doorway again, sneaking up behind him, standing over him. With his nostrils flaring as he fought to maintain his composure, he slowly eased his grip on the towels and folded them neatly around the wet clothes he'd discarded. "I'll handle it. You were messy tonight."

"Me? You're the one who was careless. I told you it was too soon, but you wouldn't listen."

"Really? A gun? Do you know how long it took me to clean up the blood?" He laid the squared package of damp clothes and towels in the bottom of the hamper before turning to face her. "I had everything under control. She was mine to use however I wanted—until you interfered."

"Do you think she would have given you what you wanted?" He went to the sink to unwrap a fresh comb. Her reflection joined his in the mirror. "She woke up, called you by name when she recognized your voice. I had to silence her."

"I wasn't finished with her."

"Oh, you were finished." She laughed.

His comb clattered into the sink. "Shut up."

"I'm the voice of reason in your sad, secretive life. I'm the only one who has always been here for you. Without me, you'd be rotting in prison. I know the lie you live and I've loved you any—"

He spun around, clamping his hand around her throat and shoving her against the wall. "I said, shut. Up."

"You won't hurt me. I made you. You need me."

What he needed was to feel in control again. His fingers tightened for a few moments until he heard her choking gurgle. But, damn her, even as her face drained of color, she barely even blinked at the dangerous torture he inflicted.

He popped his fingers open and released her. She inhaled a calm, deep breath and smiled. "You see? You know you can't hurt me, that I'm the only one who'll always be here for you." She left the room to pour herself a drink. "Now. What are you going to do about Hope Lockhart?"

Chapter Four

The whole elevator smelled of vanilla, reminding Pike of the decadent sugar cookies his grandma Martha baked for Christmas every year.

Crossing his arms over his chest, he looked down at the toffee-haired woman standing at his shoulder, resolutely watching each number light up as they rode from the garage level up to the third floor of Fourth Precinct headquarters. She'd tamed her hair back into a loose ponytail, but a handful of curls escaped to frame her weary eyes. "You don't have to do this, you know."

It was maybe the fifth or sixth effort he'd made at starting a conversation with Hope Lockhart since driving her to the station for an interview with Detectives Montgomery and Fensom. *"Get her downtown. Let's talk to her while the memories are fresh."*

If he hadn't scared the memories right out of her.

In the truck he'd gotten nothing more than a couple of nods and some wild-eyed glances back at the dog caged securely in the seat behind them. Maybe now, with Hans secured in his kennel downstairs, he hoped the skittish woman might relax a bit and they could share some normal, friendly conversation like the kind they'd started at her shop.

Well, he got conversation. But there wasn't much normal or friendly about a woman talking to a pair of steel doors instead of to him.

"I know. But I want to help. Too many people I know have been hurt by that man. I barely knew LaDonna, but it feels like I've lost another friend. She splurged on mochas every Friday, and she had this big smile. Tonight she looked like she was sleeping. Until the M.E. closed that zipper..." Pike watched the ripple of movement down her creamy throat as Hope swallowed. "She was in a bag. Like...like she was being discarded."

"You shouldn't have agreed to confirm her ID." Sure, the quick confirmation helped speed the investigation along, but very few people got to look at dead bodies outside of a funeral home. So how did he reassure her? How did he stop feeling so guilty about everything she'd been through tonight? "It's a good thing, actually—the bag, I mean. It protects the evidence as much as it honors the victim's dignity and keeps others from seeing what can sometimes be a pretty disturbing sight."

He almost startled when she suddenly tipped her head and looked up at him. Even her glasses couldn't diminish the impact of her gaze locking onto his. Her eyes were as warm with concern as they were cool in color. "Have you seen a lot of that? *Disturbing* things?"

Pike dropped his arms and reached out, feeling the need to offer some kind of comfort. But he wisely curled his fingers into a fist and kept it at his side. The last thing he wanted to do was to scare her into silence again.

"More than I want to." Yeah. There was a lot of pretty to discover about this woman if a man took the time to look. Maybe he was doing a little too much looking. Taking a cue from the champ, he turned and focused his gaze on the elevator panel. "But you learn to turn off your emotions and you just deal with the facts."

"How do you do that? Turn off your emotions, I mean." She was staring straight ahead again, too. "Maybe I live inside my head too much. But sometimes, I can't stop thinking about things. I wish I could just *do*. And not overthink the consequences or second-guess myself."

"What do you want to do?" He couldn't help himself. The woman was too much of an enigma to ignore.

She shook her head, stirring the curls down her back. She wasn't going to answer.

"Come on, now. You've just said as many words to me as you've said in the entire twelve months I've known you." He nudged his shoulder against hers. "Are you going to stop talking to me now?"

Her eyes darted up to his at the teasing request. And was that a smile? Victory. "You're awfully patient with me, Officer Taylor."

"Pike."

"More persistent than most men I know. Why do you keep trying?"

He liked a challenge? He was a sucker for a complex mystery like this woman? He just plain couldn't stand the irritation of having someone not like him or his dog? "I am determined that you're going to look at me and not think I'm the evil villain in the fairy tale of your life."

"The fairy tale?" The smile disappeared and she fixated on the K-9 Corps patch sewn onto the sleeve of his uniform. "Oh. My shop. Believe me, my life isn't a fairy tale, Offic...Pike." And then her gaze crept back to his.

"There's no Prince Charming. There's no fairy god-mother. I just try to make the magic happen for others."

"Why aren't you making it happen for yourself, Hope?" And then he did the dumbest thing he'd done all night long. He tunneled his fingers beneath the silky knot of her ponytail, stroked his thumb along the line of her jaw to her chin and tilted his face down toward hers. "Why don't you have the fairy tale?"

She shivered beneath his touch, making him feel like all kinds of ogre for holding on just a little tighter to prevent her from pulling away when he felt the tug against his fingertips. He knew better. He trained dogs for a living and was smart enough not to try to pet one until it was comfortable around him and some ground rules for expected behavior had been laid down be-tween them. But her pink tongue darted out nervously to moisten her lips and an unexpected anticipation pinged him right in the groin.

Here was a shy, secretive woman who bolted or blushed every time he came near—and he wanted to kiss her?

The elevator stopping wasn't the only thing that had him swaying on his feet.

The elevator doors opened to the bustle and noise of KCPD's early morning shift change…and two men wearing expensive business suits who stopped their re-spective pacing and phone call the moment they spot-ted their arrival.

"Hope?" Pike's hand fell away as the dark-haired man wearing charcoal gray pulled Hope off the eleva-tor and straight into a tight hug. "Thank God. Are you all right?"

"Hey." At her startled *oof,* Pike's instinct was to

step in and break it up. But her arms gradually settled around the man's waist.

Besides, when Pike tried to intervene with a hand on her shoulder, the guy with the tan suit and the phone stepped between them and flashed a business card. "I'm Adam Matuszak, Miss Lockhart's attorney. If she's going to be interviewed by the police, then I need to be present."

"Matuszak. Why do I know that name?"

Hope pulled away from the hug. "LaDonna worked for him."

The dark-haired man draped an arm around her shoulders and was already walking her away before she'd finished. He tipped his mouth close to Hope's ear to say something that made her nod. Stealing her away. Shutting her up. Warning her...about what?

"Miss Chambers was an intern at my office," the lawyer confirmed, interrupting Pike's silent observations. "I believe my building is on your patrol."

Pike nodded toward the man taking Hope away. "Who's he?"

"Brian Elliott." The tall blond attorney pocketed his phone and smoothed his lapels. "He owns my building—and several others on your beat. He's Miss Lockhart's business associate—and a good friend."

How good? Pike ignored the stirrings of something he wasn't ready to name and unbuttoned the pocket of his uniform shirt to stuff the business card inside. Seeing his shot at making inroads with Hope disappearing down the hallway, he retreated a step. "I'm not the cop interviewing her. I'm just a...friend who brought her in."

He was instantly dismissed as inconsequential. "Who do I need to speak to, then?"

With a reluctant nod, Pike led Matuszak past the sergeant's desk to point out Spencer Montgomery and Nick Fensom. The attorney immediately crossed through the maze of desks to introduce himself to the two detectives, then signaled to Hope and her *good* friend to join them.

Since the third floor of Fourth Precinct headquarters housed the detectives' bull pen, conference area and meeting rooms—Pike didn't have a desk here. But he did have a badge and access to the KCPD computers. While Hope and her well-pressed bookends settled in across from Detective Montgomery, Pike made himself at home at the sergeant's desk. He intended to find out a little more about Hope Lockhart.

Even if she wasn't going to tell him herself.

IF HENRY LOCKHART SR. was as much of a lowlife as his criminal record indicated, then it was no wonder that his daughter, Hope, would be afraid of him. He'd served a nickel at the state pen in Jefferson City for domestic assault, multiple DUI/suspended license violations and animal cruelty.

Was Hope the domestic assault? More than once? Had she been witness to repeated violence in her own home?

Pike scanned the prison record on the computer screen at the desk sergeant's counter where he stood before sliding a glance across the third-floor squad room. The morning shift was changing—detectives and uniforms were straightening their desks and signing out as the A shift reported in, poured coffees and made their way toward the conference room for morning roll call.

Still, with all the comings and goings in and out of the elevators and from cubicle to cubicle, he had no trouble spotting the woman sitting across from Spencer Montgomery at his desk. Hope Lockhart's ponytail flared loosely down her back, looking a shade richer than the camel-colored trench coat she wore and reminding him of a lion's mane. Nick Fensom stood at Detective Montgomery's shoulder while the two men who'd whisked her off the elevator flanked her.

And though he couldn't see Hope's face from this angle, he could read the rigidness of her posture and the way she stiffened when Brian Elliott patted her shoulder before pulling a chair from a nearby desk and sitting beside her. Pike wouldn't have expected Hope to have friends like that—expensive suits, cocky enough to interrupt the detectives' questions and argue with whatever accusations they were making. He wasn't sure he'd ever seen her with a man who wasn't a customer at her shop. Certainly, the brief scan he'd made of the open rooms of her apartment revealed no signs of a masculine influence in her life. There'd been a flowered centerpiece on the kitchen table and lace curtains masking the blinds at the windows. Not to mention he didn't know any man who liked to see his woman so buttoned up, covered up and pinned up that she faded into the background of his world.

Were those scars he'd glimpsed on her wrist a graphic reminder of whatever her father had done to her? Was that what she was trying to hide? And what was with her dog phobia, anyway? Sure, Hans had been bred and trained to intimidate when ordered to. But otherwise, the big shepherd was a pussycat who couldn't get enough playtime and who regularly conned Pike's mother out of extra dog treats when they went home to visit.

Pike glanced back at the screen. Animal cruelty?

The idea of such an atrocity left a bitter taste in his mouth, especially if that sort of heartless violence had anything to do with Hope's fear.

Pike felt a nudge at his elbow and looked down at the petite crime scene investigator who worked the task force with him. Annie Hermann pointed to the same group he'd been watching. "Why is *he* here?"

He assumed she was talking about her fiancé, Detective Fensom. "Nick? He and Detective Montgomery were the first two detectives on the scene of LaDonna Chambers's rape and murder."

Annie's dark curls bounced around her face as she shook her head. "No, I mean Adam Matuszak. My tall, blond, ambitious ex." She made no effort to mask her sarcasm. Pike liked Annie. She might be a bit of a flake in the personality department, but far and away, she was the smartest, sharpest thinker on their team. She'd been the first to get them a lead on their unsub by identifying his blood type and confirming they were looking for both a rapist and an accomplice who cleaned up after his crimes. "I dodged a bullet when Adam dumped me. She's the bridal shop owner, isn't she?"

"Yeah. Hope Lockhart."

"Does she need an attorney?" Annie asked. "I thought Nick said she was a witness."

"Potential witness," Pike clarified, liking Hope's friends less and less. "Do you know Brian Elliott, too?" The one who kept touching Hope's arm and shoulder, despite the way she subtly shifted posture or pulled away each time.

"He owns most of those buildings in our target neighborhood. He remodels and sells them. If I remember rightly, he invested money to help Miss Lockhart set up her bridal shop. Adam is his personal attorney—

Nick and I met them at a crime scene in one of the buildings Elliott was converting. We thought it might be the location where our unsub was taking his victims to sexually assault them." Annie's voice trailed away and Pike looked down to see where her thoughts had taken her.

"It turned out to be a staged crime scene, right?"

Annie nodded. "It was a trap. If Nick hadn't been there, I could have died."

His attention shifted back to Detective Montgomery's desk, and Pike saw Nick Fensom grab his leather jacket off the back of his chair and excuse himself from the conversation. Hope turned to see where he was going and her gaze locked on to Pike's across the room—for about two seconds before Elliott touched her shoulder and forced her attention back to whatever their attorney was saying to Spencer Montgomery. Hope nodded and answered a question. And then she was pointing to a picture in a book of vehicle makes and models on Montgomery's desk

But in those two seconds, Pike had read a plea in those lake-gray eyes. The fatigue of working through the night melted away and he stood a little straighter, leaned a little closer, felt a little more protective. She was part of the neighborhood he guarded; that made Hope his responsibility. And though she'd made it clear she hadn't wanted his help at her apartment, and she wasn't too comfortable having him touch her, her eyes had sent him a different message just now. *Help.*

Just like with Hans, it had been bred into every fiber of his being to answer that call. But help her with what? How? What did she need him to do? Or was he just imagining her distress? He hadn't read any other nonverbal cues she'd been giving off correctly. Shy—not snooty. Afraid of Hans—not him.

This is too much, please come bail me out—or *what the heck are you still doing there staring at me when whatever interest you have in me isn't as mutual as you'd like it to be?*

There was a reason Pike worked with dogs. Communication with them was so much less complicated. Eat. Sleep. Pet. Play. Work.

While Pike debated the mystery of Hope Lockhart and how he should respond, Nick circled around the counter. He shrugged into his jacket before brushing a curl off Annie's forehead. "Everything okay? Matuszak isn't giving you fits, is he?"

With their opposite personalities, Nick and Annie were the last two people Pike would ever have imagined as a couple. But together, they worked. Annie shook her head and smiled. "I don't even notice him when you're here."

Nick grinned. "Good." He shifted his gaze up to Pike. "Seems like Matuszak ought to be answering some questions instead of keeping her from talking. All we want are details about what she saw last night, and her observations of activities in that neighborhood. But as her business mentor, Elliott claims he knows her better than anybody. He says she's 'sensitive and suggestible' and wants to make sure we're not taking advantage of her or scaring her more than she needs to be. It's like facing off against a pair of big brothers."

Sensitive and suggestible? The woman had stood up to what was probably an abusive father and pulled a knife to defend herself from the things that frightened her. She'd gone to the scene of a homicide to confirm the identity of someone she knew. Pike punched Hank

Lockhart's prison record off the computer screen and turned toward Nick. "Hope may not look like it on the outside, but she's tough. She's a survivor."

"I hope so. I'd still like to get her in a room without her entourage to see what she has to say." Nick's shift was long over, too, but he had nothing but a smile when he reached for Annie's hand. "Come on, slugger. I'll drive you to the lab." With a nod to Pike, the couple walked toward the elevators. "See you at the briefing tomorrow morning. Try to get a couple hours of sleep."

"Yeah," Pike answered. "You, too."

Pike groaned when the elevator door opened and three of the five members of SWAT Team 1 stepped out, including Pike's older brother Alex Taylor. Pike greeted Trip Jones and Holden Kincaid, each of whom towered over his vertically challenged, muscle-bound sibling. As adopted brothers, Alex and Pike couldn't look more different, but they couldn't be closer, either. Growing up in foster care together had forged a bond as strong as blood between them.

And Alex took his role as big brother very seriously. He knew Pike should be home at his apartment getting some shut-eye right now.

After sending his buddies on to roll call, Alex combed his fingers through his curly black hair and stretched up on tiptoe to look over the counter where Pike stood. "Where's your better-lookin' sidekick?"

"Aren't you the funny guy." Logging out of the computer terminal, Pike grabbed his ball cap and joined his brother around the front of the desk. "Hans is in his kennel, getting some R & R."

"Looks like you had a long night, too."

Pike scratched at the stubble that shaded his jaw and nodded. "We had another Rose Red rape."

"Ah, hell." Although the task force was specifically dedicated to solving the string of assaults and related deaths, there wasn't a cop on the force who didn't care about catching the perp. "Did the victim survive?"

Pike shook his head. "Looks like the Cleaner got to her. Shot the vic. CSI Hermann thinks LaDonna Chambers was dead before the body was dumped this time." There had been too many innocent victims. He smacked his cap against his thigh and looked across the room to Hope again. A woman like that shouldn't have to live in fear of walking the streets or going to work. "I don't understand why we can't catch these bastards. He hasn't left a single fingerprint at any crime scene, but we've got the accomplice's on file. We've got the rapist's DNA, but there's no match in the system. According to the CSI I was just talking to, the only blood at this scene belonged to the vic. We can't figure out where he takes them to commit the assault or why this Cleaner goes to so much trouble to destroy any evidence of the crimes. It's a sick relationship."

"I don't know what color they were." Was that Hope raising her voice? "He was going too fast. If I had known who he was, of course I would have…" Her hands squeezed into fists on top of Detective Montgomery's desk. "He wore a hat and a surgical mask. His eyes were in the shadows." Matuszak moved in behind her chair, warning the detective not to press his client.

Alex turned to track the object of Pike's wandering gaze. "What's she got to do with it? Montgomery is lookin' intense."

"I know. They're being pretty hard on her. The woman hasn't had any sleep."

Alex tilted him a curious look. "Is she part of your task force investigation?"

"We think she saw the van our rapist uses to abduct his victims. She may even have seen the guy, but didn't get a clear look at him."

"I thought you were a K-9 cop, not a detective. Have you been asking her questions, too?"

Pike studied the toe of his boot for a moment, recalling that unexpected urge to kiss her. But he remembered the stark fear he'd seen in her apartment just as clearly. The knife and the wild eyes had reflected how well his attempt to develop a rapport with her had gone. He raised his head, wondering again if he'd misread her silent plea for help a few minutes ago. She was hanging in there with Montgomery. "Her shop and apartment are on my beat. I answered a call there last night."

Crossing his arms over his chest, Alex leaned back against the counter beside Pike. "Why don't you go over there and do something about it instead of standing here staring like a moon-eyed teenager?"

"What do you mean, do something? I'm not…" Ah, damn. Had Alex picked up on that weird attraction vibe? Without paying any mind to the flak vest and SWAT uniform his brother wore, Pike quipped back, "I can squash you, you know."

"Hey, I'm older than you—show some respect."

"Don't have to."

"I'll tell Mom."

"Mom likes me better."

Alex shook his head and laughed. "Go over there and say something. Offer her a cup of coffee or a ride home. Give her a break from the Inquisition and she'll be grateful. Is she nice?"

"Are you matchmaking?" Pike accused. "Hope and I aren't even friends. She's not my type."

He preferred getting to know a woman who might actually like him.

"You don't have a type. Besides, I don't buy that 'she means nothing to me' line. You're about to crawl out of your skin with worry, so why don't you go over there and do something about it?"

"Alex—"

"You can handle her."

"What does that mean?"

"I know how suave you are with the ladies," he teased, intimating just the opposite. "At the rate you're going, Matt and Mark will be married before you."

"They're still in school."

"That's why I'm helping you out." Alex gave him enough of a push that Pike had to plant both feet to keep his balance. "What are you waiting for, Casanova?"

"Shut up." Pike returned the shove, pushing Alex beyond arm's reach but returning his teasing grin. "It's a wonder you ever got Audrey to say yes to you."

"And yet she did." Alex flashed his wedding ring and cut Pike a break on the teasing. "Follow your instincts, little brother. There's no other way to figure a woman out. I'll see you in a week at Sunday dinner. Grandma and Grandpa will be back from their fiftieth anniversary trip. I warn you—Grandma said there'd be pictures." Alex doffed him a salute and headed toward the conference room. "Good luck."

"Yeah. See ya Sunday."

After he watched Alex rejoin his SWAT teammates, Pike looked across the desks to Hope again. He could do this without his older brother's help. He started walking before he talked himself out of the idea of taking one more stab at proving to Hope that he was one of the good guys. Besides, she'd been up as long as he had, and if he was this tired, she must be exhausted after the emotional ups and downs she'd been through in the past several hours. He'd be doing her a favor to interrupt the grill-fest of questions.

"Yes, LaDonna worked in my office, and yes, I want answers," Matuszak was explaining as Pike approached. "But I don't intend to let any woman I know be hurt like that again. Hope has told you everything she knows more than once. I won't let you put her through anything else, especially something that's not even admissible in court—like this ludicrous idea of hypnosis."

"But if it could clarify some detail from what I saw, then I'd—" Hope began.

"It won't." Matuszak shut her down and squeezed her shoulder at the same time. "You've done enough. If this…animal…gets wind that you're any kind of witness to what he's done, then he might well come after you next."

Sizing up the tailored cut of the attorney's tan suit and his willingness to scare his client in order to keep her mouth shut, Pike circled around him. Someone here was wearing some serious cologne, too. But he remembered Hope's scent was sweet and subtle. And Spencer Montgomery wasn't the cologne type. Another reason not to like these two.

Detective Montgomery acknowledged him as he joined them. "Pike?"

Hope's face was too pale for his liking. The urge to rescue her and change her perception of him flowed even stronger through his blood now. "I was wondering how much longer you'll need Miss Lockhart, sir. My shift's over and I'd be happy to give her a ride back to her apartment."

Hope's head shot up and those long tendrils danced away from her confused expression. "You would?"

"Anytime."

The wealthy entrepreneur Pike already knew to be Brian Elliott stood up to introduce himself. "And you are?"

"Officer Taylor." They clasped hands in front of Hope's face, and when he glanced down at her with a friendly wink, her pale cheeks dotted with color. Was that embarrassment at his teasing show of support or discomfort that he'd forced his way into a conversation that had already gone on too long for her? Pike forged ahead. "Hope and I have a habit of running into each other."

"Yes. I saw how you ran into her in the elevator." Scowling as if displeased by the half embrace he'd witnessed, Elliott diverted Pike's attention to the other man. "This is my attorney, Adam Matuszak."

"We've met."

They shook hands while Brian Elliott continued. "Thank you, but Hope and I are friends. I've known her for several years now. I was the first to notice her talents as a business woman with impeccable taste. I've nurtured that talent and supported her ever since. Adam and I will take her home."

Although Elliott's tone was polite enough, Pike got the idea that some sort of claim was being made. Were these *GQ* and *Forbes* cover models the kind of men Hope preferred to hang out with? The kind of men who made her feel safe? That didn't bode well for a *Field & Stream* kind of guy like him.

Still, he wasn't looking forward to letting Alex know he'd struck out with Hope Lockhart. Again. He made one last valiant effort, dropping his gaze down to Hope's. "Is that what you want? I'll take you out of here right now. Just say the word."

"I…" She glanced up at both her friend and her attorney before adjusting her glasses on her nose and narrowing her gaze at Pike. "It would be more convenient for Brian to take me. He lives in the same neighborhood."

"I drove Mr. Elliott here," Matuszak added, settling his hand on Hope's shoulder. "It's no problem to drive her, too."

Convenient. Not what he'd asked. But the dismissal was clear. She'd made her choice.

So much for Alex's matchmaking. So much for winning Hope's trust.

"Then I'm headin' home myself." He put his cap on and tipped the bill to her. "Ma'am. See you next time I'm on patrol."

Her gaze dropped to the middle of his chest before she nodded. No *thank-you*. No *goodbye*. No *appreciate your concern*.

A nod.

Pike turned away, strolling toward the elevators and trying to figure out what that woman had against him— and why it bothered him so much that she did.

Chapter Five

A solid night's sleep, a run with Hans, a shower and a shave had refreshed Pike enough to stay focused during the task force meeting early Monday morning.

At least, he was physically alert. Unfortunately, there were so many thoughts running around inside his head that he was distracted, anyway.

The graphic crime scene photos that Annie Hermann passed around indicated that the Rose Red Rapist's level of violence had escalated, and that his habitual routine was growing more erratic. It was disturbing enough that LaDonna Chambers had been abducted and sexually assaulted. But there'd barely been any defensive marks on her. Had the initial blow to the head when she'd been blitz attacked and kidnapped rendered her unconscious through the whole ordeal? If so, then why kill her?

Had something upset the rapist's routine and he'd fired the kill shot out of rage? Had the Cleaner, a female accomplice who destroyed evidence of his crimes, upped her game to the extent that she now intended to murder every victim? Was the assault no longer enough violence to sate these perverts' sick needs?

And then there was the guilt Pike had to deal with. CSI Hermann's timeline indicated that Ms. Chambers's abduction had happened during his patrol shift with Hans, just a block away from his location at the time. She'd been taken from *his* territory. On *his* watch. She'd been a woman working in the neighborhood he'd sworn to protect. A law student, LaDonna had been taken from the parking lot outside the firm where she'd been doing her internship.

Adam Matuszak's law firm.

First impressions of the arrogant blond attorney lingered in the mix of Pike's thoughts, too.

Pike reached down to where Hans dozed on the floor beside his chair and stroked the dog's warm flank, automatically seeking that grounding, don't-stress-unless-you-have-to feeling that working with the clever German shepherd gave him. But that first encounter with Matuszak and Brian Elliott still irritated him. Both men had shut down Hope's efforts to speak for herself. And while that might have been a legal thing to protect her from volunteering to say or do anything that might be upsetting or unnecessary or even potentially incriminating, it stuck in Pike's craw to think that she'd tried to make herself heard and no one was listening.

And what would he have done if Hope's high-society buddies hadn't been there to greet her when the elevator doors opened? Tunneled his fingers deeper into that glorious hair? Eliminated the distance between them? Kissed her?

Maybe his instinctive dislike for Adam Matuszak had a more personal, less noble foundation. Maybe what galled Pike was that he'd made a concerted effort these past few months to earn Hope's trust and become a friend, and—with or without Hans at his side—she'd repeatedly blown him off. Meanwhile, she aligned herself with those two suit-and-tie movers and shakers of

Kansas City society who'd answered her call in the middle of the night.

Sounded a little like wounded male pride.

That was an unsettling thought, too.

"Either he's getting sloppy or she's learning to enjoy the game, too." Spencer Montgomery's stern voice dragged Pike's attention back to the opposite end of the table where the senior detective ran the task force meeting.

Spencer's partner, Nick Fensom, sat immediately to his left. He tossed the pen he'd been rolling between his fingers onto the table and leaned back in his chair. "So they get more violent and we get no closer to solving this damn case."

"That's not entirely true, Nick." Dr. Kate Kilpatrick, the police psychologist and profiling expert who was a member of the team, was ever the voice of cool, calm reason. She patted the thick case folder sitting in front of her. "We're building an extremely strong case against our unsub, with a variety of evidentiary support. We have his DNA and a surviving witness who can identify him by voice and scent, as well as describe the site where the rapes occur—a building undergoing renovations or construction."

"Doesn't do us any good if we can't catch the perp and put him on trial," Nick argued.

Annie Hermann curled one leg beneath her and sat, trying to calm the fiancé she sat across from. "We know exactly the kind of man we're looking for now."

Dr. Kilpatrick tucked her short silvery-blond hair behind her ears, concurring with Annie's facts. "He's most likely OCD—suffering from obsessive-compulsive disorder. The surgical mask Miss Lockhart mentioned fits our profile. He has specific routines. He needs things to be spotlessly clean and orderly. And even though he functions normally in society, he has issues with successful, goal-oriented women. He's been emotionally traumatized by a woman with power over him—a mother, a lover, a boss."

"Blah, blah, blah." Nick voiced his opinions and emotions more loudly than anyone, but Pike had to admit he was feeling the same frustration.

Maggie Wheeler-Murdock, the red-haired officer who was typing notes onto her laptop, and who had a special affinity for talking to the victims of these brutal crimes, looked up from her computer screen. She directed her question to the police psychologist. "Is it possible the shorter time frame between attacks is because the Cleaner has turned the rapes into murders? She's stealing the spotlight from him?"

Dr. Kilpatrick nodded. "That could be the very relationship he's acting out on by going after these women. She's interfered with his routine. And he no longer sees himself as the most dangerous thing out there on the streets."

Pike finally had something to add. "There's danger enough." He felt all eyes at the table turn to him. "When Hans and I are out there walking our beat, you can see the fear on women's faces. It's in the way they walk and carry themselves. A lot of the businesses in that neighborhood are run or staffed by women. Now some of those businesses are closing because of the fear our unsubs have created. Trust me, I'm less worried about the economic impact than I am about what this guy is doing to the confidence of this city." He braced his elbows on the table and leaned toward the rest of the group. "We need to do something now. Go on the offensive. There are too many dead bodies—too many ruined lives—left in this guy's wake."

"Pike's right." Detective Montgomery surveyed the members of his team, sitting around the table. "We need to set up a sting that will draw this guy out."

"We need bait for a sting," Nick pointed out. "We don't have the manpower to track every potential victim he might go after."

Dr. Kate added another bit of reasoning. "It needs to be a woman our unsub sees as a specific threat to him."

Spencer shook his head. "We've only got two surviving witnesses who can implicate him. One of them is in a mental hospital. And the victim Dr. Kate mentioned—Bailey Austin—we can't count on her. Her assault was too recent. She's too fragile to put into a possible face-off with her attacker unless he's behind the glass in a lineup room."

"It doesn't have to be a previous victim, does it?" Maggie suggested. "Can't we put a female officer undercover in that neighborhood who fits his ideal victim? Make her an irresistible target to draw him out?"

"It can't be you." Dr. Kate smiled and nodded toward the baby bump that was already starting to show following Maggie's summer wedding to a U.S. Marine who'd lived in her apartment building.

Nick Fensom's gaze locked on to the dark-haired CSI sitting across from him. "The Cleaner has seen Annie at crime scenes. We have to assume she's shared that information with our unsub. He won't go after one of us."

Kate Kilpatrick agreed. "None of us can assume the role we need. As the task force liaison to the press, I have my face all over the media. He knows I'm with KCPD, too."

Pike flattened his palms on top of the table. The

team's undercover-cop idea wasn't going to fly. "This guy lives or works in that neighborhood. He knows every woman there. He'd avoid a stranger, unless we're talking about embedding someone there for several months."

Detective Montgomery shook his head. "We can't wait that long. He'll have gone after someone else by then. We need to recruit a volunteer from the community—offer her police protection, of course."

Nick Fensom snapped his fingers. "We've got Pike's girlfriend who gave us the info about the surgical mask and a detailed description of what we believe is his van."

What? Whoa. Pike raised his hands and backed his chair away from the table. "She's not my girlfriend."

Nick swiveled in his chair, his teasing grin looking an awful lot like his brother Alex's yesterday morning. "Then why did you hang out at the precinct for six hours after your shift was over yesterday?"

"Hope was my responsibility. I was the first man on the scene after she called Dispatch. I drove her in to HQ. I wanted to see the incident through to the end." Yeah. That was it. He'd stayed out of concern...because he'd be worried about anybody from that neighborhood on his watch. Right?

Clearly thinking through their options, Detective Montgomery adjusted his dark silk tie. "Brian Elliott offered to put her up in his lake house down in Branson, but she refused. She told me she wanted to stay in the city and help in any way she could."

"There you have it." Nick turned back to his partner. "Our bait."

Pike remembered the prison record he'd read. Henry Lockhart's home address had been in a small town close to Branson. Maybe that part of the state dredged up too many unpleasant memories for Hope. That was probably why she'd refused Elliott's offer.

"I'm sure she was talking about testifying in court," Pike countered. "Not…what you're suggesting."

"She's a successful woman," Montgomery argued. "Runs her own business. She's been a resident in the Rose Red Rapist's target neighborhood for a couple of years now. Hell, the press gave our unsub that nickname because of her shop."

These people weren't listening. Hope Lockhart as an undercover lure? Not that she couldn't attract a man's attention—if she loosened a few buttons on her blouse, let down her hair and actually talked to a guy. But that wasn't going to happen. He'd been trying to interact with the woman for months now, and except for those brief seconds on the elevator, all he'd gotten were some curt hellos and a knife pulled on him. "How are you going to get a man on the scene to protect her without making our unsub suspicious? If you look up *spinster* in the dictionary, Hope Lockhart's picture is right there next to it." He knew those weren't the kindest words, but facts were facts. "You can't suddenly throw a cop into her life and have anybody believe it isn't a sting operation."

Dr. Kate moved her hand to the tabletop next to where Pike's hand rested. "Your emotions are more than a little elevated when you speak of Miss Lockhart. Do you have a relationship with her?"

"With Hope?" His protest was sharp enough for Hans to raise his head.

The psychologist nodded. "If there's already a connection between you, we could capitalize on that."

Oh, yeah. He never should have touched Hope in that

elevator. "I'm not in a relationship with anybody. And trust me, if you're going to recruit her, then you need to send someone else to keep an eye on her."

Spencer Montgomery stood at the opposite end of the room, buttoning his suit jacket, looking as though he was about to wrap up this meeting. "Why? Can't you handle some personal protection work?"

"Of course." The dog rested his muzzle on Pike's knee, giving him a look that seemed to question just where this conversation was taking them. "Hans and I can guard a place or a person better than any team of men. But Hope…she's afraid of me—of us." He reached down to rub Hans's head. "And I don't work without my partner."

Dr. Kate was sizing him up as though he were a patient of hers. "Do you want me to talk to her? You know, helping her through these fears is a very legitimate way to deepen your bond with her."

"I don't have a bond."

"But you *do* know her," Detective Montgomery clarified. "You've had conversations?"

"Sort of."

"You've been seen with her?"

"Yeah, but—"

"Anybody else here know Hope Lockhart better than Pike?"

Maggie gave him a sympathetic look over her laptop. "She planned my wedding to John, but I've got desk duty until the baby comes."

Annie Hermann stuffed her files into her bag. "Sorry. Never met her."

"Saturday night's interview was the first time we've spoken." Nick Fensom tucked his pen into the pocket of his leather jacket.

"It's settled, then." Detective Montgomery closed his notebook and zipped it shut. "Make her like you."

"Excuse me?" Pike stood and Hans fell into place beside him.

"You need to become her boyfriend. I can't think of a more plausible way to work a bodyguard into her life."

"She'll never go for that."

"She'll have to if she wants our protection." Detective Montgomery circled the table, indicating a decision had been made. "Kate, you and I can have a discussion with Miss Lockhart this afternoon. We'll make it clear that we need her help to make that neighborhood—this city—safe again."

"Wait a minute." Pike strode around the table to catch Montgomery at the door. "You want me to... date...Hope Lockhart?"

The red-haired detective's cool gray eyes weren't joking. "I want you to move in with her. Pretend you're having an affair. Or better yet, she runs a bridal shop. Pretend you're her fiancé and you're planning your wedding."

"Detective—"

"We'll provide whatever backup you need—keep eyes on her when you can't. But you and Hans are going to be our front men. We can leak that we've got a description of our suspect—drop some subtle clues that lead back to her. We at least have to ask if she's willing to do it."

"You're going to put a civilian in that kind of danger?"

The detective's assessing look included Hans. "She'll have the best protection KCPD can provide."

"Sir, I've never worked undercover."

"You just have to do your job. Be there if and when

our perp comes after her. You'll still be a cop. You'll just be a cop who's in a relationship." Pike had a sinking feeling there was no argument left to be made. Hope *was* their best shot at luring the Rose Red Rapist into the task force's trap. And nobody else here could make the sting setup work. But what a setup. "Make our unsubs believe that Hope Lockhart is your bride-to-be."

PIKE WATCHED SPENCER Montgomery and Kate Kilpatrick pull out of the parking lot at Fairy Tale Bridal to merge with the beginnings of rush-hour traffic, leaving him standing on the sidewalk out front. He looked down at the alert dog sitting beside him. "I guess we're really going through with this, Hans."

Hans tilted his long black muzzle up into Pike's hand, promising his silent support. Whatever his master had to do, they would do it together. Even if it meant taking on a role neither of them had trained for— pretending Hope Lockhart was their happily-ever-after.

Pike looked up and down the street, wondering if any of the people walking to their cars, heading into shops, peeking out of office windows or warming up with a coffee amongst the autumnal reds and golds of the young trees that decorated the rooftop garden of the cafe on the corner had any suspicion of the trap KCPD was laying for the Rose Red Rapist. Was one of them their man, watching him even now and evaluating his appearance at Fairy Tale Bridal? He was the neighborhood cop, right? Would their unsub buy that he and Hope were an item? Would he believe that all those brief encounters with her these past twelve months had led to a marriage proposal and that the extra security on the premises had to do with love and not catching a criminal? There was only one way to find out.

"Fuss." At the German command to heel, Hans jumped to his feet and fell into step beside Pike as he turned back into the parking lot. "Let's do it."

After holding the door for a group of young women who were all chattering at once about the best color for a bridesmaid dress, Pike led Hans into the vestibule of Hope's shop. He paused a minute to inspect the splintered wood around the lock he'd busted to get up to Hope's apartment late Saturday night. The door swung open with barely a push, making him glad she still had the outside entrance and her apartment door upstairs she could lock for security. But he also made a mental note to pick up some wood from the lumberyard to reinforce the lock until he could get the antique door replaced and a new dead bolt installed.

Inhaling a fortifying breath and reminding himself how important this assignment was to KCPD and all of Kansas City, Pike pushed open the door to Hope's shop.

"...Ms. Carter, er, Mrs. Lonergan now, let me off an hour early to come fix your door." A short, wiry man wearing a green uniform shirt and jeans was talking with Hope across the counter at the center of the shop. Pike recognized him as an employee from the florist's shop across the street. The two businesses often handled events together, but this didn't look like a work-related discussion to him. "She worries about you, you know."

The bell ringing above his head announced Pike's arrival, but it was Hans's loping gate beside him that diverted Hope's attention from the conversation and made her cheeks go pale. She might as well get used to having them both around. She'd agreed to this charade, and that included the German shepherd as part of her bodyguard contingency. He sure hoped Dr. Kilpatrick was right, and that helping Hope deal with her fear of dogs was the best way to earn her trust.

Pike pulled off his KCPD cap and stuffed it into his hip pocket as the dark-haired man clicked his tongue against his teeth to startle Hope's attention back to him. "As I was saying, I've got tools and some wood across the street at Mrs. Lonergan's shop. You know I can be pretty handy. Bet I have it all repaired before you close."

"Thank you, Leon." Was that a smile for the other man? When she hadn't even said *hi* to him? How were they ever going to pull this off?

Leon leaned a little closer over the tall edge of the counter. "If I come back tomorrow for another couple of hours, I'll have it looking as good as new. I promise."

Hope fiddled with the belt of the navy blue dress that covered her from neck to knee and sidled to the far end of the counter as Pike and Hans approached. "You're too good to me, Leon. How much do you think it will cost? You still haven't given me a bill for that window-pane you replaced a couple of weeks ago."

"I won't take your money, Hope."

"Technically, you work for Robin, not me. At least let me pay for the materials."

"No, ma'am." The man slid an annoyed glance toward Pike and Hans, dismissing them as an ill-timed official visit, no doubt, before circling around the end of the counter to block Hope's escape—moving from friendly acquaintance to personal-space invader. "But maybe you'll let me take you to dinner tonight?"

"I thought you had dinner with your mother on Mondays," was Hope's gentle reply.

The guy's fingers tiptoed across the counter toward her hand. "I'll make it up to her. She's subbing in a bridge game tonight, anyway. I'm a free man."

Really? Was this guy hittin' on her? Had Pike completely misread her unattached status? Whatever it was, Pike had to nip the potential relationship in the bud. He walked up behind Hope, crossing behind the cash register and computer as though he had the right to do so. "She's got plans. Right, hon?"

Hope flinched at his touch when he flattened his hand at the small of her back. Or maybe it was the dog standing so close that made her visibly shiver. Either way, she wasn't helping establish any kind of cover. "Hans, sit." While the dog plopped down on his haunches, Pike extended a hand around Hope to introduce himself. "I'm Pike Taylor."

"I know you, Officer. Leon Hundley." The twenty-something man shook Pike's hand, but looked as befuddled by his presence in the shop as Hope did. He thumbed over his shoulder at the big display windows that faced the front sidewalk. "I work at Robin's Nest Floral across the street. I help Miss Lockhart out with odd jobs whenever I can. I'm trying to make some extra cash to restore my car."

And to hit on Hope. Was she even aware that Hundley had been flirting? Or was that innocence the way she shut down any man who showed an interest in her? That didn't bode well for the success of this engagement masquerade.

Pike settled his palm at the nip of Hope's waist and let his fingers fan over the ample swell of her hip, silently warning her not to bolt while he made some neighborly conversation with a local. "What kind of car do you have?"

Good. Leon noticed Pike's subtle claim, and retreated to a more impersonal distance. "A '72 Camaro."

"Sweet. Is the chassis in good shape?"

"Yeah. I painted it blue. Look, Hope and I were having a conversation. Did you need her for something?"

"No. Just dropped in to say hi."

Although he made an effort to reclaim Hope's attention, Leon seemed a little less inclined to hang around the shop and chat than he'd been a moment ago. He pointed toward Hans. "Is he an attack dog?"

"He's a police officer. He doesn't get mean or tough unless I do." Pike released Hope and turned, thumping his chest and inviting Hans to rise on his hind legs and prop his paws on him. Ignoring his stinging conscience at the gasp behind him, Pike rubbed the dog's leanly muscular flanks, sending out a shower of tan and black fur. "Do you want to pet him?"

"Maybe another time." The ploy worked. Even though Hans thought he was playing, it made an impressive show and drove the point home to Leon that the two of them weren't going anywhere. While he pulled out his cell phone, Leon backed toward the exit. "I'd better let Mother know I can drive her to bridge tonight, after all. Then I'll get started on that door. I'll let you know how much the new lock costs."

Did Hope notice that Leon had decided to charge her, after all, since she was no longer available for whatever he'd had in mind? And was she really going to stop talking now that he and Hans were here?

"Thanks, man," Pike offered as the wiry handyman headed out the door. "I'd planned to do it myself. But if you need the cash…"

"Right. I'm on it."

The bell over the door chimed before Pike put Hans in a sit position and turned to apologize to Hope. "Don't worry, I'll clean up where he shed."

But she'd already put half the length of the store

between them and was gathering up a rainbow of fabric samples from the seating area in front of a trio of mirrors.

"Hans, *platz*." Burying his frustration on a gruff sigh, Pike told the dog to lie down and strode across the shop to join her. He picked up a box from the end of one couch and had it ready for her when she turned around with an armful of filmy material.

Hope hesitated for a moment, her gaze darting back to the counter, then up to him before dropping the samples into the box. "So, how do we do this?"

He wasn't sure if she was talking about baiting a trap for a rapist or masquerading as the woman Pike Taylor loved. "I don't know. I think we just have to be seen together. Make it look like we're a couple so no one questions me being here. And don't let the handyman across the street flirt with you."

"I wasn't letting..." She grabbed the box from his hands and carried it into the dressing rooms. "Leon was flirting?"

How could a woman who must be in her early thirties be so sweetly clueless? "He wants something from you."

"Money for his car. A friendly diversion, maybe. His mother has a chronic illness. She makes a lot of demands on his time, and the medical bills don't leave anything extra for fun things—like his car. I try to help out when I can."

"Well, you need to stop providing *fun* for Mr. Hard Luck out there." Pike propped his hands at his belt when she reappeared, carrying three bridesmaid dresses. "The press leak will go out tomorrow morning. In the meantime, Hans and I will keep our eyes and ears open for any sign of our unsub. You do understand what we're asking of you, right? It won't be a cakewalk."

"You met my father. I've been victimized before, Officer Taylor." She hung the dresses up on a nearby wall before facing him again. "I refuse to be a victim again. I'm tired of losing people I know. I'm tired of living in fear."

"That's the first thing that has to change."

Her cheeks warmed with a hint of temper. "I know I don't come across as a very forceful personality, but I do have convictions—"

"I meant calling me Officer Taylor instead of Pike or Edison or Eddie or whatever you decide on."

"Oh." The blush faded. "Like when you called me *hon* in front of Leon." So she had been paying attention and hadn't gone into a frozen version of her last panic attack. With a nervous adjustment to her glasses, Hope went back to the counter, walking a wide berth around Hans even though he had laid his head down to rest and didn't seem to care. "I'm just Hope. The only nickname I ever had was 'Sis,' and you could hardly call me that."

"That's right. You said you had a brother."

She nodded and picked up a computer pad. She brushed her finger across the screen and pulled up a calendar. "Harry. Henry Lockhart Jr.—named after our father. But he doesn't claim that name. He's just Harry. He's a sergeant in the Marine Corps—an MP at a base overseas."

Pike joined her behind the counter, subtly positioning himself between her and the dog. "Then let's just agree that it's Hope and Pike for now."

"All right."

"Besides your dad, is there any other family I should know about?"

"He's not family. Not to either of us." She uttered the statement like a pledge, then set the computer pad back on the counter and tilted her face up to his. "And no, it's just me here in Missouri. Detective Montgomery said that would help make this—us—more convincing. No one should question it."

The bell jingled above the door again. Hope smiled and nodded as a mother and daughter came in. The younger woman hurried toward a princessy wedding dress in the front window and the mom followed. "Excuse me, I have an appointment."

"And we need to make our rounds. Hans. *Steh.*"

Hans jumped to his feet and Hope dived back a step, gripping the counter behind her. "You talk to him in German?"

Pike nixed the idea of telling her that leaping up onto the counter wouldn't stop Hans from getting to her if the dog wanted to. "He's bilingual. He answers to English when he's relaxed like this. But yeah, his work commands are in German. I'll teach you a few words sometime."

"Why?"

"Hans goes wherever I go, Hope. So that means you're stuck with both of us. I want him to mind you as well as me. He'll be our first line of defense if our perp comes after you." He dropped his voice to a whisper the two customers couldn't overhear. "Still want to go through with this?"

She answered with a jerky nod. "If I can help catch that predator, I want to."

Hope's skittish reaction had garnered the mother's and daughter's attention. Pike offered them a reassuring nod before glancing over to see Leon Hundley watching them, too, from the vestibule where he was measuring the broken door. Finally, he turned to the pale woman with the prim dress and too-tight bun. "I'll be back before you close. I'll have an overnight bag with me, and Hans's kennel. We'll talk more then. Lay down a few ground rules."

Pike pulled out his cap and started to leave. But with the customers and Leon watching, he knew he couldn't just walk away. *Might as well go for it.*

In two long strides, he came back. He palmed the nape of Hope's neck, catching his fingers beneath the bun, loosing a few of those decadent curls before tilting her face up to kiss her. Their lips were touching, but she wasn't kissing him back, and he supposed the hand she braced against his chest might look as if she was holding on to him. But she wasn't.

He raised his head, watched her pupils dilate behind her glasses and reminded her they were a team on this undercover op. "You might want to make this look good," he whispered.

When her hand slowly climbed up the placket of his shirt, Pike dipped his head and kissed her again. This time, her fingers curled into his collar, tugging on his shirt and the turtleneck he wore underneath, catching on the edge of his flak vest and pulling him closer as she stretched up on tiptoe. Her soft mouth parted beneath his, but did little more than submit to the force of him pressing against her.

She'd latched onto the front of his shirt with both hands by the time he lifted his head and pulled away. Her breath blew against his lips with a gentle, stuttering whisper of heat. What the heck? He felt that tiny caress like a kick in the gut as he pried her fingers from his wrinkled uniform. This was a charade, wasn't it? So why was he transfixed by those deep gray eyes peering at him over the top of her glasses? Why wasn't he moving away?

It took a nudge from Hans to get Pike to pull his fingertips from the silky bun that wasn't so tight and neat anymore. Pike plopped his hat on his head and tipped the brim before grabbing Hans's leash and heading for the door. "I'll see you in an hour."

That ought to get some tongues wagging about his claim on Hope Lockhart. That soft, shy kiss, so at odds with the fingers grabbing at his chest, had certainly piqued *his* interest.

Julia Williams

Chapter Six

"What in the world…?" Hope shielded her eyes and squinted at the bright square of light dancing on her bedroom wall. She picked up her glasses from the nightstand and put them on as she shuffled to the window to peek outside. Normally, the morning sun flooded her apartment with soft warmth and sunshine. It was one of the reasons why she'd converted this half of the second floor into her living space and had left the back half to be used as more storage for the shop below.

But today the clear autumn morning was playing tricks. While the windows facing her across the street remained dark and opaque in the shadows, the sun glinted off the windshield of a vehicle parked below on the street, nearly blinding her. For one frightful moment, her stomach clenched. Was that a white van parked in front of her shop? Was the man sitting behind the wheel watching her shop? Watching her?

A car drove past and she had to close her eyes and turn away. The light bounced from glass to glass and reflected up to her bedroom. No doubt that was the explanation for the dazzling rainbows shining in that had wakened her before the alarm. When her eyes had adjusted and she could lower her hand, Hope saw that the boxy vehicle below was a silver SUV of some type.

Not the van that had followed her home.

Breathing a sigh of relief, she shut the blinds behind the eyelet curtains and considered crawling back into bed. But she had a business downstairs that wasn't going to open itself. And she had an even more important job to do today—help catch a rapist. Detective Montgomery had said she was the city's best chance at ending the nightmare that stalked her neighborhood.

And just like on that fateful morning twenty years ago when she'd made the decision to find help for her starving, neglected brother and herself, Hope knew she couldn't hide in her room and wait for someone to rescue them. She had to venture out and save herself.

Hope tied her blue chenille robe snugly around her waist and took a deep breath before leaving her room. The polished oak planks that ran the length of the entire loft were cool beneath her bare feet. The automatic coffeemaker in the kitchen was bubbling to life and filling her apartment with the rich, warm aroma of fresh java.

But the same odd light was bouncing through her living and dining room area now. When it sliced across the white pillars and exposed brick and hit her eyes again, she tiptoed to the bank of windows facing the street and looked down. As she pulled aside the curtain and leaned closer to the pane of glass, trying to make out a face to go with the gloved hands on the steering wheel below, she heard the engine revving to life. The silver SUV pulled out of its parking space and headed down the street—not an early riser coming to work, but a late-night partier finally going home, most likely.

Funny. Generally, the patrons of the nightspots down the block and around the corner parked in one of the garages down there. It wasn't unheard of on a busy weekend to see cars parked this far up the street, and even in her private lot outside the shop. But on a Tuesday morning? Her heart rate kicked up a notch. Maybe not so funny. It was perfectly likely that the man she'd seen Saturday night had more than one vehicle. He was probably too smart to come back to her place in the van she'd already seen.

"You're making too much of it," she whispered against the glass, trying to calm her racing pulse. "He wasn't watching you. You don't even know it was him."

Still, the nervous instincts refused to completely dissipate. Reflecting lights and unfamiliar vehicles weren't the only differences in her regular morning routine. She had other reasons to be a little jumpy this morning. Her homey, countrified decor now included a large gray kennel with a steel mesh gate. The smells in her home were different, too. There was a slight pungency of dog food and heat from the beast dozing in said kennel. Even the sounds were different. In the early morning quiet before downtown Kansas City came to life again, she heard a soft, even snore coming from her guest room.

Maybe she *should* report the SUV. Just in case she was right to be worried about strange vehicles parked in front of her shop. A panic attack was embarrassing. But not responding to a real threat could be downright dangerous. Her footsteps took her back down the hallway.

She'd made a deal with KCPD—for LaDonna Chambers, for her late friend Janie Harrison, for her client Bailey Austin, for the women who lived and worked and played in this neighborhood, to end that threat. She'd made the deal to help capture the Rose Red Rapist for herself. Because she deserved to feel safe in her own home and shop. She'd gone to bed a shy woman who lurked in the background of society, and she'd woken up to a very different, unfamiliar world where she had to take action and play a starring role.

Hope paused outside the second bedroom and pushed the sleepy tumble of hair off her face. As much as her heart and conscience wanted to do this undercover job to help the police, her father's voice inside her head was telling her she was doomed to fail. She could never pull this off—being the fictitious fiancée to one of Kansas City's finest, playing the part of would-be witness to draw a dangerous man into KCPD's trap.

"You're too much of a coward, girl. Now quit thinkin' on your own and dreamin' those stupid dreams, and do what I tell you."

"Shut up, Hank," she whispered, pushing open the door and peeking inside. She'd gotten her brother away from their father's prison. She'd started her own business. She supported herself more comfortably than she'd ever dreamed possible back on that remote patch of land in the Ozark woods. She could do this, too. She could live with a man for a few days. She could tolerate his dog and get used to their habits. She could even learn to be more convincing as half of a couple.

Still, her heart beat faster and her breath locked up in her chest when she saw the big man sleeping in the bed. Pike Taylor's broad shoulders and naked chest seemed at odds with the white, eyelet-trimmed sheets and hand sewn quilt draped around his waist. A more familiar light coming through the eyelet curtains at the window dappled his skin with tiny spots of sunshine, highlighting golden spikes of hair among the sandy shades of tan and brown on his scruffy jaw and chin, and farther down, in the hair that dusted his chest and narrowed into a thin line running down his flat stomach and disappearing beneath the sheet.

Watching a grown man sleep was as mesmerizing as it was unfamiliar. Other than her brother, Harry, her father ages ago, or catching an accidental glimpse of a customer trying on a tux in her changing rooms downstairs, half-naked men weren't something she'd had much experience with. She'd never had that much muscle and testosterone sleeping in her apartment.

Hope's skin suddenly burned beneath her nightgown and robe, and her mouth went dry. She was assuming Pike Taylor was only *half*-naked. What if he wasn't? Her pulse thundered in her ears. She'd certainly never had *that* in her apartment.

The twin bronze medallions that marked him as uniquely male had puckered in the cool air and stood at attention atop the even rise and fall of his chest, mocking her inability to make a decision. Should she wake him up to tell him about the car? Politely retreat until he was awake and back in uniform?

They probably should have talked about the bathroom schedule and sleeping regalia last night while they were discussing ground rules for this charade. What if he was a sleepwalker? What if he sat up in bed right now and the quilt drifted farther south?

"It's not polite to stare."

Hope gasped as Pike's deep, husky voice startled her from across the room. He was awake? He'd been watching her…watch him? One blue eye blinked open, confirming the worst. Embarrassment heated her face as the second eye opened. "There was a car out front," she blurted. "It's gone." *Sound like an idiot much?* "I'm sorry." She was already backing from the room, pulling the door closed behind her. "I am so sorry."

"Hope? Wait. What car?"

Smooth, woman. She tucked her robe together at the neck and dashed to the kitchen. His teasing tone made it sound as though she'd been admiring the scenery. She hadn't been, had she? Not intentionally. She'd been curious. Concerned. She was just trying to get used to having a man in her home so she wouldn't freak out like… like the way she was doing right now. "Good grief."

If Pike had any doubts about her ability to pretend she was in love with him, she'd just confirmed them.

"Hope?"

She spun around the corner in her haste to get away from the door opening behind her. Her hip bumped a chair and rammed it against the table, knocking the lid off the sugar bowl and waking up the beast sleeping by the front door. Hope shrieked at Hans's deep woof and reversed course, plowing into Pike's bare chest.

Her fingers brushed across ticklish hair and warm sinew before she flattened her palms against a sculpted swell of muscle and pushed away. The heat of his skin sizzled beneath her cool hands and her vision swam with a blur of faded blue. Hope realized he had on a pair of old jeans, and the words tumbled out of her mouth before she could stop them. "Thank God, you're wearing pants."

"Huh?"

The dog barked again, either at her flighty distress or excitement at seeing his master.

Or the gun he held in his hand.

"Oh!" Hope ducked behind Pike, her fingers sliding around the bare skin of his torso as she tried to put him between her and Hans. The moment she noticed that the skin at the small of his back was smoother than the hard muscles of his chest had been was the moment she realized she was still touching him. Hope curled her traitorous fingers into her palms and clutched them beneath her chin. "Sorry. I shouldn't keep grabbing you."

"You shouldn't keep apologizing, either." Pike turned, filling her vision with his broad shoulders and chest. "It's okay. I won't break."

"No. Obviously, you're strong enough to…" Heat radiated off him in waves. Or maybe that was her own embarrassment making her feverish. "I was just caught off guard because you're hot." What did she just say? "I mean, your skin's hot. Temperature-wise. Oh, God."

He reached out and squeezed her shoulder, thankfully silencing her double entendres, keeping the heavy black gun he carried pointed down at his right side. "It's okay. I'm flattered more than I should be. Now tell me about the car you saw."

Those clear blue eyes were all business when she looked above the bare chest. Hope nodded as some of the fluster faded. She knew how to respond to that. "A silver SUV was parked out front when I woke up. I wouldn't have noticed it except the sun was reflecting off the windshield and coming into my bedroom. There was a man behind the wheel, but I couldn't see him well because of the glare." Pike was already moving across the apartment to peek out the front windows. "It's gone now."

"Did he see you look out the window?"

Pike's concise movements made her think she'd been right to be suspicious. "From my bedroom, maybe. If he was looking up. He pulled away when I opened those curtains there."

"He drove south?"

"Yes. Is that a bad thing?"

"I'll find out. Come on, big guy." Hope hugged the

white pillar beside her couch as he released Hans from his kennel, hooked the leash to his collar and opened her front door. "Stay put. Lock the door. We'll be back."

As soon as the door closed, Hope hurried after them to throw the dead bolt. She heard the doors opening downstairs and dashed to the windows to see Pike and Hans rush out to the sidewalk below. Even with Pike barefoot and wearing holey jeans, there was something powerful, vigilant, relentless about the pair's quick movements and watchful scans. They moved up and down the street, following Hans's nose before disappearing around the side of the building into her parking lot.

Several more minutes passed, giving her plenty of time to imagine a dozen different dangerous scenarios, before she heard them on the stairs again. Hope met them at the door and opened it, standing behind its blockade while Pike wrestled for a few seconds with Hans, then tossed a thick rope with a rubber ball tied to it into the living room, where the dog curled up on her braided oval rug to chew on his toy.

"There's no sign of anybody watching the place now." Pike pulled the door from her hands and locked it, exposing her hiding place before she was certain the loose dog wouldn't notice her here. But that long-ingrained phobia was of little consequence. Pike tucked the gun into the back of his jeans and started rummaging through her kitchen cabinets. "You've had company. There were footprints in the landscaping around your lot."

Hope hugged her arms around her waist. "They could be from patrons coming or going to the bar or coffee shop on the corner last night," she suggested.

"They park on the next block and take shortcuts through one of the alleys or my parking lot."

Pike shook his head. "Hans found deep footprints in the mud. Someone was standing there a long time. Facing your shop."

Shivering at the possibility that she hadn't imagined someone outside was watching her, Hope inched into the kitchen with Pike. "Can I help you find something?"

"A trash bag? This was left outside the door." He pointed to a padded envelope he'd set on the table. "I want to bag it for evidence, just in case it's important. Unless you recognize it?"

Hope shook her head. "Under the sink." She looked at the package without touching it. Her name. No return address. No postmark, either.

"Hand-delivered," Pike agreed as if she'd voiced her suspicion out loud, and shook open the plastic bag. "Just like the box of bugs. I'm guessing that whoever was loitering outside was hoping to see your reaction when you open it."

"Should I?"

"Careful. Hans seemed to think whatever's inside would be fun to play with. He didn't indicate anything explosive." Pike waited beside her while she picked up a knife and sliced open the end of the slightly bulging envelope. "Maybe it's another gift from your father?"

"I don't know if I would recognize his handwriting anymore. It was pretty illegible, like this address. But we don't even know if the bugs were from him, do we? He denied sending them."

"Most criminals would." When she glanced up, Pike shrugged an apology. "I did a little research after he threatened you the other night. I know he spent time in Jeff City. Did he ever hurt you?"

Not exactly. Hope tucked her chin to her chest and focused her attention on the envelope again. Hank Lockhart might never have laid a hand on her, but then, he'd never needed to. There were other, far more cruel ways to get an already meek child to do what a man wanted.

"Hope?"

She ignored the curious prompt and opened the package, crinkling up her nose at the rotten odor that suddenly filled the air. "I know that smell." She recognized it from one of the nasty jobs she'd had as a little girl, when her father had been too drunk to clean their tiny kitchen, and what food they'd had in the house had been too precious to share. As much as she wanted to throw the envelope away, Hope knew she had to look inside. But she prayed she was wrong. She wasn't. "Oh, my God."

"Son of a…"

Brown and furry and stiff as a board.

Hope gasped and stuffed the envelope with the dead mouse into the trash bag and scooted across the kitchen. She dropped the knife into the sink and pumped the soap to wash her hands, even though she hadn't actually touched the frozen-eyed critter.

"Hope?" Pike wrapped up the offending present and set it out of sight. "Does that or the bugs mean anything to you?"

"Mean? It means there's some sicko out there having way too much fun at my expense." She washed the knife as well, then dropped it into the dishwasher and rinsed out the entire sink, working frenetically to cleanse the frightening image from her memory.

"I'm talking about those specific gifts. Do they have any significance to you? Any hidden message?"

"I don't know."

"Hope." Pike's hands closed over her shoulders. "You need to calm—"

"No, I don't!" She spun in his hands and shoved him away. The dog jumped to his feet in the living room and barked a warning. Hope screamed and backed against the sink, hugging her arms to her chest and staring straight down at Pike's bare toes. "I'm sorry. I didn't mean it. I'll be quiet."

"Hans. Box!"

Hope flinched at Pike's sharp command, but the dog trotted obediently to his crate and curled up inside. Her gaze made it up to the belly button above the snap of Pike's jeans. "I'm sorry. I shouldn't have pushed."

"Don't apologize for having a temper. I'd be pissed off, too, if someone was sending me those crude gifts and spying on me." After closing Hans in his kennel, Pike reached for her, but grumbled something beneath his breath and pointed to the windows, instead. "Be afraid of that guy out there. Not me."

"I am."

"Which?" He braced his hands at the waist of those softly worn jeans. "You're afraid of him or me?"

Maybe she was just afraid, period. Shaking her head, Hope circled around the table to avoid him, needing time to regroup, rethink, maybe just start this whole day over again. "I'm going to shower and get dressed now. There's cereal, milk and fruit for breakfast. Coffee's made."

But Pike blocked her path when she tried to slide past him, and she had to curl her toes into the cool wood planks beneath them inside her slippers to keep from bumping into him again. "Hope, I don't need you to be quiet or to act like you don't think or feel like anyone else. I need you to talk to me. If we can't learn to communicate with each other, then I'm not going to be able to protect you. And we have to be able to be in the same room together without you bolting, or we're never going to convince anyone we're a couple."

"I know. That's why you need to find someone else to help you."

"There *is* no one else." He scrubbed his palm over his beard stubble, then leaned in, pleading or venting, demanding something she wasn't sure she could give. "This mission has already started. Someone is already watching you—watching us. Now, I know you're a society lady and I'm working-class good ol' boy, but we have to make this happen. We have to make *us* work or our perp will see right through what we're trying to do, and he'll go even deeper into hiding. How many more women will he have to hurt before we get a chance like this again?"

Frowning, she tilted her gaze up to his. "Society lady?"

Those deep blue eyes were dead serious. They could lose the Rose Red Rapist if she couldn't move past her fears and phobias and become a part of the team Pike Taylor needed her to be. Embarrassment faded. Doubt lingered. Yet the determination that had made her say yes to this plan in the first place was still there, beating steadily through her veins. Suddenly she didn't see the half-dressed man who made her so nervous, but the comrade-in-arms whom she was letting down—and the mission they couldn't afford to fail.

"Pike, I'm not a society lady. Maybe I work with a lot of them, but I grew up in the backwoods of the Ozarks. I worked my way through college. I borrowed money from Brian Elliott to buy this building and open my shop, and I'm still paying him back. I'm not... I don't..." Hope shoved her fingers through her hair and gathered it out of the way down her back. "If I concentrate, I can control the panic. I'll learn how to kiss you and have meaningful conversations and pretend I'm not afraid of Hans. Don't give up on me yet. Please. I can do this."

"Give up on you? Why would I...? Oh, Hope." Pike brushed aside a tendril that had escaped from her grasp and tucked it behind her ear. "Have you ever been with a man?"

All the blood seemed to rush straight to the cheek and ear he'd touched. She turned back into the kitchen, confessing the awkward truth. "Pike, I've never even been in a serious relationship." She stared at the turquoise glass tiles of the backsplash before reaching for a bowl of fruit and a clean paring knife. She pulled down two cereal bowls and sliced up a peach into them, needing to keep her hands busy while she talked. "I have friends who are men. And I've dated a few times— mostly business acquaintances, a couple of times in college. But if I ever felt anything more, it wasn't mutual. Or they just wanted... And no, I've never done that, either." When the peach was done, she peeled a banana and kept working. "I don't turn heads. I don't get much chance to practice. All I do is freak out when a dog comes into the room or a man tries to touch me. KCPD may have made a mistake in asking for my help."

He leaned his hip against the counter beside her, glancing around the remodeled loft. "I don't think so. You came from the hills of nowhere and ended up here? You're obviously a smart woman who knows how to work hard and succeed. You're very observant of what goes on around you." He plucked a peach from the nearest bowl and took a bite. "You don't need to say a lot of words for me to know you care about people. You're a champion of this neighborhood. You stood up to your dad the other night, so I know there's strength in you."

She stopped slicing fruit just to listen to his quiet, deep-pitched voice. His words were soothing, supportive, tapping into some of that strength inside her and making her believe, just a little bit, what he was saying. When he reached over to touch her hair again, she tilted her chin up to see his eyes watching the curls sifting through his fingers. "If you left your hair down natural like this, men would notice you. Heck, if you didn't work so hard to hide all those curves, you'd be beatin' us off with a stick."

Hope chuckled at that improbability and he smiled in return.

"You'll never convince me you're anything but a lady. I just need to teach you a thing or two about how we should interact, so I don't startle you or make you too uncomfortable. It won't be hard. Trust me, I'm not that complicated."

She sighed with regret. "But I think I am."

His teasing smile never wavered as he straightened away from the counter. "You've already mastered step one. You called me Pike without even thinking about it. And I think we're having a meaningful conversation right now." He took her hand, setting the knife down on the counter and turning her to face him. Her eyes widened as he placed her hand against that warm, beautiful—bare—skin again and held it there. "Let's work on step two."

He gently pinched her chin between his thumb and index finger and tilted her face up as he dipped his head. "Don't hold your breath," he whispered, seeing she was doing just that. "Relax." Impossible. Not if he was going to kiss her again. He stroked the pad of his thumb over the seam of her lips. "Shh. Easy."

Her lips parted on a breathy exhale and he closed the distance between them, settling his mouth over hers in a gentle kiss.

Hope stilled despite the warmth of mingling breaths and the unfamiliar pressure of his mouth pushing, withdrawing, tugging her bottom lip between his. She concentrated simply on breathing, in and out through her nose. But it was difficult to focus and her breath stuttered. Pike traced his tongue around the rim of her lips, eliciting a sigh, waking nerve endings she didn't know were there. She attuned her senses to the supple firmness of his lips and the soft abrasion of his beard stubble rubbing against her softer skin. He generated such heat wherever he touched her, the curious friction between them stoking something deeper inside, something even warmer than the brand of her fingers splayed over the drumbeat of his heart.

"Like I said—I won't break," he coaxed, kissing the lower curve of her mouth, then the bow on top. "You try," he whispered against her, his warm proximity making her feel connected even when their lips were no longer touching. "I'll go with the flow of whatever you're comfortable with. You're in control."

With a subtle nod, Hope pushed her mouth against Pike's again. She dug her fingers into his chest and circled her left hand up behind his neck, anchoring herself as she pulled up to compensate for his greater height. Her fingertips discovered the crisp line where his short hair met the nape of his neck. She ran her tongue along his bottom lip as he had done with her. His mouth opened with a husky moan from his throat that skittered along her skin and made her nipples tighten with an answering anticipation. Hope shyly touched the tip of her tongue to his and quickly drew back at the unfamiliar contact with its soft, raspy warmth, only to have his tongue chase hers and invite her to take another sample.

Okay, so this guy was a really, really good teacher. This time she cautiously took her time, sliding her tongue against his, tasting the sweet peach he'd eaten and something more, something that made her whimper and want to move closer—something so potent that it made her heart race and her thoughts go fuzzy.

When she recognized the raw desire coursing through her, Hope pulled back, dropping to her heels and releasing her clinging fingers before she embarrassed herself by forgetting the reason for that kiss. "How did I do?"

"Honey, you're a natural." His hands had worked their way into her hair, and were massaging her scalp. "Knew you were smart. Didn't expect you to catch on quite that fast." His chest heaved in and out in a deep rhythm that mimicked her own and fogged up her glasses. She tilted her eyes up to his over the rims and was surprised at how close he seemed, how close he felt deeper inside her. But his eyes were sparkling with humor, not questions. "Feeling any urge to run away?"

Hope shook her head.

"Good." He grinned before taking a deep breath and pulling back. "I think we might have to practice that lesson again."

For a split second, Hope wondered where she'd gone wrong with that kiss. But he was still grinning while he pulled his cell phone from his pocket and punched in a number. "You're flirting, right?"

"Oh, yeah." Pike winked before turning away and reporting the information about the dead mouse on her doorstep to Detective Montgomery.

Hope couldn't seem to erase the silly smile from her own expression as she finished prepping breakfast. The morning might have had a horribly embarrassing and disturbing start, but her day had improved dramatically. Not only was she in the same confined space with a trained German shepherd, but she was entertaining a distractingly shirtless man in her apartment—and not freaking out about either one.

Hope was setting two mugs of coffee on the table when the intercom beside the door buzzed, announcing she had a visitor outside. Glancing at the clock on the stove, she frowned. "Who could that be? The shop doesn't open for another hour. My first scheduled appointment isn't until ten."

Still on the phone with Detective Montgomery, and his hand back on the gun tucked into his jeans, Pike crossed to the window and peeked out. "There's a news van parked outside."

"Already? I thought I'd have some time to prepare…" for the onslaught of attention Dr. Kilpatrick had said she should expect once her name was leaked to the press as a possible connection to the task force investigation. "What am I supposed to say?"

When she approached to see for herself, Pike put out his arm, warning her to stay out of sight behind him.

"Yes, sir. Understood." The intercom buzzed again, making her think of a timer that had just run out. There was no backing out of this now. Hope looked up to Pike for guidance. He tucked his phone into his pocket and nodded to the intercom. "Go ahead and answer it. Get a name and find out what they want."

Aware that Pike was following right behind her, Hope cleared her throat, then pushed the call button. "Yes?"

"Miss Lockhart? Hope Lockhart?" A smoothly modulated woman's voice answered.

"Who's this?"

"Vanessa Owen. Channel Ten News. I've been to your shop before, remember? Right after Bailey Austin was assaulted?"

"I remember you, Ms. Owen." The dark-haired beauty had practically become a fixture in the neighborhood this past year. The female reporter's tenacious coverage of the Rose Red Rapist attacks and subsequent investigation had made her a staple on the evening news in Kansas City, and had even garnered her some national appearances for her coverage of the crimes. "It's awfully early. The shop isn't open yet."

"I'll wait, Hope. May I call you Hope?" Did she have a choice? "I'm shopping for information, not a dress. You've been holding out on me. I want you to tell me everything you know about the Rose Red Rapist."

"Everything I—?"

Pike pulled her hand off the button to mute their conversation from the reporter. "There's no time for a learning curve here. It's showtime. Are you ready?" Hope was about to be thrust from nobody in the background to headliner of the front-page news. Pike turned his hand into hers and laced their fingers together. "We're a team, remember? You can do this. I've got your back."

After a moment's hesitation, Hope squeezed her grip around Pike's, holding on as she pressed the button again. "I need half an hour, Ms. Owen. Then I'll be down."

Chapter Seven

"This isn't a good time, Hank." Hope had thought answering her phone would give the idea to the stunning brunette reporter that she had a business to run and the interview needed to be over. She'd been wrong.

"Is that the boyfriend?" Vanessa Owen drummed her dark red nails on top of the central counter in Hope's shop.

Boyfriend? Hope snapped her mouth shut as soon as she realized the surprise that must have registered on her face. With a quick no, she turned away from the curious reporter. "I have people here. I need to go."

If she had known it was her father on the line, she would have let it go to voice mail, closed her shop and locked herself in the storeroom until all these people who wanted something from her left her alone. "We're just a few minutes from your place." Hank was in charming mode this morning. But that would change soon enough if he didn't get his way. "Won't be any trouble to stop by for lunch. I'd like to catch up on all the time we missed."

"I'm busy."

"What about dinner?"

"I can't."

"What if I said I was dying?"

"Are you?" She hugged an arm around her waist and dropped her voice to a whisper.

That he didn't answer told her the pang of remorse she'd felt for a split second had been a wasted emotion. The charm bleeding from his voice confirmed it. "What if I said it was about Harry? Would that get you to listen to me?"

"I don't have time for this."

"Girl, I'm your father. I raised you." She'd raised herself. *He* had nearly killed her. "There are certain expectations and responsibilities. You have to talk to me."

"You know, actually? I don't." Hope hung up and set the phone on the counter.

"Oh, good." Seeing that the call had ended, Vanessa Owen wasted no time in asking one more question. "Could you hold that dress up beside you again?" She snapped her fingers to call her cameraman back from the shop's front door. "Damien, make sure you get a picture of this. My viewers will love the wedding dress angle. You see those shows all over cable these days, don't you? Very popular."

"I suppose." Hope blinked against the camera's bright light as she hung up the white gown on the tall hook beside the central counter. She wasn't sure what wedding dresses had to do with an interview about the Rose Red Rapist, but after two hours of questions on everything from why she'd been up so late the night she saw the van to why she thought she hadn't been singled out as a victim yet, Hope was certain Vanessa would use whatever footage and sound bites guaranteed her the biggest viewership.

"Vanessa, how much longer are you and your vultures going to prey on Hope this morning?"

Brian Elliott didn't seem particularly thrilled to have his eleven o'clock appointment delayed by the intrusion of television cameras and reporters still lingering on the sidewalk in front of Fairy Tale Bridal. And even though the bulk of the impromptu press conference had dispersed, he was still irritated enough to follow Vanessa to the counter to vent his displeasure.

"That's good, Damien. I'll be out in a minute." Once the reporter dismissed her crew and turned her big doe eyes up to meet the man who obviously knew her on a first-name basis, Hope seized the opportunity to finally evade the spotlight.

More than once, she'd repeated the information Kate Kilpatrick and Detective Montgomery had encouraged her to share with the media. But no matter what she'd said, her answers never seemed to be quite thorough enough to satisfy the reporters and curious passersby who'd stopped by to see what all the fuss was about. With a wink from Brian, urging her to go on about her business and take the respite she needed, Hope zipped the long white gown into a garment bag.

"Eloquently put as usual, Brian." Vanessa's dark red lips pouted into a smile. "You know I'm only doing my job."

Hope picked up the alterations estimate for her seamstress and pinned it to the plastic bag before draping the dress over her arm. But when she tried to slip away to the dressing rooms, Brian's attorney, Adam Matuszak, was blocking her path.

"Excuse me, Adam."

Two or three seconds passed before she was even sure he'd heard her. Barely taking his eyes off the charged debate between his client and the brunette, the blond attorney stepped aside for Hope to pass—or

perhaps just to join the conversation. "You keep showing Brian's buildings as crime scenes on the evening
news, and you'll put him out of business."

"Adam, dear. Always good to see you." Clearly, all
three ran in the same social circle and knew each other
personally. Curious as she might be about that tense
triangle, Hope skirted around the attorney and carried
the dress to the seating area in front of the three-way
mirror. She saw Vanessa's smile reflected in one of the
mirrors, and wondered if the woman's exotic beauty really was that striking, or if her hair, lips and nails only
looked extra rich next to her own mousier reflection.
"Why would I want to do a thing like that?" Vanessa
asked. "You know how much I enjoy Brian's company."

"I know how much you enjoy Brian's money."

"I'm a success in my own right, Adam. I don't need
any man's money."

"You certainly seem to be making a killing on Brian's misfortune," Adam argued. "He's trying to reclaim the run-down parts of this city, and all your news
stories talk about is the crime spree happening here.
Why don't you give some press to the historic pres-
ervation and revived economy he's brought to downtown K.C.?"

Hope carried the gown inside the dressing rooms,
but the agitated voices were loud enough to carry
throughout the shop. She was glad there were no customers on-site. There was no Pike Taylor on-site, either, but he had assured her that his detective friend,
Nick Fensom, was hiding close by, keeping an eye on
her and the shop while Pike and Hans made their routine morning patrol. He'd made a point of walking her
down the stairs to greet the reporter and welcome her
and her cameraman into the shop, giving Hope a good-

bye kiss that had gone beyond their kissing lesson in the kitchen, leaving her gasping with surprise and making sure that anyone who was up and about in the neighborhood could see that shy Hope Lockhart was a spinster no more.

With a silent warning to step up her game and a squeeze of her hand that she thought was meant to reassure her, Pike had left her to face Vanessa Owen and the gathering contingency of reporters and onlookers outside her shop alone. She knew he couldn't stay on the premises around the clock or else the Rose Red Rapist might peg him for the bodyguard he was. Still, it was a little discomfiting to realize just how quickly she'd developed a craving for that boyish grin and the squeeze of his hand around hers. And while she had no illusions that their fake relationship was anything more than a job to Pike, she was beginning to think— and hope, maybe just a little bit—that they were becoming friends.

But they would never be more than friends. Pike was a virile, outgoing, confident man, and she was... well...Hope Lockhart.

She looked in the dressing room mirror and studied her lips. They looked pink and pale compared to the lush burgundy of Vanessa Owen's mouth. The boxy cut of her brown suit hid all the plump curves that more than compensated for the skin and bones child she'd once been. Unbuttoning the top of her cream-colored blouse, Hope pulled aside the collar to look at the faded scars on her neck, shoulder and chest. They were such vivid reminders of not only her traumatic past, but of the cautious, closed-off woman she had become. While she had no trouble being attracted to Pike's tall, muscular body and rugged looks, he certainly had his work cut out for him, convincing the world that he'd fallen so in love with her this past year that he'd moved in.

"You're never gonna amount to anything, girl. Now put those highfalutin ideas right out of your mind and fetch me a beer. That's all you're good for."

"Shut up, Hank." Temper brewed in her veins. When was that ugly voice ever going to stop talking in her head? "I have a job to do. LaDonna and Bailey and all those other victims need me to pull it together." She straightened her collar and refastened her blouse, going back to unhook the top two buttons and let it fall open in a modest effort to play a more believable mate for a man like Pike. She pulled a belt from a returned tuxedo order and cinched it around her waist, nodding approval at the hourglass shape it gave to her figure. "Pike's doing his part." She talked louder than the demeaning voice inside her head. "Stop thinking about who you were and who you wish you could be, and do your part, too."

That meant she couldn't spend the rest of the day hiding in the dressing room, having philosophical discussions with her reflection and avoiding the tension in the other room. Hope picked up three dresses a customer had tried on earlier, and quietly returned them to the racks while the debate continued at her front counter.

Adam had moved closer to Brian and Vanessa, still arguing that the Rose Red Rapist attacks were motivated by some kind of vendetta against his employer. "It's awfully convenient that these assaults have all taken place in this neighborhood."

"Interesting theory," Vanessa drawled, sounding more amused than curious. "You think that these attacks are all part of a giant conspiracy to devalue Brian's investments? Instead of, say, that he lives in this area, or that this is where he can find the successful professional women he targets?"

"I'm just saying there's more than one person benefiting from this guy's reign of terror over the city." Adam pointed an accusatory finger at the reporter. "It put you on the radar of every national news bureau, didn't it?"

"That's enough, Adam." Brian pushed his attorney away in a protective gesture. "Vanessa is only doing her job."

"And I'm doing mine. You hired me to protect you and your interests, Brian. This woman is taking advantage."

"Boys, boys."

Hope watched as the woman in the taupe silk pantsuit stepped between the two men, tapping a dark red nail against both chests.

"You and I will have to discuss the rapist's possible motives beyond terrorizing women sometime, Adam." Vanessa dismissed him before turning to Brian. "Are we still on for dinner tonight?" To Hope's surprise, she stretched up and kissed his cheek, leaving a brand of burgundy lipstick on his skin. "Later. After the broadcast. I'll bring the wine."

Brian took a handkerchief from his suit jacket and wiped away the stain with a handsome smile. "Don't keep me waiting too long."

Hope hugged the last dress she held as Vanessa walked her fingers up Brian's lapel and tapped his lips. More than discovering that her friend and the reporter were apparently an item, Hope was stunned by the woman's smoothly flirtatious moves. Was that the kind of teasing maneuver Pike expected her to make?

That the world expected to see between a couple like the one they were pretending to be? "Don't I always make it worth the wait?"

With a deep sigh, Brian pressed a kiss to Vanessa's finger. "Always. Tonight, then." Folding up his handkerchief and tucking it into his pocket, Brian turned to the tall, dark-haired woman waiting patiently by the front door. "Adam? Regina? Shall we get on with our business?"

Regina Hollister, Brian's executive assistant, stepped forward when summoned. Her eyebrow arched as she passed Vanessa, giving Hope some idea of what the businesswoman thought of her boss's paramour. But any hint of a personal emotion was quickly replaced by cool efficiency. Pulling up the sleeve of her charcoal-gray suit, Regina checked her watch. "I'm sorry, Brian, but we need to go now to make your lunch with the mayor. I'll reschedule your appointment with Miss Lockhart."

Hope hung up the dress and returned to the counter to finish up the meeting that had never had the chance to get started. "That's okay, Brian," she assured him. "I'm a little talked out for the day, anyway."

"I can imagine." Brian buttoned his tailored jacket and leaned in to kiss her cheek, giving her a whiff of the strong cologne he wore. "Sorry we got so sidetracked. We'll work out those easement regulations so you can get that bigger parking lot you want. I know you'd like to get construction started before the winter weather hits."

She nodded. "If I can."

"How about I have Adam pull the necessary permits and construction contracts and have him contact you with some initial estimates? Adam?"

But the attorney didn't immediately respond. He was

at Hope's front window, watching Vanessa strut down the sidewalk, leaving her news van behind. What was she up to now? Where was she going?

Before Hope could come up with any answers, Adam spoke. "What did you say that van you saw looked like, Hope?"

"White. Boxy. Silver bumper."

Adam pointed through the display of fall-colored bridesmaid dresses to the vehicle out front. "You cover up the logos on that van and what do you have?"

Hope walked up beside him. Channel Ten's shiny rear bumper gleamed in the sunlight. The make and model were the same. But that couldn't be the same vehicle, could it? The van she'd identified had rusting wheel wells. She'd seen it late at night, through tired eyes. Could she have mistaken the brown trim for rust in the dark? She adjusted her glasses at her temple and looked through the van's side entry, up to where the cameraman, Damien, sat behind the wheel. He was sipping coffee, steadily meeting her curious gaze through the front window.

Hope recoiled back a step. Damien wore no stocking cap, no surgical mask. But his dark eyes…they watched…

There was always somebody watching.

The temperature in the shop suddenly seemed to plummet. It was probably just the cop outside, protecting her, that she sensed. But this—she peeked through the mannequins in the window, scanning up and down the street—this felt like something more. Something sinister.

She yelped when Brian palmed the center of her back, halting her unconscious retreat. "Enough, Adam.

You're frightening her. Besides, I'm quite certain Vanessa is not the Rose Red Rapist."

"This isn't a joke. I know KCPD is looking for a man." Adam had been studying her reaction, too. "What about someone else on the Channel Ten News team? It wouldn't surprise me if Vanessa knew the rapist's identity and was covering for him so she can keep reporting the story and making headlines."

"That's horrible," Hope whispered. "What woman would do something like that? That monster needs to be put away."

"Mr. Matuszak." The sharp voice of rebuke came from Regina Hollister this time. "On behalf of women everywhere—shut up." Then she looked to her boss and tapped her watch. "The mayor?"

Brian circled around Hope to stand toe-to-toe with his attorney, warning him. "I won't hear another word against Vanessa's character."

Despite his superior height, Adam seemed to understand who paid his salary and relaxed his defensive posture. "You're right, of course. I know Vanessa means something to you. She and I dated a couple of times before I got wise to her. I'm just trying to spare you the pain I went through. As I said before, I'm looking out for your best interests."

A moment more passed before Brian smacked Adam's shoulder and nodded. "That's why I pay you the big bucks, Adam. Thanks. Don't worry. I understand the kind of woman Vanessa is. I've got both eyes wide-open."

What kind of people formed a relationship with someone they couldn't trust? Brian Elliott was an attractive, wealthy man—he could have any woman he wanted. Adam Matuszak, as abrasive as he was, would be considered a catch, too. How did he feel about his boss dating his ex? Was he jealous? Or was he truly concerned that Brian would get burned, too?

And why did they have to bring all their drama into her world when everything was already such a frightening mess?

The bell chiming above the shop's side entrance offered her the diversion she needed to interrupt her thoughts for a few minutes. "Excuse me, I have a customer."

Brian nodded as she left them at the window. "I'll have Regina call you. We'll show ourselves out."

Hope smoothed her hand against her neck, battling the urge to button her open collar and hide like the turtle she was used to being. *Stay out of your head, Lockhart.* She quickly pulled her hand down and headed toward the woman who was admiring a display of beaded evening purses.

She recognized the brassy blonde chauffeur who'd been with her father the other night. So much for keeping her father out of her life. "Nelda, is it?"

"You're Hope, right? We didn't get to meet the other night." Her smoky voice was friendly enough. She extended her hand. "Nelda Sapphire. It's my stage name. For my blue eyes. I'm a dancer. Well, I used to be. I own the place now." She tilted her head to one shoulder, indicating the door. "That's where I met Hank."

Hope wasn't about to judge Nelda on her name or profession or the overprocessed pouf of her hair—only on her taste in men. Had Hank duped Nelda, promising some sort of caring relationship with the same empty words he'd used with his late wife and children? Or was the woman fingering the expensive purses in a business partnership with Hank, working with him to beg or con whatever money they could out of Hope?

A glance beyond Nelda confirmed the worst. The older woman hadn't come alone. Her father stood out in the parking lot, finishing off a cigarette. "How can I help you?"

"You're going to give me a good deal, aren't you?" Nelda's smile seemed sincere. "You know, the family discount?"

Giving Nelda the benefit of the doubt, Hope politely corrected the status of her relationship with her father. "I'm sorry. I think Hank may have misled you if he intimated that I'd be doing him any favors."

Nelda shifted on the ridiculously high heels she wore. "You know your father regrets what happened between you, don't ya, sweetie? He didn't really come to Kansas City for a handout. He wants to work, to earn the money you give him. He's awfully handy with repairing things and cleaning up. It's hard for an ex-con to get a respectable job that pays much. But we thought that maybe, since you're family—"

"No. I'm sorry."

The friendly smile vanished. "Then I hope that lady out there is paying him for all those questions she's asking. We need money."

"What lady? Oh, no."

Hope dashed to the vestibule and pushed her way out the second door to the parking lot before the inner door had fully closed. Why hadn't Vanessa Owen gone back to the TV station? Instead of prepping for the evening broadcast, she stood in the parking lot, shivering against the autumn chill while she chatted with her father—and hung on to every word.

Her father, of course, was eating up the attention. "I

ain't proud of what I done. But I served my time. Hope's stubborn like her mama was. She ain't forgiven me yet. But she's got a good heart. She will."

Forgive? Yes. Her peace of mind demanded it. Forget? Never.

Hope walked up behind her father. "Why are you talking to Ms. Owen? She doesn't even have her coat. I'm sure she needs to get back to the TV station to finish her report."

"Nonsense. I have plenty of time." Vanessa hugged her arms in front of her against the cool temperature, but her smile never wavered. "Your father and I are getting acquainted."

Hank dropped his cigarette to the asphalt and ground it out beneath his boot before facing her. His leathery face creased with a smile she didn't believe. When he reached out to hug her, she put up her hands and backed away. That was a charade she couldn't play. Hank laughed when he turned back to the brunette reporter. "My girl was always makin' up stuff in her head. Like she wanted to be a princess or there were witches in the woods."

Vanessa's assessing gaze darted over to Hope and back. "Do you think she made up seeing the Rose Red Rapist?"

"Well, it's gettin' her lots of attention now, isn't it?"

"Do you think I want this kind of scrutiny in my life?" Hope wondered if Hank could see that Vanessa's amused smile never reached her eyes. She wondered if she smelled booze on his flannel shirt and denim jacket because he'd already been drinking that morning or because he hadn't changed from the night before. "This man is not a reliable source for any news story. I saw what I saw. The van, the driver, everything. I didn't make up any of it."

But Vanessa truly was the shark Adam Matuszak had accused her of being. And she was on the trail of a juicy sidebar to Hope's story. "You've got a bit of a charming country boy accent there, Mr. Lockhart. What part of the state are you from?"

"I asked you to call me Hank, ma'am." He pulled a pack of cigarettes from his pocket and tapped out another smoke. "You ever been down to the lakes around Branson? Deep in the Ozark Mountains?"

"How about I buy you a cup of coffee, Hank, and we talk someplace warmer? You can tell me all about those mountains." She waved to Damien in the news van and pointed down the street before linking arms with Hank and pulling him into step beside her. "Did your daughter grow up there, too?"

"Hank, no one needs to know—" Hope chased after them, but a bright flash of light blinded her as soon as she reached the sidewalk. Hope threw up her hands to protect her eyes, remembering for a split second the mysterious flashes that had wakened her in her bedroom that morning.

"Gabriel."

"Vanessa."

Before Hope could blink her vision clear and push aside her nerves, Vanessa Owen was trading cheek-to-cheek air kisses with a handsome, black-haired man wearing jeans and a corduroy sports coat. The camera and plastic ID badge hanging around his neck identified him as another reporter. "You're a few steps behind on this scoop, aren't you, Gabe?"

"I don't think so."

"Let's do lunch sometime and compare notes."

"Sure." The male reporter watched Vanessa and Hank walk off together toward the coffee shop on the corner before shrugging. "When hell freezes over."

Hope was torn between following her father, to shut him up about the pitiable past she'd overcome, and retreating to the shop to hide from his lies. But the second reporter raised his camera again and she put up her hands to shield her face. "Don't. Please."

"Fair enough." He lowered his camera and pulled out a pad and pen. "Gabriel Knight, *Kansas City Journal*. I got the shot I needed. Unlike my colleague Ms. Owen, I'm not into sensationalism. I'm all about getting the real story." His blue eyes seemed to size her up and find her wanting. "So KCPD finally has a witness who's going to wrap up this fiasco of an investigation for them."

"Fiasco?" The urge to defend the people she was helping proved stronger than the desire to flee. "The task force has made huge strides in identifying the rapist." She repeated one of the talking points Kate Kilpatrick and Detective Montgomery had given her to share. "I'm just one little cog in the wheel that represents all the hard work they've done to protect this city."

"That task force has been pursuing their serial rapist for over a year now. Where are their results? Why isn't a picture of the man you saw splashed all over my front page?"

"I didn't get that good a look at him. The sketch artist's picture wasn't...conclusive. It could start a panic. People might start turning in any man on the street who vaguely fits the description." Hope curled her toes inside her pumps, standing her ground when Gabe Knight tapped his pen on the edge of his notepad before he wrote down whatever observation he'd just made about her.

"But *you* could identify him if you saw him again." His piercing gaze reminded her of the intensity of another pair of eyes, leaving Hope feeling vulnerable, defenseless.

Lying didn't come easily under that challenge. "I think so."

"And the van?"

"Absolutely."

But the reporter was shaking his head. "There's something more going on here. What aren't you telling me?"

She'd spent the whole morning battling Vanessa's questions, and after a few minutes, this man had already done more to rattle her composure. "What do you mean?"

The reporter narrowed his gaze as though studying her through a microscope. "What makes you so special? What secrets are you hiding?"

"I'm not hiding anything." A movement in the corner of her eye turned her attention to the floral shop across the street. Leon Hundley was there in his green uniform shirt, carrying a tray of flower arrangements out to the delivery van. He'd stopped his work, no doubt watching the parade of people in and out of her shop. When their eyes met, he set the tray in the back of his van and took a couple of steps toward her. But his attention turned up the street and he stopped. A moment later, Pike's black-and-white K-9 unit truck was pulling into the parking lot beside her.

But Gabe Knight seemed oblivious of Leon's concerned interest or the brawny uniformed cop climbing out of the truck he'd hastily parked. "A woman who calls her father 'Hank' and hates seeing him walk away with a reporter as much as she hates seeing him at all? There's a story there."

"You were spying on me?" Goose bumps scattered over Hope's skin as she swept her gaze up and down the street. She felt eyes on her even now, and she hated it. The lights, the reporters, her father, her friends...and someone else. *He* was watching her. But from where? Who was he? Someone on the street? Someone hidden? Someone she knew?

"The press conference is done, Knight." Pike loomed up behind the reporter, the broad shoulders of his black uniform dwarfing the other man. "No more questions."

"Pike." Relief crashed through Hope, and she reached for his hand as he came around to stand beside her. She didn't realize how badly she'd been shaking until she felt the anchor of Pike Taylor's grip closing around hers. "I'm glad you're here."

His sharp blue gaze ran over her face. "You okay, honey? Did this guy upset you?"

Honey. Right. He wasn't here to pull her back from the brink of another panic attack. He was here to play the part of the concerned fiancé.

Disappointment joined the roller coaster of emotions that left her feeling drained. But when she extricated her hand from the false comfort of Pike's grasp, he draped his arm around her shoulders and hugged her to his side, as if sensing her retreating into her shell or getting ready to run. "You're cold." When she didn't respond, Pike turned his interrogation on the reporter. "Are you pestering my fiancée, Knight? She agreed to give a statement to the press, but she doesn't have to answer any questions she doesn't want to."

The wall of heat pressed against Hope felt as foreign

as the hard shell of the flak vest Pike wore beneath his shirt. And the crisp, starchy scent of his uniform was more basically male and more enticing than the eye-watering potency of Brian Elliott's cologne had been. Yet the same intriguing sensations that left her feeling so unsettled and out of her depth seemed to fill her with strength and a quieting sense of calm, as well. They didn't have to be a real couple. She could accept comfort from a friend, couldn't she? She could latch onto this much-needed support from her partner on this mission. Slowly, she wrapped her arm behind his waist and leaned against Pike's treelike strength. She was as aware of the gun and handcuffs and other survival equipment strapped to his belt as she was the tapered waist and abundant heat emanating from the man himself. Next to this man, she was safe.

Despite the protective shield of Pike's arm around her, Gabe Knight still didn't seem to be in any hurry to leave. "I have one last question, Officer Taylor."

"What's that?"

The reporter looked up to Pike and down to Hope, then farther down to the hand she clutched at her side. "If you two are engaged, where's her ring?"

Pike's grip tightened on her shoulder, the only indication that he'd been caught off guard by Knight's question. But with eyes watching and her eagerness to get rid of the reporter combining with her determination to get past this crippling timidity, Hope blurted out, "It's at the jewelry store, getting resized."

Pike squeezed her shoulder again, perhaps out of gratitude this time, as he followed her lead. "That's right. It's my grandmother's ring."

Hope flared her fingers in front of her face. "She had small hands."

"I see." Gabriel Knight tucked his pen and pad back inside his jacket. His expression as to whether he believed the ruse or not was hard to read. "Congratulations to you both. I look forward to seeing the announcement in our paper. May I?" Before either of them could answer, he'd raised his camera again and snapped a picture of Hope and Pike standing side by side. "I'll send you a copy." With a nod in lieu of a goodbye, he turned and climbed into a silver SUV sedan parked beside the curb. "So many secrets."

Holding her breath, holding on to Pike, until the last intrusion on her morning drove away, Hope finally inhaled a deep breath that pushed against him. "What does he mean by that? Do you think he knows what we're doing?"

Letting her pull away, though taking her hand so she couldn't immediately leave, Pike turned to face her. "Knight's a sharp one. If he senses there's more to a story, he'll be relentless in uncovering it. Plus, he's been supercritical of KCPD's handling of the Rose Red Rapist case."

"Why?"

Pike pulled off his ball cap and smoothed his hand over his hair. "I don't know. Something makes it personal for him."

Hope trembled at the idea of one more person keeping a closer watch on her than she'd like. "Do you think he'll blow our cover and tip off your unsub?"

The breeze caught a loose tendril of hair and blew it onto Hope's forehead. But Pike's hand was there to smooth it back into place. "We won't let him, okay? What's this?" He traced the same finger along her throat to the notch of her collarbone, tickling her skin as he took note of the extra couple of inches of skin she was showing. "You're changing your looks on me."

He'd noticed the difference of a button and a belt? She hoped that was a good thing. "I was studying other women today, trying to emulate how they dressed and acted around men. I'm trying to be more convincing as your bride to be."

"You did great with Gabe Knight just now. I'm kicking myself that we didn't think of a ring to go with our cover story."

Just then the door to her shop swung open and Nelda Sapphire came running out. Well, *running* was a relative term, considering the way she shuffled down the street in those high platform heels. "Hank! You get back here!" Nelda ran right past them with nary a look or word of acknowledgment. Instead, she clutched her bag beneath her breasts and shuffled it into double time. "Where is he going with that woman? You're not leaving me! You owe me!"

The cursing blonde climbed into her compact car and made a U-turn to follow Hope's father down the street. Pike thumbed toward the car as she drove past. "Promise me you'll never change to that extreme."

Hope drew in an easier breath and smiled with him. "I won't. I couldn't handle the shoes."

Pike's laughter faded as he tucked his cap into his back pocket and settled his hands at the nip of her waist. He pulled her half a step closer, dipping his face toward hers to whisper, "Seriously, though. Are you okay? I had no idea the reporters would still be here. Nick gave me a call and said you had some hangers-on. When he described your dad and Blondie there showing up, Hans and I booked it back over here."

"Hans is in the truck, I'm assuming?" Hope debated

where to rest her hands in order to complete this public embrace for whatever audience they had. Her hands bobbed from Pike's shoulders to his biceps and finally came to rest against the Kevlar armor on his chest.

He nodded. "You didn't answer me. How are you doing?"

She stared straight ahead at the contrast of her pale hands against his black shirt. "Pretty well, I think. I haven't run away or pulled a knife on anyone—yet." Instead of laughing at the joke, Pike fiddled with that stray curl again, silently waiting for her to continue. "I said everything Dr. Kilpatrick and Detective Montgomery asked me to. I'll be on television and in the newspapers. The whole city is going to know who I am now. *He's* going to know."

Hope was decidedly uncomfortable standing in the circle of Pike's arms in front of her shop where anyone on the block could see them. And while his abundant heat and gentle hands excited something feminine and fascinating and unfamiliar in her blood, it was the movements and shadows in windows and vehicles along the street that really made her nervous.

"Do you feel it?" She voiced the tension humming through her.

"Feel what?"

"Someone watching." She tipped her head back to see his sharp gaze swinging back and forth. He was looking, too. "Do you think I'm paranoid?"

That clear blue gaze settled on her. "No. I've felt it, too. Since moving in last night. Like we're living in a glass house. Someone's got to be watching the place to know when they can drop off those creepy gifts without me seeing him or Hans hearing him. But just the same..." His hands tightened at her waist and he pulled her into his chest, winding his arms behind her back and resting his chin at the crown of her head.

Her arms caught between them and she whispered against the KCPD logo embroidered on his chest, "Did you see someone? What do you need me to do?"

"Easy, partner. I need you to let me hold you for a minute. I need to know that you're safe and that this isn't the craziest idea KCPD ever had." Pike's fingers slipped into the hair at the nape of her neck and tugged several curls from the clip she wore. Then they tunneled beneath to cup her head and pull her more snugly against him. "Okay?"

Hope nodded. She willed herself to relax against him. "I'm okay with that."

And then she realized it didn't take any will at all to turn her cheek to the strong beat of his heart. She didn't have to think twice about sliding her arms around his waist and drifting closer to the imprint of his harder hips and thighs against her body. Her breasts pillowed against the wall of Kevlar and man and she had no desire to run away from the comfort and strength he provided.

Pike's shoulders seemed to fold around her, blocking out the things that frightened her. He rubbed his chin against her hair and pressed a soft kiss to her temple. "You're not alone, Hope. It's you and me, remember? This guy's going to try to come after you, but he won't get to you, understand? I won't let him."

Whatever the reason behind this show of support, Hope curled her fingers into the back of his shirt and held on. She needed to feel safe for a few moments. She needed to know she'd made the right decision to agree to helping the police.

She needed to hear him say it again, in that deep, husky voice that danced across her eardrums and soothed the fear from her heart. "You're not alone."

Chapter Eight

"I don't like it." Pike squatted down in front of the shattered windowpane in the vestibule at the bridal shop. Hans was right there in his business, too, sniffing the broken glass littering the floor, whining in his throat as Pike pulled his flashlight from the back pocket of his jeans. Those dark brown eyes were trying to tell him something about what had happened here, but nothing beyond the signs of a routine break-in were making the dog's message any clearer. "What is it, boy?"

Hans sat and dipped his nose toward the corner where the frame around the busted pane met the adjoining brick wall. The dog's long black muzzle moved closer and closer to the dangerous shards of glass—a strong enough hit on something that Pike swung his light around and leaned in closer.

The nose never missed a trick. There was a stain of viscous red liquid clinging to an arrow point of glass protruding from the window frame. "Our guy cut himself."

Pike snapped a few pictures with his cell phone and texted them in with the report he'd made earlier. Then he patted the dog's flank and pushed to his feet, drawing the shepherd away from the crime scene. "Good boy." He bent down to ruffle up his fur before pulling the dog back into the shop. The intruder's injury probably wasn't the main reason he'd aborted the break-in. "You did good, Hansie. Bad Guy didn't get in. You did real good."

Hope was standing inside in the darkness of the closed shop, still wearing her trench coat and hugging her arms around her waist. "The one hour we were gone for pizza is when somebody breaks in? He's definitely watching the place."

"I know." Pike unhooked Hans's leash and harness and tossed him a crunchy treat from the pocket of the canvas jacket he wore. "I know it's what we were hoping for, but I hate to say it. Our man's taken the bait."

At her audible gasp, Pike reached over to flip on a light switch to flood the store with light and hopefully alleviate some of Hope's fear. Just as he'd imagined, she was pale as a ghost and keeping a wary eye on Hans to see where the dog settled down to enjoy his snack. But then those lake-gray eyes moved back to him, and he could see that, although she was rightfully concerned, she wasn't on the verge of wigging out on him as she had done in the past. "I did a quick walk-through while you two were outside. It doesn't look like anything has been taken or vandalized."

Not for the first time, he wondered exactly what had happened in her past to cause those panic attacks, and what it took for her to control them. He knew one thing, though, the woman was a fighter. Whatever he, KCPD, her father, those damn reporters or the Rose Red Rapist himself threw at her, she kept coming back for more. Pike never would have expected that kind of tenacity from such a shy, feminine woman. But he admired it. He liked it.

He was beginning to notice and appreciate a few too many things about the neighborhood spinster. Things that kept distracting him from the idea that this was an assignment he was working on, not his "let's be friends with everyone 'cause you got no game" love life.

But when he zeroed in on the patient expectation behind Hope's glasses, he remembered she was looking to him for protection and guidance through this undercover op, not another kissing lesson.

"Hans tracked the scent to the sidewalk across the street, but we lost the trail. The perp probably climbed into a vehicle and drove north. It'd be easy to get lost in city traffic if anyone did spot him." Pike shed his jacket and rolled up the sleeves of his chambray shirt, physically reminding himself that this was work. He propped open the door and took a closer look at the mess they'd come back to. Whatever the intruder had been after, he hadn't gotten through the newly replaced lock that led up to Hope's apartment, or through the second door that led into her shop. The most likely reason the perp had turned tail and run was stretched out on his belly and licking treat crumbs off the tile floor. "I'm guessing Hans scared him off. He's a better deterrent than your alarm system." He aimed the flashlight at the wire tacked to the molding beside the door. "Which looks like it's been cut. Camera's out, too."

"And we're sure it's him?" Her voice was closer now and he turned to find Hope standing in the shop doorway, holding a broom and dustpan, ready to keep moving forward. Definitely a fighter. But Pike had seen the worst the Rose Red Rapist and his accomplice could do. No matter how tenacious Hope might be, she didn't stand a chance on her own against them. Pike needed to make her understand that she was part of a team.

"Sorry." He took the broom and dustpan and set them just inside the door. "We'll have to wait for the CSIs to secure that blood sample, dust for prints and check for any other trace before we can clean up."

"Oh. Right." She plunged her hands inside the pockets of her coat, marked where Hans was lying and that the dog was stationary and headed over to the counter, where she pulled down a long ivory dress and carried it toward the fitting rooms. "Then I'll finish cleaning up in here while we wait."

Inhaling a deep breath, Pike resigned himself to his most difficult challenge yet, and followed her across the shop. "Hold up, Hope." He came up behind her in the mirror. He settled his hands lightly at her waist and looked at their reflection in the mirror. She hugged the simple, lacy dress in front of her and met his gaze in the mirror. He liked how the deep V of the neckline would reveal an enticing bit of skin, but the lace on top would keep her all covered up and ladylike. "You'd look beautiful in this."

A rosy hue of self-consciousness crept up her neck and warmed her cheeks. "Thank you." She blushed beautifully, without any false modesty, and he added that to the growing list of things he liked about this woman. He even kind of liked the rush he got, knowing something he said or did could cause all that pretty, porcelain skin to turn rosy. "Have you ever worn a tux?"

He nodded above her head. "Just once. My brother Alex's wedding."

"I bet you made a handsome figure all dressed up like that."

Pike chuckled. "Except for that noose of a tie and the shoes that pinched my feet, it wasn't altogether the worst wardrobe experience I've ever had."

"You're not a suit-and-tie kind of guy?"

Although he still wore his gun and badge on his belt, the jeans and work boots he wore now were pretty much the only uniform he had outside of his black KCPD regs. Unless he was truly off duty. Then it'd be running or fishing gear. "How'd you figure that out?"

Her lips softly pouted together when she smiled and something hitched inside him. Oh, yeah, he wouldn't mind a little more schooling in *that* department. But, tempting as it was to uncover a little more of the innocent passion hiding behind the spinster facade, Pike had something more important they needed to accomplish first.

"I think we need to have another lesson." He heard her breath catch when he reached around her to take the gown and drape it over the sofa.

"On what?"

"Trust. And what we can do to keep you safe."

She spun around with an apology stamped on her face. "I don't blame you for the attempted break-in. I know it takes me a little while to relax around new people, but I trust you."

Pike reached for her hand. "I need you to trust my partner, too."

Hope planted her feet and pulled against his grip. "I don't know if I'm comfortable—"

"Shh."

Hope's eyes widened like twin moons as he turned his head and whistled. Hans jumped to his feet and loped across the shop. His toenails clicked on the hard tile floor.

"Come on, boy. Up." Pike tapped his chest and the beast rose on his hind legs and propped two tawny paws on Pike's shoulders. He panted with excitement as Pike rubbed his hands along Hans's jowls and neck. "I always think he looks like he's smiling when I do that."

Sadly, the instant he'd released Hope's hand to pet the dog, Hope had darted away to hide behind the trio of mirrors. "Dogs don't smile."

"One step forward and two steps back, eh, buddy?" Pike's shoulders lifted with a deep breath. In a firmer tone, he pushed the dog down and ordered him to sit. Then he brushed off his hands and turned to Hope. "Come here. Hans is part of this undercover op, too, so we have to do this."

Hope couldn't seem to release her grip on the mirror. "Have to?"

"He won't hurt you. I promise." Pike held out his hand, asking her to trust him with this, too. He stretched his arm out farther. "He's part of your protection team, Hope. I need Hans to be able to do more than guard the place when we're gone. If, for some reason, I can't be there when you need me, Hans is my backup."

"Why wouldn't you be there…?" There was no blush on those pale cheeks now. "Oh."

He was her first line of defense. But he wasn't her only line of defense. "Hans doesn't know how to quit. If something happens to me, he'll protect you."

He waited patiently, never taking his eyes from hers. His patience paid off when she finally moved away from the mirror and laid her palm against his. He bit down on the urge to say, *Good girl,* and curled his fingers around hers to pull her up beside him, not two feet from the watchful eyes and black muzzle with all those teeth that seemed to terrify her.

Pike started talking before Hope's fear took hold and she ran from him again. "It's smart not to approach a dog you're unfamiliar with. But I know Hans and how he behaves. A dog's owner or handler should always clue you in on a dog's behavior before you jump in to pet him or play with him."

"That makes sense."

"Curl your fingers into a fist and let him sniff your scent before you try to touch him." Pike demonstrated what he wanted her to do. But when the dog's long red tongue slopped out over Pike's fist, Hope jumped back, digging her fingers into Pike's forearm as she ducked behind him. Hans's midnight-brown eyes shifted to her jerky movements and she retreated another step. But Pike pulled her right back to his side and the dog turned his attention back to him. "Most dogs bite because they're startled, not because they're inherently aggressive. Some breeds do attach their loyalty to one person or pack unit, and can be protective, but most of them will simply avoid or ignore an outsider unless you startle him or threaten his person or pack in some way."

Hope squeezed her hand more tightly around Pike's grip. "But some guard dogs *do* attack."

"If that's what they're trained to do. Unless he's got some mental defect, with enough time and consistency, and if they've been properly socialized, pretty much any dog can be trained to behave the way you want him to. So whether he's a safe dog or a danger to others usually depends on the owner." When she didn't respond, Pike leaned closer and nudged his shoulder against hers. "I'm thinking maybe you haven't been properly socialized, either."

A deep breath eased from Hope and she bumped him back, understanding he was teasing her. "Are you training me like the dog?"

"It's what I know how to do. Hans, *steh*." The dog lurched to his feet and Hope darted behind Pike. Her fingers clawed into the back of his shirt, and Pike's skin jumped where the ten needy imprints dug in. For a split second he was aware of breasts and grabbing hands and Hope's warm body clinging to his. But despite the instant, thumping urge that heated his blood, Pike made himself stand rock-still. He spoke to her in the same calm, articulate voice he'd used with the dog. "Now you tell him to lie down."

Her fingers tightened above his belt.

"Say his name and the command in a firm voice. You don't need to yell, just be succinct."

"He won't listen to me."

"The command is 'Hans, *platz*.'"

The big German shepherd tilted his head to one side, as though questioning who Pike was giving the command to. "Hans, *platz*," Hope whispered into the back of his shirt.

Pike reached behind him and pulled Hope in front of him. "You'll have to say it so he can hear you."

The dog was looking up at her now. And though she backed that sweet, round bottom right against his groin, Pike resisted the urge to do more than cup Hope's shoulders and encourage her to try again.

"Hans. *Platz*." Hope repeated the command in a stronger voice.

With what looked like a nod of his large, masked face, Hans stretched out on the floor at her feet. The warm vanilla scent of Hope's hair swept past Pike's nose when she tilted her head back to beam a smile at him. "He did it."

Pike squeezed her shoulders before moving to stand beside her. "Now reward him for obeying."

"How?"

"Treats. Playing a game—although I don't think

you're ready for tug-of-war quite yet." Pike squatted down beside Hope and mussed the dog's fur on top of his head. "Or pet him."

"I can't."

Pike tugged her down to her knees beside him. "You're the bravest woman I know, Hope. If you can stand up to the Rose Red Rapist, you can pet ol' Hansie here."

While she processed that reassurance, Pike placed her hand on top of Hans's head, and using his fingers to guide hers, showed Hope how to pet the warm, furry head.

"Easy." Stroke once. Again. "That's it. Did you know that petting a dog is supposed to lower your blood pressure?"

"I doubt they'd want to include me in that medical study." Despite the sarcasm, she took over the gentle massage, and Pike gradually pulled his hand away.

"He's warm like you," Hope observed, continuing the gentle strokes on her own. "Hairier, of course."

"I hope so."

"And his ears are so soft." Hope's grip on Pike's knee eased as she lengthened her strokes out to the dog's shoulder. Although Hans was panting lightly, he seemed to enjoy the tentative massage. "We had two dogs when I was little. Short-haired. Bigger than Hans." She swallowed hard and her fingers pinched his knee again. "Maybe because I was a little girl, they seemed bigger than they really were."

Was she opening up to him about whatever had triggered this phobia of dogs? Pike brushed a tawny curl away from Hope's cheek, silently urging her to continue. "What were their names?"

Pike felt the tension radiating off her. Hans sensed

it, too, judging by the whine in his throat. Her fingers twitched in Hans's fur. "Hank called them the baby-sitters."

His fingers stilled at her temple. Little girl. Big dogs. *Babysitters?* His gaze dropped to the scars on her wrist. He had a very bad feeling about where this conversation was going. "And?"

Her vision glazed over. Her hands clenched into fists. *Ah, hell.*

Sensing the change in the woman petting him, Hans raised his head, pushing his cold wet nose against Hope's arm. Pike saw curiosity, concern. But when Hans stretched his mouth open in a yawn, exposing those long rows of teeth, Hope saw something else.

"No, Jack!" She jerked back as a memory surfaced and terror consumed her. She tumbled into Pike, knocking him on his rear. "Stop!"

"Hope? What the…? Who's Jack? Hans, *bleib!*"

The dog froze, but Hope was moving. She pushed at Pike's shoulders, scrambling to her feet, fleeing toward the nearest door.

Pike got to his feet and grabbed her hand. "It's okay. You were doing great. Hans was liking it. That was a yawn. He's relaxing."

"I'm not." She swung around, punching at his wrist to free herself. "Let me go!"

"Hope?" Her eyes were wild, her skin flushed, her movements pure panic. "Hope!" She fisted her hand again. Enough. For both their sakes, Pike cinched his arms around hers like a straitjacket, lifting her off the floor, snugging her right up against his chest and pinning her while she shoved and twisted against him. Even though she lost one high heel, her kicking feet were still doing some damage. One caught Pike between the shins and tripped him onto the couch. Taking advantage of the opportunity, Pike rolled into the deep leather cushions, cocooning her thrashing body between his and the back of the couch. He put his lips against her ear and whispered her name. "Shh. Honey, you're all right. Hope? Hope."

"Stop it!" she yelled at whatever demon pursued her. "Please!" she wailed. Her running legs tangled with his. Her pounding hands fisted in his shirt. "Don't—"

Pike caught Hope's face between his hands and closed his mouth over hers. Something desperate, something clever and maybe something completely selfish had flashed through him as her fear turned into sobs. He wasted no time with a patient tutorial. He forced her lips apart and plunged inside—giving, taking, demanding. The initial shock of the kiss snapped her out of the panic and stilled her struggles.

Hope's deep gray eyes opened and locked onto his. His breath steamed through his nose as he lifted his mouth to ensure that she was back in the present. Here. With him. Not afraid.

In the next breath, a very different sort of urgency erupted between them. Hope wound her arms around Pike's neck and pulled him back into the kiss. Her chest and hips slid against his, seeking the full body contact he'd forced on her moments earlier.

Pike thrust his tongue inside her hot, open mouth, drinking in her eager welcome. He palmed her butt and twisted them to a more comfortable position on the couch, with her lying partly beneath him, giving his hands easier access to discover all the secrets of her lush, womanly body. While her lips skidded across his jaw, sampling a taste here, experimenting with a nip there, Pike freed the rest of her hair from its confining clip and sifted the silky tresses through his greedy fingers.

"What should I do?" she whispered in a moist, breathy caress against his neck that sent an electric current straight down to the south side of his belt buckle. She closed her teeth gently around his earlobe and Pike groaned at the delicate maneuver that was somehow shy and bold at the same time. "Is that okay?"

"Oh, yeah, honey." He kissed her lips again, praised her, thanked her. "Told you you were a natural."

While her fingers roamed curiously across his shoulders and chest, Pike worked his gun from its holster and set it safely on the floor beside them. He went back to remove her glasses, and her eyes widened like beautiful lakes warmed by the stars. "You're liking this, too, right? I mean you'd tell me if—"

He silenced the foolish protest with another kiss, telling her with his lips and hands and hardening body just how much he was liking what she was doing to him. Pike hoped to God she knew the difference between those intimacies they'd done for show and the serious reality that was happening between them right now.

Any sampling of her shy kisses, any suspicion about her hidden curves and beauty, was coming to life and going far beyond his expectations with each needy grab of her hands, each stroke of her tongue that grew bolder and bolder against his, each soft groan of pleasure that hummed in her throat. His pulse thundered in his ears. His fingers burned to discover every inch of her. He was a thirsty man, getting drunk on the finest whiskey that no other man had been privileged enough to taste.

He vaguely remembered the panic that had set them on this course—the dog, the break-in, the tension that must have been simmering between them for months. There was only now. Here. Hope.

And it wasn't enough. Sliding his hands down between them, Pike loosened the belt and buttons of her coat and pushed it open. He smiled against her mouth as he met the soft wool of her suit jacket. He unhooked that belt and worked the buttons free. Her fingers were in his hair as he uncovered the layer of cotton blouse. Pike moaned his frustration and stole another kiss before resolutely attacking the buttons there. And then he was sliding his hand inside and palming one of those full, beautiful breasts. He squeezed at the silk and lace covering it until it poked to attention and drew his lips toward the tempting peak.

"You're so pretty, Hope." She gasped when he closed his mouth over the pebbled nipple, wetting it through the slip and bra she wore. "So, so pretty."

She arched against him, then quickly drew back, no doubt discovering the eager bulge behind his zipper. "I don't know what… I can't even think. I want…"

"It's okay, honey. You can touch me." Her instincts were good. She'd already unbuttoned his shirt and slipped her hand inside to brand his skin. "Do whatever you want. Or if this is going too fast, we'll stop right now.

"But you…" Her hand drifted down his side and cupped his hip. A few inches closer and she could finish him with a hand job. Pike groaned in anticipation but held himself still. He wouldn't push her. He wouldn't do anything that might frighten Hope and spoil this perfect moment. "You're…" Her face colored a beautiful shade of pink. "…ready."

Oh, man, was that an understatement! But there was

something equally important going on here. That trust he'd always wanted from her was growing stronger.

"I won't break, remember?" He tunneled his fingers into her hair again, loving how dusky and pretty her eyes looked up close like this. "I can stop. You're driving me crazy, but the timing's not right. Not yet," he promised, in case she was thinking, for one naive moment, that he didn't want her with every fiber of his being. He gathered the blouse and suit and coat together and pulled them over her. "Not yet."

Her fingers fumbled at the buttons of his shirt, trying to do her part to ease the throttle back a couple of notches between them, but failing miserably. "I'm driving *you* crazy?"

He laughed at the incredulous statement coming from those delectable, kiss-stung lips. "My brother says I haven't got any game when it comes to women. I'm better with dogs and fish and my hunting rifle." He caught her hand and stilled the distracting fingers against his chest. "But you, Miss Thing, are a real talent."

"Your brother's wrong." The knot furrowing between her eyebrows told him Hope was dead serious with that compliment, and Pike leaned in to kiss the worry spot. "You can be very charming," she insisted.

Maybe to a thirty-two-year-old virgin with panic attacks and trust issues who was just now discovering her sexuality.

But Pike's grin faded when a telephone rang.

"Is that yours or mine?" Hope patted her clothes, but with her trench coat and jacket tangled between them, she was having trouble even locating her pockets as the phone rang again. "It's mine."

Pike was content to cuddle and hold on to the connection beyond their task force mission he and Hope had just made. "Let it go."

"At this hour?" Her cheeks were flushed again, and she was pushing at his chest and the couch behind her, struggling to sit up. "It's my life intruding. My stupid past keeps trying to ruin any chance I have at a future."

He felt the vibration of her phone against his thigh and eased out a weary sigh. The moment that had just happened between them was gone. Forgetting his own discomfort, he swung his feet to the floor and sat up. "What does that mean?"

She shot to her feet as the phone rang a fourth time. "Someday, Pike, you'll find out what a sad, screwed-up life I have."

"Had," he corrected, pulling her phone from her coat pocket and handing it to her before she could find it. "There's nothing wrong with you."

She answered on the fifth ring. "Damn it, Hank! Leave me alone—"

Hope's entire body went suddenly and utterly still.

Pike was on his feet in an instant, sliding an arm behind her waist and lowering his ear to listen to the mechanically disguised voice on the line. "Who's Hank?" The tinny voice laughed. "And here I thought you were a good girl. You're an opportunistic slut, just like the rest of them." There was an ominous pause. "You be careful."

When a click ended the call, Hope collapsed against him. "Pike?"

"Get in the dressing rooms and stay out of sight." He took the phone from her and tucked it into her pocket before shutting her inside. Then he scooped up his gun from the floor and ran to kill the lights, check the doors and peer through the windows to account for every car, pedestrian and window with potential eyes on Hope's shop.

He saw nothing suspicious, no one showing more interest in Fairy Tale Bridal than they should. But he could feel it in his bones that that pervert had been watching them on the couch, that he was watching the place right now—that he'd taken a shy woman's hard-won sense of confidence and composure and shaken it right down to the ground.

Pike glanced back at the long leather couch, feeling a little shaken himself at how fast and how far Hope Lockhart had gotten under his skin. But he made the man recede and the cop in him take over. Finishing the sweep, he holstered his weapon and pulled out his cell to call the task force leader.

The senior detective picked up on the first ring. "Yes?"

"Montgomery? Pike Taylor." Hearing the noise of precinct HQ in the background, Pike checked his watch. It was just after eleven o'clock. Didn't the guy ever sleep? Pike wasn't sure he could now. "He's on the hook. He's coming for her." No need to clarify the unsub they were talking about. "He just called and threatened Hope."

"I'll notify the others. Nick and Annie are already en route to process the scene. I'll be there ASAP."

"No. You can't send in the cavalry yet. Remember? Too big of a police presence may scare this guy off. Let's just address the break-in with a routine response."

"But if that blood you mentioned matches the DNA in our system—"

"It'll match. It's his. I know it is."

"Then let me send—"

"No. The guy is long gone. Hans can track him by scent now, and he's not here."

"Are you sure you don't want more backup?"

"I'm sure. I'm not putting Hope through this for nothing. If he goes underground and we don't catch this guy now, she'll never be able to stop looking over her shoulder."

"How's she holding up?"

"Like a champ, given the circumstances." Pike's long strides carried him quickly back to the dressing rooms. He trailed his fingers along the smooth leather on the back of the couch, slowing his steps, then stopping— processing what his instincts were trying to tell him. With the height and angle of that couch, the perp shouldn't have been able to see anything from the street or parking lot once he and Hope had stretched out together. Either the two of them making out was a lucky assumption on the caller's part, or...

"Make sure Annie brings something to sweep for hidden cameras, too. We may have a spy right here in the shop." Pike thought about the funny little guy who'd been flirting with Hope that first day. He turned toward the flower shop across the street where the guy worked. What was his name? Leon? Hope said he'd been doing odd jobs around here for months. How easy would it have been for him to hide a camera in here? Pike raised his gaze to the ceiling above him. Would Leon have access to Hope's apartment, too?

Hope was waiting anxiously for him at the dressing room door as soon as he pushed it open. Her clothes were rebuttoned, cinched up tight. But she'd lost the clip for her hair, and the long curls fanned around her shoulders, leaving Pike with the impression she didn't have all her protective emotional armor back in place yet, either. "Is help coming?" she asked.

Pike reached for her hand and she squeezed both of hers around his. "Don't send any backup," Pike repeated, for Hope's understanding as well as the detective's. "Not yet. He's taken the bait, but he's not in our trap yet."

"Roger that." As irritated as Spencer Montgomery sounded at being ordered by a younger officer to stay away from a crime scene, the senior detective let Pike take point on this. "We'll keep our distance. But call for backup the instant you need us. In the meantime, do your job, Taylor."

That went without saying.

"Yes, sir. Hans, *pass auf!*" Holding hands wasn't good enough. He verified Hans was standing guard at the door before pulling Hope into his chest and wrapping his arm around her. Her arms snaked around his waist to hold on and he pressed a kiss to the crown of her hair. "We'll keep her safe."

Chapter Nine

Hope would never have imagined that she could be afraid inside a church. Nor would she ever have expected to see Pike Taylor being afraid of anything besides sticking his oversize foot in his mouth.

But he'd been reluctant to let her leave the shop after lunch. *"There won't be anyone around to keep an eye on you,"* he'd argued.

"No," she'd gently corrected him. *"You and Hans won't be there to protect me. But I won't be alone."*

And she wasn't. Hope had her bride-to-be client, the client's mother, the minister, her friend Robin Lonergan to consult on floral arrangements and Leon Hundley, one of Robin's employees, at the church with her.

The planning meeting for the client's summer wedding was going smoothly. Everyone had shown up on time. There'd been no strange requests and the autumn sun outside was bright enough to illuminate the interior of the spacious sanctuary without turning on any lights.

And yet Hope couldn't shake the idea that there was someone else here with them—someone moving through the denuded trees and orange-red shrubs swaying in the breeze outside the church windows, peeking in, or clinging to the shadows in the farthest corners of the building where the sunlight couldn't reach.

Hope startled when a branch scraped against the window near the end of the pew where she was sitting. And even though she should be taking notes about what floral displays the church would allow in the sanctuary, her attention fixed on the movement outside until she saw the mourning dove that had landed in the tree and shaken the branch suddenly take flight again.

Her brave words from that morning might come back to haunt her. Even with the German shepherd beside him, a tall, rugged cop on the premises right about now would go a long way toward dispelling this anxiety that fueled her imagination. *"Just like you told Detective Montgomery. I can't have cops around me all the time, or we'll scare this guy off. And you have to patrol the neighborhood like you do every other day or he might suspect we're up to something. Try not to worry, Pike. I'll be surrounded by people the entire time I'm gone, or I'll be in my car."*

"Try not to worry, she says." Pike had reached into her coat pocket and pulled out her phone. He punched in his number and put the phone back in her hands. *"Call me when you leave the church and come straight home. I'll meet you here. And if you sense anything hinky while you're away from me, call. Push one number and I'll answer."*

She'd nodded, touched by his concern. Then he'd palmed the back of her neck and pulled her onto her toes to plant a hard, quick, very personal kiss on her mouth. And there hadn't even been an audience except for the omnipresent dog.

"I'll be here." And he had been until she'd given

directions to her assistant running the shop, and had driven away.

Hope could still feel that kiss. The same way she could still feel the arousing heat of his hands moving over her body from the night before, and remember how uniquely different and altogether exciting the hardness of his long, lean body had felt beneath her exploring hands.

She was learning just how seriously the man took his job, and she truly believed she couldn't have been assigned a more skilled and dedicated protector. She could even understand the logic behind his repeated efforts to help her get along with Hans.

So where did that make-out session on the couch last night fit in? Even she wasn't so naive to think that had been part of their undercover charade. But was the passion that had flared between them just a case of convenience? A man got horny and she got curious enough to test the simmering sexual needs she'd kept buried inside her for far too long? Or was there something more tender, more caring evolving out of the friendship she and Edison Pike Taylor were forging between them?

Another flurry of movement, from the center aisle of the church this time, stirred Hope from her thoughts. Their meeting was breaking up. People were leaving. With one more glance toward the window, she stood to say goodbye to her clients and assure them she had their next appointment in her planner.

While the minister walked the two women out, Robin summoned her assistant from the back of the church. "Leon, would you take those sample arrangements back to the van while we finish up the paperwork?"

"Yes, ma'am." Leon strolled to the front of the church

and started packing the decorative arrangements into boxes and stacking them up on a dolly.

Robin tucked her short dark hair behind her ears before carrying a spray of silk carnations up to the altar to set them into one of the boxes before Leon finished up. "Oh, and my husband and daughter are coming to pick me up here, so you can head on back to the shop. I know you worked over lunch to help me set up here, so unless Shirley has any new deliveries that need to go out, go ahead and take the rest of the evening off."

"Will do." Leon closed the top box and pulled his uniform cap from his hip pocket. "Thanks, Ms. Carter." His neck reddened above the collar of the green company shirt he wore. "Er, I mean Mrs. Lonergan."

"That's okay, Leon," Robin assured him. "I'm still getting used to the name change myself."

"Yes, ma'am." He settled the green cap over his short dark hair and winked to Hope. "See you later."

"Okay." She smiled back and then gathered her notebook and color cards and dropped them into her tote bag.

"You were a million miles away." Robin waited at the end of the pew for Hope to join her.

"I wish. Sorry if I got distracted at the end there. I got stuck inside my head, overthinking things."

Robin linked her arm through Hope's as they followed Leon out. "What are you worried about? Surely not this wedding?"

"Not at all." At the task force's request, to ensure that the truth of what they were doing wouldn't accidentally get out, Hope hadn't been allowed to share the details of their operation with even her best friend. But Robin had to know there'd been some big changes in Hope's life recently. Surely, it wouldn't hurt to share a little of why she was so distracted these days. "Someone broke into my shop last night. Disabled the alarm system and the camera."

"Oh, my gosh. Are you okay? Was anything stolen?"

"I'm fine."

"You should have told me."

Hope grinned as she pushed open the front door of the church and headed down the concrete steps to the parking lot. "Oh, right. I've been a third wheel my whole life, Robin. You and Jake haven't even been married a month. Like I'm going to be the one to interrupt your honeymoon." She squeezed Robin's arm, letting her know she didn't feel slighted in the least by her friend's preoccupation with her new husband and adopted daughter. "Besides, I think the dog on the premises scared the intruder away."

"That's right. The scenery at your shop has changed recently. Officer Taylor sure has been hanging around a lot." Robin hugged her arm tighter, leaning in with a shamelessly nosy question. "Is he as scary as you thought he was? What's he like?"

"Blunt. He likes to tease." Hope felt the warmth creep into her cheeks at her next thought. "And he's a really good kisser. Of course, I don't have all that much experience—"

"That's okay. You know what you like and you like how he does it? Then he's a great kisser. I'm so happy for you. I knew if the right guy came along, he'd see you for the treasure you are."

After their first introduction at a neighborhood business development meeting three years earlier, Robin had quickly become Hope's dearest friend and confidante. She hated lying to her about her relationship with

Pike. "I guess I kind of figured I'd be growing old by myself. My feelings for Pike have really surprised me."

That part, at least, wasn't a lie.

"Trust your instincts, Hope. Trust your heart. Sometimes love comes at us in unexpected ways, from unexpected places." Robin turned her attention to the big brawny man unfolding himself from behind the wheel of the extended-cab pickup that had just pulled in. Jake Lonergan's less than handsome face reminded Hope of the thugs who terrorized the good guys in any of a dozen movies she could name. But he'd proved hero enough a few months earlier when Robin and her infant daughter's life were in danger. "You might be surprised at just how happy you can be."

"Ladies." Even a smile did little to change the harsh contours of Jake's scarred-up face, but there was nothing but adoration shining from his pale eyes as he leaned in to kiss Robin and take her bag for her. "Emma's asleep in her car seat, so I'll leave the truck running." Hope smiled as he leaned over to drop a kiss on her cheek, too. "Did Robin tell you that Emma's on the verge of crawling now? She's got scooting across the floor on her bottom mastered, but I know she's going to roll over and take off any day now."

Jake looked less like an infant girl's father than anyone Hope could imagine, yet she'd never seen a man take to daddyhood the way the former DEA agent had. "Do you have any new pictures?"

"A few."

"Liar." Robin gave him a nudge toward the truck to load her things. "He's taken hundreds."

Jake shrugged, unable to deny his guilt. "'Bye, Hope."

"'Bye, Jake."

Robin wrapped her arms around Hope and squeezed her in a goodbye hug. "I swear that man would put a crown on Emma's head if her neck could support it."

Hope hugged her back. "Jake is a wonderful father." Just like one she would have wished for growing up. "Emma's lucky."

"She wouldn't be with us now if Jake hadn't been around." Robin's loving smile flatlined and she had a serious, sisterly word for Hope. "You make sure you stay safe, too. With everything that's happened in our neighborhood? Now to hear you've been broken into?"

"I'm fine. Really."

"Well, don't hesitate to call us if you need anything. Anytime of day or night."

"I won't."

Robin's smile was back. "And we're going to have you and Officer Taylor out to the house sometime for dinner."

"Oh, that's not—" Hope reminded herself to smile and keep the charade of her relationship with Jake as real as she could make it. Dinner with friends would be a normal couple thing, wouldn't it? "Okay. Talk to you soon."

Hope said goodbye and loaded her things into the backseat of her car before climbing in behind the wheel. She'd just pulled her keys from her pocket purse when a sharp rap on her window startled her. With a shrieking gasp, she dropped her keys to the floor.

"Leon." She muttered his name with an apology, picked up her keys and started the car before rolling down the window. "Yes?"

Leon hunched into the open window, pulled his cap into his hands and smiled. "Yeah, um, I was just wondering if you had plans for tonight. Since the boss is letting me go early, I thought we could get a bite to eat somewhere, or something."

Really? They'd known each other for two years, and he'd picked today to ask her out? Hope forced her gaping mouth to close. Even without the charade of a fiancé to maintain, she wasn't interested in a date. "I can't."

Leon thumped the side of her door and straightened. And then he was leaning into the window again. "It's him, isn't it? I knew I'd lost you."

Lost her? Had he been under the impression that she was ever his to lose? "You and I have barely spoken about anything except repairs at my shop and our jobs. We're friends. But that's all we'll ever be."

His brown eyes narrowed into slits that made her lean away from the window. "After I did all those things for you, like fixing your door. I would have come and sprayed for bugs or set traps for you, too, just so you wouldn't have to dirty your hands."

Bugs? Traps? As in mouse traps?

"You sent those awful gifts?" Hope gripped the wheel and stopped retreating. She'd been grossed out, confused and terrified by the creepy bugs and dead rodent—and by the knowledge that whoever had left them must have been watching her shop and apartment very closely. This didn't make any logical sense. "You've been sabotaging things at my shop as an excuse to come over and spend time with me? What, so you could save the day and be my hero? I thought you were being a nice friend. I offered to pay you for your time." Her stomach got a little queasy at the twisted means of courtship. "Those gifts frightened me."

He reached into the car and curled his fingers over hers on the steering wheel. "I just wanted you to need me the way I need you. You would never talk to me, so I had to make up a reason for you to come out of your shell."

And she thought she'd been backward about meeting someone and developing a relationship. She slid her hand from beneath his and articulated the truth as succinctly as she knew how. "Leon, I don't feel the same way about you. I'm sorry." Confusion moved through disgust and went straight to anger. "You broke into my shop last night, didn't you? You made that phone call?"

He plunked his cap back on his thin brown hair. "What are you talking about?"

"Did you break in the window to my shop and cut the alarm wire? Did you spray-paint over the security camera? Pike's dog could have killed you if you'd gotten all the way inside."

"Oh, so now everything that goes wrong in your life is my fault? I suppose you're going to report me to that cop you've been shackin' up—"

"Did you break in?"

"No! I was at my mother's last night."

"And you didn't call and threaten me?" Hope's indignation waned as other, more disturbing, possibilities ran through her head. If Leon hadn't installed the tiny camera Pike's friend, Annie Hermann, had found hidden inside a light at her shop, then who had? The list of suspects who'd have that kind of access to her shop was short. The list of anyone interested enough in her life and business to go to that kind of trouble was even shorter.

"Hundley." Jake Lonergan's massive shadow fell over Leon, and the short man with a sick idea of romance froze for a second before taking a step away from Hope's car. "You've got some deliveries to make for my wife, don't you?"

"You're not my boss, Mr. Lonergan."

Jake crossed his arms over the front of the form-fitting black sweater he wore. With that heavyweight boxer's body and scarred-up face, Jake Lonergan in intimidation mode was scary enough to make Hope shrink away, even though he was defending her. "If my wife tells you to do something, you do it. Understood?"

With Jake daring the much smaller man to argue with him, Leon quickly gave up the fight. "See you around, Hope," he said, sneering. "If anything else goes wrong at your shop, you get someone else to fix it."

"I will." He scurried away to the flower shop van, sparing one contemptuous glare toward Hope before shifting into gear and speeding out of the parking lot.

She was still running through a list of names of men who had access to her shop when Jake braced his hands at the open window of her car. "There's something about that little weasel I've never liked. Call your boyfriend. Tell him you're on your way. Robin and I will wait until you leave."

Boyfriend. Right. The undercover ruse was working if both creepy Leon and her true friends believed she and Pike were a couple. Wishing more than she should that her time with Pike Taylor wasn't a lie, Hope looked up and smiled. "Thanks, Jake."

Robin and Jake followed her out to the highway before turning off to their home in the country outside the K.C. area. Hope waved them a thanks and continued toward downtown.

As the miles passed, she was torn between simmering resentment at the unnecessary fear Leon had caused her, and a fear that ran much colder, much deeper, when she thought about someone even more devious, more dangerous stalking her. Leon's misguided efforts would have provided the Rose Red Rapist a perfect misdirection to throw the police off their ability to track down his movements and his threats against Hope. He could have been watching her from that very first night she'd spotted his van.

Could the lights reflecting in her apartment, and the movements in the shadows around her, be attributed to Leon Hundley? Or were Leon's crude attempts to work his way into her life a convenient distraction for the police while a more secretive threat watched her from unseen vantage points and hidden cameras? Maybe Leon was a really, really good liar—and her would-be suitor and the serial rapist were the same man. The one thing she was certain of was that she needed to get home to Pike and tell him about Leon's disquieting confession.

Hope rounded a wide turn on the interstate to head south toward the city, and found herself veering a bit into the passing lane. She tapped on the brake to turn off the cruise control. Although the light on the dash blinked off, centrifugal force was still making her lean toward the door. "Slow down, already."

She tapped on the brake without detecting any change on the speedometer. If anything, as the straight stretch of highway dropped into a valley, she was picking up speed. "Really?"

The third time she pushed, the pedal went all the way to the floor and she went faster yet.

"Oh, my God."

She had no brakes.

Panic bubbled up in her throat, but she swallowed it down and gripped the wheel harder, judging the thankfully empty stretch of road, the brown grass median to her left and the trees climbing the steep hill to her right. She tapped on the useless pedal again. "What do I do?"

Turn off the engine? Then she'd have no steering.

Shift to a lower gear? Not at this speed!

"Call me. I'll be here."

Hope risked taking her hand off the wheel to pull her cell phone from her coat and punch in Pike's number. She'd clicked it to speakerphone and dropped it onto the seat beside when Pike picked up. "Hope?"

She put both hands on the steering wheel again and raised her voice so he could hear her. "Something's wrong with my car. I can't slow down."

She pitched forward when she hit the bottom of the valley and raced up the next incline at breakneck speed. "Pike?"

"Where are you?" She could hear hurried footsteps and measured breathing. Pike was running.

She gave him the highway number and closest exit she remembered passing. "I'm heading up a hill now. I'm losing some speed, but not much yet. I'll try to pull off. But if I reach the other side—"

He muttered one swift, succinct swearword, then started giving orders. "Put on your blinkers and make sure you're buckled in. I'm calling highway patrol right now. Listen to me. Pump your brakes. Sometimes you can rebuild the pressure." He went through a list of things to try to compensate for the damaged brakes.

But none of them were going to do her any good.

Hope's eyes went to the rearview mirror, and her breath locked up in her chest.

A white van crested the hill behind her, rapidly closing the distance between them.

"Pike?"

"I'm on my way."

He'd be too late.

HOPE'S HAND TIGHTENED around Pike's. "Wait."

Ignoring the audience of waiting patients, visitors and staff in the east lobby of the Truman Medical Center, Pike stopped the nurse pushing Hope's wheelchair toward the exit and knelt beside her. He knew it wasn't the crowd inside that made her nervous, but the onslaught of cameras and reporters waiting in the parking lot outside that put the shadows of fear into her eyes. Pike brushed a curling lock of hair away from the deep purple bruise on her forehead. "You say the word and I'll get you out of here through some back hallway or employee exit. You just spent a night in the hospital. You don't have to talk to these people."

She adjusted her glasses at her temple, and for several tense moments, those beautiful eyes looked straight into Pike's soul and tried to tell him something. But then she blinked and the message was hidden behind the dutiful tilt of her gaze up to Detective Montgomery, who stood on the other side of her chair.

Hope's grip pulsed around Pike's, and her pale lips smiled. "Yes, I do. I know what I'm supposed to say. I just need a second to gather my thoughts and steel my nerves. That's the whole point of this, isn't it? Using me to bait the trap? We wanted his attention focused on me so he'd come after me. I won't give up now."

"The bastard tried to kill you."

"He didn't succeed." But the burn on her forearm from the air bag, the bruising from her seat belt and the bumps and scrapes over the rest of her body told him the outcome of sailing over a ditch and flying up a brushy hillside to finally wedge her car between two trees could have had a very different outcome. "The truck driver who stopped to help me said he saw a man running to a white van parked on the shoulder of the road when he pulled up. The trucker must have scared him away before he could get to my car and..."

Finish the job. Pike nodded. He'd been there when the EMTs had pulled a dazed and bleeding Hope from the wreck. "Remind me to give that guy a medal."

"Pike?" Hope's gentle fingers brushed across his rough jaw, reminding him he still needed a fresh uniform and a shave after his vigil in the chair beside her hospital bed. Why was she smiling at him? After all KCPD and the Rose Red Rapist were putting her through, how could she still be brave enough to smile? "It's not the first time I've been afraid of something and did it anyway because I had to. I may not be a firecracker on the outside, but I can be tough when I really need to be."

The old scars Pike had seen along her shoulder, wrist and collarbone each time a nurse had come to check on Hope's progress through the night made him think this wasn't the first time she'd cheated death. They also made him seethe with something akin to a protective rage when he thought of her father and her fear of dogs and how they all must tie into that painful childhood and grown-up panic attacks she didn't like to talk about.

The woman shouldn't have to keep fighting for survival. Pike tilted his head to the astutely patient detective eavesdropping on their conversation. "Montgomery, help me out."

But it was Hope who answered. "Pike." With another gentle touch, she turned his gaze back to hers. "I have to do this. Just promise you'll stay with me."

He nodded. Yes. Screw the charade. He wasn't leaving her to patrol his beat or attend a task force briefing. He wasn't going to family dinners or football games with his brothers. He was staying right by her side until that slimy, cowardly cockroach of a man who'd done this to her was in jail and could no longer hurt her.

Hope inhaled a deep breath. "Okay. I'm ready."

Pike pulled her fingers to his lips and kissed them before rising and taking the nurse's place behind the wheelchair. "Let's get it over with."

Hope's friend Robin had brought jeans, a sweater and a flannel-lined knock-around coat for Hope to wear home. Yet Pike could feel her shivering in the afternoon sun the moment the first light flashed and the barrage of questions started. With Spencer Montgomery, Nick Fensom and Kate Kilpatrick keeping the reporters at a barely respectful distance, Pike pushed the chair out to the far curb and bit his tongue while the press had at her.

Vanessa Owen pushed to the front of the pack, urging her cameraman in beside her to get a shot of Hope's bruises and bandages. "You claim the Rose Red Rapist ran you off the highway."

Hope squinted against the bright light. "I know it was him."

"You saw his face? You were careening down the interstate at eighty miles an hour and you took the time to look at the driver's face?"

"I wasn't going that fast. I was already having car trouble. I'd slowed down."

Gabriel Knight was there, too, with his notepad and cynical voice. "That unpopulated stretch of highway north of the city where your car broke down is pretty far from the Rose Red Rapist's usual hunting ground."

"He must have planned it." Her chest rose and fell more rapidly as her breathing quickened. "The police found brake fluid at a church where I was attending a business meeting. They believe my car was sabotaged."

"Are you sure you're not just a bad driver, Miss Lockhart?"

Her knuckles were turning white on the arms of the wheelchair. "His van clipped my bumper, sending me into the ditch. I'm lucky I didn't roll my car."

"Forget the accident, Gabe. What did he look like?" Vanessa Owen took center stage again. "You say you saw the Rose Red Rapist. You're certain it's the same man you identified last weekend, near where LaDonna Chambers was found raped and murdered?"

"Yes."

"What did he look like?"

Pike stepped in when the brunette's microphone got too close to Hope. "Enough. The woman could have died. Cut her a break."

"What about the other women who died, Officer? Don't their families deserve to know who this man is? Don't the rest of us have a right to know from whom we should protect ourselves?" With a smile that was more shark than serene, the reporter retreated a step. "Miss Lockhart, give us something. Was he tall? Short? White? Black? Dark-haired? Blond?"

"A white man." Hope's voice sounded small.

"How old was he?"

"I…" She lowered her head, tilting only her eyes toward the camera. "He wore a surgical mask."

"So you didn't see his face."

Her chest heaved with a deep breath. "I saw enough."

"What color were his eyes?"

"Did he say anything to you?"

She twisted her fingers in her lap. "He didn't speak."

"Did he touch you?"

Her head shot up. "He tried to kill me. He walked up

to my car...after it crashed. He... I heard him coming through the brush... I tried to get out, but..."

Pike could see the panic stirring in Hope's pale skin and trembling mouth. If she hadn't run out of patience yet, he had. Ignoring the cameras, the questions and his superior officer, Pike scooped Hope into his arms and lifted her from the chair. "She's done answering questions."

"Miss Lockhart!"

As soon as Hope curled her fingers into his collar and laid her head against his shoulder, Pike carried her across the driveway to his truck.

Kate Kilpatrick took over the press conference and diverted most of the reporters' attention to her. "Please. Miss Lockhart's car was totaled. She's lucky to be alive. She needs her rest."

"Can *you* give us a description?"

Dr. Kate's voice faded in the distance. "For obvious reasons, the police don't want to give away all the details of these crimes. But we are looking for a white male, late twenties to forty—"

"I can walk." Hope's lips moved against Pike's neck in a weary protest, but he just held on tighter. He didn't set her on her feet until they reached the black-and-white K-9 truck. And even then, it was just long enough to get the door unlocked and open before he lifted her onto the passenger seat. "Where's the beast?" she asked, looking into the backseat.

Pike reached across her lap to fasten the seat belt. "My brother Alex took Hans for the night. He'll drop him off at your apartment once we get there."

With Hans gone, what fight she had left seemed to drain right out of her. "I hope that was enough. I tried." She squeezed her eyes shut and turned away from the crowd.

"You did great." He pulled a stadium blanket from under the seat and covered her up. "I'll get you home, Hope. Just as fast as I humanly can." He smoothed her hair off her face and earned a nod of appreciation, or maybe just understanding, before Pike closed the door and hurried around the hood.

A stern-faced Spencer Montgomery stopped him in his tracks. Pike pulled up to his superior height, ir-ritated by protocol and unspoken accusations and his own guilt. "Detective?"

Spencer Montgomery couldn't be intimidated. He pulled back the edges of his jacket and propped his hands at his waist. "Don't mess this up, Taylor. We need our perp to think she knows exactly who we're after."

"She said enough."

"Are you getting emotionally attached to this woman?"

"Yes, sir."

"Yes, sir, you won't blow this sting operation, or yes, sir, you have feelings for her?"

The promise of the coming winter chilled the late-morning air. But there was something as warm and cer-tain as it was unfamiliar filling Pike's chest when he looked inside the truck to see Hope huddling beneath the blanket. He nudged aside the detective before open-ing his door and climbing in beside her. "Both."

Chapter Ten

The cut on his forearm stung like the annoyance Hope Lockhart had turned out to be. He tossed back the whiskey in his glass and poured himself another while the woman who'd doctored his wound sat on the edge of the bed, towel-drying her hair.

"Be a love and pour me one of those, will you?" she asked.

For several seconds, he stood at the drink cart, his hand fisting around his glass so tightly it should have cracked. He drank that shot down, too, needing the sharp burn of the liquid to cut through the anger stirring in his blood and poisoning his thoughts. When he could think again, he poured himself a third whiskey, and filled a glass for her before taking the drink to her.

"I told you to let me handle it." He nodded toward the television they'd just turned off. "Now it's all over the news. Hope Lockhart is talking."

With a smile that was as smug as it was seductive, she clinked her glass against his, then drank the whole thing down like a man. "I've given you the perfect alibi, taking the van out to north Kansas City for you while you were here in town. You should be grateful."

Grateful? To a woman?

He took the glass she handed him back to the cart. He tried to simply set it down, but couldn't help himself. There were maids to do this kind of thing, but he picked up both glasses and carried them into the bathroom, where he washed them in the sink, removing saliva and fingerprints and any other contaminant that might linger. He dried them with a towel until they sparkled, lined them up, just so, on the counter, then washed and dried his hands until they were pink and chapped and just as clean.

He pulled a bottle of vinegar from his toiletry bag and poured the liquid over his hands, sterilizing them before rinsing again. Then he dabbed on enough cologne to mask the tangy scent and returned the glasses to the drink cart.

He might be a sick man. But he wasn't a foolish one. "I don't like that you made the decision without me. I've been keeping a close eye on Hope. I don't think she knows as much as the police claim."

"Didn't you hear her at that press conference?" The robe the woman wore barely covered the curves of her body as she stood and sauntered across the room to him. This woman tempted him. Repulsed him. She was good at her job and good for him, and he hated that he needed her. She'd hurt him deeply, yet he couldn't walk away. He owed her far too much and she knew him far too well. "She saw your surgical mask."

"Because you wore one today."

"Because she saw you that night. I never got that close to her car, or she'd be dead by now." She touched her fingers to his jaw, and his skin crawled, even though he knew she'd just come from the shower. "She knows the color of your skin. She may know more, but she's too broken to share it."

"You think Hope is lying?"

She pulled the towel from her hair and tossed it onto the bed. "You obviously do, too, or you wouldn't be spying on her."

"Then why hasn't she called me out? She knows me."

"She's afraid of you." She combed her fingers through her hair and shook the dark layers behind her back in a move that was probably meant to entice. But all he saw was the damp wad of towel soiling his bed. "I've looked her in the eye, just like you. That woman's afraid of her own shadow."

"Then we have nothing to worry about."

She faced him, backing up that beauty with cold, hard logic. "We have everything to worry about. Haven't you ever read fairy tales? The ugly duckling turns into a swan. The poor little ash girl becomes a princess. She'll change. She'll snap out of this stupor she's in. She'll come up against something or someone she fears even more than you. It may not be today or tomorrow, but one day, she'll name you for the ogre of the story you are."

"Ogre?"

The bitch smiled. "How many women have you raped? You're not exactly hero material, are you?"

"And you're no princess."

"I don't claim to be. I've always taken whatever steps are necessary to get what I want and to protect the people I love. I'm a survivor. Are you?" She tucked her fingers into the belt at his waist and inched closer to him, close enough for the heat of her body to seep into his. "Do you want me to take the necessary step of killing Miss Lockhart? Or do you plan to wait for her to destroy us?"

"I'll take care of Hope myself."

"You'll have to get rid of the boyfriend, too, because I think dead is the only way he'll let anyone get past him now." Her fingers moved behind his zipper. Despite every urge to deny her affect on him, his body leaped in response to her touch. "Think about it, darling. Have you ever killed a man?"

"I've never killed a woman, either. That's all on you."

"You just destroy lives and let them live with the physical and mental pain you inflict. Isn't my way kinder?"

He fisted his hands at his sides, refusing to give in to her seduction. "There's not a kind bone in your body. I never asked you to clean up what I do. I never made a mistake before you got into my head and turned me into some kind of misogynistic lunatic. I never asked you to take care of me. You're a selfish, ambitious bitch like every other woman I've known."

She pressed her body against his and smiled. "And yet you stay with me. You keep coming back to me because you know I'm the only one who understands you—who can handle what you need to do."

"Stop it!" He picked her up by the shoulders and threw her onto the bed. "I don't need *handling!*" When she dared to sit up and reach for him, he flipped her onto her stomach and pushed her face into the pillow. "You make me sound like a child who needs to be taken care of. I assure you, I am no child."

She rubbed her bottom against his traitorous response to her cunning wiles, and he jerked back, giving her a few precious moments to raise her head up and catch her breath. "I protect you because I love you. I do it because you won't take care of yourself. There's nothing I won't do for you, darling."

Then she made the mistake of looking at him. He

never liked to see a woman look him straight in the eye—as though she was his equal, as though she had the right to challenge him.

He grabbed her by the hair and pushed her face back into the pillow. "Then stay away from Hope. *I* want to be the one who punishes her for betraying me. Say you understand. That you'll do nothing more to interfere. Say it!"

Her muffled voice struggled to answer. "Yes. I understand. You want to take care of Hope."

"No. I *need* to be the one who does it. Your part in this is finished. She's mine. Understood?"

He pushed harder until the only answer she could give was a nod.

He left her gasping for air on the bed as he strode from the room. The hunger was eating through his blood now. The rage consumed him. And there was only one way to curb the sickness and assuage his need. The rational part of his brain knew he'd just been manipulated into this. And yet that only fueled the compulsion to prove he was the one in control of his life.

Hope Lockhart wasn't the submissive speck on the wall he'd thought her to be. She had knowledge of things that could ruin him. And that gave her a power over him that no woman had a right to.

He grabbed his keys and slammed the door on the way out. The gasps from the woman on the bed had turned to laughter. But he refused to hear her.

It was time to prepare for the hunt.

HOPE STIRRED RESTLESSLY as she dozed, unable to fall into the deep sleep she needed.

There were still parts of her body that were a little tender after smacking her head against the window and being jostled in her seat as her car had banged across the ditch and bounced up the hill. But she'd found a comfortable position in her own snug bed, was plenty warm beneath the sheet and quilt and even had on her old, comfy favorite—a white cotton nightgown.

But sleep eluded her because she couldn't shut down the images in her head. A white van filling up the space in her rearview mirror. Shadowed eyes above a stark white surgical mask. Golden lights bouncing off her bedroom walls. And that crawling sense of someone watching, someone she couldn't see, someone tracking her down and closing in just as surely as two red heeler mixes running down a frightened girl on a dirt-packed road, knocking her to the ground, tearing at her skin.

Hope gasped as her childhood memory blended with the grown-up nightmare of this past week. She rolled onto her back, forcing her eyes open and letting them adjust to the dim illumination from the streetlamp outside her window.

Her gaze settled on the tall silhouette of the man leaning against the doorjamb to her bedroom. Instead of being startled, she smiled. "It's not polite to stare."

Pike's low-pitched chuckle reached across the room like words of comfort. He unfolded his arms and straightened, taking a step closer to the glow from the curtains. He was still a blur until she picked up her glasses from the bedside table and put them on. His blue eyes were warm as he came into focus, but she could see the marks of fatigue lining his face. "I don't want to let you out of my sight again. Ever. This guy is more ruthless and resourceful than I imagined. I thought you'd be safe away from this neighborhood. He must have followed you out of the city."

Despite the disturbing topic and the distance of the

room between them, their voices sounded hushed, intimate somehow, in the dusky light. Maybe it was the connection to another human being who truly understood what she was going through that made this perfunctory conversation feel so soothing. "Or he knows my schedule. He knew where I'd be."

"That means he's someone you know." His shoulders lifted in a weary sigh. "Doesn't make me feel any better."

She wasn't the only one whose life had been turned upside down this week. "You need sleep, Pike."

"I've got one job, Hope. Keeping you safe. I blew it."

"I don't blame you." She pulled the covers to her chest and sat up in bed. "From the beginning, I understood the roles we had to play. You're the neighborhood cop. I'm the wedding planner. You moved in to protect me while I'm here, but if you follow me all over the city, then this guy will never make his move and you'll never catch him. Right?" He shifted on his feet, remaining silent. "And you did save me. You told me how to slow down my car. Your voice kept me from panicking. I could be dead instead of a little dinged up around the edges."

"I can see the bruises on your forehead and shoulder from here. Sorry, honey. You can't talk me out of feeling guilty." He came to the side of her four-poster bed, bringing the worn comfort of his flannel shirt and jeans into view. She could also now see the gun and badge strapped to his belt—and the concern he wore like the uniform and body armor she usually saw him in. He plucked the covers from her hands and shook the wrinkles from them. "Lie back down. I'll wait a little longer, until you fall asleep."

"But I can't sleep. My brain won't shut down. And you can't stand there forever."

"Watch me." The man took his job seriously enough that she had no doubt he'd stay at his post for days if he had to, no matter what it might cost his health or peace of mind.

But she didn't need the bodyguard keeping watch over her to chase the rapists and killers and from her dreams tonight. She needed something more than the gun and the badge. "Pike, would you stay and talk to me?"

A grin creased his scruffy jaw. "What have we been doing?"

She pulled the covers from his hands and patted the quilt beside her.

"Oh." The edge of the bed dipped when he sat and took her hand. "Better?"

Instead of being grateful for the interlocking fingers she'd grown to love, Hope pushed up onto her knees and threw her arms around his neck. "Now I am."

For one self-conscious moment, she thought she might have misread his caring nature, or that she'd pushed the limits of their charade too far. But with a breathy groan against her ear, he wound his arms around her and drew her up against his chest, lifting her off her knees and cinching her up so tight against his warmth that she felt the imprint of every button and belt buckle through the thin cotton of her nightgown. He rubbed his sandpapery jaw against her cheek and neck, catching loose tendrils of hair between them, kindling tiny sparks of friction that danced across her softer skin.

In the next moment, Hope was back on her bottom in the bed and Pike was leaving her. She quickly reached

for his hand, instantly missing his strength and heat.
"Pike—?"

"Shh." He squeezed her hand, whispering as he
smoothed her hair away from the knot at her temple.
She reached up too late to stop him from pulling her
glasses off her face and setting them back on the nightstand. "I guess neither one of us is sleeping unless we
do it together, right?"

Together? Wasn't that what she'd been subcon-
sciously asking for? She held her breath when he
stooped down to untie his boots. After he stripped off
shoes and socks, the belt followed. She started breathing again, quickly, but soon realized her anxiety came
from anticipation, maybe even a hint of impatient curiosity, not nerves or fear. Not of Pike. No, this man
would always take care of her, she realized, as he carefully set his heavy black gun and badge on the bedside table. He might teach her things the same way he
trained his dog, and speak plainly without a sugarcoat-
ing for anything, but his heart was pure gold. The shirt
buttons came next, and Hope squinted in helpless fas-
cination while he peeled off the blue plaid flannel and
hung it on one of the bedposts. So much bare skin. So
much man.

Although the jeans stayed on, he unsnapped the
waist before sitting down beside her and sliding his long
legs beneath the sheet. The mattress shifted and Hope
tumbled into that wide expanse of naked chest. But
the shock of warmth and hardness and Pike's unique
musky scent quickly gave way to curiosity and then
need. When Pike gathered her in his arms and lay back,
Hope tentatively turned her cheek into the pillow of
his shoulder. Her hand hovered above the terrain of his
chest, feeling the warmth from his skin. But she was

unsure exactly where to put it until he caught it and pressed it against the sleek arc of muscle over his heart.

"Breathe, Hope." His voice was husky and deep in the twilight above her. "If you don't relax, I'm going to think I'm scaring you, and neither one of us will get any sleep."

Her breath rushed out on a noisy sigh and her body closed the last bit of distance between them. Hope idly wondered if Pike could feel her breasts pillowed against his side through the thin layer of cotton knit that separated them the way she could. She'd never been draped against a man before. She liked that he was a furnace and that she seemed to be softer in places where he was harder so that their bodies could snuggle so closely together.

He must be just as aware of her body, too, because he seemed to know when she finally grew comfortable with the physical intimacy. "That's better. So what do you want to talk about?"

Her toes played nervously with the soft denim that hugged his calf. "Anything. I can't shake the feeling that he's out there, watching me. All the time. He knows everything about me and I…I don't know who he is."

His fingertips stroked up and down her arm. "No one's going to get to you tonight. My brother Alex is on one of the KCPD SWAT teams. He's perched on the roof of your friend Robin's flower shop, keeping an eye on things so we can get some sleep tonight."

"Is Hans here?" she asked.

"On the rug in your living room."

"And your brother's across the street?"

"Yes."

Hope braced her hand against Pike's chest and

pushed herself up. "So we're well protected. Why aren't you sleeping?"

"I thought you wanted to talk."

She remembered how warm her hand had been, clasped inside his in that chilly hospital room. "You were at the hospital all last night, weren't you? You need your rest."

His eyes hooded as he dropped his gaze to her chest and traced his fingertip across her collarbone. "How'd you get these?" The scars. With the slack neckline of her sleeveless gown, a man didn't need twenty/twenty vision to see them when they were this close, even in the semidarkness. "I knew you had them on your wrist, but when you were wearing that hospital gown, I saw... Some of these are skin grafts, aren't they?"

If she hadn't been snugged in the cocooning heat of the bed and his body, Hope might have frozen up. If his arm hadn't locked her against his side, she might have rolled away. If those handsome blue eyes weren't shadowed with pain, she might have closed her mouth and retreated to that quiet, lonely place inside where she normally hid from the world.

But she did none of those things. She could feel the sudden tension in him, saw the self-deprecating grin that never reached his eyes. "Asked the wrong question, didn't I?"

"It's okay." She cupped the side of his face and pressed a kiss to the corner of that false smile. He deserved to know why she was such a screwed-up woman, why he'd had to fight so hard to get her comfortable around Hans, why she had so little experience with trusting relationships. If Pike Taylor would put his life on the line for her, then the very least she could do was tell him the truth.

But it wouldn't be easy. She settled back down against him, clutching her arms between them. "My mother died in childbirth with Harry," she began. "I wasn't even two yet. I suppose Hank tried to keep us together as a family for a while. But he was never the same man after losing Mom. He blamed Harry, and I was a nonentity taking up space in the house. He started to drink and...never seemed to stop after that."

Pike groaned in lieu of a curse or condolence, and turned onto his side, throwing one of his legs over hers and drawing her more snugly into the hug of his body.

She breathed in his clean, musky smell that was simple, unadorned man, finding strength in his patience. "I became useful when I got old enough to take care of Harry and the house."

"How old were you?" His lips brushed against the crown of her hair.

"Six? Seven?" She relaxed her clenched fists and let her hands settle against the planes of his chest. "Hank drank a lot of the grocery money. He drank the mortgage payments until we were booted out of our home and went to live out in a cabin he had on one of the lakes near Branson. I kept it clean, fixed meals when I could—I was a stellar microwaver and sandwich maker."

Instead of laughing, Pike grunted a curse. "Didn't you have any family to help? Where were the social workers? My grandmother was sick with cancer for a long time, but I never doubted that she was doing her best to take care of me. Until she just couldn't any longer. I went into foster care when she went into hospice."

"She must have loved you very much."

"It was mutual. I lucked out twice in the family department with Grandma Pike and the Taylors." He went quiet for a few minutes, and Hope sneaked her right arm around his waist, holding on while he worked through his remembered grief. But then his fingers were sifting through her hair again, urging her to continue. "Did someone help you?"

Hope nodded. "My second-grade teacher reported us to DFS when I ran out of clothes that fit me. Things got better for a while. Harry and I got regular meals at school. Hank kept a part-time job with a rock-and-gravel company."

"What about the scars? Did Hank…?"

She felt the tension vibrating through every clenched muscle of Pike's body.

"Did he hurt you?"

"Not directly."

"What the hell does that mean?" The massage on her scalp stilled and Pike pulled back far enough to tilt his head down to meet her gaze. "Hope?"

She shook her head and burrowed back beneath his chin. She couldn't share the rest of it, looking into those suspicious, caring eyes. His arms stayed around her until the doubting moment passed and Hope knew she would never, ever find another man who could make her feel the trust and, yes, the hope and love that this man's blunt honesty and endless patience had nurtured in her heart.

With that stark admission of the feelings blooming inside her distracting her from the nightmarish pain this story usually invoked, Hope dug her fingertips into the reassuring warmth of his chest and finished it. "The summer I turned ten, Hank got fired for drinking on the job. Whoever his latest girlfriend was dumped him and he went on bender after bender. He'd leave the house for days sometimes. But…we had these two dogs he called the babysitters. Jack and Jilly. Doberman/heeler mixes. I suppose they were pets once, but he didn't take any better care of them than he did us."

"That son of a bitch." Pike's arms jerked around her and she laid a placating hand against the restless thump of his heart. "Babysitters?"

"Hank didn't want to lose his welfare benefits, or get in trouble with the police, so he didn't want anyone wandering onto the property or us leaving the cabin to let someone know how bad things were." For the first time tonight, tears stung her eyes, and her throat felt gritty. "Harry was so hungry that day. He was crying, and there was nothing in the house." The tears spilled over onto Pike's chest. His muscles flinched with every drop, but he said nothing. "I'd hidden a few dollars from Hank—from cleaning the neighbor's cabin—and I thought it might be enough for some milk and bread, maybe a jar of peanut butter if I could get to the store."

"But you had to get past the dogs?"

She nodded. His breathing quickened to match her own. "I fished an old, rotten meat bone out of the trash and tossed it into the yard. The dogs were starving, too. I thought I could sneak past."

"Ah, hell. Ah, hell, baby." He knew what was coming as surely as Hope.

"The dogs were doing their job. They were hungry. I smelled like garbage from the trash. And Hank came home."

"Get her!"

Footsteps pounding on the hard-packed dirt.

Tearing flesh.

"Harry was nine years old. He got Hank's gun and shot Jilly. A nine-year-old had to defend me. And I…" She couldn't breathe. She couldn't think beyond curling into a ball to protect her neck, beyond grabbing a rock and swinging it at Jack's head. "The neighbor lady heard the shot and I—"

Suddenly Hope was pulled from the nightmare by the demanding pressure of Pike's mouth against hers. "I knew you were a fighter." His body pressed her into the bed and he threaded his fingers into her hair as he kissed away the evidence of her tears. "If I had known what all you've been through, I'd never agree to this charade to draw out the Rose Red Rapist. It's too much, honey. It's too much."

Hope's hands went to his chest, instinctively bracing against his heavier weight. Then his mouth opened over hers and her fingers latched onto skin and muscle as her tongue darted out to meet his.

Fear turned to excitement. Despair turned to anticipation. Pike Taylor's fierce brand of caring chased away the nightmare and drew her back to the here and now.

Hope arched her neck as his lips skidded along the pulse at her throat, cooling the path abraded by his beard. "I'd have done it anyway," she gasped, startled by the heat pooling inside her with each rough caress. "When Detective Montgomery said I had the power to help put away that madman, I'd have volunteered, anyway."

"I know." His lips grazed her collarbone, finding nerve endings among the scarring there. Or maybe there was something in her brain that was responding to the needy tug at the strap of her nightgown, pulling it away from her shoulder so the trail of his beard and lips and tongue could continue there. The tips of her breasts beaded and rubbed against his chest, making them ache for a stronger, more insistent touch. Something sweet and hot coiled at the juncture of her thighs as his words and kisses and body caressed her skin. "You're kind of stubborn that way. You're the toughest fighter I know." He lifted his head and looked her in the eye. Even without her glasses, he was close enough to see the dilation of his pupils against the cobalt and sky-azure of his eyes. "If anyone can survive this mess, it's you."

Stubborn. Tough. A survivor.

It was as beautiful a compliment as Hope had ever received.

"Pike?" She pulled her hair off her feverish face and tucked it behind her ear. "Would you…? Can we…?"

"One of us had to ask." With a laugh, he reclaimed her mouth and rolled her onto the bed beside him.

For several minutes, there were no more words. He worked at the buttons of her gown, pressing a kiss deeper and deeper between her breasts until he groaned. Unsure whether that was frustration or arousal, she opened her mouth to ask. He held up one finger, warning her not to speak, then reached down to grab the hem of the gown and push the whole thing off over her head.

The gown flew away into the blurry darkness. The swift need of his actions startled her, excited her. But she had little time to savor each discovery of the tension building between them and inside her.

"If these aren't the prettiest things I've ever seen." Pike's hands and mouth were quickly on her breasts, squeezing, tasting, exploring the tender skin the material had hidden from him. She cried out with delight when his hot mouth closed over one aching peak and pulled it gently between his teeth. "Damn pretty."

Hope tried to keep up with every brush of his lips, every tease of his fingertips, every demand of his body. She skimmed her palms down his flanks, swirled her tongue around his taut male nipple, teasing it with her teeth the way he had her. When he bucked in response, she kissed the delicate spot and moved across his chest to see if the other was just as responsive.

Hope felt more and more feminine, more and more powerful with each sharp intake of breath, every quiver of responsive skin beneath her hands. Soon she became aware of his sturdy thigh pushing between hers. She moaned when he rubbed against her. The pressure inside her womb was sudden and intense, as if every blood cell in her body was racing to the spot to see what these new, overwhelming sensations were all about.

She was equally aware of the bulge in Pike's jeans, pressing against her hip. She was squeezing her thighs around his leg, instinctively seeking some kind of release, when he propped himself up on his elbows above her. Pike was breathing as hard as she was, so their chests kept meeting, retreating, touching again and robbing her of sense each time. His voice was husky and raw and as potently sexy as the rest of him. "Have you ever had a man in your bed, Miss Lockhart?"

Slowly, feeling the blush creep into her cheeks, she shook her head.

Pike leaned down to kiss her hard and quick as he pulled his wallet from his back pocket. "Well, get used to it. 'Cause I'm not leaving."

Taking her cue from the hands stripping her panties down her legs, Hope unzipped Pike's jeans and helped him shuck them and his boxer-briefs before they, too, sailed away into the night. Accidental, purposeful, gentle, urgent touches and whispered words filled the next few moments until Hope lay beneath him. His fingers stroked her hair, his eyes reassured, as he gave her the time she needed to get used to the feel of his hips cradled against hers, his thick, hot shaft pulsing against that most sensitive part of her.

"I'll try to be gentle," he promised. "But if anything hurts, if anything scares you, you tell me."

Hope looked up with all the love filling her heart. This was right. *He* was right. She slipped her arms around him and boldly reached down to palm his butt. "It's time to stop talking, Pike."

And then he was spreading her knees apart, nudging at her entrance, sliding inside, slowly, deeply, perfectly.

Hope gasped at how tightly he fit, how completely he filled her up, how close she could feel to one special person. Once the initial pain eased and she stroked the line of his jaw, he started moving inside her. Hope's breathing quickened. Pike's mouth was on her lips, her neck, her breasts. She gripped his back and found a rhythm that matched his. The pressure between her thighs grew almost unbearable. She wanted…she needed… "Pike?"

"That's it, honey. Let it happen."

He reached down to press the sensitive nub where they were joined and she cried out with the force of her release. While she crested the hill and marveled at the waves of tiny aftershocks pulsing inside her, Pike moved. Trusting her instincts, wanting him to know the same rapture she felt, she hooked her heels behind his thighs and opened herself to the driving force of his need. Seconds later, his arms tightened around her and he groaned against her neck. With one last thrust he tumbled over the edge inside her.

Pike collapsed on top of her and, for a moment, Hope hugged him tight around the neck, sensing that his weight and scent and the slick heat between them were the only things that could ease the sharp sensations still firing inside her. But then Pike pushed himself up, gave her a quick kiss and plopped down onto the bed beside her. He was struggling to even out his breathing, too, as he reached for her hand. "Thank you, Hope. Thank you for letting me be your first."

A few minutes later, after Pike had excused himself to the bathroom to dispose of the condom and come back with a washcloth to clean them both, Hope was still lying in the same spot on the bed. Her thoughts were floaty and the air in the room was cooling her skin. "I'm completely spent. And so relaxed. Is that normal?"

Pike laughed in the darkness and climbed back into the bed. He gathered her into his arms and pulled the cover up over them both. "That just means we did it right."

Feeling content, weary, alive and safer than she'd ever been, Hope turned her cheek into Pike's shoulder and let her eyes drift shut. There was no pretend about her feelings for Pike. This was a man she could trust. This was a man she could love.

And she did.

But the feelings were too new, too unfamiliar for her to put into words. She could barely make sense in her own head how she could, in the span of a week, lower the emotional barriers that had guarded her through so much of her life. For now, she would simply be grateful that he was kind and she was safe.

With her hand resting against the steady beat of Pike's heart, Hope fell into a deep, dreamless slumber.

SEVERAL HOURS LATER, revived by the most solid sleep he'd had in a week, Pike awoke to the brightness of the streetlamp outside the frilly curtains at the window. He slipped on his jeans for a quick check around the apartment, verifying that everything was locked and secure. He went to the front window and saluted the thumbs-up from his brother Alex on the roof across the street. He exchanged some words and licks from Hans before letting the dog settle back onto his favorite rug and returned to Hope's bedroom.

He stood in the doorway, inhaling deeply as he watched her sleep. Her hair fanned like a glorious silky mane across her pillow and the exposed curve of one beautiful breast. The cool air in the room smelled of vanilla and sex, stirring something possessive and provocative inside him.

He'd had no idea when he was stuck with this assignment a week ago that things would get personal, complicated. He wasn't a complicated kind of guy. He'd had sex before, but not like this. He'd tried relationships before, but never with anyone with so many layers and secrets and hang-ups and curiosity and courage as Hope. He'd dated prettier women, more experienced women, women who actually talked to him the first time they'd met.

But he couldn't remember any woman getting under his skin and getting inside his head the way Hope Lockhart did.

"So what are you going to do about it, Taylor?" he whispered into the shadows.

This was supposed to be a job. He had a mission to complete. The safety of his beat, maybe of the entire city, rested on his shoulders. If he was smart, he'd grab his gun and badge, take a cold shower, brew a pot of coffee and sit up with the dog in the living room, keeping watch.

Instead, he unsnapped his jeans and dropped them

on the floor before crawling under the covers with Hope again.

She stirred when he brushed that decadent fall of hair away from her porcelain skin. Those big lake-gray eyes opened like shadowy pools in the darkness and she reached for him. "Hey. I was thinking..."

"Uh-oh." He shouldn't get this kind of rush watching a blush stain her cheeks and creep down her neck. He shouldn't be this curious to see just how far down that blush could go. "What is it?"

"I know that some people do it more than once. Could we? I may never get this chance again."

The tips of those lush breasts were already teasing pebbles against his chest, waking his body. "I doubt that, honey."

"Please?" She was doing that ticklish thing with her toes again. "If you have another condom, that is. If you want."

Yeah. He wanted.

It was swifter, needier, this time as he pulled Hope on top of him and taught her a couple of new things about making love. He made it as good as he knew how, driving her to the edge of her release as she took him right to the brink with her.

And when he drove himself home inside her, pouring out the essence of everything in him, Pike knew something had changed. Terribly. Irrevocably.

This woman wasn't just his to protect.

She was his.

Chapter Eleven

Pike felt a sudden chill when Hope rolled away, taking her sweet warmth and half the covers with her.

"Is that your phone or mine?" she asked.

His.

Hope turned on the lamp beside her and tried to find her glasses and cell while he pulled his jeans down from the bedpost. He didn't need glasses, the lamp or the dusky, predawn twilight to see his phone screen flashing like an alert, or to have a bad feeling about why anyone would call at this hour.

He pushed the talk button and tucked the phone between his ear and shoulder, slipping into his shorts and jeans as soon as he read Alex's name on the screen. "What is it?"

He had a very bad feeling before his brother even spoke.

"Just spotted a white van with a silver bumper half a mile north of your position," Alex reported. "It's headed this way. Do you want me to intercept it?"

This was it. He was here. The Rose Red Rapist was coming for Hope.

And Pike was damn well going to put a stop to that man's reign of terror over the city. And her.

"Negative," Pike answered, grabbing his shirt. "Call Montgomery and give him a sit-rep."

"You need me to call in backup? SWAT Two is on duty. The team could be here in ten minutes."

"Pike?"

He threaded his holster onto the belt of his jeans and hurried to the window, barely hearing the soft whisper from across the bed. Alex's SWAT training and gear gave him a tactical advantage Pike couldn't match. But he parted the curtains and peeked through the blinds anyway, hoping to glimpse a target where he could focus the red alert pumping through his blood.

But beyond a few parked cars, traffic was almost nonexistent. Their unsub would see the cops coming and disappear back to one of the nearby thoroughfares or the interstate. "Negative. Too big a presence will scare this guy away. Besides, this is our bust. We've been working too damn long and hard on this case. We'll take him down."

"Understood, little bro." Despite the nickname, Alex was all special weapons and tactics right now. "I'll maintain my position and give you an update if he changes course. Good luck, Pike."

"Thanks for having my back, Alex."

"Roger that. Taylor out."

Pike tucked the phone into the front pocket of his jeans and dropped to the bed to put on his socks and boots. Half a mile away? Maybe two or three stoplights to catch him between here and there? If he was lucky. Pike had a matter of minutes—seconds, maybe—to gear up and get into position to catch this guy. He quickly tied the second boot and stood.

"Is it him?" Hope had pulled the quilt with her off the bed and wrapped herself in it to bar his path out the bedroom door. He'd already seen the lush beauty of her full figure, and had caressed every one of her scars, so he doubted it was modesty that made her cover up. She was afraid. Shutting down. Hiding herself from the world that had done her such harm again.

He needed to say something. He needed to tell her that she meant something to him and that last night was hot and that maybe, one day, when life was sane and safe for them again, they could…what? What was he going to do? What did he want to do about Hope?

"I gotta go." Seriously? That was the best he could come up with?

That knot of consternation dented the skin above her glasses. "Okay."

Frustrated by his inability to say the right thing at the right time, and feeling the clock ticking down as the van approached, Pike snaked his hand behind her neck and pulled her up onto her toes, planting a hard kiss on her soft mouth before setting her aside and darting into the hallway.

"You're a fighter," he called out over his shoulder. "Remember that. Hans! *Hier!*"

He grabbed his keys, his flak vest and the leash as the big dog bounded to his side. Pike suited up, before putting the harness and badge on Hans. Hope had followed him out, still clutching the quilt to her breasts and bottom, still looking at him with the fear and questions in her eyes.

Say something.

The phone vibrated against his thigh. His brother was calling again. The mark must be close now. "I need you to lock the doors behind me. Stay put. I'll be back."

Then he and Hans were out the door and running

down the stairs. He opened his truck and put the dog inside as he took Alex's call. "What's up?"

"The van's stopped at the light at the top of the street. He'll go past you in about thirty seconds." Pike started the engine and pulled the truck up to the edge of the parking lot entrance, leaving his lights off to stay hidden until the last possible moment. "I'm ready."

"Montgomery was at HQ. He's on his way. Fensom's already en route." The tenor of Alex's voice changed to that of a soldier, ready for battle. "Light's changing. I'm on my way down to back you up."

Pike felt the same cagey readiness running through his veins. "Roger that. Taylor out."

Phone in pocket. Breathe deeply. Grip wheel.

"And here...we..."

Go!

As expected, the boxy white van slowed in front of Hope's shop. But the driver must have spotted Pike's truck, even in the shadows. With a squeal of rubber clawing to find traction on the pavement, the van driver pushed his lights up to bright, momentarily blinding Pike, and floored it.

Since he'd been made, Pike flipped on his own lights and the siren and pulled out onto the street as the van sped past. The truck bounced over the curb and picked up speed to gain ground on the van. With the T-intersection at the south end of the block, the unsub was going to have to either slow down or fly around a corner and risk rolling the van. Either way, Pike intended to stop him.

Thankfully, there was little traffic, but the driver was already pushing his luck, fishtailing into the side of one parked car as he veered into the opposite lane to try to make a wider turn. Pike pushed the accelerator closer to the floor and held on tighter. The guy whipped back into his lane and bounced off another car, shooting up sparks as metal scraped against metal.

Pike saw a couple turning the corner on the sidewalk up ahead. Their looks of panic were unmistakable as they jumped back toward the shelter of the nearest building. Another car screeched to a stop and shifted into Reverse, backing out of the intersection as the two vehicles raced toward it.

"Slow down!"

Pike's engine roared with power. His siren screamed in his ears, but he could still make out other sirens in the distance. Too far in the distance. And Alex was at least half a block behind him.

"We've got to stop him, Hansie." The dog was panting in rhythm with the charged adrenaline pumping Pike's heart. "It's you and me."

He quickly glanced ahead. Nobody knew this part of town the way he did. He knew every citizen, every corner, every curb. Coffee shop on the left. Dance bar on the right. Yarn shop straight ahead. They were all closed for the night, but owners lived in the apartments above them. Security guards sat in offices and patrolled their buildings. A couple of homeless guys liked the alley off to the east when the night wasn't too cold. If traffic was clear, that left the abandoned warehouse around the corner to the west that hadn't been reclaimed yet.

Target acquired.

He called in the location, updating the chase to Dispatch, alerting traffic cops to clear the streets, telling his task force teammates where they could finally get their man. He reported his intent and hung up the radio.

Pressing the accelerator down to the floor, Pike

raced up behind the van, targeting the left side of that shiny steel bumper. Closer. Closer.

The van's brake lights flashed. "Gotcha."

Pike rammed the truck's front end into the rusting taillight of the van and sent it skidding around the corner. With a big white target and a clear sidewalk in front of him, Pike T-boned the van. It jumped the curb and Pike hit his brakes, letting the truck's momentum shove the van straight into the crumbling brick facade of the abandoned building.

His seat belt caught and held as the truck's front end crumpled and the windshield cracked. Hans woofed in protest at the wild ride and abrupt stop.

But they were both okay, and the damn van wasn't going anywhere. One rear wheel was shredded and one in the front wasn't even touching the ground.

"Hans, *bleib!*" Pike reassured the dog of the need to stay put, unhooked his seat belt and climbed out of the steaming truck.

He drew his Glock as he ran to the front of the van. "KCPD! Take your hands off the wheel!" He opened the folding door and charged up the steps, his gun pointed straight at the driver's head. "Payback's a bitch, isn't it? You run my girl off the road—I run you…"

The adrenaline short-circuited into confusion. Gray hair. Prison tats. This wasn't right.

"Officer Taylor." Hank Lockhart massaged his shoulder and ran his tongue along the lip he'd split open, having smacked one or both on the bloodied side window.

Pike glanced into the back of the van. Empty. Spotlessly clean. And there were no other seats inside. This didn't make sense. Where…?

The gray eyes might be bleary with pain or booze, but the old coot was laughing.

The amused, malevolent sound galvanized Pike and he leveled his gun at the ruddy target of the bastard's nose. Questions could be answered later. "Hands up, Lockhart."

There were lights flashing in the corner of his vision now. Help had arrived. Not that he'd need it to take this lousy excuse for a man down. As soon as Lockhart's hands settled on top of his head, Pike holstered his weapon and pulled out his handcuffs. He slapped one end around Lockhart's wrists and reached for the other hand.

"Ow, man." Lockhart swore as Pike jerked his injured arm behind him and locked the other cuff around his wrist. "I really took a shot to my shoulder."

"And your daughter took on a pair of starving dogs because of you. I don't hear her complaining." Cars were stopping, and guns and detectives were charging forward as Pike dragged him out and shoved his face into the side of the van. Pike kicked the old man's legs apart and searched him, pulling out a pocketknife, a wallet and a thick long envelope. He ripped it open and found a stack of hundred-dollar bills inside. "Where'd you get this?"

The old man turned his head with a smug grin. "I'm gettin' my money out of that girl one way or the other."

Pike braced his forearm behind Lockhart's neck and shoved him back against the van. "What are you talking about?"

"Taylor!" Spencer Montgomery holstered his weapon as he jogged up. With a nod, his partner, Nick Fensom, jumped inside the van to give it the same once-over

Pike had done. He took the cash and knife Pike handed him. "Is this our guy?"

Pike stepped back, shaking his head as the senior detective spun the culprit to face him. "This is Hank... Henry Lockhart Sr."

"Hope's father?"

Nick jumped down from the van's steps and holstered his weapon. "My grandmother doesn't keep her bathroom as spotless as that van. The whole thing reeks of disinfectant." He pulled out his cell phone. "I'll call Annie to bring her kit. Whatever was back there has been cleaned within an inch of its life." He nodded to the gray-haired man in handcuffs. "Who's this douche?"

"Our eyewitness's father." Montgomery pulled his cell phone from his suit jacket and pulled up a picture. "The van matches Hope's description. But he's not our guy. She'd have recognized her own father, wouldn't she? Even with a mask?"

Pike glanced behind him, taking in the skid marks and wreckage, unmarked vehicles and black-and-whites with flashing lights blocking off the three-way intersection. This was one hell of a show for downtown Kansas City at five in the morning.

One hell of a distraction.

Suspicion lit a fuse inside him. "Run his priors," he advised the senior detective. He walked out past the back of his truck, gazing as far up the street as the streetlamps and strobe effect of the flashing lights would let him. What was out of place? What was missing? "Lockhart did time in Jeff City. I'm sure he was incarcerated for at least some of the Rose Red Rapist assaults."

His brother Alex walked up with Nelda Sapphire in handcuffs. "This one was following you in a compact heap of junk. Didn't think much of it until you did your fancy driving. Once you crashed, she pulled off in an alley and started running the other direction."

"Not a word, Nelda," Hank warned.

"Shut up." Pike and Detective Montgomery both had the same idea.

"Probably his getaway," Pike guessed, rejoining the others. If this was their unsub's van, the one Hope had identified, there were only a couple of reasons why Hank would be driving it. And the coincidence that he'd stolen this particular van wasn't very likely. "Drive the van someplace and drop it off, then she picks him up."

"This isn't your guy?" Alex asked.

No. But he could lead them to him.

"Tell me about the money, Hank." Pike resisted the urge to drive his fist into that split lip and opted for a threat Hope's opportunistic father might answer to. "We've already got you on speeding, reckless driving, assault, attempted assault—"

"What? I never."

"—and accessory to rape and murder. How much time do you want to spend with your old friends in lockup?"

"Tell him, Hank," Nelda urged. Mascara ran down her face as she cried. "Or I will."

Surrounded by two armed detectives, a cop in full SWAT gear and an angry Pike who used every inch of his six feet four inches of height to back the coward against the van, Hank finally muttered something useful. "Some guy paid me five thousand to drive his van past Hope's shop."

"Some guy? What guy?"

"I don't know." The guy looked smaller and meaner, backed into a corner like this. But he knew he had no place to go. "He found Nelda and me sleeping in her car last night. Black pants and a jacket was all I could see in the side mirror. Came at us from behind and knocked on the window. Said he saw me hanging around Hope's shop a couple of times. Told me not to turn around and look at his face, and for that kind of money, I didn't."

Decoy.

"Hope." Pike ran to his truck.

That's what was off. There'd been no cars parked in front of Hope's shop when the van drove past. And he'd just spotted a light-colored SUV there.

Even the unflappable Spencer Montgomery revealed a spike of temper. "You set up your own daughter?"

"She wouldn't help me, so I helped myself."

Montgomery grabbed Hank Lockhart and handed him off to a pair of approaching uniforms. "Get this trash out of here."

Pike's truck was toast. The shop wasn't that far. He opened the back door and grabbed Hans's leash.

"Taylor!" Detective Montgomery caught the door and closed it after Hans jumped out.

"Pike?" Alex fell into step beside them as they jogged across the intersection. "Talk to me, bro."

"Get everyone back to Fairy Tale Bridal. He's going after Hope."

Then there was only Pike and his partner and a long city block to run. "Go, boy!"

HOPE DIDN'T WASTE any time after Pike and Hans left. She pulled on underwear, jeans and a sweater, and grabbed her phone and keys before unbolting the door and running barefoot down the stairs.

Whatever was going on was something bad. And even though she had questions about last night with

Pike, and even more questions about tomorrow, she knew that something big was breaking on the task force investigation. Pike needed to deal with the danger his brother had alerted him to, and he needed her to nod her head and do what he said.

She pulled open the door at the bottom of the stairs and immediately turned the dead bolt on the outside door of the vestibule, securing access to both the shop and her apartment. She peered out the door into the rose-tinted darkness of early morning and saw that Pike's truck was gone. There'd be time to ask questions later, she hoped. Time enough for Pike to come back safely. Time to wrap up this hellish mission and end their fake engagement.

Hope held on to the door handle and stretched up on tiptoe, trying to see over the fence and hedge that lined the parking lot. Were those flashing lights bouncing off the tops of the buildings? Pike's was one truck. Just how many emergency vehicles were out there? What was going on? Was someone hurt? Was Pike?

Obeying common sense as much as curiosity, she unlocked the inside door to the shop and went in to check the front door and windows there. Her bare toes made no sound on the cold tile and carpeting, and she left the lights off so no one would be alerted to movement inside the store.

She peeked through the mannequins in the window display and saw a black-and-white police car with flashing lights parked sideways across the street, down by the coffee shop. Had there been an accident?

Without stopping to ponder an answer, she continued to the front door between the displays and jiggled the handle. Locked. Good. She was safe.

Now she could spend a few seconds pressing her

cheek to the glass to see farther down the street. Where was Pike's truck? All she saw were police cars and flashing lights. She almost smiled with relief. Had they caught the Rose Red Rapist? Had the sting operation worked?

Hope breathed a sigh of relief and pulled her phone from her pocket. How needy and inappropriate would it be if she called Pike right now and asked him for answers? Asked him to come back to her? Asked him...

The scent of a powerful cologne, tainted with undertones of vinegar or disinfectant stung her nose.

Oh, God. Her pulse thundered in her ears. She wasn't alone in the shop.

Had someone snuck in before she'd gotten the outside door locked? Who else would have a key?

She slipped her thumb over the screen of her phone and pushed Pike's number and the call button. Fear kicked into panic and her fingers trembled as she tried to slide her key into the lock to get out the door. But the reflection taking shape behind her in the window warned her it was already too late.

Screaming at the familiar white mask, Hope turned to defend herself. But his arm was already swinging. He hit her in the side of the head and she was unconscious before she hit the floor.

"HOW LONG DO you think it's been?" Detective Montgomery asked.

Pike didn't have time to piece together clues and figure this out intellectually, so his brother answered. "Fifteen minutes, twenty, tops, sir. Pike left the building at 5:10 a.m. I picked up Miss Sapphire at quarter after. It's not five-thirty yet."

"The street's blocked to the south, so he had to go

north. Traffic Patrol would have spotted a speeding car, so he can't have gotten far. I'm calling in every favor I've got for this manhunt." Montgomery pulled out his phone. "Nick's already going door to door. Maggie Wheeler, Dr. Kate and her friend Sheriff Harrison are on their way. I'll contact Dispatch and get every available uniform here ASAP."

"Belay that phone call, sir." Rank didn't matter when it came to Hope. Pike was giving the orders now.

They didn't need manpower. They didn't need men.

Pike knelt beside Hope's glasses and shattered phone and let Hans sniff the white nightgown he held in his gloved hand. "I need you to do this for me, boy. I need you to find her. Please."

The German shepherd whined and tilted his head to one side. Pike could tell from his excited panting that he had the scent and was ready to work. But his partner wasn't used to being asked. He was used to being led. Pike pushed to his feet and opened the shop's front door.

"Hans! *Such!*"

HOPE CAME TO with a start. The pungent liquid splashing on her chest and neck acted like smelling salts, piercing the fog of her headache and waking her to the cool lights of the room above her.

Above?

Automatically, she reached up to adjust her glasses. But both hands came up, and she hissed at the sharp pinch at her wrists. They were duct-taped together.

Half-blind? Bound?

Fear sharpened her senses further and Hope squinted to bring something—anything—into focus. Colorless walls reflected a single light hanging overhead. From the angle of things, she must be lying on the floor. She couldn't make out any windows, couldn't tell if it was morning or night.

But her other senses worked just fine. The cold liquid hit her belly and she shrieked. Vinegar? She jerked away from the smelly dousing and rolled over a sheet of plastic that popped and crackled when she moved. Beneath the plastic, something padded protected her from the hardness of the brown floor. A mattress. The air was chilly and stale, with no moving air. And she was shivering because her sweater had been cut or ripped and pushed aside, leaving her in a bra and blue jeans for protection and warmth.

And then she saw the black shadow moving past her feet and remembered the reflection in the glass.

Hope startled, tried to scoot away. But a strong hand clamped over her ankle and pulled her back into place. She was going to die. She was going to be horribly violated, made to suffer and then she would die.

"Where am I? Who are you? Why are you doing this?" she asked in rapid succession. Oh, God, she was in terrible trouble. Where was Pike? Did he know how much she loved him? Would it matter? Did she have any chance of saving herself? "Do you have my glasses? I can't see," she admitted as the first hot tear ran across her cheek to her ear.

The man laughed.

Finally, he spoke. "I've been such a fool." Five simple words and she felt light-headed again. Sick to her stomach. Heartbroken. She knew that voice. All this time…so many conversations. And she'd never had any idea of his dark, dangerous secret. "You never saw me at all that night, did you? With those eyes, in the shadows, you never really could. And to think I believed the lies you told."

Hope blinked away the tears that burned her eyes. "Brian? Brian Elliott? You're…"

"Yes." Something silky soft and sweetly fragrant touched her nose and she jerked away from the sickening caress. A red rose. "I'm the devil the police can never catch. I'm the man terrorizing the women of this city. I'm teaching every greedy, selfish witch that she's not everything she thinks she is. I'm the Rose Red Rapist." He crawled over her, dropping the rose beside her as he came into view. He was wearing that glaring white surgeon's mask over the bottom half of his face. But the eyes above the mask were dark and clear, and sadly familiar. "But you're never going to tell anyone that."

He reached down and unsnapped her jeans. When the zipper began to slide apart, she shook off the shock of never knowing what an evil man her mentor and friend had been—of never even suspecting how sadistic he could be. "Stop it!"

She bucked beneath him, clawed the air to stop his hands. But she was helpless. Trapped.

Brian picked up a bottle, although she couldn't make out the contents. "Women are filthy creatures, you know. You can't trust them." He poured the liquid onto a cloth and she realized that was the vinegar mixture he'd thrown on her earlier. Hope sucked in her breath when he laid the cloth on her stomach and started to bathe her. "They take everything you have—your money, your trust, your heart—and they grind it into dust beneath their feet. They use you. They humiliate you."

She arched her back, trying to escape the cloth sliding over her skin. "I never did."

"I thought you were different, Hope. I made you into the success you are. I coaxed you out of your shell and taught you to trust your vision. I gave you a building to live and work in—"

"I bought that building." She snatched at the cloth, but he pulled it beyond her reach. "You invested in my shop."

"I never thought you would betray me. You were always so dutiful. So appreciative."

"I worked hard to get where I am. I thought you were proud of me."

"I was. And then..."

"What? What did I do, Brian? What did any of those women you hurt do to you? Bailey Austin? LaDonna Chambers?"

"You're all like Mara."

"Your ex-wife?" He freshened the washrag and slipped it beneath the elastic of her panties. "Why are you doing this?"

"You humiliated me. You played me for a fool."

"Stop it, Brian." She tried to sit up, but he shoved her back down. "You don't want to do this."

"I've never heard you talk this much before, Hope. I don't like it." He reached across her and came back with a box cutter that he trailed against her cheek.

Hope jerked her head away from the sharp blade. "The police will find you. You won't get away with this."

"I've gotten away with this for years. A mousy little slut like you isn't going to change that."

She heard the ripping sound of tape before she felt the vibration of a slamming door from somewhere beneath them. "Where are we?"

"Shut up."

"Brian—"

"Shut up!" He slapped her across the mouth, stun-

ning her long enough for him to press a piece of duct
tape over her mouth. He jerked her jeans down her hips
and Hope screamed helplessly behind the tape.

Do something. Make a noise. Help them find you.

If there was ever a time in her life she needed her
voice to be heard, it was right now.

While Brian unhooked his belt, Hope reached up
and peeled the tape from her lips. "Help me! Help—"

When his fist came down, she raised her hands to
deflect the blow. Brian grabbed her wrists and pushed
them over her head, tearing skin beneath the tape as
she thrashed and screamed. He lay across her, reaching for something. She kicked. She twisted. She heard
the clatter of heavy objects hitting metal and wood. He
grunted. She jerked. Brian sat up, his weight straddling
her body and crushing the breath from her lungs. He
raised his hand and she saw the hammer he'd pulled
from the toolbox beside her.

Hope screamed.

"KCPD!" She heard a loud bang and the splintering
of solid wood. Brian turned. "Hans! *Fass!*"

A blur of black and tan leaped at billionaire Brian
Elliott and knocked him to the floor.

Hope tumbled off the mattress as Brian cursed and
screamed. She'd heard ferocious snarls like that once
before in her life. Even dazed and frightened, without her glasses, she knew exactly what was happening. There was the initial blow that knocked the wind
and sense from a body. The bruising punctures. The
tearing skin.

"Hope? Hope!" Pike pulled Hope to her feet and
tucked her behind the broad wall of his back. "How
bad are you hurt?"

"I'm okay," she whispered. She pulled up her jeans

and fastened them as best she could with her clothes wet and her hands still bound. She curled her fingers into Pike's belt and moved with him as he pointed his gun at Brian Elliott. "I'm okay," she repeated with more strength.

"Hans! *Platz!*" In a heartbeat, the growling stopped and the big dog sat back on his haunches and lay down.

"Damn." Brian writhed on the floor, clutching his injured arm to his stomach. "Filthy beast! You've killed me."

"Shut up, Elliott, or I'll let him do it."

"I need to wash. I need to clean it off."

Pike inched closer with the gun and pressed it against Brian's skull. "Don't move."

Other than breathing hard and moaning in pain, Brian didn't.

"Come here, baby." Pike shifted his gun to one hand and reached behind him to hug Hope to his side. "How many doors do I have to break down to get to you?" He pressed a kiss to the crown of her hair and then turned his attention to the man bleeding on the plastic-covered mattress. "Brian Elliott, you are under arrest for kidnapping and assault on Hope Lockhart. Other charges will be filed against you. You have the right to remain silent." More footsteps stampeded up the stairs and blurry figures she couldn't recognize charged into the room. "You have the right to an attorney. If you can't—"

"We've got it, Taylor." Hope recognized Spencer Montgomery's voice. "Nick, cuff this bastard." The detective's red hair came into focus as Pike backed away from the man on the floor. "Are you okay, Miss Lockhart?" He looked over his shoulder and shouted, "Let's get a bus here and have this woman looked at."

She nodded and he faded away again as Pike turned

her away from the black uniforms and plainclothes officers storming into the room. "Come on, honey. You've done your part." He pushed her several steps out of the way while he holstered his weapon and ripped apart the Velcro fastenings on his flak vest. "You've done a hell of a lot more than we had the right to ask of you."

"I can't see anything, Pike. I feel so lost."

"Here. Probably should have left them at the crime scene, but…" The first thing Hope saw when Pike slipped her glasses onto her nose was the clear blue gaze of his eyes. They were dark with concern, lined with fatigue—and the most beautiful sight she could hope to see.

Joy and relief rushed through her before caution and common sense could, and Hope stretched up onto her toes and looped her bound arms around Pike's neck. "You found me. You saved me. Just like you promised."

His arms cinched around her back and he lifted her clear off the floor, turning his face into her hair. "Hans found you. He followed your scent across two city streets and up three flights of stairs. He's the one who saved you."

Hope struggled to find the floor again, to stand on her own two feet and frame Pike's anguished face between her hands. "Who trained Hans? Who busted up that door so he could get to me? Who never gave up on me?" She pulled his head down and kissed him, just the way he'd taught her how. "Thank you," she whispered as she settled back on her feet. "Thank you."

Without a *you're welcome* or *no problem* or *my pleasure, ma'am,* Pike pushed his vest over his head and dropped it to the floor. He picked up the very box cutter Brian had threatened her with and sliced through the tape on her wrists. Then he pulled off her ruined sweater and replaced it with the blue flannel shirt he wore.

And while Pike buttoned her up, the rest of the room came into focus. They were at a construction site. She recognized the two-by-fours framing open walls that had been covered in plastic.

"Secure this location," Montgomery ordered. There were several voices talking now. Clipped commands and "yes, sirs."

"This crazy guy has created his own sterile room." That was Detective Fensom. "He could move this setup from building site to building site. No wonder we could never come up with a crime scene. Annie's going to have a field day processing this one."

"So let's get everyone out of here before we contaminate any more of it." Spencer Montgomery was clearly the man in charge. "Get Chief Taylor on the line and wake up the commissioner. I'm escorting this guy downtown myself."

"I want a doctor and my lawyer," Brian protested.

"Bring Miss Lockhart, too."

"Yes, sir," Pike answered, catching a T-shirt that one of the uniformed officers tossed to him, and slipping it on over his head. "Need anything before we go downtown?" he asked her.

Another kiss? A chance to erase the guilt that lingered in his eyes? But what if he didn't want her to ask those things, anymore? They didn't have to pretend to be a couple anymore.

They were a cop and a shopkeeper.

They were friends.

"Yes, wait." She couldn't leave yet, not without the rest of her protection team. "Hans! *Hier!*"

The German shepherd jumped to his feet and trotted over to her. *"Setzen!"* He sat down beside her and Hope knew an urge to drop to her knees and hug him around the neck, too. But training was a slow, repetitive process. And she still had a ways to go to completely move past those long-ingrained fears. But she did reached down and scratch around his soft, furry ears. "Good boy, Hansie. Good boy."

If Pike hadn't laced his fingers with hers just then, she might have burst into tears. Instead, she latched onto the strength of his hand, to the strength he'd revealed inside her.

She had a feeling she'd need every last bit of that strength to get through the rest of the day—maybe, to get through the rest of her life.

"Thank you, Hans." She petted the dog one more time, then headed to the door with Pike on her left and Hans on her right. She was safe. Kansas City was safe. It was enough. "Thank you both."

Chapter Twelve

How long were Spencer Montgomery and Nick Fensom going to keep grilling Hope?

When Pike stepped off the elevator onto the third floor at Fourth Precinct headquarters, her curly mane of toffee hair was the first thing he spotted. Without the overbearing assistance of either her attorney or her mentor, Hope was sitting across from Detective Montgomery at his desk, going over some kind of paperwork. Maybe it was just the formal approval of her statement. And maybe the detectives were demanding something more from a brave woman who had already given far too much.

They had Brian Elliott dead to rights on kidnapping and assault charges, thanks to Hope. And the task force was certain they could get him on the multiple rape charges now that he could be compelled to give a DNA sample to match the evidence they had on file at the crime lab. If they got a witness to come forward who could put Elliott at any one of those previous crimes, they'd have a slam-dunk case for the D.A.'s office, and the man would never get out of prison.

Pike leaned against the sergeant's counter, scrubbing the tight muscles of his jaw as he watched over the conversation from a distance. Even though the detectives had let her shower and put on a borrowed set of gray KCPD sweats after Annie Hermann had taken her clothes and Pike's shirt, and processed Hope for evidence, the grueling marathon of wrapping up the details of the task force investigation had to be wearing her out. Hell, Pike was exhausted. And he hadn't been struck in the head, kidnapped and nearly assaulted.

She'd sat through the task force briefing with his team, eaten a lousy cafeteria lunch and identified Elliott in a lineup, first with, and then without, that neurotic surgical mask he'd been wearing that first night he'd nearly run her off the road with his van. Pike had even had time to run down to the locker room to shower and shave and put on a clean uniform while Hope met with Commissioner Cartwright-Masterson and Pike's uncle, Precinct Chief Mitch Taylor, to receive an official departmental thank-you for a citizen going above and beyond to help serve and protect her community.

They'd have to feed her dinner soon if they kept Hope here much longer. And Pike wanted that opportunity for himself. He wanted to take her home, at least. Let her change into something demure and girly, and run around barefoot. He wanted to tuck her into bed and watch over her and teach her a thing or two more about making out and making love—or maybe he'd let her teach him since she seemed to have such a flair for making him crazy in all the right ways.

"Earth to Edison." A bump on his shoulder roused him from his thoughts. "Yo, Pike."

Pike pushed away from the sergeant's desk and looked down to see his brother Alex grinning up at him. "Now what?"

He knew that look. Alex was cooking up something

that was going to either embarrass him or put him in his place.

"I was just wondering how long you were going to stand here looking at that woman before you work up the nerve to go over there and do something about it."

"Do something about what?"

Alex punched him again. "How much you love her."

Pike shrugged off Alex's annoying attempt to get a reaction out of him. "It was a fake relationship, Alex. An undercover op."

"Uh-huh." Alex crossed his arms in front of him, mimicking Pike's stance. "I saw the look on your face when you realized Elliott had her. That wasn't worry that you'd blown the assignment—that was a man who had his heart ripped out of his chest because he thought he might lose the woman he loves."

Surprised by his brother's serious tone, Pike released a heavy breath and admitted his fear. "What if it was just a job to her? Hope doesn't have a lot of experience with men. Now that she knows she can do anything she sets her mind to, be with anyone she wants—what if she decides I'm not what she wants?"

"Seriously?" Alex shook his head. "You're a Taylor. You're KCPD. You're *my* brother. She'd be crazy not to want you."

Something warm and free from doubt blossomed inside Pike at his brother's vehement defense. He grinned his appreciation. "You're getting soft on me, Alex."

Hope and the detectives all stood and shook hands, giving every indication that at last they were done.

"Me? Soft?" Alex nudged Pike forward, quickly moving past the mushy stuff. "I'm not the one who's afraid to tell a woman that he loves her. You go up to her, maybe take some flowers, think about your favorite greeting card and what it says. Tell her she's pretty or sexy or—"

Pike palmed Alex in the face and shoved him away. "I got this."

SO THIS WAS it.

Hope had stayed as long as she could at precinct headquarters, waiting for the chance to share a private conversation with Pike before they had to return to their normal, *real,* lives tomorrow. Before they went back to being the neighborhood cop and the shy shopkeeper he tipped his hat to.

Now he was closing the door to one of the meeting rooms behind him, filling up the small space with his size and earthy scent and easy confidence. She paced off the length of the conference table, wishing she had time to change into something more feminine, wishing she wasn't bruised and scarred and so embarrassingly new at this personal relationship thing.

"Pike—"

"Hope—"

They had started together.

Her cheeks heated with embarrassment. "You go ahead."

"No, you first."

Fine. She could do this. She tugged the sleeves of the sweatshirt she wore down over her fingers and curled the long cuffs inside her fists. "I just wanted…" She tipped her face up to his and smiled. No need to be nervous when what she had to say was true. "I wanted to thank you."

He leaned his hip against the table and sat on the corner. "For what?"

"Saving my life. Being patient. Teaching me not to

be so afraid of dogs." She moved a couple of steps closer and gestured toward the detectives' desks beyond the door. "Thank you for finally getting my father out of my life. And for showing me how to love. You were my first, Pike. In more ways than you'll ever know."

"Like I said, you have all the right instincts, honey. You just needed the confidence to act on them." He plucked at a nonexistent piece of lint on his black slacks. "What do your instincts say about us?"

If she could survive this past week, then she could find the courage to say three words. "I love you." His fingers stopped playing and his head jerked up. "But I want you to know that I would never hold you to any sham of a relationship. If all we can be is friends, I'm okay with that."

"I'm not."

"Excuse me?"

Pike reached for her hand and pulled her closer, adjusting his position so he could pull her between his knees and slip his fingers inside her baggy shirt to rest his hands at either side of her waist. "Look, I'm going to say this just as plain and direct as I know how. I love you, Hope Lockhart. You deserve a happily-ever-after more than any woman I know." He twirled a fingertip into a long tendril of hair that had fallen across her cheek, and tucked it back behind her ear. She leaned her cheek into his hand when it lingered there. "If you'd be interested, I'd like to hire your services to create the wedding of your dreams. I'd like you to be the bride and I want to be the groom. I'll even put on one of those damned tuxes. I want the real thing with you."

"Yes."

"Yes? This is what you really want, too? I'm a real catch. I talk to dogs, I like to fish, I don't always say what I mean." Sarcasm bled into his voice, but she refused to hear it.

Hope slipped her fingers around his crisp black collar and drifted closer to the addictive warmth of his body. "But you *do* what you mean. Let me make this just as plain and direct as I can, too. My answer is yes." The doubts around her heart vanished like magic and she leaned in to meet his kiss. "*You're* my happily-ever-after."

* * * * *

She's loved and lost — will she ever learn to open her heart again?

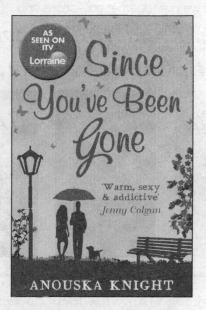

From the winner of ITV Lorraine's Racy Reads, Anouska Knight, comes a heart-warming tale of love, loss and confectionery.

'The perfect summer read — warm, sexy and addictive!'
—Jenny Colgan

For exclusive content visit:
www.millsandboon.co.uk/anouskaknight

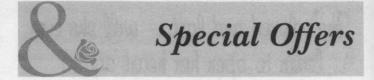

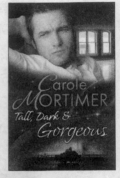